D1391747

WHITE LADIES

BY FRANCIS BRETT YOUNG

FRANCIS BRETT YOUNG

WHITE LADIES

LONDON
WILLIAM HEINEMANN LTD

FIRST PUBLISHED 1935

PRINTED IN GREAT BRITAIN
AT THE WINDMILL PRESS, KINGSWOOD, SURREY

For
Eddie Marsh
with the gratitude
of a Georgian Poet
and the affection
of a Friend

CONTENTS

BOOK ONE

BOOK TWO

BOOK THREE

BOOK FOUR

BOOK FIVE

BOOK SIX

Note.—Though the events and situations described in this book are by no means uncommon, the place and the people involved in its fate are entirely imaginary and unconnected with any living person.

BOOK ONE

GENESIS OF A HEROINE

THE Tinsleys' fortune had its origin, no doubt, in the luck which led them to settle, without permission, on the land called Hayseech: a triangular expansion of the valley that connects Mawne with Halesby at the point where the Lapsley Brook slips into the Stour. Their name, which was later to become so widely advertised on the sides of clanking mineral-trucks in railway-sidings, makes its first public appearance in judicial records of the mid-eighteenth century: none too creditably, for they were stiff-necked, litigious, and usually in the wrong.

As for Hayseech itself: if it were ever worth calling anyone's property it probably belonged by rights to the Pomfrets of Mawne Hall—not the Victorian-Baronial Hall, with stucco battlements and quatrefoil windows, which later became the seat of Walter Willis the ironmaster, but its predecessor, a rambling mass of red Tudor masonry, securely set among hanging woods on the opposite bank of the Stour.

By the time when the Tinsleys first began to assert themselves, the old Pomfrets, having kept up their heads (more or less) for seven hundred years, were beginning to feel the effort. Planted there in the reign of Rufus as a sturdy exotic sapling, the family tree had

3

profited by its sheltered obscurity and made no more rootage than was necessary for the immediate weathering of such major tempests as the Wars of the Roses (which providentially missed them by thirty odd miles) and the Great Rebellion—in which they had prudently made the best of both worlds by fighting, or rather expressing their willingness to fight, on either side.

Had the Pomfret stock been possessed of sufficient vigour to thrust its radicles downward into the subsoil, where, all unsuspected, lay buried the ten-yard coal, with veins of ironstone and pockets of lime side by side in proportions physiologically balanced for the nurture of giants—had the Pomfret stock been a trifle sturdier and its roots sufficiently inquisitive to explore and to tap these astonishing treasures, its memory might have survived to this day as something more than that of a name. But the Pomfrets had had enough of life. By seventeen-seventy, when the Tinsleys first made themselves unpleasant, protesting, by virtue of their long, undisputed occupation of Hayseech against its enclosure, the Pomfrets were too bored, too tired, and possibly too scornful to wrangle over trifles.

What *was* Hayseech anyway? A mere, rushy triangle of waste land whose marches had never been thoroughly cleared of the oak and birch of the Mercian Forest; sour acres, neither drained nor tilled within human memory, where a gentleman with a gun

(if he were lucky) might pick up an odd brace of snipe or a bittern, or bring down a heron winging heavily homeward to the Shrawley heronries. There was water, indeed: the brook trickling down from the dismantled mill at Lapsley to lose itself in all that remained of one of the Abbey's fishponds now narrowed by silt to the dimensions of a mere pond. A source of potential power? Country gentlemen were not accustomed to think of water in terms of power. Even supposing such power could be developed, how should it be used by the Tinsleys or anyone else? They were a prickly race; but sportsmen didn't shoot hedgehogs. Even wise dogs left them alone. The land they had squatted on, apart from the question of Pomfret prestige, was barely worth the cost of enclosing, much less fighting for. If these Tinsleys were such fools as to waste their time fencing the god-forsaken tract, they might as well do so!

Thus the Pomfrets contemptuously omitted Hayseech from their private Enclosure Act, and the Tinsleys possessed themselves of it without further hindrance. The Pomfrets continued to decline in a dignified fashion, and the Tinsleys to exist—from hand to mouth, as the meanest sort of small farmers.

But early in the nineteenth century, when the Pomfrets had gone—Mawne Hall empty, their barony extinct, the remains of the family retreating in dudgeon to Worcestershire—the conditions of life in the Stour valley suddenly changed. War flared out over

Europe, and the ultimate smoke of the conflagration blew into the triangle of Hayseech. Before this, the Tinsleys (save the earliest, who had felled what remained of the Pomfrets' oaks to burn charcoal for smelting) had had little truck with their industrial neighbours. They had lived on the verge of the great fossil forest of coal without being aware of it: but now the whole civilized world (as it was called) began to clamour for malleable metal in the last, the fiercest battles of the Iron Age. Half the inhabitants of North Bromwich and Wednesford were busy fashioning flint-locks for guns, burnishing welded barrels and grinding blades for sabres. In Halesby and Dulston ten thousand nailers toiled day and night with their wives and children forging nails for the hoofs of chargers. In Wolverbury an equal number of loriners made cast-iron bits and stirrups and saddlers' ironmongery. All these industries grew hungry and greedy for their raw material, iron; and the basin of the Black Country, as yet green, where the coal and the ore and the limy flux lay waiting, was filled with the fume and ferment of a monstrous activity. Smoke blackened and made acrid the air that the Tinsleys breathed; flame-belching furnace-throats reddened their sky at night. In the valley of the Stour, at their very door, new factories arose. Men ignorant but shrewd, such as the Bulgins of Halesby and the Hacketts of Mawne, were quick to exploit the power of falling water. Wherever visible coal could be found it was dug and coked to feed

furnaces, and the iron that flowed from their vents, before it grew cold, was hauled over quagmires of gritty ooze to the long sheds where rollers flattened it into sheets, or batteries of thudding water-hammers shaped lengths of rod.

II

THE Tinsleys of those days took no part in this red harvest. Though potentially more vigorous, they were as little adaptable as the Pomfrets. As yet there was no greed in their blood. Unable to retreat, they watched the convulsion grudgingly, but made no attempt to profit by it. They were men of the soil, temperamentally averse from bletching their hands with industry. The first tide of development and prosperity swept past them unheeded; it left them as poor and contented as they were before. It was only in the eighteen-twenties, when the wars were over, that Josiah Tinsley, the first of that name, discovered, in sinking a well, the presence of blue clay for brick-making in the Hayseech subsoil.

He made use of it, first of all, to rebuild his own dwelling: that rude earth-floored structure of mud-brick and adze-shaped oak which his squatter ancestors had set up originally on the Pomfrets' land. The erection of this new and far more hideous house stirred the seeds of possessiveness in Josiah's heart to germination. Its unwonted dignities suggested a higher standard of life; the new standard of life demanded a certain supply of ready money such as he had neither desired nor dreamed of when he lived by his land.

The obvious expedient was to make more blue bricks and sell them; and this was easy, for the hordes of new labour now settling and multiplying at Mawne and overflowing the old town of Halesby needed buildings to house them and paving for footpaths and courtyards.

A man quicker-witted than Josiah could have made a quick fortune; but his mind was slow-moving and bucolic, incapable of seeing beyond present needs. If he was not intelligent, he was, at least, industrious and tenacious. He worked, and his family with him, as long as light served, digging clay from the pit and shaping the stuff into bricks as a dairymaid bats her butter; firing his brickill (as they called it) with shaly coal shovelled from an inferior outcrop nearby; hauling his new-made bricks to the builders' yards in his own farm-cart. His labour was one of dank discomfort demanding infinite patience; yet, in the long summer days, Josiah, his wife and the children, could turn out as many as a thousand bricks a day. They were of an unsightly purple, the colour of raw ox-liver; but when once they were baked they became hard as furnace slag or volcanic rock.

Bricks of any quality were welcome to the contractors running up jerry-built back-to-back boxes in the "courts" of Mawne and Halesby; but Josiah Tinsley's were easy to handle and made for eternity. More than one of the builders, sniffing a "good thing," made him proposals: they would buy his claypit, erect modern machinery and install him as manager. But

Tinsley had his own ideas—not of the value of Hayseech but of its sacredness as a family possession. He was not going to run away as the Pomfrets had done.

Wealth—fortunes, that is, on the scale of those amassed by the gun-barrel makers now turning their war-time plants to the making of tubes for water and steam and coal-gas—meant very little to him. He *was* making money, unconsciously—far more than he knew what to do with. It accumulated steadily, surprisingly, as the clay-crater deepened. For some years he stored it in a hiding-hole cunningly constructed beneath the brick floor of his brew-house, till the thought of it got on his nerves and he carried it one day to the new bank at Halesby—two thousand, seven hundred odd pounds in sovereigns and guineas—and casually dumped this avalanche of gold on the mahogany counter.

From that moment—for banking, in those days, was not confidential—Josiah Tinsley became known in Halesby as a "hot" man. The district, though it bustled with energy, still lacked capital. He found himself approached by his neighbour Hackett, of the Mawne Gun-barrel Works, whose thudding water-hammers could be heard in the night at Hayseech.

"If you want some use for your brass, Jo Tinsley," Hackett told him. "I can handle it for you. If you care to trust it to me I'm prepared to guarantee you twelve per cent on it. Better still, why not come in with me over the brickyard as well? You ought to get shut on this clay-dabber-dick affair. You've got water-power running to waste. I can find you the right sort of labour and fit you up with machinery. The new shops and housen I've planned could take all your output for the next five years. You and me can share what we save on the job. Just you think that over."

Tinsley shook his head. "I've got all I want, Mr. Hackett."

"That's fool's talk. No man in his senses has all he wants. Twelve per cent. That's handsome, damn it."

"Yo' can keep it, gaffer. The brass means naught to me."

"The brass wunna mean naught to your family I reckon, Tinsley."

"That's their look-out, then. As long as it's mine I stick to it. And the brickill too. Yo' bain't the first beggar what's come smelling round after that."

"If you had a son, I reckon he'd have summat to say about it," Hackett said brutally. It was one of the prerogatives of new wealth to "talk straight," as they called it. But when he had spoken he laughed nervously, for he knew he had touched Tinsley on the raw. He had begotten two sons; but one had died in infancy and the other on the threshold of manhood in the dire scarlet-fever epidemic of eighteen-forty.

"I've got ne'er a one," Tinsley said, "but I've got a wench what's worth half a dozen o' your boys, Mr. Hackett, from what I've seen on 'em. Her'll stick to my brass as tight as me, you make no mistake."

"You wait till she's married, then see," Hackett laughed.

"Married? What are you talking on? What would our Bella want to get married for? 'Asna 'er got a good home? And who would keep house for *me*? Our Bella dain't give her mind to that stuff; her's a reg'lar lad-wench."

"Well, just think it over," Hackett said. "If you change your mind you've only to come and tell me."

Josiah Tinsley did think it over. It was, perhaps, the first time in his life that he had seriously thought about money. Of late he had left the ordering and collection of accounts to his daughter Bella who, thanks to the new British School at Halesby, had learnt to read and write. Though he still treated her as a child, she was now a woman of thirty, a blonde, big-boned creature, fashioned on generous lines which made her father, whom age was beginning to shrink, look mean and misshapen. The years of hard labour in the brickfield had not warped her body but developed it, and her divorce from womanly vocations had given her face—a wide, honest face with frank eyes, firm mouth and magnificent teeth—a handsomeness the quality of which was masculine and heroic. That was why, when Hackett spoke of her marrying, Jo Tinsley had smiled to himself. It would take a man of exceptional strength and courage to possess himself of this Valkyrie ringed in by the smoulder and fume of the Hayseech brickill!

That part of his conversation with Hackett which related to Bella was quickly dismissed from his mind, but the other part stuck in it obstinately. It pricked him because his neighbour had treated him patronizingly, as a big man speaking to a small; and, little conceited as he was, no Tinsley could stomach patronage. He had spoken the truth when he said that his brass meant nothing to him. At that moment it meant very little more than the material bags of gold coins which he paid into the bank for convenience as they accumulated. Now he began to think of it differently: as stuff whose possession gave a fellow with no particular distinction (who *was* Hackett, anyway?) the confidence, if not the right, to patronize men as good as himself with familiar insolence. He disliked Mr. Hackett; it was part of the Hayseech tradition to dislike newcomers, even if they only came from the next village. What was more, he distrusted him. If a fellow like Hacket was prepared to finance the brickworks it was not out of neighbourly benevolence: there must be a sight more in the business than he chose to let on, and if anyone was going to exploit Hayseech and make money out of it, he should be no stranger.

A month later—for all his processes of thought were slow and cautious—he reported the conversation to his daughter.

"Hackett talked about putting new plant up," he said, "what dost think on it, wench? The stuff's there, but we conna deal with it."

"Hackett's right; but I wouldna trust him."

"No more would I."

"The stuff's ourn, not his!"

It pleased him to hear her say that: there spoke a Tinsley!

"Hackett mentioned your getting married," he said, and watched her narrowly. Though he knew nothing for certain he didn't believe in smoke without fire.

Bella threw back her fine head and laughed. "Behappen he's someone in mind? When I see the mon that can master me it'll be time to think about that, Dad. I'm not the sort what gets married to wear the breeches. But what Hackett says about the brickill— that's right. I've thought that this long while."

"Thou hastna said naught, wench!"

Bella laughed. "I dain't meddle or mak in other folk's business. I know better nor that."

"I gass it'ld cost a fair penny."

"Yo've plenty of brass, Dad."

"Well, I reckon I'd better set about it then. The sooner the better."

Jo Tinsley set about it. Within five years, the Hayseech brickworks became a substantial business. Once started on the wheels of mechanization it acquired an automatic momentum. Not that the Tinsleys' manner of life was modified by success. They still lived, the father and his daughter, still unmarried, in the ugly house Jo Tinsley had built with his own hands in early manhood; they still rose at dawn and laboured, ant-

like, till sunset, though their calling now was that of
Egyptian taskmasters. Every penny of profit that
rolled in, five thousand pounds of it, rolled back into
the pit out of which it came.

First of all, taking Hackett's hint, Jo Tinsley
developed his water-power; but this primitive mechanism as the claypit deepened proved inadequate, giving place to a Soho steam-engine, its circular boiler fed
by the brook and its furnace fired from the shaly outcrop of coal that still heated the kilns. Soon the pocket
of clay had been bared over a surface of half an acre
and the crater sunk fifty feet deep. From its bottom
the newly-dug clay was hauled upward in trucks by
a steam-winch and cable working over an inclined
plane, then tipped into the hopper that fed the
mechanical kneading-troughs and the cylinder from
which, like a sausage, the clay emerged ready for
moulding. Here women worked at the benches twelve
hours at a shift, ankle-deep in wet sludge, their figures
and faces and hair bespattered grey as death. Two
and eightpence a thousand bricks Jo Tinsley paid them
—it was less in the red-brick industry—and the
nimblest could shape as many as a thousand a day.
But the two children (or "pages") who staggered with
fifty-pound loads, half-balanced on the head and
half-clutched to the stomach, from the troughs to the
bench and from the bench to the drying-sheds, drew
a shilling a day apiece from the moulders' earnings.
Ten women worked in Jo Tinsley's moulding-shed,

and turned out, between them, an average of sixteen thousand blue bricks a day. There was a good deal of sickness among the moulders and their "pages," which kept down the average; for the moulding of bricks was a fine art, and beginners were not only clumsy but apt to get tired. One heard a good deal of silly talk about child slavery in those days; but Jo Tinsley's conscience was clear: the "pages" in his moulding-shed only worked overtime when a rush of orders made it necessary. From six in the morning till six at night on six days of the week were their regular hours. Their Sundays were practically free: all they had to do was to turn the drying bricks which had been moulded on Saturday. Those who worked barefoot in the puddle had no call to take cold when once they got used to it: what was more, the practice saved shoe-leather; and in winter, the proximity of the ovens warmed the sheds.

In the provision of that warmth, he considered himself a public benefactor. On sharp nights out-of-works would congregate and play cards or pitch-and-toss in the glow of the kilns. Jo Tinsley didn't mind their enjoying his surplus heat, provided they didn't drop off to sleep and die, like the French bear-leader who once lay down with his bear by his side and never woke up again. The parish had buried the man, but washed their hands of the bear; and a dead bear lying about was a pretty considerable nuisance in a business where time spelt money!

During the winter, indeed, the shed-work slowed down from want of light. Since the establishment of Hackett's new forge and shops, with their black-belching chimneys, and the new Great Mawne Colliery, with its perpetual smoulder of slack, the sky over Hayseech had darkened and lost its old clarity. On January days, when the dabs of damp clay from the kneading-troughs froze on their way to the bench, the moulding-women and their "pages" worked in the half-light of tallow-candles stuck in stalagmites of their own congealed grease. It was eerie to watch the death-grey figures in this light: the grim women slapping the moulds and the "pages" softly threading to and fro bare-footed like tiny ghosts.

Bella Tinsley superintended this female labour and kept it on the move. She was well qualified for the job; in earlier days, she had moulded many thousands of bricks herself. It was she who measured out the pounds of candles and kept an eye on them; for in winter voracious "pages" had been known to develop an Eskimo taste for tallow. It was she who inspected the bricks in the drying-shed; for defective ones did not count in the moulders' score. It was she who checked the loads as they left the yard, took orders, apportioned the output, and distributed wages on Saturday night. After work, when the yard lay deserted except for the men on night-shift, who kept the kilns fired, she would retire to the living-room of the house, which had been turned into an office, and busy herself with a rough-and-ready accountancy which was, in fact, no more than a check on her amazing memory. Once or twice, as the business grew, Jo Tinsley suggested employing a clerk; but Bella would have none of it: a clerk would draw eighteen shillings a week and waste good money; what was more, she didn't want any young man knocking round the house —one old one was nuisance enough!

Jo Tinsley laughed, and gave her her way. He had spoken the truth when he boasted to Hackett that his wench was worth half a dozen boys. As they grew older, side by side, he was amazed and almost intimidated by his daughter's efficiency in organization, her acuteness in matters of money. It was almost as though the development of the Hayseech "brickill" had liberated in Bella a store of energy that had lain dormant, like the buried coal-measures, awaiting the right means of expression. Once or twice, attracted by the growing wealth of Hayseech, men had dared to approach her with clumsy overtures of courtship. They did not stay long. Bella Tinsley knew how to handle them.

"Is it me or the brass you're after?" she asked them frankly but not unkindly—and such was the directness, the compelling candour of the creature that they were forced, as a rule, to admit some part of the truth.

Then she smiled, and Bella Tinsley's smile had a charm beyond its unexpectedness, being gentle and faintly sad. Her voice, too, had tenderness in it.

"Nay, lad," she would say. "When I marry I shall

reckon to better myself, and I 'av'na set eyes on the right mon yet. No offence intended. Behappen I bain't what's called the marryin' kind."

Such was the general opinion. Bella Tinsley was now thirty-five, and women who worked as she did aged early. Was she a woman at all, or just a lad-wench, as her father had said?

III

THE problem was solved in secret, unexpectedly, and by a stranger.

In that prime of the Iron Age the black-country coal-field had begun to draw labour from all over the Western Midlands. The need was not filled, as in Lancashire, by mass-migrations or by the importation of gangs of workmen from Ireland. The drift was un-organized, and perhaps more natural. As industry grew it steadily sucked in the man-power of the adjoin-ing countryside, like a slowly-expanding sponge. All the roads that led to North Bromwich and its black neighbours were scattered with stalwart young men, with bundles on their backs, who had left the byre or the plough or the woodlands to try their luck in the land of promise. They came, above all, from the country of rolling hills and woods west of Severn, where a race of hereditary smelters of metal had declined with the ending of the charcoal iron-trade on the Shropshire border.

Jasper Mortimer was one of these. Where, exactly, he came from or what were his origins he never un-folded; he was a man of dark, brooding soul, slow and sparing of speech till the day of his death. All that the people of Mawne or Halesby knew of him was that he took the road and came eastward in search of a fortune in the year eighteen-fifty, a tall, dark-visaged man in the pride of his early manhood, with all his belongings on his back.

He followed the road that all raiders have taken since the days of Caradoc (by the name he bore, he had Marcher blood in his veins) crossing Severn below the Forest of Wyre at Bewdley; and the eve of his passage found him footsore at nightfall on the crown of the Clents, that range of hills that divides the green lands from the black. Sprawled there, in a brake of dry fern, he lay on his belly and looked downward. Immediately at his feet lay dense oak-woods, a gulf of darkness: the extended coppice through whose tangles the brook trickled down past Lapsley Mill to Hayseech. But beyond that dark zone, mounting into the sky as it seemed, for earth lay as black as air, there appeared a spectacle of infernal majesty: all the furnace-towers of the Black Country massed in fiery eruption. Those nocturnal splendours have faded now; but in the mid-nineteenth century the best part of five hundred blast-furnaces pointed their open throats to heaven like black howitzers bombarding a sky mantled fantastically and ringed and ridged with the low-hanging purple cloud of their own monstrous creation. Every muzzle white-hot at the lip, they poured forth their flowers and jets and streaming torrents of flame. When one group faded to flickers of summer-lightning, another broke forth, suddenly

born in the darkness, like a masked battery opening
fire. And beneath the high turmoil of this celestial
bombardment, like a sea of molten metal (which indeed it was), the sanded beds of a thousand puddling
furnaces swam with a more tawny light; so that the
whole of that sunken amphitheatre, twenty miles wide,
resembled nothing so much as a seething crater in
which the crust and substance of earth were being
reduced to a flux of red-hot lava.

Even to eyes accustomed to its majesty this scene
was impressive. In the mind of Mortimer, attuned to
the gentle hues and green silences of the border hills,
this panoply of fire aroused a strong exaltation. Its heat
and fierceness corresponded with some element hot and
fierce in his own dark nature, and called to it. The
spectacle of this vast reservoir of smouldering heat
and simmering power, the thought of the wealth sur-
passing all dreams that flowed from it, excited and
challenged him. His mind shook itself free from the
rustic taboos of custom and station by which he had
been bound. Amid the throes of an industrial upheaval
such as this he felt that a man of determination and
courage started level with his "betters." Birth, breeding, even education counted for nothing. Here the race
was to the swift and the battle to the strong; each man
for himself, and the devil take the hindmost! Aware
of his own strength and power to endure, he had an
almost prophetic confidence in himself and his future.
Beneath him illimitable riches lay sparkling like a

spilt casket of treasure; it seemed that he had only to stretch out his hand and pick up what he could. In that age of opportunity such illusions were not uncommon.

Refreshed and elated he rose. As he descended the hill-side, the spectacle sank with him till the last furnace-flame had set. Nothing survived of its glory but a red reflex momently flushing and waning in the sky, and from the earth an occasional mutter of sound like far thunder. From that sublime vantage-point he dropped to surroundings in which he felt more at home. Along the edge of the wood there was a smell of oak-leaf mould. He heard a chuckle of tumbling water, and the sharp yap-yap of a fox. He passed the mill-house at Lapsley standing empty amid thickets of nettles and entered the apex of the triangle of Hay-seech where the kilns shed a downward glow and the characteristic reek of baking clay hung acrid on the air. At this hour the brickyard appeared to be deserted, for the ovens had just been fired for the night; but beyond them, in Jo Tinsley's house, a single, uncurtained window shone. Mortimer, drawn to it like a moth to a candle, drew near. This was the first sign of habitation he had found since sunset. He was tired and had no idea where he was. At the best he might find a bite of food and bedding for the night, at the worst the direction of an inn or a lodging-house. He approached the window.

A young woman sat with her back to him writing

B

in a ledger by the light of two candles. On the table beside her were neat piles of coins, silver and copper. Her face was invisible, but the shape of her body pleased Mortimer, for it had vigour as well as grace, and the colour of her hair above the strong white neck was that dull gold of wintry beech-leaf which above all others had the mysterious power of inflaming him. Women coloured like that, he knew, were disposed to like him as he liked them. He tapped at the window, and she turned round, peering out into the glazed blackness with puzzled eyes. Her face disappointed him, inhibiting the mood of indefinite desire; she was older than he had imagined—probably older than himself. She came close to the window and saw him. After a hurried glance at the money on the table, she opened it, not in the least afraid.

"Who are you?" she said sharply. "What brings you here? What do you want?"

"I've come down from the hills," he said. "I'm a stranger to these parts. This was the first light I saw, so I came to it. I'ld like to know where I am."

Her face hardened. "This is Tinsley's brickfield, and you'll find the road to Mawne at the bottom of the holloway. You've no business mooching about a place in the dark. We don't want no tramps here, so you'd better hook it, lad."

She spoke harshly, but her eyes were not harsh. In spite of herself they unconsciously approved of this stranger. He was taller than she—that of itself was

unusual among the men she was wont to command;
for the Black Country physique is gnarled and stunted.
Of an opposite type, he possessed, like herself, the clear
stamp of a physical aristocracy. His eyes, too, had no
trace of servility. They were dark and deep-set in
craggy orbits that seemed blacker because of the pallor
of fatigue which made his brow pale—a pallor
accentuated again by the vigorous growth of hair on
head and cheek and chin. She liked, too, the gravity
of his mouth: the lips full yet firm with an odd combination of strength and childishness. She had never
seen a man like him. And he was tired in spite of
his strength. It seemed a pity that such a fine man
should be tired. She repented of her harshness.

"Where have you come from?" she said.

"A long way. Out of Shropshire."

Her eyes took in his decent clothes and clean linen:
"You don't look like a labourer."

"I'm not. My dad owns his own farm."

"Then why do you come here?"

"The land is too slow for me. And I saw the light
in the sky: the light from the furnaces. On the hills
you can see that light fifty miles away."

"And where are you going?"

"I don't know. Somewhere hereabouts, I reckon.
I'm looking for work."

"There's no job for you here," she said quickly.
"We've more hands than we want."

He laughed, and his mouth became charming.

"Who said I wanted to work here?"

"Well, I'm only telling you." She was taken aback by the question, not being used to men laughing at her. She said brusquely: "If you go down past the kilns you'll find the road as I told you. Behappen you'll find work at Hackett's. Good night to you."

Still smiling, he stood his ground. "I should like to work here," he said slowly, "now that I come to think of it."

For the first time she felt herself at an advantage. "I've told you we've nothing for you," she said scornfully. "Why should you want to work here?"

"Well, I have my fancies, the same as others. This place'ld suit me. You can make me a job if you want to, I seem to think. I'm a strong man, and I'm no fool. You'd better think on it."

Bella shivered. The dank air that blew in through the open window and fluttered the flame of her candle was icy cold.

"I'm not going to stand here starving, anyway," she said brusquely. Then she weakened: "If you want a job here, you'd better come round in the morning."

"Then where shall I sleep?"

"That's no business of mine. If you like you can sleep in the brickill anant the ovens. It's warm there, and you won't be the first."

"Is there a public handy where I can get food?"

"There are plenty of beer-shops in Halesby, if you've the money to pay. But I doubt you'll be wanted. They'd rather sell beer nor fittles. Are you hungry?"

"Hungry? I'm regular clemmed," he said. "Not a bite since morning."

She turned her eyes quickly to the table with the money on it. He broke in: "No, I don't want *that*. I'm no beggar, missis. But if you could find me a crust of bread and a drink of water, I wouldn't say 'No'." He laughed: "Though perhaps you're scared of being alone with a stranger? All that money about. . . ."

"I'm not scared of any man living," she answered contemptuously. "If you're hungry you'd better step in. Go round to the door, and I'll get you summat to eat. It's time for my supper, anyway."

When he entered the room she had disappeared. The piled gold and silver and copper—the brickill's week's wages—still lay on the table: more money than he had ever seen at one time in his life. But what impressed him more than the quantity of money was the fact that she had left it. That showed that she trusted him. It was unusual to find a woman whose nature was big enough to take risks. No woman he had ever known would have done that. A fire blazed fiercely in the grate and a kettle sang. The heat warmed his sinews and took the numbness from his limbs. He felt lazily complacent, well pleased with this end to his journey.

When the woman re-entered the room, he saw, with some satisfaction, that she had smoothed the dead-

golden hair whose colour attracted him. She had tied
on a clean white apron which showed her slim waist
and the generous curve of her breast, and the excitement of this odd adventure had not merely flushed
and softened her face but made it look young and
eager, restoring the illusion he had lost when she
turned and faced him. His dark eyes watched with
approbation the purposive movements of her body and
deft hands as she cleared the table and spread the
rough linen cloth with the coarse fare of the district:
a rib of green bacon and a quartern cottage-loaf of
seconds bread; but as she moved to and fro Bella
Tinsley's own eyes were lowered and rarely met his:
they were modest—he had almost said humble—nor
yet did she speak till she had finished laying the table
and poured out two glasses of thin beer.

"Come," she said. "You had better eat. It's getting
late."

They sat down on opposite sides of the table and
ate in silence. The food and the liquor completed
the comforting process the heat of the fire had begun.
Mortimer's appetite was enormous. By the time he
had eaten and drunk his fill he felt on good terms with
himself and the world. It tickled him to see himself on
the verge of some incalculable adventure in which this
woman opposite, so strangely subdued and silent in the
candle-light, was concerned. It struck him as odd, yet
characteristic of the whole affair, that he had no idea
to what or to whom he owed this impulsive hospitality.

What was she doing alone in this isolated house on which he had blindly stumbled? Was she married or widowed? He could see no ring on her finger. Why had she invited him to share her solitude? That was equally mysterious, though perhaps it might be explained by the increasing physical attraction which he felt and which filled with a strange intensity the silence between them.

As soon as the meal was over she cleared the table methodically and locked up the money in a cupboard. He sat gazing at the fire, not looking her way but always conscious of her quiet movements. At last she came near and placed a pair of worn slippers to warm on the hearth. A man's slippers. He took this as a hint for him to be going.

"I suppose these are your husband's," he said. "Are you expecting him?"

She laughed softly. "My husband's? What made you think I was married? They belong to my dad; but he's away in Wednesford. I'm not expecting him back to-night or to-morrow. I could see that your boots are soaked, so I brought them for you."

"You've sharp eyes," he said, "and a kind heart as well. Do you live here alone with him?"

"Alone since my mother died. That's fifteen years ago."

"And the brickyard belongs to him?"

"Yes. The brickill belongs to us."

"If I take off my boots," he said, with a curious

glance at her, "I shan't feel like moving. It'll be a raw night outside, in spite of the heat of the kilns."

"I've been thinking of that," she said calmly—and her voice, it seemed, had the quality of their strange, tense silence. "I've been thinking—if so be that you've a mind to stay here, you've no cause to go. There's an empty bed in Dad's room if you like to use it, and I've no objection."

"That's all very well," he said. "But what about *him?*"

"I've told you: he's away in Wednesford. Better take off your boots. If you leave them anant the gleed they'll dry in the night."

He obeyed, aware of her standing there and watching him. The relief from the grip of soaked leather was unbelievable. When he had pulled on Jo Tinsley's slippers, he looked up and smiled. Their eyes met; but no smile answered him. Her face was serene and grave; for the first time he found it beautiful. She took up a candle from the table and moved towards the bedroom door.

"I will show you the room," she said. "At Hayseech we go to bed early. It's nigh ten o'clock, and I have to be down in the sheds before six in the morning to check in the men and women and set them to work."

She opened the door, holding high the candle. Mortimer rose and followed her. The bedroom was bare and low-ceiled, with no furniture but a chair and a double iron bedstead; but the walls were whitened with lime and the room smelt sweet, and the sheets on the bed were as invitingly clean as the starched table-cloth off which they had eaten.

"If I pass through here before it's light," she told him, "you needn't disturb yourself. I sleep in the room beyond, and there's no other way through. But you've no call to stir before I've come back from the sheds and got you your breakfast. Now I shall leave you."

She spoke as she turned to the inner door, without looking at him. Mortimer spoke and stopped her.

"I've not thanked you," he said, "as I should. I've forgotten my manners."

"Oh, that's naught," she said hurriedly. "There's no call for thanks. I'm glad you came here."

"It's a rum go, when you come to think of it: me turning up out of the dark. It was enough to scare you."

She smiled. "It takes more nor that to scare *me*. That's the way things happen. Now I'd better be going. You look tired. Sleep well. Good night."

"Aren't you going to leave me a light?"

"You can have this, if you want one."

She held out the candle. Mortimer advanced and took it together with the hand that held it.

"I'm not so sure that I do," he said slowly, gazing steadily at her.

Then he smiled, and blew out the light.

IV

ARABELLA's marriage to Mortimer, which took place two months later, marked the real turning-point in the genesis of the Tinsley fortune. Though her father and she had laboured unsparingly to lay its foundations, their vision and their powers of development were limited. Hayseech, at this point, resembled an orchard whose powers of self-fertilization were limited and possibly waning. To achieve the full fruition of which it was capable, perhaps even to survive, it needed a brisk pollination from an alien strain.

Jasper Mortimer provided this: not wholly to the satisfaction of Jo Tinsley. It had been something of a shock to him, first of all, to find the dark stranger installed in his home on his return from Wednesford. He accepted the accomplished fact because, now that he had begun to grow old, Arabella was stronger than he, but grudgingly, still supposing that the arrangement was a mere whim and temporary. When she proceeded to marry Mortimer out of hand he cut up rougher.

"What d'you want to get married for," he asked, "at your time of life?"

"For the best of reasons," she told him, with a laugh. "I've got to marry him."

The wench had no modesty. You would have said that she gloried in it. She had, indeed, re-created a shadow of the youth which, cooped up at Hayseech, she had never enjoyed in its proper season. She was gay, she was tender; she glowed with a kind of wild radiance which made Tinsley sometimes add jealousy to his dislike of the son-in-law she had thrust on him.

But even though he grudged his influence, Tinsley couldn't dispute the adaptability, the mental and bodily energy Mortimer brought to their business. He swept through the stagnant air of Hayseech like a livening wind. This amazing marriage, together with the prospect of a child, had concentrated into a single channel the indefinite force which had driven him from home. If Hayseech was not yet the property of his wife and himself it soon would be, and no time was to be lost, out of deference to Tinsley's prejudice, in making the most of it. His quick mind grasped the fact that for want of imagination and energy opportunity had already been wasted. This was the golden moment: within a short space the boom in the malleable-iron trade might be over. Every rising barrack and factory in the Black Country clamoured for Tinsley's blue bricks. As many as were made could be sold before they were dry. Some day soon the demand might slacken and prices fall. It was their duty, while the going was good, to quicken production.

By this time the clay scooped daily from the bottom

of the pit was as much as the existing machinery could comfortably raise. Rain-water and hidden springs seeped into the crater, so that half of the power available was wasted in pumping. The obvious course was to uncover the whole extent of the clay-pocket's surface and start new dry workings. Under Mortimer's supervision they stripped another half-acre. On the edge of their digging they struck coal.

This was not surprising. The outcrop of Hayseech had been casually used by the Tinsleys for the last fifty years. The seams they had dug were thin and mingled with shale: tolerable fuel for the baking of bricks and useful for little else. But the coal which the new digging exposed was a different matter. It was the so-called Brooch Coal: a four-foot seam of high quality was the Brooch Coal's calculable output: with a four-foot seam, say five thousand tons per acre in all! By the time that Bella's first child, a daughter, was born, the Brooch Coal had been verified over an area of more than five acres. Twenty-five thousand tons of coal at a sovereign a ton at the pit-head!

And this was not all. Jo Tinsley would probably have been contented to take this gift of the gods at its surface value. Mortimer, backed by the faith and fiery energy of his wife, stopped at nothing. While Bella, at home, proudly held the fort and controlled the growing business, he ranged far and wide over the district in search of new knowledge. His black eyes devoured all they saw, and never forgot; his shrewd tongue picked the brains of men more experienced than himself. He began—and in this, again, his wife helped him—to understand the difficult Black Country temperament and speak its harsh dialect. He had a way of communicating his enthusiasm and inspiring confidence, and a reputation for justice; so that when the Brooch Coal began to be raised in quantity there were many old miners in Mawne who came knocking at the door of the Hayseech office for work.

At this time, indeed, in the prime of his manhood, Jasper Mortimer certainly presented an attractive figure. There is a daguerreotype portrait of him in the mid-eighteen-fifties preserved in the offices of Josiah Tinsley and Co., Ltd., at Hayseech, which might be chosen as a typical representation of the successful Victorian manufacturer: tall and spare, not an ounce of surplus flesh on his sinewy body; black-haired and black-browed, with a strong growth of curling whisker. His head is thrown back; his eyes (which in such portraits are usually glazed by the paralyzing duration of the pose) have an intense, level gaze, not precisely sceptical, but challenging, and there is a challenge, too, in the slightly hard, pugnacious setting of the lips.

His wife worshipped him and was immeasurably proud of him—of his hardness no less than of his rare tendernesses. Their union was a firm offensive and defensive alliance. All their material interests (and they had no others) were identical. Her only regrets

were that she was older than he, that they hadn't
met sooner, and that their only son, the second
child of the marriage, died of croup (it was probably
diphtheria) in infancy. It seemed as if the Tinsley
stock in the male line were destined to extinction. Five
years after their marriage she produced another
daughter, Arabella the second. After that it was too
late.

By this time the seams of the Brooch Coal in their
original workings were becoming exhausted, and Jo
Tinsley, long since consigned to the background, had
died leaving thirty-odd thousand pounds. But the
development of Hayseech, as Mortimer knew, had
hardly begun. Below the Brooch Coal, all over the extended estate—for before its secret was out they had
spent their last penny in buying adjacent properties—
lay seam below seam of amazing mineral wealth. Beneath the Brooch layer, in every shaft that he sank,
Mortimer discovered, as he had hoped, the Thick Coal,
the great ten-yard seam: thirty thousand tons of
marketable coal to the acre—and the original acreage
of Hayseech had now been increased from ten to
thirty! There was the Roofs Seam, the Top Slipper,
the White Coal and the Lambs: all adapted for use in
the most delicate of local industries, from the annealing
of a needle to the welding of gun-barrels, and fit to be
used uncoked in the smelting furnaces. Beneath these
lay the Heathen Coal, the best coking coal in the
district; and between and below these two measures,

incredibly apposite, appeared vast deposits of the Gubbin Ironstone, the New Mine Ironstone, the Blue Flats Ironstone: raw material for the creation of a new and gigantic industry.

It came of itself, this new spurt of development—now that the growth of Hayseech moved by geometrical progression—at the moment in the world's industrial history best prepared to receive it. New mined ore from California had flooded America with gold that would furnish two armies impartially with British rifles and field-guns and road-rails and every machine and trinket of metal that the men of the North and South were too busy fighting to make. Mortimer threw himself into the press with volcanic energy. New mine-shafts were sunk; new head-gear began to spin; the cages were shot up and down the twin shafts like busy shuttles. Now the mineral-railway, detached from the Halesby branch line at Mawne Road, crossed the Stour on two high girder bridges and wound into Hayseech. An officious squat locomotive, the "Arabella," bustled to and fro, shunting trucks from this line to that and whistling shrill warnings to sooty colliers jumping the rails to escape her and turning sooty faces and pale eyes to swear at the nuisance. But the little engine puffed on, shrieking every few yards, and the shunted trucks clanked in a thunderous *feu de joie*, shot free, running loose to the sidings where trolleys rumbling along on their endless cables like black insects following the twists of their leader in single file climbed the

ramps and tipped each its appropriate load of Brooch
Coal for household burning, of Brazils for reverbera-
tory furnaces, of Heathen Coal for coke, and coarse
Bottom Coal for lime-burning. Other railway-trucks
were packed daily with thousands of blue bricks which
still issued unceasingly from Josiah's bottomless claypit. But no truck which left the sidings now returned
empty. In those days an even greater weight of
material poured into Hayseech than left it: new
trolleys and cutting machinery and pit-props for the
work underground; iron girders to carry the workshop
roofs and corrugated galvanized sheets to cover them;
lengths of metal tubing of different calibres to distri-
bute gas, steam and water; curved plates of forged
steel and rivets by the ton—for now, by the side of the
colliery head-gear, where ironstone lay heaped in
mounds the colour of dried blood, three cylindrical
towers of black metal were swiftly rising: Jasper
Mortimer's new hot-blast furnaces for the smelting of
pig-iron.

He was moving, logically, in advance of his time,
towards the grandiose conception of an establishment
that would be complete in itself, self-supporting and
self-contained; a works that could handle metal from
the state of ore to the finished forging—towards the
stage later to be known as "integration," in which
the fluctuating costs of raw materials could no
longer affect him. Every penny of the fortune which
Josiah had left him went into it. His credit was

pledged to the hilt, but he borrowed cheaply: there was no difficulty in finding money for a man who possessed thirty acres of ten-yard coal!

They still lived, Arabella and he and the two children, in the mean house, no more than a cottage, which Josiah had built; they still kept no servant. Indeed, there was no room for one, and Arabella despised a woman who could not do her own housework. It was with the greatest reluctance that she had abandoned her active share in the management of the works, whose gradual extensions enveloped their dwelling so closely that there was no more silence in it by day or by night nor freedom from the smell of fire and the fine drift of coal-dust. It stood there like a solitary rock, gradually submerged by the rising tide.

Hayseech was no longer a fit place for the bringing-up of children. In a few brief years the whole aspect of the valley had changed. Of old its thickets of gorse and scattered hawthorns had given its neglected acres a quality of wildness and secrecy; and, indeed, it was secret, for the cart-track which penetrated it from the holloway assuredly led nowhere, petering out, amid clumps of grey-green rushes and drifts of mare's-tail, at the foot of the fishpond and the edge of the wood. Foxes barked in the night there and sometimes an otter whistled; rings of rising fish dimpled the water's surface and, rarely, a nightingale sang. Now there was hardly a blade of green in its whole extent. All the surface-soil, and with it the gorse and the may, had

been stripped to uncover clay or coal and heaped into
banks where only the niggardly weeds of the waste
found rootage. Through the heart of it ran a road of
crushed slag, the main strand of a network of minor
ways faced with cinders crossed here and there by
narrow-gauge rails, on which the trolleys ran to and
fro on their purposive way to the tips, and broad-
gauge rails where the mineral-wagons shunted. The
fishpond itself had been narrowed still further by
dumpings of ballast. The exhaust of the great beam-
engine that hauled the cages discharged itself into it:
its surface lay iridescent with oily scum, opaquely reflecting the spindly head-gear of the pit's main shaft
with its spinning-wheel and the barren mound of the
steadily-growing spoil-heap. The brook, still falling
to the Stour, was now no more than a ditch; its bright
pebbles blackened and beslimed, its waters milky with
clay or reddened with ironstone. All the trout which
once lurked in its bays had sickened and died; no life
remained in it. And all over this blighted scene there
hung heavy or languidly moved, with the ebb and
flow of polluted tidal water, an air that was acrid to
the tongue and charged with hot fumes of burning
slack and oily smoke of bituminous coal; so that the
trees which had held their own stubbornly for
centuries were choked, shed their leaves, and died
back from the tips of their branches; so that Spring,
when it visited them now, brought no birds with
whimpers of nesting or torrent of love-song, but

Winter possessed the wood eternally in a dumb Decembral silence.

Neither Mortimer nor his wife was aware of the death and desolation they had brought to Hayseech. There was new life, of another sort, monstrous life, in the perpetual motion of turning wheels and the hot respiration of furnaces that broke into flowers of flame. Before the American war was ended three of these were in blast, fanned white-hot with the gases released from their own combustion, each capable of producing five thousand tons of iron pig in a year. Mortimer fed their red throats incessantly with the ironstone he had raised. Already his restless mind had run on to the day when the pig-iron should be puddled and refined and forged on the spot by the steam-hammers whose concrete emplacements were settling in their pits before the foundations of the sheds which should cover them had been laid.

It was the proudest day of his life when the components of the first of these giant hammers arrived: the proudest and the most bitter, for, that night, Arabella died.

V

HER loss weighed upon him more heavily than those who condoled with him guessed. This dark-visaged man, apparently so composed, so self-possessed in his grim efficiency, was, in fact, in this one relationship, oddly tender and sensitive. She had contributed far more to their fifteen years' partnership than the material for the fortune his imagination had foreshadowed. From the strange moment of darkness when she had surrendered herself so mysteriously to his arms, she had given him a complete and utterly unselfish devotion. Wisdom, too, and a ballast of strict common sense which had steadied the sweep of his ambition. There was no step in the early development of Hayseech to which she had not contributed an equal share. In its first stages she had worked at his side— literally worked with her hands. Later on, when the children came, she had still clung to her office as business manager, dealing with correspondence as it arrived and always paying the hands on Saturday. After this there had come a time when she could not keep pace with the man she had made or with the business which escaped from her hands like an unbottled *djinn*. There was a point at which mere native shrewdness was not sufficient, at which instinct had to give way to intellect;

and here Mortimer, with his remarkable brain, shot off ahead of her and, almost, out of sight. Even then, if she was bewildered, Arabella had not been discouraged. She had plodded dustily in the rear, contented that, if the pace slackened, if he checked for a breathing space, she might still catch up with him, or hoping that if he should be forced to turn back he might find her waiting for him. It is doubtful if Mortimer, in the glory of his strength, even realized the strain which her un-relaxed effort cost her. Arabella was nearly ten years older than he. At the time when her second child was born she was over forty. What was more, in spite of the strength and hardihood which had been part of her original attraction to him and the apparently in-exhaustible energy which she poured out ungrudgingly on his behalf, she was not so strong as she seemed. No child working, as she had worked, in the Hayseech brickill, no young woman, standing day after day in the slime and dankness of the moulding-sheds, could be said to have had a fair start in life. For a number of years pride and courage born of her love had con-trived to mask every sign of the strain that was telling on her. For his sake, she had refused to grow old. Yet old she was, far older than her years, and the effort of concealing it made her feel older still. When, after the birth of the second child, Mortimer gaily announced to her that the site of their house could no longer be spared—it was to be covered by a new block of offices—and that he had prepared plans for

the building of a new one, more in keeping with their
station, on the slopes of the higher land he had bought
on the Halesby side, she could have cried for vexation.
. He was so boyishly fired by the project that he did
not notice her distress.

"You see, Bella," he said, "quite apart from the fact
that it don't look right for people like us to be living
in a cottage like this, it'll be better for you and the
children in every way. More fresh air and less noise."

She gazed at the plans and shook her head.

"It looks terribly big. How shall I ever keep all
them rooms clean?"

He laughed. "You won't have to, my wench.
You'll have servants. And it's just about time. You
ought to have had them long ago."

"Servants, Jasper? You know I could never abear
the lazy bissoms. I like things done my own road, and
the only way to get that is to do 'em yourself. Put it
off for a bit, Jasper," she begged him.

"How contrary you are! Here I go, trying to give
you a slap-up house of your own with hot water and
gas and all and no expense spared—trying to give you
the chance of a rest for the first time in your life, and
you take it as if I'd asked you to go to the work'us! If
you go on talking like that I shall think there's summat
wrong with you and send for the doctor."

"No, no," she said. "I'm all right." (She was terrified of doctors.) "I only wish you could wait till next
year."

"Why next year? What difference 'ld that make? You don't know what's good for you, that's your trouble," he said, with a laugh. "And I want the land we're standing on. I can't wait. As a matter of fact, if you want to know, we've started digging the foundations."

Nothing that Mortimer touched at Hayseech ever went slowly. On the top of the slope the walls of the new house soon began to rise. Arabella watched them with a sinking heart. The place seemed to her enormous. It was a building of a kind much fancied by mid-Victorian architects, a mansion in the Tudor manner decorated with numerous scutcheons, as yet innocent of emblazonment, and mullioned windows. Its interior was the latest thing in decoration, being lined with panelling of orange pitch-pine and served by a pitch-pine staircase, and the windows were lavishly variegated with real coloured glass, geometrically disposed, and with transfers of mediæval scenes in the manner (though not in the taste) of the early pre-Raphaelites. The whole building was, in fact, the architect's counter-blow to the stucco-baronial grandeurs of Mr. Willis's new Mawne Hall.

When the time for moving drew near, Arabella set herself, with a heavy heart, to furnishing it.

"You can let yourself go," Mortimer said. "I'm not sparing expense. When we put in for big contracts we shall have to do some entertaining, and I look on this house as part of the necessary advertisement. Now you'll be able to enjoy yourself."

For his sake she pretended to enjoy herself. She was not feeling well. When she walked up the hill to the new house, she had to stop; her breath seemed to leave her. And the staircase inside made her breathless, too. Mortimer himself was too busy at this time to trouble his head about domestic matters; but the two children enjoyed the excitement, running all over the echoing, empty house and shouting, entranced with their own noise. They were beginning to get on her nerves; she hated herself for being cross with them, but couldn't help it. One day, alone in the house, she turned giddy and fainted.

This frightened her so much that she stole away and consulted the chemist in Halesby who had generally prescribed for the moulders in the brickill. He listened to her from behind his counter as she whispered her troubles to him. The shop was full of shawled women and snivelling children.

"It might be the heart and it might be the kidneys, Mrs. Mortimer," he said, and he gave her some black pills coated with yellow powder marked: "One, three times a day." Bella took the pills in secret; for she knew that if Mortimer guessed she was taking medicine it would worry him. She had hopes and faith in the chemist's medicine; but somehow taking it didn't seem to make much difference. Her legs felt just as leaden, swelled just the same, though fortunately her skirt was so long that nobody could see them. And always, with the pressure of a nightmare, the new great house and the threat of servants lay on her mind. She stood in the draughty hall, smelling the undried plaster and gazing at the little heaps of swept shavings, and the hopelessness of ever getting it clean appalled her. One day she caught cold; the cold spread to her lungs. The doctor, examining her chest, was shocked by the state of her heart, as well he might be.

"Have you ever had rheumatism, Mrs. Mortimer?"

She couldn't remember. In the old days, working in the damp clay of the moulding-sheds, she had known too many aches and pains to take much count of them. When her lungs became choked with bronchitis, the poor heart had to meet a strain which it couldn't bear. Before she guessed she was dying her pulse faltered and stopped. The district was greatly disappointed by the meagre character of her funeral: just the hearse and one four-wheeled cab, and no flowers to speak of!

VI

But the pulse of the works neither weakened nor faltered for an instant. It would take more than the death of a woman to break its gigantic rhythm. Jasper Mortimer knew this and embraced the necessity as a duty. Arabella, he consoled himself, would never forgive him if he allowed Hayseech—which, after all, was her trust to him—to fail through the weakness of an unseasonable grief. He missed her enormously, though far less than he would have missed her if she had died ten years earlier. In those early days he had consulted her and bowed to her advice; of late he had, rather, expounded to her and claimed her approval. Still, even though he knew that this approval had been given automatically, he felt the lack of it: even when he knew he was infallible he had got into the way of being told so. He felt, more than all, the lack of somebody to think aloud to in the grey of dawn or last thing at night. He had always been, but for Arabella, a lonely man. Now his loneliness was a desolation.

People supposed he would re-marry quickly, as a matter of mere convenience: a man of his wealth and standing could "suit himself" easily. Regard for the dead was all very well, but might surely be overdone in the case of a well-set-up man without a grey hair on his head and with a fine new house and two girls, one nine and one fifteen, suddenly left on his hands. Some nice comfortable middle-aged woman, a childless widow perhaps, would meet the situation. There was no lack of candidates or of canvassers to urge their qualifications.

But Mortimer did not re-marry. As for the furnishing of the house, he handed that over for completion to a firm of upholsterers in North Bromwich who were prepared to give estimates for providing a proper setting for a prominent industrial magnate on the usual scale. For its conduct he engaged a housekeeper, a woman of experience, but, regrettably, a stranger (he was not going to have his house made the gossip of the district) who dealt easily with those servants whose advent Arabella had dreaded so deeply. For the children he employed a series of governesses who disputed with the housekeeper for the children's affections.

Mortimer's business acquaintances took it for granted that he made love to his governesses. When their wives lamented his neglect to provide his girls with a stepmother, they winked and leered and said there was safety in numbers, though they couldn't understand how a man with such opportunities hadn't made a more prepossessing selection.

Mortimer was not concerned with the looks of these ladies, nor were they his mistresses. He had already one single exacting mistress: Hayseech. Now that his

wife had died he became, more than ever, absorbed in
it. For by now his ideal of the "integrated" concern
was taking shape. The new Companies Act provided
his various activities with a convenient frame. All the
components of his group of associated industries—The
Blue Brick Co., the Hayseech Collieries, the New
Midland Iron and Steel Co., The Hayseech Lime and
Coke Co.—were now merged in the great concern
which, partly out of sentiment and partly because the
name had been so long familiar, he had christened
Josiah Tinsley and Company, Ltd. This was the name
which finally appeared on the wagons which were to
be seen and subconsciously remembered throughout the
extent of every railway system in the United King-
dom; the name which was stamped upon girders and
bridges in savage continents and upon the skeletons of
the iron ships that carried them overseas. On the board
of the new company there were directors to whom he
had allotted the holdings necessary for their qualifica-
tion—mostly foremen or managers or clerks in the
works whose fortunes had risen with them—but the
control of policy and more than ninety-seven per
cent of the ordinary stock were still vested in the hands
of one man: Jasper Mortimer.

He became something of a figure in the district,
this man of fifty with his tall, spare figure, his strong,
pale emaciated features, so much older than their age,
in their frame of stiff black hair and eyebrows and
whiskers. He had adopted a fashion of dress which

made him look taller than he was: a full-skirted frock-coat, buttoned high at the neck, with a starched collar and a black satin cravat, and a tall black felt hat, rounded at the top and encircled with a deep band of crape. He was respected, but never liked, by men of his own position. He walked brooding, it seemed, in a cloud of dark meditation; he neither made jokes nor laughed at the jokes of others; never dined, if he could help it, away from home; never gave a penny to any organized charity or political party—at a time when other "new" men, such as the Willises and Hingstons and Hacketts, were vying with each other in gestures of public munificence. This singular resistance to the temptation of courting popularity gave him the name of a miser; and, oddly enough, this reputation did him no harm: the Black Country respected (except in the case of that funeral) a man who refrained deliberately from "making a splash," and men working at Hayseech were paid higher wages than most in the district. What was more, though he never frequented the "society" of his peers, Jasper Mortimer was always accessible, as his wife and father-in-law had been, to the humblest of his workers—more accessible to them, indeed, than to his own children.

He had never taken paternity very seriously or the children as anything more than a casual by-product of a marriage whose real purpose had been the acquisition of Hayseech. He would have liked to have reared a son, but mainly for the sake of the continuity in the ownership of the property and the management of the business. As for his daughters, his attitude towards them in their infancy had been grudging and even irritable. He was jealous of the time (and perhaps of the affection) which Arabella gave them; for being devoted to one woman, the first and last, he could not tolerate a divided devotion on her side. If he found the two children a nuisance he had an excuse in the inconvenience they must have been to so busy a man in such a diminutive house.

They had no reason to be fond of him either; for he appeared to them as no more than a dark, brooding figure on whose appearance the house fell quiet, like a spinney over which a hawk hovers.

After the death of their mother they saw even less of him than before. He was a grim and anxious man. With the end of the Civil War in America there came a slump which the Prusso-Danish and the Austro-Prussian Wars did little to relieve. It was a ticklish time for Josiah Tinsley & Co. The overhead expenses of their enormous establishment went on; it seemed as if they had bitten off more than their customers could chew. Melancholy prophets in North Bromwich declared that the Iron Age was over. At Hayseech two of Mortimer's new furnaces stood cold. What made things look blacker than ever was the invention of the open-hearth process for the making of steel in which the phosphoric ores of Hayseech could not be utilized. All the ore suited to the new process was mined in Cumberland. It became clear to him that if he wanted to make open-hearth steel, the metal of the future, he must set up new plants in the North or nearer the coast where sea transport would cheapen the cost of ore. For the second time he was faced with a situation that demanded the risking of all his accumulated capital and the making of new debts. For the second time he threw down a glove to Fortune. He bought a site and erected new works in South Wales.

During that anxious time Mortimer left Hayseech every Tuesday morning, and rarely returned before Friday night. To the children—Harriet was now seventeen and Bella thirteen—he was more of a stranger than ever. The only occasions on which they saw him were at meal-times when, in silence, he occupied the head of the table, and on Sunday mornings when, as a matter of routine, they walked over the fields behind him to the box-pew he rented in Halesby Church, and later, according to custom, inspected their mother's grave. Even then he appeared unaware of his intimidated retinue, and when Sunday dinner was over he left them immediately to prowl round the works: a world into which the two little girls had never been allowed to penetrate.

Their neighbours were sorry for them. Everything that happened in the grand new house at Hayseech was material for gossip in Halesby. It seemed a pity, too, that Mortimer himself got so little benefit from the society of two such nice-looking, well-mannered girls. The elder, Harriet, or Hattie for short, "took after" him: she was tall and old for her age, black-haired, hazel-eyed, with the pallid, fine-textured skin that often accompanies this colouring, and, already, a hint of a moustache. In her, as in Mortimer, the dark Celtic gene was dominant; but her nature was shy and compressed, as were her thin lips, and this instinctive stiffness throttled the vitality which might have coloured her looks and made her, in an arid way, beautiful. These suppressions were the fault of her upbringing. From their earliest childhood she had not been allowed to mix with other children: not merely because Hayseech was so physically isolated, but because her mother, who had begun her life as a working woman, felt ill at ease with neighbours of their own station, whom she regarded as too "grand" for the likes of herself, and equally fearful of the work-people, in whom familiarity might possibly breed contempt. Mortimer, again, had ambitious ideas on the subject of education. Though he couldn't be bothered with their company, he was anxious to fit his children for the state of society to which his own future position would call them, so that the governesses he chose were invariably what are called "ladies," elderly women of a severe and precise gentility. The two girls were brought up in a tradition of old-fashioned propriety in speech and deportment. Their tongues were free from the Black Country accent and idiom which he himself used, and they had the attitude towards life of daughters of a "county" family.

Hattie, doubtful of herself and instinctively retiring, quickly adopted her governesses' prim manners as a protective coloration for her shyness. Assuming the domestic responsibilities of an elder sister, she became, at eighteen, a passable imitation of a well-connected middle-aged spinster. Arabella's nature proved less amenable. She was her mother's daughter—and therefore, so far as he took any notice of either, her father's favourite. She had inherited her mother's colouring—the white skin, readily suffused with quick blushes, the dead-golden hair—to which Mortimer had been so susceptible. If her body had not that instinctive grace and fineness, suggestive of race, which made strangers sometimes speculate on her father's origins, it had a certain glowing vitality whose warmth served to accentuate her sister's coldness. Like the first Arabella, she was a creature of impulse: swift to anger and swiftly forgiving; at once prejudiced and generous; bewildering in her quick alternations of passion, yet always, in the main, large-hearted. Even as a child she could be mulishly obstinate—that defect (or virtue) derived from both sides of her odd heredity—but her obstinacy, unlike her sister's, proceeded from a surplus of feeling rather than from an excess of caution and was so salted with humour that, without any warning, she was ready to laugh at her own extravagance and to relapse into a gentle sub-

c

missiveness that was disarming because it was so child-like. Above all, she was naturally affectionate, so demonstrative in this as to make her sister wilt with shyness; and her affection, when once bestowed, hardened into an adamantine loyalty, illogical, impervious to persuasion or scorn or reason—to anything, indeed, but the softening influence of a similar affection. Though, in her gusty, passionate way, she loved her sister, their two natures resembled a positive and a negative pole, each conveying electrical current of high potential, and their governesses, living in the gap that separated them, were subject to a bombardment of blue sparks and crackles which reduced these well-mannered ladies to a state of apprehensive bewilderment.

VII

DURING the years of his daughters' adolescence all Mortimer's energies and attention were absorbed in his new challenge to Fortune, his open-hearth steel-works at Pandypool in South Wales. He had other embarrassments, the chief of which was the flooding of the lower levels of the Hayseech Colliery, an ever-present menace in that wet coal-field. It was not till the spring of eighteen-seventy that he began to see his way clear. He had even begun to flatter himself with the idea of enjoying, for the first time since the building of the new house, a normal domestic life.

Hattie was now in her nineteenth year, and Bella sixteen. Miss Beagle, the last of the series of governesses, had announced her intention of resigning her ticklish post: and no wonder, for life in the smoky, fire-girt cloister of Hayseech—in that house which no stranger entered from one year's end to another—was neither various nor entertaining. Her charges, she said, were by now equipped with the modest degree of accomplishment befitting young ladies. Bella, she admitted, was still something of a problem: the quickness and precocity of her mind had not been applied to the acquisition of useful knowledge and domestic science; she was, in fact, a "handful" and led the whole household "a dance." But then, she was young, and age would bring sobriety. Hattie, on the other hand, was a mirror of all the virtues: serious-minded, polite, and, above all, an excellent housekeeper, fit to take her place at the opposite end of any gentleman's dining-table.

Mortimer listened to her gravely: the prim old cat amused him. He laughed to himself when he heard of Bella's waywardness. Her mother, after all, had been a woman of character with a mind of her own, as witness the incident of their marriage—a story which Miss Beagle would certainly not have found edifying. He had a feeling that this younger daughter of his, with her smiling eyes and humorous mouth and those little mannerisms which often, with the ghost of a pang, recalled to him the rapturous Arabella of their first love-making, might be a charming companion for the leisure of his declining days. (He thought of them thus; for, though he was still short of fifty, he had compressed and expended in the last twenty years as much energy as would last most men the best part of a lifetime.) And then, just as he had begun to think of taking his ease and enjoying it, he found himself snatched up again into a pitch of activity that made all his previous labours appear insignificant. This time it was no question of flinging a gage to Fortune, but of struggling to keep pace with the shower of favours she threw at him.

One stifling evening of mid-July, so windless that

the smoke from the works hung motionless over the pit of Hayseech in long streaks, like the tattered shreds of a sable catafalque, the two sisters awaited his return to the supper-table in vain. His lateness was unusual. When he was at home his life had the regularity of clockwork. Hattie, always inclined to be apprehensive of evil, grew anxious at his delay; but Bella laughed at her. "You would think the man wasn't old enough to look after himself," she said. But day died out of the sky, and still Mortimer did not come. Hattie wanted to run down to the office at the works and find out what had happened. "If you do that," Bella told her, "he's bound to come in at the back and you'll miss him." It was now quite dark—unusually dark for that season of the year—and preternaturally still. From the west beyond the hills, the sky was washed with summer lightning; nearer at hand it was lightened from time to time with jets of flame released from the furnaces of Mawne and Hayseech or the amber reflex of boiling "pig" pouring into the puddling-beds; and each of these illuminations, momently flashed on the sky, outlined the invisible pall that still hung there in tatters with lurid light. It was mortally quiet. Even the corncrake which faithfully frequented the neglected fields below Lapsley Mill had gone dumb. The only sound that reached their ears was an occasional mutter of far thunder or the rumbles, resembling the bubbling of a pent volcano, which came from the works.

In an interval of silence they heard heavy steps on the cinder pathway, and Mortimer entered the house. His face was haggard, his dark eyes dilated with excitement. He carried a paper map which he spread on the table and scanned as he ate. Throughout the meal not a word was spoken: the girls themselves were almost too scared to eat. They supposed something dreadful had happened—perhaps a colliery disaster; but the excitement in their father's face was that of exultation, not of distress. At length he pushed back his plate and began to talk with an unusual animation. His long, grimy forefinger pointed to the map, darting hither and thither, or rapped the table nervously. Here, he said, was MacMahon at Strasbourg, here Canrobert at Châlons, here Marshal Bazaine at Metz. Here, close to the Rhine, Moltke was already detraining his Second Army. "This means war to the death," he said, "a long war—the longer the better! Do you understand? Whichever side wins or loses it's the same to us. This is the day for which I've been waiting. They can have whatever they want, either side, at a price!"

It's an ill wind, they say, that blows nobody any good. The Franco-Prussian war blew a hot *scirocco* which fanned every ember in the smouldering Black Country into incandescence. Not merely the gun-barrel-makers, but locksmiths and brassfounders, makers of picks and shovels and edge-tools and harness and curry-combs and buttons and optical glass, found their books choked with orders. New factories sprang up in odd corners of the waste, and each factory demanded equipment with power-machinery. The glut of new money to be had for the asking encouraged spending and fostered a taste for luxuries. Manufacturers' wives fancied hand-made jewellery and workmen's wives cheaper trinkets stamped by machinery. The whole district, which lately had languished, burst into an efflorescence of flame, a pandemonium of hoarse-breathing furnaces and hissing steam-pipes, of spinning-wheels and writhing belts, of machinery that stamped and hammered and rolled and ground and squeezed and sliced perpetually. And beneath all this riot, in the fossilized forest-swamps of the ten-yard coal, an unseen army, mole-like, burrowed in Plutonic blackness. Every one of these industries clamoured for fuel, for iron to build their machines and for bricks to house them.

This was, in fact, the iron-trade's culminating period of triumph, and Mortimer, with his "integrated" concern at Hayseech and his new steel-works in Wales, had the world at his feet. There was not a single product of his pits, his kilns or his furnaces that failed of an eager market. All the stocks of pig-iron, which he had accumulated unwillingly with no purpose but that of keeping his furnaces hot, were swept away from him in the first months of the war. In eighteen-seventy, iron was selling at eight pounds a ton; by the end of 'seventy-two the price had touched sixteen and continued to soar. Prosperity on this scale was frightening. The effort to keep up with it exhausted and aged him so much that he was almost thankful when at the end of four years the German-dictated Treaty of Peace was signed. He was an old man of fifty-three; his hair had turned white. Now, at last, he would settle down to the enjoyment of life and of his daughters' society. But it was too late. He had missed his chance. There was only one daughter left.

Arabella had gone. The occurrence was as natural as that a ripe pear should fall to the ground. No creature so vivid and ardent could fail to attract attention (or to return it) even though she were hidden in a spot as cloistered as Hayseech. Whenever she emerged—as, for instance, in church—young men's eyes had begun to wander towards her. This distressed her sister extremely.

"I think it's disgusting, Bella," she said. "If things like that happened to *me*" (things like that did not happen to Hattie) "I should sink into the earth for shame."

Bella laughed. "Well, I can't stop them looking at me, can I?" she said. "If it does them good, it doesn't hurt *me*. I think it's a shame that girls of our age don't know any young men."

"Well, the least you can do if it happens again," Hattie said, "is to keep your eyes down. If you don't, they'll think you're encouraging them. As a matter of fact I'm positive I saw you smile. If they were people

of our own class like the Hingstons or Willises . . .
But they aren't; they're just nothing more than the
riff-raff of Halesby, clerks and shop-assistants and
so on. As Miss Beagle said . . ."

Bella laughed; she had a light silvery tinkle of a
laugh which her sister considered not merely frivolous
but vulgar.

"Miss Beagle? That horrid old pussy-cat? You
know, Hattie, you hated her just as much as I did; but
now that she's gone, thank heaven, you do nothing
but quote her. If you don't look out you'll turn into
a Beagle yourself. As for 'people like ourselves':
that's just rubbish. You knew perfectly well we're
nothing to boast of in that way. Mother worked in the
moulding-shed herself: she told me so lots of times.
If it comes to that, your Hingstons and Willises aren't
much better either. If Mother made bricks, Mr.
Willis's father laid them. And I'm not going to be
grand, however much you try to force me. I like
people for what they are, and I want to know heaps of
them. I happen to be made like that."

"You're too young to know what you're made like,"
Hattie said scornfully. "And if Mother did work in
the brickill you needn't raise your voice when you say
so, and amuse the servants. After all, I'm only doing
my duty by warning you. I don't *want* to tell
Father . . ."

"If you did, I'ld kill you, Hattie. What a mean
thing you are!"

c*

"You know perfectly well he wouldn't like us getting mixed up with these Halesby people."

"All right, when I do get mixed up with a Halesby young man, I'll tell you and you shall have the pleasure of telling him. And much good may it do you! Hattie, darling, don't look so pitiful or I shall cry."

Still laughing, she kissed her sister impulsively. Hattie smiled and shook her head. "It's all very well; but I never know when you mean what you say."

"That's quite easy. I never do, darling."

"But you *will* be more careful, for my sake? People are apt to be misunderstood."

"Yes, they are indeed, pet. What a difficult world we live in!"

It was much easier for Hattie than for her, Bella sometimes reflected; for Hattie, it seemed, asked so very little of life: just to manage the house, as, of course, she did to perfection—not a speck of dust on the varnished pitch-pine banisters or the panelling whose knots made it look so like a cut pineapple; not a halfpenny out in the balancing of the weekly accounts nor a second at meal-times; not a moment wasted in all the day from its misty dawn to its blood-red Black Country sunset, since Satan, as the Beagle said, found work for idle fingers (Bella wished she knew what work!) and knitting or crochet or macramé-work, or, in strict moderation, performing the works of Mendelssohn on the piano, constituted the proper and ladylike use of leisure; not a speculation of any kind; not a thought, not a dream!

And Bella's life, at this season, was all dreams and discontents and vague aspirations which made her oddly restless and sometimes irritable, particularly with poor Hattie whom she knew to be so much better than herself. She found it hard to believe that the life which her sister accepted with such complacency and apparently enjoyed was really worth living. When Hattie sat knitting or played the piano or ransacked the files of accounts for a missing halfpenny it hurt her so much that she could have shrieked. All these painful industrious activities seemed to lead nowhere, or rather to revolve, round and round, like a squirrel in a cage. Hayseech was the cage, not a particularly gracious one either; and outside, outside . . . Well, who could say what was outside? One could only guess at the brave exaltations and dangers through the fugitive suggestions contained sometimes in a phrase of music or the colour of a flower or the timbre of a stranger's voice, or, above all, in the carefully-chosen volumes which constituted their reading—such as the poems of Longfellow and the Poet Laureate's Mariana in the Moated Grange and Maud's sweet poison, Scott's romances and a strictly-limited selection of Lord Byron, which did not include *Don Juan*. No novels were tolerated save the earlier productions of Mr. Dickens, on whom death had lately conferred the seal of respectability, and such works of Thackeray as Miss Beagle considered to be the least cynical, and as could therefore, out of respect for his style, be admitted on sufferance. Indeed, in the little old house where the sisters had been born, there had been no books whatever but an annual prophetic almanac and a volume interpreting dreams, which constituted the whole of their mother's library of reference; while their father's reading was limited to the daily newspaper (which he kept to himself), the *Iron Trade Gazette*, and occasionally the Old Testament.

For this reason, apart from her curious and romantic disposition, certain writings acquired for Bella the fascination of forbidden fruit.

She would probably never have heard of them but for the war, whose horrors (so delicate is conscience!) had impelled the wives of local munition-makers to arrange sewing-parties for the manufacture of dressings which might be hurried to France and applied to the wounds that their husbands' missiles had inflicted. The new Mrs. Willis—*née* Hackett—was the most energetic of these sensitive ladies, and the Mortimer girls were invited to Mawne Hall to share in her charitable labours. Here, modestly plying her needle and listening, Bella heard of the existence of novels at the mention of which Miss Beagle would have shuddered and fainted: a book called *Jane Eyre* and another called *Under Two Flags*, lately published, whose mysterious authoress, a lady named

Ouida, touched the limits to which the rebellious passion of modern womanhood could go.

Inflamed by these whispers, Bella wrote to a book-seller in North Bromwich and ordered the two volumes. It was a ticklish business concealing her secret from Hattie; each morning, until they came, she rose early and met the postman; when they arrived she hid the parcel in a drawer where Hattie's prying fingers were not likely to penetrate. At night she opened it with an enthralling sensation of guilt (how the paper crackled!) and having chosen the newer and the more shocking of the pair, *Under Two Flags*, found herself transported into regions in which Passion held undisputed sway over human behaviour; into the lives of creatures with whom she knew she had more in common than with the pallid heroines of Dickens and Tennyson; into emotions, vicariously enjoyed, which seemed nearer to her nature than those she habitually experienced. The scenes of this newly-discovered country did not strike her as tawdry nor the figures that inhabited it as theatrical; they were, rather, an exhibition on an exalted plane of her own repressed aspirations. There, splendidly, but for the iron bonds of circumstance, went Bella Mortimer.

She began, in secret, to dream about love, no longer as an abstraction but as a concrete experience; and these dreams filled an eager mind which her condition of life had condemned to drabness and emptiness with a variety of enchanting (if second-hand) experience. If she resembled her mother physically Bella's spirit had certainly inherited a glimmer of that imaginative ardour which had fused the daring dreams of her father's youth into the superb reality of Josiah Tinsley and Co., Ltd. Jasper Mortimer, in his own way, was an artist, and the new Hayseech—an *Inferno*, if you will, or *A City of Dreadful Night*—his masterpiece. It seemed almost as if his willed abstention from beauty, subdued for a generation, had found release in the soul of his second daughter and bred in it an even intenser hunger for what he had forsworn.

Bella's secret reading, high-pitched and tawdry as it was (and in part because it was secret), went to her head and dizzied her. It had the effect of crystallizing her cloudy emotions of adolescence into a medium through which she perceived a new world, a world magnified and bedecked with magic colour. It had something of the quality of a world seen from upside-down, in which familiar shapes acquired a new definition and familiar colours a novel intensity. She saw her father, whom she had previously taken for granted and rather dreaded, as the handsome and rather saddened figure that he was: a lonely man, burdened with riches, who had loved and lost. She saw her sister, whom she loved at intervals, as a poor creature affected with blindness, moving unconsciously—and this was rather unfair, for Hattie, after all, was only twenty-three! —towards an arid spinsterhood. She saw the new house at Hayseech, which, before visiting Mawne

Hall, she had considered not merely vast but extremely grand, as the abomination of bastard Tudor in variegated brick and faked stained-glass which it undoubtedly was. She saw the works—and here vision failed her, for, especially at night, they had their own sombre magnificence—as an unpardonable sin against the light and sweetness of life. She saw, for the first time, what she had oddly failed to notice before: the astonishing, secret beauty of the country that edged the grey slough of the works' vitriolic erosion: the recesses of Uffmoor Wood, virgin Arden still; the quiet turns and swift stickles of the Lapsley Brook, as yet undefiled, with its bottom of amber gravel or tawny sand where trout hung quivering in mid-water with tails waving like weed, or startled by a shadow darted this way and that in arrowy alarm.

There was no end to the wonder of this lonely, this newly-discovered Eden—to the surprise that choked her when first she beheld (why had she never seen it before?) foam bursting from soot-blackened boughs in the cherry-orchard behind the sightless windows of Old Mawne Hall (left empty by the Pomfrets half a century since); to the rapture of blue reflected from sheeted hyacinths in the wood beside Lapsley Mill (now falling to ruin); to the joy which stole into her heart with the cuckoo's song, wafted drowsily over the sorry fields where sick ponies brought up from the pits cropped wan April buttercups.

To this young, lonely heart so eager and sensitive

only human love was lacking, and when love came to her she accepted it blindly, as her mother had done before her. Judged by the standards of her favourite authoress Bella's lover was no more romantic than the occasion of their meeting and falling in love; but that made no matter: her sentimental imagination gave him an heroic stature and invested the commonplace affair with subjective magic.

He was a young man of twenty-six, eight years older than herself; a draughtsman in the office at the works. His origin was undistinguished, and his name Rupert Small. At Hayseech Small was something of a misfit, having reached his modest position, at a salary of two pounds a week, without any mechanical vocation—nothing more, in fact, than a certain aptitude for drawing. He was one of those unhappy sports which an industrial community produces, out of subconscious protest, perhaps, against its own materialism: an amiable creature, unfitted through lack of original vitality for the hurry and stress of industry, and handicapped by a vaguely injured leaning towards the arts and graces of a smoother age. The fate of such by-products, unseasonably produced, is usually tragic. They have as little chance of survival as the pallid and sappy suckers that spring with pathetic hopefulness from a fruiting stock. It was disastrous for Small that he had been born, an indifferent artist, in the heart of an industrial area in which every manifestation of art was regarded with contempt if not with hatred. It was even more disastrous that he should have met Bella Mortimer.

He was a little man, dark and pallid as Mortimer himself, but without a vestige of that fierce energy which lurked beneath Mortimer's blackness like heat in a coal. At the most he was capable of diffusing a mild warmth which glowed, in moments of enthusiasm, in the shy eyes sheltered behind his spectacles. His face, in a woman, might even have been counted beautiful. Its features revealed a real refinement of line, the mouth, in repose, showing the formal sweetness of early Greek heads in marble. His body was neatly made and he had sensitive hands with tapering fingers and filbert nails, quite different from the severely practical finger which generations of manual labour had fixed as the Tinsley type. His mind, without any great vigour, was quicker and subtler than those with which Bella had previously had contact. Indeed, it is quite possible that the contrast between his delicate mechanism of body and mind and her own, so full-blooded and so much more coarse-fibred, enhanced his attraction for her; but what drew them together when once they had met, with a greater power than any mere allurement of physical opposites, was a community of loneliness: the fact that each was a friendless romantic isolated in grimly unromantic surroundings. When once Bella had fallen in love with him, not one of these reasons counted. All her reserves of unspent energy, all her inherited tenacity were displayed with the determination her mother had shown on a similar occasion. Rupert Small had no more chance of escaping her love than a gazelle in the claws of a hungry lioness.

They first met quite by chance on a Saturday evening in early summer by the ruins of Lapsley Mill. Bella saw him sitting there sketching in water-colour, and an inevitable curiosity impelled her to approach and to watch him at work, for of all the arts this, to her, was the most mysterious. When she asked if he minded her watching, he laughed and said no. So she sat there, wide-eyed, on the edge of the broken mill-dam in the dank smell of water-weed, and watched his deft fingers moving. For her, artists were people who only existed in novels (like dukes and guardsmen) and the stranger seemed to her a visitant from another world, since no artist, surely, could exist within miles of Hayseech and at any moment he might vanish. As he worked, a little self-consciously, she began to talk to him; and her questions were so naïve and childish that he answered them easily. It was the first time since he had come to Hayseech that he had opened his heart.

He had been born, he told her, in Bromsberrow, eight miles from Halesby. His parents were dusty little people, small manufacturers of sorts; but that kind of life hadn't appealed to him (how should it?) and his heart had been always in drawing. There was no art school nearer than North Bromwich, and study was expensive. That was why he had passed from a firm of ornamental glass-workers in Stourton to his present post in the drawing-office at Hayseech. The pay in the engineering trade was better, and he needed money. When he had saved enough, he was going to study seriously.

"But what do you draw at Hayseech?" she asked him.

"Oh, things that you'ld never believe. The work's purely mechanical. A matter of rules and compasses. It consists of blue-prints and so on for the engineers' designs. But I do them quite well. I think I earn my money. Some day I shall earn money by drawing what I want to draw. Things like this."

His voice pleased her. It was light and melodious, and his speech was not disfigured by the Black Country twang. She watched his picture growing under his hands and she watched his face.

"But where do you live?"

"I live in lodgings in Halesby. The people are decent and my room is reasonably clean. But that's all. Do you know, you're the first person of my own kind I've spoken to since I came here? Who are you, by the way? I didn't imagine that anybody like you existed in these parts."

She evaded his question—the idea of mystery pleased her—and went on to ask if he often came to the Lapsley Valley.

"Very often," he told her. "Whenever I can get away. It's my only escape. From the first moment I found it I fell in love with this place. It's so quiet you can hardly believe you're less than a mile from those furnaces. At this point there's nothing between you and the hills, and if you climb to the top of them —perhaps you don't know?—you can see right down into Gloucestershire and over to Wales. Nothing but green, for seventy or eighty miles: only think of it!"

Bella was moved. She had never heard anyone speak like this. Even in the Willises' drawing-room at Mawne people spoke (and thought) as though the edge of the globe were North Bromwich, with London as a neighbouring and slightly disreputable planet. His words winged her fledgeling imagination. She was transported in the spirit over those leagues of greenness.

He stopped suddenly, as though he felt he had spoken too freely, and looked at the sky.

"The light's failing," he said, "and I've no idea what the time is. I shall have to go home. Do you live near here? You won't mind my asking you, will you?"

She laughed. "Not a bit." For one moment her mind was divided: should she tell him that she was the daughter of his employer, the great Jasper Mortimer? It would create a superb effect—but perhaps an effect of the wrong kind: he might be intimidated: one of the qualities that appealed to her most in him was his diffidence. It suited her mood and her nature better to be mysterious.

"Not far from here," she replied.

He pressed her: "In Halesby?"

"No, no. In the other direction."

His face fell. "That's a pity," he said. "We might have walked home together. Do you know, you're the first girl—very nearly the first living soul—I've spoken to since I came here?"

She was glad to hear that. If he knew many people he might question them and find out who she was.

"I can go just a little way with you, if you like," she said, and they walked on together, rarely speaking, along the edge of the dusky wood in an air that was drenched with spring, marshy odours of trodden rushes and mint and dewy grass, until the trees became sparse and a current of air moving up the valley blew into their nostrils the essential smell of Hayseech— hot, acrid, devitalized—and the vault, as night fell, alternately flushed and darkened as with the systole and diastole of an invisible heart.

"That is beautiful too," he said, gazing upward. "I want to paint those things as well, although I hate them."

But now Bella scarcely heard him. Her mind was engaged with the strategy of a mysterious retreat.

"You had better go on now," she said. "I can find my way home."

"It's dreadfully dark," he said. "I don't like leaving you behind. Hadn't I better come with you?"

"No, no, please. I'd much rather you didn't."

"Then I may never see you again."

"But why not?" she said tenderly. "Surely you must finish that picture some day. You'll be coming to the mill again."

"Not before next Saturday, I'm afraid. If I did come then, is it possible that you will be there?"

She knew that she would be there, but dissembled, saying: "Perhaps . . ."

VIII

ALL summer lay before them. While the works at
Hayseech approached the climax of their astonishing
development—that year Mortimer erected three more
blast-furnaces and doubled his acreage of workshops
—this minute human fire burned in secret beyond the
edge of the smoke-pall. It was the secrecy of their
love-making that gave it, for Bella, its particular spice.
She saw it as a condition transcending normal human
experience and dramatized herself as the heroine of a
unique romance. It enchanted her to think that her
sister, poor thing, was too innocent or too stupid and
her father too grimly absorbed in the making of money
to suspect the existence of the miracle which had transformed her life. The contrast between their world of
workaday cares and her own enraptured state was as
dramatic (and therefore, to her, as exciting) as that
between the fire-blackened area of the Hayseech works
and her cool green solitude.

For some months she imposed her darling mysteries
on Small. It pleased her to remain for him a sort
of heavenly visitant, Eros to his Psyche—and there
was more in the parable than appears at first sight!—
the discovery of whose earthly identity might dissipate
their rapture. When, at last, he forced her to declare

herself, he was more frightened than pleased; for the grandeur of Mortimer's name and the grimness of his swart-visaged figure filled him with terror. If the affair came to light, he might easily lose his job and forfeit his prospects.

His attitude was less heroic than she would have desired; but by this time Bella was in love with him— even with his weakness—and no timid lukewarmth on his part could cool her passion. She laughed at his fears of her father: *she* wasn't afraid of him. A love that could wilt beneath such imaginary shadows was a poor sort of thing. And because she was so much stronger than he, she had her way with him.

Like her mother before her, oddly innocent in her desire, she had chosen her man and now no caution could stay her. No doubt, as in the case of the unfortunate Miss Beagle, she "led him a dance." It was she, invariably, who called the tune, though he paid the piper. She was exacting, petulant, yet often amazingly tender; half mistress and half protectress, half mænad, half nymph. She absorbed him, she preyed upon him, and yet she mothered him; for an instinct if not in body she was ages older than he. Their embraces were nursed in darkness or pallid moonlight; they loved like shy creatures of the night, for now that Hayseech had reached its greatest output Rupert Small could not count on an hour of freedom in daylight. They met in the quiet Eden of Uffdown Wood, where the furnaces' sudden lightning coloured the sky like flashes of gunfire, and the rumble of wheels and clashing of couplings and thudding of hammers reached their ears like the rumour of those far battlefields for which the works' deadly merchandise was destined. But of these they knew nothing, nor cared.

So summer passed: for Bella in an oblivious ecstasy, for Small in a rapture always tempered by anxiety; he was timid by nature and her possessiveness alarmed him. Autumn came; the days shortened; and soon it was winter: the dank Black Country winter in which all light seemed to be extinguished by smoke-laden fog. The skies grew so dim and the ways so mired that they could no longer grope their way through the woods to meet. Bella fought against these frustrations: she was so used to having her own way that she refused to accept them. Her ruthlessness alarmed him. There was no knowing, he felt, where this adventure might end.

It ended, of course, in the manner which might have been expected. After that nothing less than marriage would satisfy her. She was far less excitable now, but more tenacious than ever. The culmination of the affair had given her a composure, a sort of virginal serenity, which was new to him. Her insistence on marriage perturbed him, for it implied a threat to his liberty. Like most artists—particularly small ones—he was selfish in self-defence. When he hedged, she rallied him gently:

"Why do you look so scared, darling? Even if we do marry, nobody need know."

"Then why marry?" he argued. "If we marry we should live together, and we've nothing to marry on, anyway."

"Dad has plenty of money."

"I can't see myself facing *him!*"

Bella laughed. "Well, you needn't face him. You can leave that to me."

"That's all very well! My turn will come next."

"What a coward you are! He isn't so terrible as all that. I'm sure I can manage him."

"Well, I wish you wouldn't try to."

In some ways he gauged Mortimer's nature better than she did. The moment of her confession was ill-chosen. On the evening when she broached the subject her father was tired and irritable. The war was nearing its end and the activity of Hayseech had passed its climax. Werder's pressure had forced the French Eastern Army towards the Swiss frontier. On that very day Clinchant had marched them over the border to be interned. Mortimer, looking ahead, perceived that his own iron harvest was over. He, too, had to face a retreat. This was no season for the disentangling of domestic difficulties.

When she began to speak he hardly bothered to listen to her, but as soon as he caught her drift all his own perplexities found release in a burst of anger such as she had never known.

"What do you mean, wench?" he cried. "What damned nonsense is this?"

He jumped up from his chair and towered over her like a black thundercloud. This was essentially a repetition of a similar scene which had taken place twenty years before. With the same blazing face, the same determination, the first Arabella had announced her intention of marrying him. But that he had forgotten.

"We have talked it all over," Bella was saying, "and decided to marry."

He laughed harshly. "Then the sooner you get that maggot out of your head the better. Who is he? Who is this damned blackguard? I've never heard of him before!"

"He works in the drawing-office."

"What? Under my very nose? You're only a child. You don't understand what you're talking about. Marriage . . . marriage indeed! I shall see that the fellow's sent packing at once."

"If you send him away," Bella said, "I shall go away with him."

"Then go, and be damned to you!" he shouted and swung out of the room.

He went down to the works immediately—in action he never hesitated—and turned out the head of the drawing-office.

"You have a fellow named Small, Rupert Small. What d'you make of him?"

"His work's good. I should say he's a cut above most of them. A smart chap, I should say."

Mortimer grunted. "Too smart for my liking. Get rid of him at once. He can go to-morrow."

"Very good, sir. What about wages? He'll be entitled to a week."

"Wages? Wages? Not a penny if I know it!"

"I shall have to explain, sir."

"There's no need for that." Mortimer laughed. "He'll understand. The war's over, or near it; we shall have to consider expenses. I'm going to cut down your staff by twenty per cent. Send me a list to-morrow of the men you can do without, but deal with Small first."

When he came home next evening Bella had gone. That she would be as good as her word and follow her lover was the last thing he had expected. It was what they call in Halesby a nasty smack in the face for him. Mortimer took it hardly; but in ordinary life as in business he hated half-measures. His will was as adamantine as hers. She had made her bed and must lie in it. Neither in his life nor after his death should she touch a penny of his. When she wrote to him seven months later and told him that he had become a grandfather ("We have christened her Arabella, just to keep the name going," she said) he tore up the letter and threw the fragments away. Hattie picked them up out of the fireplace and pieced them together. She was not envious of Bella's escape—

Hayseech was sufficient for her adventurous spirit—but she did envy Bella her baby and wished she could see it. It was improbable, she thought, that she would ever have a baby of her own. She took note of the address, and, with a deep sense of guilt, replied to Bella in secret; but the answer which reached her at last was written in a strange hand. Rupert Small wrote to say that on the day her letter had arrived his dear wife had died. Hattie cried all day. Still distressed and red-eyed when her father came home that evening she handed him Small's letter in silence. He read it through twice and then handed it back to her. Not a word was spoken.

IX

But although he said nothing, either then or afterwards, Jasper Mortimer's mind must surely have been full of bitterness if not of remorse. In so far as he took any notice of his children, his younger daughter had been his favourite. The elder, admirable housewife as she was, meant very little to him. There was nothing in her nature that reflected his own or even the first Arabella's, and neutrality, of all qualities, was the one which least appealed to him.

After Bella's death he retired more than ever within himself: a grim and solitary figure, detached from all human relationships; a mere incarnation of the iron efficiency of Hayseech, which, now that the wars were over (for good, men said), began to consolidate its position, by the side of Hingstons' and Hacketts' and Willises', as a formidable, cumbrous and slowly-declining giant.

Though his wealth did not increase (and he had no desire for it) many honours came to him. He was invited to stand for Parliament and refused a baronetcy offered to him by the Liberal Ministry in eighteeneighty. He became the acknowledged head of the heavy industries and President of the Iron and Steel Institute. At the end of his term his fellow-members presented him with his portrait. It was hung in the board-room at Hayseech behind the chair which he occupied at the table as Managing Director, portraying a spare, sinewy old man, with a back like a ramrod, a clean-shaven face, heavily furrowed, and a magnificent head of vigorous snow-white hair above coal-black eyebrows. A stern face, with cavernous eyes which had kept their fire, though the full, pugnacious lips had thinned to a line that denoted weariness rather than suffering. A figure of great dignity, and, indeed, of simplicity, but old for his sixty years.

The years which had aged him were those of the "great depression," in which the output of coal fell by half and the mining of ironstone dwindled even more quickly; for, as pit after pit was worked out and abandoned, the water, accumulated in their depths, drained into the galleries of their neighbours. In this period many of Mortimer's competitors went under. Josiah Tinsley and Co. felt the pinch, but survived by reason of the foresight which had anticipated the coming of steel and prepared to meet it. He was still, as always, amazingly single-minded. Hayseech was his only god, and he grudged it no sacrifice.

Hattie's youth was one of the burnt-offerings paid to this Moloch. She lived on in the new house at Hayseech—they still called it that, though it was no longer new—in the isolation of a nunnery. She was "getting on" now, as they said, and her chances of "getting off" (if ever there had been any) dwindled year by year.

Bella's fate, in any case, had taught her the folly of
independence; and though he neither showed nor pro-
fessed any affection for her, she had a real affection for
her father, regarding him, in one way, with filial reverence, and in another with maternal care. After Bella's
departure she had accepted celibacy as a vocation and
assumed the habit of spinsterhood. In the last quarter
of the nineteenth century women aged early; and in
the thirties Hattie resembled, in her dress and demeanour, a middle-aged woman, never departing from
the fashions she had acquired under the tutelage of
Miss Beagle in her girlhood: an era of black satin
bodices and tight corsets and voluminous skirts; of
closed windows, crocheted antimacassars, macramé-
work, gentlemen's smoking-caps; of clasped photo-
graph-albums and Henry Wadsworth Longfellow
and Felix Mendelssohn-Bartholdy. She had watched
the "new" house grow shabby from over-cleaning, its
mahogany acquiring a glossy patina; she had ordered
the Sunday sirloin on fifty-two Fridays of each year;
eaten it cold on Monday and hashed on Tuesday and
minced on Wednesday, and racked her brains over
feeding her father on Thursday and Friday, until
tripe and onions relieved her anxieties on Saturday,
and on Sunday morning the smell of the roast pervaded the house again. Every day, when her father
had finished with it, she just "glanced through" yesterday's paper, following the movements of the Queen
from Windsor to Osborne and from Osborne to

Balmoral. She was not, as her sister had been, a "great reader." The house was nearly as innocent of books as it had been in her day, though a small shelf of volumes had accumulated in the drawing-room, more or less automatically, like silt. She took practically no exercise apart from her two walks to Halesby Church on Sundays; yet, because of the politeness of her appetite, retained her figure. Visitors rarely came to the house, and she had no friends among the neighbours to whom she bowed in the churchyard on Sunday mornings. The Mortimers had always "kept themselves to themselves." Her life, in the ordinary sense of the word, was no life at all; yet she lived it with dignity and without discontent. And her servants, although she "kept them in their place," adored her, not as the museum-piece which she was, but as a human being.

As for Mortimer's life, that was even more mysterious. Although, from the day of her death, Bella's name was never spoken, his silence, in this case, was most probably his characteristic expression of a deep emotion. As his riches accumulated and his honours increased—perhaps, more than ever, when he refused Mr. Gladstone's baronetcy—he must often have wondered what was going to happen to Hayseech when he died. In the end, no doubt, he decided that the future was hardly worth thinking of. His duty, so far as it went, was towards the great concern's anxious present and the interests of the shareholders

D

who had supported him during the bad times and to whom he considered himself responsible.

As he neared seventy his enormous vitality began to fail; but though the works absorbed every ounce of his strength, he never spared himself. It was at a quarterly meeting of the board in the new terra-cotta offices in the year eighteen-ninety-four that he gave a slight gasp, a grimace of pain, clutched the arms of his chair, and died. At the inquest the cause of his death was recorded as Angina Pectoris. He was seventy-two years of age.

Mortimer's death created a considerable sensation in the Black Country. He was one of the figures of whom the district was proud. The principal subject of popular discussion was his will. He was known as a man who had never spent a penny in luxury or ostentation. Bets were made on the figure of his fortune. It was generally supposed that he would beat old man Hingston, the baronet's father, by a good many thousands. Some people went so far as to speak of the sum in millions.

When the terms of the will were published the Black Country gasped with surprise. Jasper Mortimer had died, comparatively, a poor man. His property, apart from his interest in Tinsley's, was negligible. Every penny he made out of the business had always gone back to it, and as the value of Josiah Tinsley and Co.'s shares had steadily declined, his whole holding was assessed at the surprising figure of less than a hundred and forty thousand pounds.

The will was an odd one. It had been made in the last decade of his life. After numerous benefactions to elderly servants of the firm (but none to charity) and an annuity of five hundred a year to his daughter Harriet, the remainder of the estate was bequeathed to his grand-daughter, only child of his "beloved daughter" Arabella. By the terms of the will she was required to adopt the surname of Tinsley.

Such was the genesis of the Tinsley fortune and the heredity of its heiress, Arabella the Third.

BOOK TWO

EXODUS OF A HEROINE

I

Until the surprising day when she succeeded to the Hayseech property, in her twenty-third year, Bella Small had not been aware of its existence. Her father had rarely spoken to her of her mother. The portion of his life which had begun with that April passion and ended so cruelly, a year later, with her birth and the loss of his wife was one that he shrank from remembering. He was a sensitive man, at the mercy of his quick imagination; and that period with its extremes of exaltation and suffering, of beauty and terror, had a nightmarish quality which, even in memory, he knew his nerves would not stand.

In the first bewilderment of his loss he had taken the new-born baby to the only refuge he knew, the home of his parents in Bromsberrow. He had no feeling for the child; his heart was still sore, and its existence seemed a poor exchange for what he had lost. Singularly helpless in practical matters and faced, in any case, with the necessity of earning some sort of a living, he had deposited her there thankfully and moved on to London in search of oblivion and new work in surroundings that did not remind him of his disaster.

Small's parents received the infant gladly. She was

their only grandchild. His mother, a pinched, active woman of fifty-five, was enchanted to renew her youth in the care of this new pet, for she was a motherly woman, whose instincts had been starved of their sole means of expression for the best part of twenty years, and to her Rupert's baby was a godsend; while his father was thankful for anything that would "keep the old woman quiet" on the cheap, and permit him to live in peace. He was an elderly, easy-going man, with an enormous besom of a beard which concealed a weak mouth and chin. His main interests were the breeding of fancy pigeons and float-fishing, a sport which he indulged in long sessions on the tow-path of the "cut"—the North Bromwich and Worcester canal —or on the verges of lakes and ponds in which farmers or local gentry fired extravagant hopes in him by occasional permissions to fish.

By trade he was a nail-master, having inherited, in the third generation, a small business and a warehouse on the edge of the market town of Bromsberrow, from which he supplied the nailers of the neighbouring villages with rod-iron out of which at their domestic forges they stamped and hammered into shape the wrought-iron nails that were still largely used to fix horse-shoes. Though this trade was decreasing, all the little red cottages adjoining the warehouse were fitted with lean-to nail-houses, so that from the first Bella's ears were accustomed to metallic noises: the clank of bundles of rod-iron driven up to the yard on flat carts and wheeled away in barrows, the tinkle of musical anvils and the click of the nailers' hammers. Such sounds, together with the cooing of pigeons in the warehouse loft, made an undertone to her childhood.

It was, generally, a happy and a healthy childhood; for the air of the village was sweet and its people kindly. Her grandmother, softened by age, was more indulgent than a mother would have been; and the child adored her grandfather. In spite of his ferocious beard, he was the gentlest of creatures, with very little to say and that so little worth listening to that his wife rarely took any notice of what he said or replied to his questions. When she snubbed him he had the habit of humming a tune to himself to cover his confusion, and for the same reason, forestalling (as it were) her disdain, he would begin and end his remarks or questions with a charming and rather foolish laugh which he used so often that it ended in becoming part of everything he said.

He was not nearly so clever as his wife or as their son, Bella's father, whose talent bewildered him. This sense of inferiority made him much happier in the company of Bella than in that of her father or her grandmother; and Bella, with a child's or an animal's instinct for recognising friendliness, touched and flattered him by obviously preferring him to all other human beings, regarding him from the point of view of a small animal which makes friends and plays with a big one. Bella's trust and affection were the greatest

D*

compliment that Mr. Small had received since his
marriage. He could speak his thoughts to her (whether
she understood them or not) without being snubbed,
and did so by the hour, making her the confidante of
all sorts of secrets about his plans for outwitting the
big carp that basked in the pool at Stoke Priory and
the tricks of shady professional pigeon-fanciers and
the slump in wrought-iron which had begun to hit
him so hard.

"You see, Bell," he would say confidentially, "it's
all because of these bloody Belgians. Wire-nails I
grant you: yes. They have their uses; they're nice to
look at and handy for knocking-up boxes and that, and
I don't pretend to compete with them. But cut-nails,
no, Bell. There was never a cut-nail made yet—you
mark my words now!—that could stand up to its work
like a hand-forged wrought spike or rose or brush-nail
of the type I can quote you this week at seven shillings
a hundredweight—and that's a shilling less than they
fetched ten years ago. But these bloody Belgians, you
know, they're so downy you never know where you are
with them. They're like those old carp I was telling
you about t'other day. Stewed wheat, gentles, wasp-
grub or brandlings, it's all the same to them. They
turn up their great fat noses at baits that are fit for a
king. They just take a look and a smell and then they
turn round and wink at you. I give you my word, they
do. But do you think your gran will believe that a
carp can wink? Not she! She's a septic, Bell; that's

what she is—a septic. Now just wait till I've got these figures totted up; I've been through them, bost it, three times and they always come different. Then we'll have a look round, you and me; and if your gran isn't looking we'll pop over and see Sam Waldron."

"Having a look round" with her grandfather was one of the greatest treats of Bella's childhood. She went everywhere with him: into the dim store where the sixty-pound sheaves of rusty rod were piled and weighed and distributed (some of them came, no doubt, from Hayseech) and the eyes of a cat with its family of half-wild kittens that "looked after" the rats shone green through the piles of rod-iron like jungle tigers; into the office upstairs, where her grandfather kept leather-backed ledgers spread out on high desks and interviewed buyers and (secretly) arranged his fishing tackle; into the warehouse where the finished iron was re-weighed and nails stored in sacks; through the yard, a fascinating jumble of rusty scrap-metal which three generations of Smalls had casually dumped there; out along the street of red cottages that straggled downhill into Bromsberrow; up gravel paths edged with old-fashioned pinks and sweet-williams and lad's-love, and love-lies-bleeding, and love-in-the-mist; into front parlours smelling of musk and geraniums in pots, the nail-houses smelling of iron, where aged men like Sam Waldron talked as they worked—(*click-click-click-clock*—and the nail jumped out of the bore—*click-click-click-clock*)—while the coals on the hearth glowed red as the bellows wheezed. Wherever he went—if she could escape—she went with him, sometimes riding on his shoulder, high up in the world, with his beard tickling her legs, sometimes clasped to a waistcoat that smelt of clove-scented ground-bait, sometimes trotting beside him like a puppy, with one hand in his.

Her father, it seemed, had fallen on his feet in London. The fashion for "new art" was beginning and he had found a well-paid job decorating glass fire-screens and milking-stools and painted furniture. Apart from this mechanical labour his original work had improved, the shock of the tragedy having somehow galvanized his spirit; a number of his landscape drawings had been exhibited and one or two sold. In the first years of Bella's life he had spent his holidays sketching at Bromsberrow, though that made little difference to her, since he was awkward with children and regarded his own daughter detachedly as an obscure and inexplicable phenomenon. But later, when his pictures began to sell a little better—he had discovered a formula that fell in with the current ideas of drawing-room decoration—he forsook his parents, with whom, indeed, he had very little in common, and took his holidays abroad.

He must still, in some odd way, have been attractive to women, particularly to women of a strongly possessive nature; possibly his shattering experience of romance made him chary of committing himself and encouraged pursuit. When Bella was ten, however, he announced his intention of marrying a widow rather older than himself with two children of her own and a comfortable private income. Her two children were, providentially, nearly "grown-up," and her income would prove extremely convenient for an artist whose talent had never been properly appreciated. This lady, he wrote, was a great admirer of his work and understood his temperament. The only obstacle to the project from her point of view was the existence of another child by his first tragic marriage. He proposed, in short, to abandon Bella entirely if his parents would be good enough to adopt her and take her off his hands. It would be better, he felt, for both of them, since it was not as if the child knew him or cared for him. Indeed, she had had scant opportunity for doing either.

His parents were delighted. They would have been far more distressed if he had suggested their surrendering Bella. The child had entwined herself round the structure of their declining years—Mrs. Small was now sixty-five and her husband over seventy—and her attachment had given both of them a vicarious prolongation of youth without which life would lose its savour. They had never been very well off, and of late the wrought-iron nail-trade had shrunk catastrophically. Still, having reached an age when it was reasonably safe to live on their capital, they decided to make the most of it by giving the child the benefit of an education a little better than they could rightly afford and thus fitting her to earn her own living when they were gone.

By this time Bella's body and mind had passed from the indeterminate state of babyhood into a definite shape. She had matured with amazing rapidity, as children brought up by elderly people will. In her early teens, indeed, she was much less of a child, in many ways, than her grandfather, whose limited effectiveness continued to decline in a gentle curve (along with his business) towards an amiable dotage. Bella's precocity was a source of pride and wonder to him. She was "an old-fashioned body," a "cust one," he said in his Worcestershire dialect—Shakespeare had used the same word for his Katherine—"as peart as a parcel of monkeys" and "as sharp as a packet of needles." His flatteries on her pertness were firmly discouraged by her grandmother: they made the child bold, apt to get "above herself" and inclined to "show off."

When she first went to school, in fact, Bella's manners were atrocious and her person unattractive, presenting a mixture of the odd physical strains that had gone to make her. She was little for her age, small-boned like her father but lacking, save in her hands, his refinement of shape, verging, in this, toward her mother's coarser and more generous type. The colour of her hair, again, was that of the previous Arabellas, dull-gold with a streaky burnish of bronze:

and in dramatic contrast to this her eyebrows—above long-lashed eyes that were large and of so dark a grey as to seem black—had the raven hue and swallow-wing curve of her grandfather, Jasper Mortimer's. Her disposition showed a similar mingling of strains. All that she drew from the Smalls was her father's æsthetic sense. This declared itself not in any aptitude to the practice of the arts, but in an instinctive sensitiveness towards beauty of shape and colour unusual in a child of her age. Without any instruction she had a taste that discriminated unhesitatingly between plastic beauty and ugliness, though music, in the performance of which her deft fingers enabled her to give an illusion of brilliance, meant nothing whatever to her.

Besides Mortimer's eyes, she had much of his restless energy and some of his moodiness, which, illuminated by spurts of her mother's flaming impulsiveness, made her a freak of contradictions and contrasts which puzzled and harassed the Miss Bakers, to whose School for Young Ladies in Bromsberrow she was first sent.

Hypatia House was a highly select establishment. In theory its membership was limited to children of the Titled and Professional Classes. Unfortunately, in Bromsberrow, there were no children of the first category available, and only six or seven of the second; so that the Miss Bakers found themselves forced to lower their standard and accept a number of pupils who were Young Ladies only by courtesy: the children of superior tradespeople and small manufacturers, among whom Bella Small scraped in by the skin of her teeth.

The Miss Bakers, like the Witches in "Macbeth" and the Fates, were three in number, and their qualifications for instructing the young were purely social. Miss Agnes, the eldest and grimmest, whose temper suffered from recurrent attacks of migraine, had once indeed been employed as an under-governess in a noble household; but Miss Hetty, the second, who "ran" the house, knew nothing about anything in the world but housekeeping, and Miss Penelope, who gave instruction in the Graces—Drawing, Music, Poetry, French, Fancy Sewing and General Culture—based her claims to familiarity with these subjects on faulty memories of a three months' journey through France and Italy as companion to an invalid lady. The education provided by the three Miss Bakers was inferior in every respect to that of the National School; but Mrs. Small was enchanted when Bella was granted the privilege of enjoying it.

Bella was less conscious of the privilege than her grandmother. She was a wild little thing. The social correctness of Hypatia House oppressed her; and its pupils, the first middle-class children with whom she had been brought into contact, seemed incredibly tame and childish in their acceptance of its conventions. Her quick mind and her parrot memory made lessons easy for her, so that she had plenty of spare time in which to indulge her sense of the ridiculous. At first, naturally enough, she was subdued. The Miss Bakers regarded her as "such a sweet little thing," sitting there, so quietly demure, with her big black eyes; but the big black eyes took in more than they guessed; their glance was critical; and the mind behind them, impish and amused, was less simple than the Miss Bakers imagined.

Little by little they began to realize what a snake they had let loose in their dovecote. They had had "difficult" children to deal with before, but never, in their lives, a child who had developed naughtiness to such a fine art. Bella despised the two younger Miss Bakers and disliked the elder. Yet, by well-timed exhibitions of sweetness and submissiveness, she contrived never to fall out with more than one of them at a time, so that she always had a working majority in her favour, convincing each, in turn, that the others had misunderstood her, and tempting each with a vision of reclaiming her from her wicked ways.

Each lady's scheme of reclamation was different. Miss Agnes was convinced that the only right way to deal with such children as Bella was to Break their Wills. She took every opportunity of doing this, particularly on days when a headache made her desperate; but, in trying to break Bella's will, she strained her own will to breaking-point; she had never encountered a will quite like Bella's before.

Miss Hetty strongly disapproved of her elder sister's methods; she was a soft and amiable creature entirely possessed by a frustrated maternal interest which she could hardly have lavished upon a less promising subject. *Her* theory was Curing by Kindness—which suited Bella's book admirably, since it allowed her to make sympathetic capital out of Miss Agnes's brutal attempts at Breaking her Will and to obtain secret consolations from Miss Hetty's larder. Miss Penelope, the youngest sister, had no use for Will-Breaking or Curing by Kindness. Her formula for Bella's regeneration was Changing through Christ; and Bella, on the whole, preferred this method to the others, for whenever Miss Penelope went down on her knees and prayed for her, she enjoyed a suspension of the teaching routine, which bored her. Miss Penelope's method had picturesque—not to say grotesque —elements which the others lacked. It was less exacting to be prayed for than bullied or pampered, though neither religion nor bullying nor pampering affected her conduct in the least.

It took the three sisters the best part of two years to realize and to admit to each other the futility of their several methods—by which time Miss Agnes was convinced that Bella Small was a hard, insensitive child and quite incurable, Miss Hetty that she was heartless and calculating, and Miss Penelope, more mystically inclined, that she was probably possessed of the devil. All three agreed finally that she should not be allowed to return to Hypatia House next term. The reason for this decision, conveyed in a letter cross-written in Miss

Agnes's peaked hand, was not their own inability to subdue her, but the evil influence she was said to exercise over their other pupils.

Bella's grandfather regarded this letter as a good joke against the Miss Bakers; it was no more than could have been expected after putting a spirited child under a lot of tame cats. But Mrs. Small was upset. The other children would tell their mothers that Bella had been sent away, and the mothers would talk. She put on her best lace mantle embellished with jetty bugles and hurried to Hypatia House, where the Three Fates gave their judgement antiphonally like a Greek chorus.

"At Hypatia House," Miss Agnes began, "we are accustomed to dealing with the children of gentlefolk; children whose Wills have already been Broken, as they should be, at home . . ."

"Responsive, affectionate children," Miss Hetty continued. . . .

"With the love of their Redeemer implanted in their hearts," Miss Penelope said sadly.

"While Bella, Mrs. Small, I am grieved to say, is by nature stubborn, and apparently ungovernable by discipline . . ."

". . . or by kindness, Agnes dear . . ."

All three wagged their heads. Mrs. Small looked from one to another. She asked timidly: was there nothing more definite than this against Bella?

"Indeed there are several things," Miss Agnes replied, "which I, for one, hesitate to mention."

"Mrs. Small had better be told, Agnes dear."

"It is our duty as Christians to tell her."

"First of all, foul language. The child has used words, Mrs. Small, which have never, never, been heard before in Hypatia."

"Words beginning with 'd,' Mrs. Small."

"Even worse than that. A word beginning with 'b' and ending with 'y.' You can guess what we mean, perhaps?"

Mrs. Small could guess quite easily. Both were part, in fact, of her husband's colloquial vocabulary.

"And we are concerned, Mrs. Small," Miss Agnes went on, "not only with words but with deeds. Bella has one mitigating feature: she is not an habitual liar. She has confessed to these deeds, in fact, with a brazenness that is almost more distressing, if less sinful, than prevarication. She has leanings which in a child of our sex are depraved and unnatural. She has frequently been observed in the company of working-class Boys, and in shocking circumstances. It would be unfair to mention the names of other witnesses; but my sister Penelope will tell you one incident which she observed herself. Go on, Penelope . . ."

"It happened last week, Mrs. Small, the day after school broke up. I was crossing the fields on my way to evensong when I heard vulgar laughter proceeding from the banks of the brook. I immediately looked the other way, for I know that young men sometimes bathe there; but before I had time to turn I realized that these were *not* young men. They were a rabble of boys, and among them one girl whom I was shocked to recognize as Bella. They were not bathing but paddling, and the girl had not only taken off her stockings but held her skirts uplifted. My sister Hetty, who is prone to see good in everything, has suggested that Bella may have been wearing pink under-garments. That may possibly be so, I admit, though I understand hers are Turkey-red; but what I saw gave me a distinct impression of . . . limbs, bare, unclothed limbs!"

"And you must admit, Mrs. Small," Miss Agnes broke in triumphantly, "after an incident like that we owe it to Hypatia House, to our other pupils and the parents who have entrusted them to our charge, to be firm . . ."

". . . though, of course, not vindictive, Agnes . . ." Miss Hetty said hurriedly.

". . . or uncharitable."

Mrs. Small was silent. She had an enormous respect for the Miss Bakers as the final arbiters, in Broms-berrow, of erudition and good taste. At last she said humbly: "If you won't take the child back again, I hardly know what to do with her. Perhaps you'll advise me?"

"Advise, no," said Miss Agnes firmly. "That is a responsibility from which we should, all three of us, shrink. But you may follow the dictates of reason, Mrs. Small. Bella cannot return here. There is no other establishment in Bromsberrow of which we can honestly approve. She is unusually clever: it would be wrong to deny her the advantages of advanced education, and unfair to relax control. The only alternative that remains is to send her to a boarding-school removed from the pernicious influences and associations whose results have compelled us regretfully to take this unpleasant step. If you wish, we will give you a list of suitable establishments."

"I'm afraid a boarding-school would be very expensive," Mrs. Small said dolefully.

"When it is a question of Saving a Brand from the Burning," said Miss Penelope, "no expense should be spared."

II

In the following September, three months after her
fifteenth birthday, on the day when her grandfather
began to fit up his pike-tackle, Bella was sent to the
school called St. Monica's, in Alvaston, the politest
suburb of North Bromwich. St. Monica's had been
approved of by all three Miss Bakers as an ideal to
which even the best of their pupils might aspire. It
was an establishment run with strict discipline tempered by kindness and permeated, to Miss Penelope's
joy, by a subdued flavour of ritualistic Anglicanism
which blew into it, no doubt, from the Oratory on the
other side of the Halesby Road, where the great
English cardinal lived.

It was an expensive school. The fees were far
heavier than anything the Smalls had contemplated,
and could only be met by calls on their dwindling
capital; but the Miss Bakers' rejection of Bella had
made her grandfather obstinate and anxious to put
them to shame by "going one better" at any price.
After all, he argued, the child needn't stay at St.
Monica's for more than two or three years, by the end
of which time she would emerge as a product superior
in finish to anything that had ever emanated from
Hypatia House. Her grandmother, more realistic in

money matters, would have preferred, before committing herself, to have enlisted the help of Bella's
father, who, supported by his wife's income, was now
doing well; but the old man's pride jibbed at this: his
son was another person whom he wanted to put to
shame; having taken Bella over he would make a lady
of her without Rupert's permission or help.

The Bella who returned to Bromsberrow after her
first year at St. Monica's was very different from the
leggy, mischievous little girl who had paddled with
boys in the brook. In twelve months she had lost so
much of her natural tomboy impulsiveness as to appear
demure. Though her hair still hung in the plaits required by the school's regulations, she had gained
several inches in height, and the period's cuirass of
canvas and whalebone did not conceal the fact that
she had become a woman.

In this sudden maturity the various conflicting
strains had now reached an equilibrium which was to
settle and fix her "type." Of her father's inheritance
nothing remained save a general neatness of body and
limb and a refinement (if not a regularity) of feature
which, combined with her mother's quick and vivid
colouring, gave her face the piquancy that, in youth, is
a fair substitute for beauty. Yet by far the most striking
part of her physical make-up derived from her grandfather Mortimer: her coal-black eyebrows and lashes
were now more strictly defined, and the grey-black
eyes beneath them were as handsome as his, with some-

thing, too, of his tragic mysteriousness.

She had become, as was natural at her age, extremely self-conscious: she knew herself to be striking, if not quite beautiful, and took trouble to make the best of herself, deliberately subduing her native wildness to a practised serenity of bearing closely modelled on that of the music-mistress at St. Monica's, a young woman named Boldmere, for whom she had conceived the first passionate devotion of her life.

It was Miss Boldmere who had awakened in her the religious emotion which the youngest Miss Baker's persuasions had previously failed to arouse—not because Bella herself had become more susceptible to mysticism, but because Bella was in love with her (as Miss Boldmere intended she should be) and yearned to resemble her in everything, and because Miss Boldmere's tactics were so much more subtle than the ingenuously devout Penelope's, spicing her sensual wiles (in which the experience of her calling made her an innocent adept) with a cunning appeal to Bella's æsthetic sense, an important part of her nature which had never before found expression.

It was unfortunate for Miss Boldmere's designs that in music, the art in which she was directly concerned, she drew a blank: Bella wasn't musical and, definitely, never would be. But in poetry, in pictures, in a romantic appreciation of natural beauty, and through these, in those mystical ardours which were Miss Boldmere's sublimation of what she would have been revolted to hear described as a sexual libido, the child's heart became open and eager and deliciously responsive.

As a consequence, when she came home for the holidays that summer, Bella found herself referring all thought and speech and behaviour—in others as well as in herself—to Miss Boldmere's standards; and the result, though it gave her a sense of superiority, was embarrassing. Up till then she had always considered her grandparents' house as a paragon among homes. Now, she found it shrunken and dingy and painfully lacking in graciousness, an impossibly un-romantic environment for her regenerate self. It was strange, she thought, that she had never realized the meanness and ugliness of the yard with its confusion of rusty débris, the shabbiness of the little office up-stairs in which, incredibly, she had spent the happiest part of her life. Hypatia House, once palatial and elegant, had declined to the status of a smug little suburban villa without any distinction.

A change of the same kind had overtaken the people of Bromsberrow. The Miss Bakers, for instance, whom she had regarded with a certain degree of awe if not with reverence, stood revealed, on her next encounter with them, as a trio of mere grotesques, with their old-fashioned clothes and their mincing manners; while their elder pupils, whom Bella had previously considered "grand" or "smart," had become rather "common"—not at all the sort of girls Miss

Boldmere would approve of.

She would have been happier if this detached and critical judgement could have spared her own relations. But it didn't. When she considered them through Miss Boldmere's eyes she was shocked into thanking heaven that Miss Boldmere had never seen them and hoping that she never would. Her grandmother, she found to her surprise, was no more than an ordinary, lower-middle-class, working housewife with a spare uncomely figure and bony red hands; while her grandfather, who had been the particular idol of her childhood, turned out to be a slovenly, snuffy old man with an infantile mind, a stupid laugh, and a beard smelling strongly of stale tobacco which revolted her whenever he attempted his too-frequent embraces. In her heart she was ashamed of them both, and this made her ashamed of herself, for her conscience told her that Miss Boldmere, however much she disapproved of her grandparents, would have disapproved of this attitude even more. It was a dreadful thing to find the two people to whom one owed everything, distasteful and pathetic. Yet, in the endless letters she wrote to her and often tore up (so little of her devotion was expressible in words) she could never confess her fault—for that implied letting Miss Boldmere into its cause, of which she was equally ashamed.

Through the long summer holidays her self-consciousness made her acutely unhappy and lonely. Not a soul in Bromsberrow could enter her introvert's world.

She had nothing to read, save the volumes of poetry and devotion which Miss Boldmere had lent her and two heavenly hurried letters which her idol wrote to her from Italy where, in the company of a detestable rival, she was spending a month in the study of Florentine Art.

The arrival of these letters and Bella's evident exaltation aroused suspicion in her grandmother's shrewd mind. She remembered the history of her daughter-in-law's passionate love-affair which had ended in a hasty marriage at the age of eighteen. Bella was mature for her years, and who knew what might have happened in North Bromwich? She guessed they were love-letters (which, in a sense, they were) and lay in wait for an opportunity to examine their contents. When she found them, at last, under Bella's pillow, she was equally relieved and staggered by Miss Boldmere's medley of religious exhortations and luscious endearments combined with an effusive essay on Renaissance Art and the towers of San Gimignano. It was sufficient for her to know that the correspondent was not a young man, and she communicated the discovery with acute satisfaction to her husband.

He, too, had been bewildered by the change in his little pet, but was inclined to put it all down to the mistake they had made in sending her to a boarding-school. She was no longer the delightful child who had been content to "mess about" and waste time with him like a friendly puppy, or listen gravely to his

complaints about Belgian competition or the wariness
of carp, and laugh at his feeble jokes, but a stranger,
withdrawn and possibly critical, in whose watchful
eyes, whatever else there might be, the sweet trust and
friendliness of childhood no longer abode.

This was sad, for the time had come when he really
needed Bella as something more than a plaything.
Amiable and kindly as he was, he had never possessed
much vigour of body or intellect; and now that age
had begun to tell on the reserves of both, his plight
was even more pathetic than Bella, distressed by her
own disillusion, knew. During the last few years the
wrought-iron nail-trade had taken its final precipitous
plunge towards extinction. One by one the sources of
income on which he had counted faltered and ran dry.
Buyers no longer "dropped in" to the warehouse for
a chat and a "glass of wine and a biscuit," leaving
orders behind them; and even if he had had marketable wares to push—which, alas, he hadn't—he was
too old to take the road in search of new trade. His
tragedy was that of many humble manufacturers who
had succeeded to a small "family" business in the easy
years of the mid-century boom which had made Hayseech. In youth and in middle age he had never known
the need of bestirring himself, and now that old age
had come he had lost the power to move. Even
physically, his manner of life became more and more
static. He found it an effort to disentangle his fishing-
tackle or to concentrate his attention on the bobbing

float. It was much easier to stay at home in comfort and make vague plans for the future or ruminate on the past, during which, as likely as not, he would drop off to sleep in his chair by the office fire.

One evening, during the following autumn, when he had failed to come in for his tea, Mrs. Small found him sprawled in his chair and breathing so heavily that his snores shook the air, and when she disturbed him she could not rouse him. She ran down and called their next-door neighbour, old Waldron, the nailer, who hurried as fast as his weak hams would carry him to call the doctor from Bromsberrow. There was nothing to be done but to carry Mr. Small to bed, where he died, three days later, having never recovered consciousness. It was a good thing, the doctor said, that he hadn't died suddenly; for that would have meant an inquest. *Cerebral Thrombosis*, he wrote on the certificate. A merciful end.

Bella knew nothing of all this until the eve of the funeral. It would have been cruel, her grandmother decided, to involve a young girl in its sombre preliminaries. A telegram addressed to their son in London drew no reply until two days later, when a letter came saying that his wife was ill and that he could not possibly leave her.

Bella herself received the news from Miss Boldmere, to whom the head-mistress, Miss Cash, had deputed the awkward duty of breaking it. Her choice might have been happier, for during her second year at St. Monica's Bella's attitude towards the music-mistress had been modified by the pressure of new interests and a stiffening of the hard core of common sense which was Mortimer's dower to her. She had by now ceased to view her former idol through the rosy mist which Miss Boldmere's flattering intimacies had conjured up so skilfully in her younger mind. There was something clear-cut in her nature that rebelled against sloppiness of sentiment; and Miss Boldmere, who had looked forward to this mission as an opportunity for reconciliation in an atmosphere made sweetly tense by the moment's emotion, was doomed to a sharp disappointment.

"The child was like granite," she informed Miss Cash regretfully afterwards. "Of course I tried all I could to break the news gently and gradually; but those great black eyes of hers saw through me at once. Her composure seemed unnatural, almost uncanny in a girl of her age—though, really, I might have expected it. During the last term or so, her whole disposition appears to have changed completely. At times her . . . I hardly know what to call it: it isn't exactly insensitiveness . . . her deliberate coldness towards me, I fear, in particular—and I really don't think I deserve it, Miss Cash—has been almost frightening. She's more like a woman of fifty than a child of seventeen."

"Well, you told her. What did she say?"

"She simply wouldn't *let* me tell her. She knew all

about it before I came to the point. She said, quite
coldly: 'You mean my grandfather's dead?' Just like
that: not a suspicion of a tear or a change of colour!
Then she said: 'Well, he's over seventy, and I don't
think he was awfully happy. Poor Grannie: she's the
person who'll feel it most.' I said: 'Don't you feel it
too, darling?' I won't say she laughed, but she smiled.
I think she did that to hurt me: I do, honestly, Miss
Cash! She said slowly, just as if she were calculating
exactly what she *did* feel: 'No, I don't think I do, Miss
Boldmere, not terribly, you know. He's probably
much happier now than he was before.' And this rather
took the wind out of my sails, because that, more or
less, was what I was going to tell her, though I *do*
think it ought to have come from me rather than her,
and I'm perfectly sure she was speaking in a hard,
matter-of-fact way—I mean, that it didn't come from
any religious feeling."

"And then?"

"Well, Miss Cash, to tell you the truth I hardly
knew what to say: she seemed so—untouchable, so to
speak. I just told her that her grannie expected her
home for the funeral, and asked if she had any black
clothes. She said no, she hadn't; but she supposed
there'ld be time to get her maroon frock dyed. I told
her I thought I could find her a coat and skirt—she's
about my size—and she thanked me quite nicely. Then
she said: 'Miss Boldmere, do you think this means I
shall have to leave here altogether?' And I told her,

of course, that I couldn't say anything about *that*. 'Because I don't *want* to leave here a bit,' she said."

"That was very nice of her, poor child."

"Well, Miss Cash, it was and it wasn't. If she'd said she'ld hate leaving *me*, or you, or her friends, it would have been quite different. But she didn't. In my humble opinion she was just thinking of herself."

Miss Cash hesitated. "Poor Bella! She's an odd, lonely child," she said.

"All the more reason for her to respond to affection," Miss Boldmere replied.

"From what the grandmother has told me, I gather that she has no other relations—none that count, anyway: her mother's dead and her father re-married. I'm interested in Bella Small, and always have been. She's pretty, in a way; she's intelligent, and she's enormously strong: that's what you call hardness . . ."

"If you'd seen her and heard her this afternoon!"

"Yes, I know how you feel. She isn't the child you knew when she first came here two years ago. And she never will be, Miss Boldmere, you may take that from me. I think Bella has the makings of a remarkable woman. I shall be as sorry as she is if her grandmother is forced to take her away. However, we'll see. Has she gone to the station?"

"Yes. She went half an hour ago. I offered to go with her, but she told me I needn't."

"There are times when people prefer to be alone, Miss Boldmere. That doesn't imply any criticism of

E

yourself or lack of appreciation for your kindness. It's just a protective colouring. You're so terribly sensitive, aren't you?"

Miss Boldmere sighed and threw wide her hands in a little gesture of despair. Her weak eyes, behind the strong lenses of her spectacles, were full of tears.

"And you're another hard one!" Miss Boldmere thought.

III

BELLA had chosen to go to the station alone because her feelings were far too near the surface to bear Miss Boldmere's assaults on her emotions with equanimity. She had been deeply moved (though not in the way Miss Boldmere would have desired) by hearing of her grandfather's death. Though she hadn't exactly "loved" him—that was the word people used to cover such different feelings as that which had made her mother elope with her father and Miss Boldmere open her heart to Christ—his suddenly ceasing to exist afflicted her with an almost physical sensation of cold helplessness—as though a glacial hand clutched and held her. People died, she knew, every day of the week: she was reminded of that on Saturday afternoons when the high black-horsed hearses with their florid carvings of draped urns and swags and plumes and their barbarous equipment of professional "mutes" moved slowly, at a ceremonial trot, up the Halesby Road. (Later on in the day they came bowling briskly home again; the driver, a pipe in his mouth, touched up his black-plumed horses and the "mutes" found their tongues and cracked jokes.) But for Bella death was a horrible, dank thing that happened to other people and other people's relations, never to oneself

or one's own. Thus, while she was shocking Miss Boldmere with her defensive affectation of callousness, a
strange sense of insecurity and disquietude troubled
her, like a November fog that veils or, more terribly,
distorts familiar surroundings and breathes into the
heart an inexplicable icy loneliness.

This sensation of awe was mingled, oddly enough,
with an irrepressible feeling of adventurousness.
The catastrophe had broken the rhythm of her fixed
life, which should have been engaged at that moment
with Victor Hugo's *Hernani*, and dissolved it into
something fluid and incalculable. At breakfast that
morning she had been nothing more than herself, Bella
Small, an average schoolgirl in the top class at St.
Monica's; while here she was, eight hours later, a
prominent (if not the central) figure in one of life's
major tragedies, driving down to the station alone in
the splendour of a four-wheeled cab with straw on
the floor, and dignified by the grown-up black tailor-
made Miss Boldmere had lent her, whose faint and
characteristic perfume of White Rose was enough to
convince her that she was no longer herself. It was
hard to believe that the cabman and the clerk in the
booking-office could be unaware of her costume's
dramatic significance or of her own importance.

On the platform, indeed, a young man in a Norfolk
jacket showed interest of another kind. She was aware
of him following her up and down the platform while
she waited for her train to be shunted in, and at the

end of one turn, he smiled and made as if he would raise his cap till he saw how Bella's face hardened and quickly covered his overture by transferring the smile to another direction and scratching his head. At that moment Bella would much rather have been regarded as a tragic figure than as an attractive young woman. It was the fashion just then at St. Monica's— a fashion encouraged by Miss Boldmere—to consider flirtations rather "silly" and to treat the sentimental advances of adventurous young men with studied aloofness; but though she tossed her head in the correct manner Bella was none the less flattered by the interest she had aroused. If she wasn't exactly pretty in a conventional way, she knew she was "striking"; she was aware that her unusual colouring—pale gold hair, black brows and eyelashes, combined with the vivid complexion that belongs to brunettes rather than blondes—made people, particularly men, look twice before their eyes left her. It struck her now that this quality of contrast must surely be heightened by the "black" Miss Boldmere had lent her. It seemed stupid of her, with her instinctive tastes, not to have realized this before; but she was pleased to think that in future she would have an excuse for wearing mourning for just as long as she wished, thus emphasizing her state as a person whose grief entitled her to unusual respect and also "making the best of herself."

The first of these fortunate distinctions (if not the second) found its reward at Bromsberrow station, where a porter who guessed who she was, though she didn't know him, showed her delicate attentions that made her feel like a person of consequence.

"We're all terrible sorry to hear your bad news, Miss," he said. "Mr. Small was a kind old gentleman; he'll be missed in Bromsberrow. He always had a kind word and a laugh for everybody, no matter who. Ay, I've often carried his tackle in the times he used to go fishing, and sent off his pigeons. A regular old sportsman he was: there's not many of 'em left."

The man spoke so feelingly that, for the first time in her life, Bella began to feel proud of her grandfather whom she had lately despised. Was it possible, after all, she wondered, that she had misjudged him when she thought of him as a rather slovenly, uninteresting, uneducated old man with a beard that smelt of tobacco? "A laugh for everybody . . ." That laugh had got on her nerves; it was a silly laugh—there was no denying it—yet that was the thing that people remembered him by when they spoke of his kindliness. And all of a sudden, as she sat in the broken-down fly jolting over the rutted road on her way to the house of mourning, she was overwhelmed with an acute, an intolerable remorse. Now she saw no longer her grandfather's silliness nor even his slovenliness, but only the goodness, the simplicity, which she had been too self-conscious and too proud to appreciate. During the last summer holidays she had been selfish and wicked enough to avoid him, she might even have hurt him, the poor old thing, with her brutal callousness. And now it was too late: she could never make him amends, never humiliate herself, as she passionately desired, nor return him the kindliness which he had given her so sweetly, so ungrudgingly, ever since her babyhood. By the time that she reached the warehouse she found herself crying. This was the real bitterness of death: its utter irrevocability.

Now, the mood of adventure, in which she had flattered herself on her own importance, had vanished. She was pale and humble before a majesty that made her feel light and vain and little to the degree of insignificance. Though she knew she could never now make amends to that poor old man, she resolved not to incur a new burden of regrets in the case of her grandmother, who, she supposed, being much the same age, would not long survive him.

Yet when, virtuous in these resolutions, she entered the house, she found that her grandmother was not so easy to patronize. She was sitting in the front room, where the reek of the old man's tobacco was mingled with an odour of chrysanthemums, in the company of their nearest neighbour, old Mrs. Waldron. Bella had expected to find her grandmother overwhelmed with the sort of emotion which she herself had discovered on the way from the station. Mrs. Small, on the contrary, was much more composed than Bella herself or than Mrs. Waldron. She looked, it was true, very little and shrunken in her mourning, the old-fashioned moiré silk which she kept for funerals. Its blackness gave her lined face framed in her scanty grey hair a pallor like that of old ivory; and her voice, too, seemed somehow shrunken in its quietness. When Bella impulsively kissed her, holding back her tears, she patted her reassuringly. It was she, it seemed, who must teach a lesson in strength.

"I'm glad you've come, child," she said. "We feared the train would be late. It's been very foggy to-day, particularly this morning."

"Ay, indeed it has," Mrs. Waldron agreed.

They went on talking about the weather!

"But I expect the child's ready for a cup of tea," her grandmother said at last, with a kind of wan brightness.

"Don't you stir yourself, Mrs. Small," Mrs. Waldron said. "I'll see to the kettle."

"Thank you kindly, Mrs. Waldron. And I daresay Bella will cut us some bread and butter. There's a new pat on the slab in the larder, Bella, and the bread's in the pan as usual. Would you like to make yourself some toast and dripping, Bella?"

She said this so meekly, so kindly, that Bella could almost have cried. Toast and dripping had been one of the treats which she and her grandfather had shared on cold afternoons in November—afternoons such as this—when he came in blinking and rubbing his hands after pike-fishing; the old man ate it greedily, the dripping glistened like oil on his bread; but the reflec-

tion that they would never again eat toast and dripping together brought tears to her eyes. It was little
inanimate commonplace reminders of that kind which,
all through that desperate evening, threatened the
composure which, taking her cue from her grandmother, she tried to assume. They affected her even
more than her consciousness, in the background, of the
dead man lying alone in the dark upstairs. Wherever
her eyes turned, she met them. On the mantelpiece
stood a bundle of paper spills which, when she was a
child, he had taught her the trick of making: she could
see his blunt clumsy fingers now, and hear his
triumphant laugh when the spill was curled. There
was a pipe by the side of them from which the ashes
had not been knocked out. What on earth could they
do with things like that? Bella wondered. They might
give them away to old Waldron. But would anyone
really like smoking a dead man's pipe? There were
two of his hats hanging up in the hall, and a shabby
overcoat, and another, nearly new.

"How useless clothes are," she thought, "when once
you are dead, and what a pity he wasted money on
buying a new one. But of course he didn't know he
was going to die. We none of us do. It might happen
to me to-night just as it happened to him and to
Mother. She wasn't much older than me."

The thought formed itself thus and gave her a
momentary shiver; but in her heart she knew she
wasn't really going to die that night, or ever, for that

E*

matter. This idea of death was only an ugly chimera that shadowed and chilled her momentarily, then vanished like a bad dream. Yet she was thankful that night when her grandmother suggested that she might sleep in her room. It would have been more than her nerves could stand to sleep alone in that house in the dark—though that, too, was unreasonable; for surely no gentler creature than her grandfather had ever lived, and he was even more gentle now. Mrs. Small slept like a child while Bella's open eyes stared into the black of night.

It was a sad little funeral. There were conventions of procedure to be observed—as, for instance, that the "family" should not see the coffin being carried downstairs. Mrs. Waldron, who was not merely a professional "layer-out" but an acknowledged expert in all these forms, saw to it that none of the proprieties of lower middle-class death were violated. She herself would not "follow" the funeral, but would stay behind to air the house and sprinkle the room upstairs with disinfectant. Bella felt these activities of Mrs. Waldron's to be revolting; the old woman appeared to extract such pride from her ghoulish rôle; but her grandmother seemed to submit to them willingly. At a quarter to two Mrs. Waldron poked her head into the front sitting-room and summoned them to depart. They stepped out into the hall together. The old man's hats and coats were still hanging there: Bella wished they had been taken away. There was a large mirror too in which, as they hurried past, she could see the reflection of her own pallid face. Last night she had been ashamed of thinking how well black suited her. Now, against her will, the same satisfaction recurred.

They stepped into the cab. Her grandmother and she were the chief and only mourners; but when they reached the churchyard a little crowd had assembled of aged women in shawls and young women nursing babies and tottering old men who had worked all their lives as nailers and dealt with her grandfather. At the lych-gate a small deputation from the Broms-berrow Angling Club, dressed in black and carrying bowler hats in their hands, awaited them. It was a golden November afternoon; all yesterday's fog had vanished. The hills stood out clear against a soft sky; birds sang, as though spring had come; and through the still air (the bell had stopped tolling now) yellow leaves of horse-chestnut and elm and blotched fans of sycamore detached themselves from the branches of the churchyard trees and fell with the soft patter of an April shower on the ground and the mourners' figures and into the grave. Bella had never before felt the solemn peace of autumn so deeply. It was beauty rather than sorrow that dimmed her eyes.

When the last words had been said and they turned away, several strangers spoke to her. They called her "my dear," as though she belonged to them and their world, and their gentleness touched her. Yet she knew, in her heart, that this small village world was not really hers and that their friendliness could not reclaim her. Its leisurely life would flow on and on eternally, yet she would not share it; for at this moment when she passed out through the lych-gate she instinctively felt she was turning her back on her childhood, stepping out into a new kind of life no less mysterious than death.

Even so, returning to the sad house in which, despite Mrs. Waldron's lustrations, the smell of chrysanthemums still lingered, she was confirmed in the resolution she had formed overnight. It was her duty, as long as her grandmother lived, to stay with her. It was not easy to announce her intention. She dreaded the danger of some untimely word destroying the precarious composure in which Mrs. Small was still wrapped. She began to wish that Mrs. Waldron had not left them alone; the presence of any third person might have provided her with an excuse for breaking the unbearable silence in which, with a mute automatism, this old woman picked up the snapped threads of her normal existence, moving here and there like a ghost, so meek and so lonely, performing the tasks that had been neglected during the suspension of the last three days. The spectacle of this mechanical absorption of the bruised brain in commonplace things was more pathetic than her previous inaction. It was so deliberate that Bella did not even dare to offer her help, though her heart was hurt when she saw

Mrs. Small take up the pipe from the mantelpiece and knock out the ashes and then, as carefully, replace it. At some unknown terrible point, she felt, there must surely come a moment of reaction equally dreadful for both of them; but the evening wore on, and the dreadful moment never arrived, nor were the words of devotion she had planned to speak spoken before her grandmother, relaxing at last, suggested with a weary smile that they should go to bed.

And next morning it was she, not Bella, who opened the subject.

"We must look up your train for North Bromwich, my child," she said. "I think you'll find a time-table in Grandpa's office, though I'm afraid it mayn't be up to date."

Bella moved to the door obediently, then turned. "Grannie darling," she said, "I can't bear leaving you like this, all alone. Hadn't I better stay with you? I'd much rather."

The old woman spoke gently. "That's nice of you, Bella. I know what you feel, and I'm glad that you do feel like that, child; but I'd rather you went. There's no need to worry about me. I shall be quite happy . . . quite happy," she repeated, "or as happy as I ever shall be again . . ."

"But, Grannie . . ."

"Yes, darling. I know you want to help me. But you can't, you see. Nobody can help me. If I were ill, it might be different; but I'm not: I'm perfectly well and able to look after myself. If I need anyone else, I know Mrs. Waldron will come in and help me. Besides, I'm quite sure your dear grandpapa would have wished you to go back. It would be a wicked waste, too, because your school-fees were paid in advance up till the end of the term, and I want you to take advantage of that while you have the chance. You see, I don't know how we're left—I suppose, in any case, we shall have to sell Grandpapa's business. If we can, that is; I'm afraid there's not much business left; and in that case I might not be able to send you to school any more. Of course things may turn out better than I think; your dear grandpapa never discussed business matters with me. Now be a good girl, Bella darling, and do as you're told."

She spoke, Bella thought, as though she still considered her a child. And she was not a child any longer, much less so than yesterday! She knelt at the old woman's side and fondled her hand.

"I shall simply hate going, Grannie," she said. "Won't you let me stay? If it's going to be as bad as all that I ought to be earning my living in some way or other."

Mrs. Small bent over her, smiling, and kissed her forehead with cold, lax lips.

"Run along to the office, darling, and look out your train," she said.

Bella obeyed, reluctantly; but for long after this the memory of that cold kiss and of the grey-yellowish

face, so furrowed and patient, continued to haunt her.
Before she had never thought of her grandmother
as having any age. Now she knew that she was old—
far older, indeed, than her grandfather—and little,
and so frail that her attachment to life appeared as
tenuous as that of the yellow leaves which had
detached themselves and fallen without a shudder on
the graveyard path.

IV

At St. Monica's everybody was exceedingly kind to her, as if recent contact with the majesty of death had given her a social distinction. There was even a brief and sober renewal of her friendship with Miss Boldmere, who had been so thoughtful in helping her over her mourning that Bella could hardly reject her sentimental advances. She liked being flattered and made a fuss of: what she jibbed at was being invited to pray, in unison, for her grandfather's soul; for even if she had believed in purgatory she could never have brought herself to consider that state unpleasant in the case of that kindly, gentle, good little man, than whom, surely, no more innocent creature had ever walked this earth. Miss Boldmere was deeply hurt by Bella's refusal to pray with her. This showed, once again, how hard the child's nature was. Not even the death of her nearest and dearest relative could soften it.

Towards the end of the Christmas term, Miss Cash, the headmistress, sent for her. Such interviews at St. Monica's were unusual, for the school, with its numbers of day-girls from Alvaston, was enormous, and the headmistress's duties were mainly administrative.

Bella knocked at the door of her private sitting-room and Miss Cash's brisk voice said "Come in!" She was standing in front of the fire and smoking a cigarette, which, in the year eighteen eighty-nine, was sufficient of itself to give the interview an unusual character. "Sit down, and make yourself comfortable, Bella," she said, "I want to talk to you."

The room in which Bella found herself was different from any she had known in its combination of masculine comfort with feminine graces. To Victorian eyes it seemed oddly empty. It had a plain beige carpet and cream-washed walls with no pictures on them save a number of large photographs of classical and medieval sculpture, a steel engraving of the Parthenon and, above the mantelpiece, a *della Robbia* plaque. The room's circumference was lined with a deep belt of white-painted shelves full of books. The closed curtains showed one of those formally complicated patterns of foliage in white and indigo produced by William Morris, and the sofa and easy chairs were upholstered in linen printed with the same design. Apart from these the room had no furniture but a Chippendale mahogany table from which an oil-lamp shaded with apricot silk diffused gentle light, and a small sofa-table in front of the fire laid for afternoon tea, where a silver kettle steamed above a spirit-lamp.

It was a room at once gracious and ascetic, resembling, in this unusual combination, its owner.

Miss Cash might have been any age between thirty-five and fifty. She was a tall, slight, brittle woman, with a peculiarly colourless quality of hair and skin that made her ageless. There was age in her voice, which was so quiet as to seem always tired, but youth in her bright, dark eyes and in the bird-like alertness of her beautifully-proportioned and, somehow, virginal figure which in movement instantly transformed the elderly owner of the voice into a young girl. Her speech, in which every syllable had the definition of a cameo, was surprising to slow minds (for her mind moved as quickly as her body) and often barbed with a delicate irony which was generally misunderstood by women, though admired (and feared) by men. This explained, perhaps, why she had never married; for in youth (if she had ever been anything but ageless) she might easily have dazzled with her mischievous fancy, her vivid phrasing, and the sly humour that made her cheeks dimple with the ghosts of smiles that faded before they were born. Even now, resigned (or at least devoted) to spinsterhood, Miss Cash had not relaxed her pride in the neatness of her person. She showed it in the well-cut shoes that "set-off" her shapely ankles, in the elegant French gloves that emphasized the beauty and delicacy of her capable hands, to such a degree that her smartness impressed (and slightly intimidated) the matrons of North Bromwich, who, although they counted themselves proud of being provincial, were not above hoping that some of Miss Cash's smartness might be communicated, as it were, by contact, to the daughters they committed to her charge.

Bella, too, was impressed, but less intimidated than thrilled by this, her first intimate contact with her headmistress. Miss Cash's room seemed to her beautiful—and that a room should be beautiful of itself was a new idea to her, for none had excited her acute, undeveloped æsthetic sense before. Its combination of spaciousness with intimacy and cool dignity enchanted her the more because it appeared to fit its owner as perfectly as her French gloves. In these, her proper surroundings, standing there like a man in front of the fire with the shameless cigarette in her lips, Miss Cash attained a new value. She was no longer the remote and essentially cold headmistress, but a warm human being for whom, Bella felt, she could experience an instinctive adoration, so different in kind from that which she had formerly given to Miss Boldmere as to be its antithesis. Here was a woman completely emancipated—as witness the cigarette!—yet obviously feminine, without a shred of sentimentality or diffuseness; a woman instinct with style; an aristocrat no less in culture than in feeling—as witness the skill with which she now put her visitor at her ease.

All these qualities instantly, if faintly, evoked eager responsive vibrations in Bella's consciousness. With her usual impulsiveness she accepted Miss Cash at first sight as an expression—on a higher plane—

of her own aspirations; as an example of what, in a flash of new vision, she conceived her own nature to be. She fell straight in love with Miss Cash's room, her pictures, her curtains, her voice, her enunciation, her hands, her ankles and her spirit—so deeply in love that she became appallingly shy.

"But before we talk, Bella dear," Miss Cash was saying, "let us have some tea. Do you like China? I hope you do. Very well, then. Suppose you pour out for us. I'm afraid you've had a rather rough time this term. Yes, I know all about it. I don't see very much of you girls—there are far too many of you— but I always keep my eye on you. Were you fond of your grandfather?"

Bella hesitated. "He was awfully kind to me, Miss Cash."

Miss Cash smiled. "Ah, I see. You went to them as a baby, didn't you? And your father remarried. He's a painter. I've seen some of his work."

Bella was thrilled. The fact that Miss Cash had seen some of his work gave her father a novel importance.

"Is it very good?" she asked hopefully.

Miss Cash laughed. "No. It's not very good. Not particularly strong, I should say; but he has great sensibility. I wonder if you have. Have you?"

"I don't think I could paint. I mean I don't awfully want to."

"And your music, according to Miss Boldmere's

reports, is 'brilliant but soulless'."

"Well, you see, I don't really *like* music, Miss Cash."

"That is honest, anyway. What *do* you like, Bella?"

"I don't think I've ever thought about it. I like poetry, sometimes. And pictures. I love those pictures of *yours*," she added quickly.

"You mean the photographs?"

"Yes . . . sculptures and vases and buildings and solid things—the sort of things you can touch. I'm awful at explaining."

"You explain yourself perfectly. Your tastes are expensive. You should have been born to great possessions. So should I, but I wasn't. I'll confess I love touching things too. Do you like being here, Bella?"

The question took her by surprise.

"I think this is the loveliest room . . ." she began.

"Yes, it is nice, isn't it? But I didn't mean that. I meant: Do you like being at St. Monica's?"

"Why, of course I like being here, Miss Cash!" (She wanted to say: I should be happy anywhere where you were.)

"I asked you that question," Miss Cash went on slowly, "for a particular reason. You know that your grandmother's ill, Bella? As a matter of fact she's been ill for several years—since long before your grandfather died, the doctor tells me."

"Then oughtn't I to be with her, Miss Cash?"

"No. You can't be with her. She's in hospital now. She was taken there several weeks ago. You were not told about it because she was anxious you shouldn't know. She has had an operation for . . . well, that doesn't really matter . . . but I'm afraid it's not done her much good."

Bella gasped. "You mean that she's dead? Oh, why didn't you tell me?"

"No, no. She's still living; but I'm afraid she won't live very long, and she certainly won't go home again. That was why I sent for you. You see, you can't go home either: the house is closed. So I was going to ask you if you'd like to stay here, with me, Bella."

"For Christmas? With you, Miss Cash?"

"Well, I shall be here. The position appears to be rather complicated. You have no mother. Your father, fortunate man, is living in Italy; and even if he'ld like to have you himself, I gather there are . . . difficulties. The whole question of what you are going to do next term will have to be discussed. Your grandfather was not a rich man, and I'm afraid his business, whatever it was, has not been very prosperous. When the lawyers went into the matter they found, apparently, that there wasn't much business left, and very little money. Then your grandmother's illness, naturally, has entailed an expense which couldn't be avoided; which means, of course, that you'll have to earn your own living. Not that I think

that's a pity. On the contrary. The world's full of
useless women. In a town like North Bromwich, with
more money than taste, they're not even ornamental.
Three-quarters of the girls we turn out from St.
Monica's will be just like their mothers, poor things.
You ought to make something rather better of your
life than that, Bella. You're intelligent, you have
glimmerings of taste, you're not bad-looking, and—
I think—fairly sensible. How old are you?"

"Seventeen."

"Well, of course, you're a child: that is far too
young to give one any idea of what you might make
of yourself. And I don't know you, do I?"

"I don't think I know myself."

"Nobody ever does, thank heaven! However, if
you stay with me through the Christmas holidays, we
shall be able to learn quite a lot about one another
if not about ourselves. Let's consider that settled,
Bella."

Miss Cash smiled. It was, Bella thought, a
peculiarly lovely smile, like thin sunshine striking over
bleached winter pastures. There was always, in Miss
Cash's smiles, a tinge of faint mockery—though
whether they mocked herself or the person to whom
she smiled or the world in general from which, even
in her enthusiasms, she seemed somehow detached,
Bella could never tell; nor did she pursue her
enquiries, for the mystery of Miss Cash's detachment
remained till the end one of her major charms.

V

THERE were other elements in this astonishing woman which continued to puzzle and fascinate Bella, not only during the enchanted interlude of those Christmas holidays, when they were hardly ever separated, but also throughout the three succeeding years she spent at St. Monica's. Miss Cash could be cruel, quite ruthlessly, consciously cruel. She could be cold: there were days when her brittleness was the brittleness of ice. She could be childlike, with a gay, adorable, kittenish humour. She could be grim and old, with a humour that bit like vitriol. She could be dreamy, subdued by beauty to a gentle ecstasy. She could be so intense that the heat of her feeling could radiate itself like a spiritual incandescence. She could be tender and affectionate—though never sentimental —and at such times, all other aspects of her protean personality were quickly forgotten.

It was this side of herself that Miss Cash displayed more particularly during the first month they spent together. She was in a delightful holiday mood and anxious to forget everything connected with St. Monica's. She was more readily tender towards her companion perhaps because, in the first week of the New Year, Bella's grandmother died in hospital, and

her loneliness was appealing of itself. She did not
let Bella know until the funeral was over. Bella was
shocked.

"But why didn't you tell me? I'm sure I ought to
have been there, Miss Cash," she said.

"Why ought you to have been there?"

"Well, people in Bromsberrow will think it funny."

"What are the people in Bromsberrow to you,
Bella? You've told me you have no friends there.
I don't suppose you will ever set foot in Bromsberrow
again. Why should you, after all? And in any case
funerals are nothing more than a horrible superstitious
survival from the middle ages. If you're a Christian
you're presumed to believe in immortality, in which
case 'paying respect,' as they call it, to the soul's
empty shell is illogical. And if you don't believe in
immortality, what does it matter what people do with
your body after you're dead? The whole practice is
revolting. If people mourn for me—and I don't suppose anybody will—I'd much rather they did it in
private instead of parading their grief for the satisfaction of a lot of gaping neighbours. As for letting
young people full of life like yourself be dragged
by sheer conventionality into these horrible macabre
exhibitions, I think it's a crime against decency. I was
sent to my own mother's funeral, I was a girl at the
time; but now that I look back on it I know that it
was wrong and cruel to send me. The memory of it
haunted me for months; it hurts me still. Some day,

when the world becomes civilized, there won't be any more funerals. The people we love will just silently disappear from the earth, but not from our thoughts. It's only the material aspects of death that are terrible, and yet those are the ones primitive people like us are forced to insist on! If I had my way I'ld make funerals and mourning illegal. Now do you see why I refused to let you be harrowed and exhibited? If you're not grateful to me you ought to be!"

She spoke brusquely; yet, for all this violence, she was aware of the child's lonely bewilderment—it was more this than absolute grief, for, of the two, she had been actually more attached to her grandfather—and softened it by filling her mind with new sensations and interests. There was a selfish element in this kindness, no doubt, for this strange woman, too, was lonely, and the company of Bella, so young and vivid and impressionable in all her enjoyments, may have been to her the source of a vicarious enthusiasm more intense than any her spirit could have achieved of itself. She was an artist in her way, and the shaping of the child's nature, so fluent and flexible, may have given her that creative illusion which, through want of maternity, had been denied her. And she did her work skilfully, without waste of material, turning Bella's mind only into those activities and sensations which she guessed would be profitable through her knowledge of its limitations.

Miss Cash found the relationship amusing, but to

Bella it was a great deal more than that: it meant a sudden widening of interest and experience. It seemed as though the closed windows of her soul's house had suddenly been flung open to fill her lungs with sweet air, to satisfy her eyes with vistas of unlimited freedom. Bella's freedom, of course (though she did not know it), was relative, being narrowed by Miss Cash's personal interests; but it seemed so much wider to her than any she had believed to be possible that she was transported and bewildered.

During the whole of that month they were hardly ever apart, together penetrating whole tracts of spiritual territory, in what, because they were new to her, seemed to Bella startling and perilous feats of exploration. During the daytime they went for long walks: sometimes through Warwickshire lanes where bare branches made a bridge for leaping squirrels; sometimes over the spine of the Clents, that miniature range which divides the basin in which the Black Country fumes and smoulders from the mountain-girdled green of the Severn Plain; returning thence, wintry sunsets glowing behind them, to the welcoming warmth and secrecy of Miss Cash's blue room, which was now no longer an arcanum of mysteries but a natural setting for this new, gracious mode of life.

Sometimes they visited galleries and gazed at pictures. In those days the despised pre-Raphaelites were coming into their own, and Miss Cash, who had known Burne-Jones and seen Rossetti and Swinburne, and actually penetrated the Gothic glooms of William Morris's house, was in the position of a disciple justified by their resurrection. Sometimes they made pilgrimages to the great churches that lay within reach: Worcester, Gloucester, Lichfield and Tewkesbury; and those visits were an even richer experience, for Miss Cash knew a great deal about architecture, and this art appealed more directly to Bella than any other—though, indeed, everything she saw in Miss Cash's company was enriched and coloured by the inward light of her adoration.

Yet even more enchanting than these expeditions were the long quiet evenings when they settled down to long talks or silences, or to reading aloud in the warmth of the fire and the apricot glow of lamplight and the aromatic smoke of Miss Cash's cigarettes. They read together a great deal of poetry and sometimes novels, particularly those of Meredith, who was not only a poor relation of Miss Cash's beloved pre-Raphaelites but also, like herself, an active Feminist. Her dry wit delighted in Meredith's brittle artifice and his fastidious evasion of the physical aspects of love, the treatment of which, in Hardy's novels, revolted her. Whenever, in their reading, they approached this subject, Miss Cash became restless and irritable. It was one, she gave Bella to understand, that bored her, and vitiated every work of art into which it intruded.

Bella regretted this; for love, theoretically, was a

topic about which she was acutely interested and curious, and anxious for information; but the faintest allusion to it was enough to bring to Miss Cash's face an appearance of cold discomfort and into her voice a rasping impatience; and since the light of Miss Cash's countenance was the sun in her present heaven, Bella reluctantly abandoned her enquiries.

Indeed, the only occasion on which, during that wonderful month, any coldness arose between them, was directly connected with this fierce taboo. They had been returning from a wintry walk over the hills by train, when, at the station called Mawne Road, a young man had entered their compartment. He was a good-humoured, clean-looking young man, Bella thought, with kindly blue eyes which, from the moment he joined them, showed an interest in herself which seemed natural and flattering. As the train left Mawne Road, and plunged into the fiery wilderness of the Black Country, he began to invite conversation with overtures which to Bella seemed innocent and friendly (she liked his voice, too) but which Miss Cash discouraged with the most acid of syllables, so unfairly and rudely, Bella thought, that it seemed only fair to make some polite amends. He was talking, with a sort of awkward enthusiasm, of Hingstons' great works where the open-hearth steel-furnaces illumined the smoke-pall with splendid reflections; he spoke of them with proprietary pride, so that Bella, guessing that he was somehow connected with them, smiled back and asked one or two questions, leading him on. As they talked, Miss Cash's set face became greyer and grimmer, her black eyes had a look of blank hatred. When they reached North Bromwich and the kindly young man opened the door and took off his hat to watch them dismount, Miss Cash rose and darted from the carriage precipitately with lowered eyes. Bella smiled and thanked him and said good evening and hurried after her. But by now Miss Cash was scudding along the platform with the rapidity of the Red Queen. Bella was forced to run as fast as she could to catch her up; but when, a little excited by the encounter and puzzled by its end, she tried to slip her arm through her friend's, Miss Cash, with an irritable jerk, detached herself. All the way home in the bus she maintained the same frozen silence. When Bella timidly spoke to her she would not even reply, and when they reached St. Monica's she shut herself up in her bedroom.

Bella sat down to supper alone. It was a miserable meal. Even the room which she loved had become cold and unfriendly, as though the pictures and furniture shared their owner's vexation. When she could bear its atmosphere no longer, Bella stole through the dark passages and knocked at Miss Cash's door. There was no answer. For a moment she was alarmed by the thought that Miss Cash might be ill, perhaps even unconscious. She opened the door and entered.

"What do you want?" Miss Cash said in an icy voice.

"I was worried about you, Miss Cash, I wondered if something had happened."

Miss Cash wriggled on the bed and laughed harshly. "Something had happened?" She mimicked the anxious voice. "If you had any vestige of sensitiveness you'ld know what has happened! Don't come near me, please. I don't want you."

"Mayn't I bring you some supper?"

"If I'd wanted any supper I should have rung for it. You'll oblige me by leaving me alone."

"But Miss Cash . . ."

"Miss Cash . . . Miss Cash. . . . You needn't go on repeating my name like an idiot. If you want anything, say so quickly and leave me."

"If I've done anything . . . anything to displease you . . . I'm most awfully sorry."

"Awfully? What does that mean? I wish you'ld learn to talk English." Miss Cash sat up in bed in the dark and glared at her. "You know perfectly well what you've done. Why did you leer at that man and lead him on like that with your inviting eyes?"

"But I only . . ."

"Of course. You only picked up the first man that happened to grin at you in a train! Didn't I see you smile at him? Even when I got out of the carriage you had to stay behind and chatter."

"I just said good evening and thanked him."

"Thanked him for what? For grinning at you and making a fool of you? If you'd asked him for his name and address I shouldn't have been surprised. I thought better of you than that. No doubt I was mistaken. You're as common as I might have expected. You'd better go. What are you waiting for now?"

Bella turned slowly; but before she had reached the doorway Miss Cash called her back. "Shut the door," she said, "and come here. I can't feel you in the dark. Where are you?"

"I'm here."

"Then come closer."

She took Bella's hand and drew her towards her. "Oh, Bella," she said—her voice cracked. "Bella, how could you torture me like that? You're the only thing I have in the world, and then . . . and then . . ." Miss Cash was crying like a disconsolate child . . . "you go smiling and flirting with the first strange man you see!"

After this there was, naturally, an emotional reconciliation which Bella, though she was touched by it, found almost as difficult to understand as Miss Cash's fierce outburst of jealousy. Why Miss Cash should have been jealous of her she couldn't imagine. But since jealousy that reached this mad degree was, in a way, a compliment, she felt it incumbent on her to affect a penitence which she didn't feel; at which Miss

Cash, having gained her point and being possibly ashamed of her tears, suddenly returned to her senses and became once more her ordinary self.

"It's twelve minutes to ten," she said. "You'd better go to bed."

And she said good night just as if nothing unusual had occurred.

Nor did she ever mention it again, though Bella often thought of it as an indication of something not wholly natural or admirable in her idol's composition. She often thought too of the nice young man in the train who had so obviously found her attractive and whom she had liked. During the next year or two, when, thanks to Miss Cash's generosity, she stayed on at St. Monica's, first as a pupil, then as a sort of supernumerary teacher and finally as Miss Cash's secretary-companion, she took pains to avoid a repetition of such painful incidents; but the idea of love in the abstract often invaded and possessed her thoughts. In the books that she read for herself, love played a predominant part. Several of the girls who had been senior to her and had left St. Monica's were married. Miss Cash relaxed her severity so far as to send them wedding presents, yet always spoke of these back-slidings with detachment and a faint bitterness, as of something a little discreditable which, thank heaven, could never happen to Bella or herself.

And Bella, who found these occasions exciting and romantic, though she dared not confess it, often won-

F

dered what had caused this odd kink in Miss Cash's
mind. She was generally inclined to attribute it to a
reaction from the disappointment of some early, unhappy love-affair; for surely, as a young woman, Miss
Cash must have been devastatingly attractive to men.
And the more Bella thought of this, the more she
pitied her; which, again, made a curious change in
their relationship, since a person who could be pitied
was not above criticism as Miss Cash had been in the
earlier stages of her devotion. Little by little, Miss
Cash was shedding those attributes of divinity with
which Bella's gratitude and enthusiasm had invested
her, till at last, in moments of clearer vision, the one-
time goddess stood revealed as a faded middle-aged
woman, of imperious and uncertain temper,
pathetically nursing an illusion of emancipated youth
and freedom and daring in what was really the arid life
of a confirmed old maid.

In essentials Miss Cash could hardly have changed
since she was a girl at Newnham and Bella a baby.
Her interests were only a little wider in scope, not in
quality, than those of the rapt Miss Boldmere,
mystically wedded to Christ, or of the other mistresses
on whom she imposed her tyrannies. And Bella, in
whose veins life moved and glowed with an increasing
urgency, came gradually to see that the routine of St.
Monica's, with its petty content of shifting female
loyalties and little intrigues and jealousies and suppressed emotions going round and round perpetually

like squirrels in a cage and leading nowhere, was the very negation of life.

Among these the jealousies troubled her most of all, for her position as Miss Cash's confidante made her peculiarly subject to them; but what finally determined her to break free from St. Monica's at all costs was her consciousness of inexorably passing years, and a growing conviction that if she did not escape in time she, too, must submit to becoming another of the figures she pitied in that blind alley: another Miss Boldmere; at the best, another Miss Cash.

The performance was less easy than the resolve, for Miss Cash was still formidable. One evening, towards the end of her fifth year at St. Monica's, she faced it and took her plunge.

"I have been thinking a lot just lately," she said, "about my future."

Miss Cash laughed. "Your future, Bella? What on earth do you mean? *You've* nothing to worry about."

"But I do worry, Miss Cash. You see I'm neither one thing nor the other. I feel I'm not getting anywhere."

Miss Cash lit a cigarette. "Well, where do you *want* to get?"

"I don't know. That's the worst of it. And if I go on as I am I'm afraid I shall never find out . . . not until it's too late."

"I can't see what you're driving at, Bella. I don't

understand you. As a matter of fact our plans are all settled. I didn't tell you before because I wanted to give you a surprise. We're going to Italy. I should like to spend Christmas in Rome."

Bella gasped. "Oh, Miss Cash, what a lovely idea! How sweet of you!"

"Well, I told you I'ld take you there some day, didn't I? And I always *do* keep my promises."

Bella was silent. Embarrassment had quickly succeeded her first sensation of pleasure. She was thinking: "If I let her take me to Italy, I shall be deeper and deeper than ever in debt to her. I shall never free myself, she's making escape impossible. I shall have to stay here for the rest of my days; and I can't . . . I can't!"

Miss Cash spoke sharply: "I asked you a question, Bella. Why don't you answer me? What's the matter? I hope you're not ill!"

(Miss Cash, who was never ill herself, had a horror of illness.)

Bella smiled. "No, I'm perfectly all right. And tremendously grateful. I'm grateful for all you've done for me. I owe everything to you. But. . . . You see . . ."

"Indeed I can't see. I'm totally in the dark. What *is* the matter with you?"

"I've been thinking, and I've come to the conclusion that I oughtn't to stay here much longer."

"Not stay here much longer? My dear child,

what on earth are you talking about? Are you mad?"

"Not a bit. Oh, Miss Cash, it's so difficult to explain. You see I have all my life in front of me, and if I go on and leave it too late . . ."

Miss Cash's pale face went ashen. She crushed out the glowing tip of her cigarette. When she spoke, her words were brittle and thin like icicles.

"You mean . . . you're tired of me?"

"Oh, of course I don't mean that. I've told you already how grateful I am for your kindness . . ."

Miss Cash laughed. "This is an odd sort of gratitude! Do you expect me to beg you to stay? If you think you're difficult to replace you're mightily mistaken! I suppose, by the letter of the law, I owe you some money. I'll write a cheque at once and send it to your room. You'll oblige me by packing your things and going at once. To-night."

"But, Miss Cash . . ." Bella was laughing nervously with tears in her eyes. "I didn't mean that I wanted . . . I was only thinking . . ."

"What you thought doesn't interest me. I object, on principle, to having disloyal people under my roof. You will go at once. I'll telephone for a cab to be here in half an hour's time. So, please hurry up."

Miss Cash turned her back on her. Bella gazed at it helplessly. She knew there was nothing more to be said. Yet, at that moment, her most powerful emotion was one of pity. She was looking at the back of a proud, bitter, hopeless old woman.

Miss Boldmere, her weak eyes goggling with excitement, helped Bella to pack. This was the third occasion on which she had assisted at a similar scene. This particular one seemed to her a fitting judgement at the hands of Providence on Bella for having deserted her. But she was a Christian, and therefore forgiving. She was also curious to know what, exactly, had happened. But in this she was disappointed. Bella never told her.

VI

BELLA slept that night in the house of one of her early friends at St. Monica's who lived in Alvaston but had been disqualified for the continuance of Miss Cash's favours by marriage. For the first time in her life she was standing alone and on her own feet; and the sensation, though novel and exhilarating, was also frightening. She had no money save the cheque which Miss Cash had scrupulously given her and a small sum in the bank—rather more than a hundred pounds—which had come to her as the remains of her grandparents' little estate. She was not even qualified to earn her living as a teacher or secretary, for Miss Cash, though she plumed herself on her own emancipation, preferred her subordinates to be wholly dependent on herself. As a final resort, Bella supposed she could fall back on her father; but Rupert Small had by now faded out of her life so completely that she didn't even know his address.

Yet her dominant emotion on escaping from St. Monica's was relief. The effect of Miss Cash's society on her spirit had resembled that of those cumulative poisons which slowly and insensibly produce paralysis. It was not until she had left it for good that she fully realized how she had grown to dislike St. Monica's, and how even more deeply, without being aware of it, she had feared and hated her benefactress. She was thankful that Miss Cash didn't know and could hardly guess where she had gone; for if she changed her mind and wanted her back again, appealing to her pity as well as to her sense of gratitude, Bella doubted if she could summon enough strength to refuse her.

Marjorie Astill, the friend with whom she had taken shelter, was a jolly, uncomplicated creature, blonde, plump, rich, easy-going, a trifle vulgar, and mercifully untroubled with the least sensibility. She liked having Bella in her house, for she had no children, and her husband, a brewer, was never at home in the daytime; she herself was entirely devoid of inward resources and knew no means of amusing herself but spending money foolishly—a diversion of which her husband complained but was rather proud. The couple were still quite affectionate, but rather bored with each other.

"Of course you can stay here as long as you like, Bella," she said. "I'm a grass-widow most of the time, and when Reg comes home it does him good to see a new face in the house. He likes and admires you, you know; and you're good for him too: you keep him awake and make him use his intelligence."

Keeping Marjorie Astill's husband awake was not an exciting vocation. In any case Bella could not have tolerated sharing her friend's life of matinées and shopping-excursions and small-talk and overeating for long. In the end, through the Astills' influence, she succeeded in finding a post as governess-companion in what was called a "good" family.

Her new employers—their name was Fladburn—were a typical product of the industrial revolution in the English provinces, having made their fortune during the two previous generations out of brass. Like many of the leading North Bromwich families they were Liberal Noncomformists, and connected, though only politically, with the ruling Quaker and Unitarian oligarchy. They were not merely high-principled people, with two generations of unchallenged respectability and good works behind them: they were acutely aware of it. There was no problem of social experiment or reform in housing or education or research into industrial diseases (such as the brass-founder's ague, to the incidence of which they had contributed) in connection with which the name—and the subscriptions—of the Fladburn family did not appear prominently. Their wealth was probably enormous; they used it generously and intelligently, partly out of the convictions of a sensitive social conscience, partly out of a self-righteous pride that knew how to pose as humility, and partly because, as their shrewd forbears had discovered, nothing paid better in business in the long run than a sustained reputation for benevolence.

No Indian caste was more strictly closed than theirs; and having interbred for three or four genera-

F*

tions, they had succeeded in evolving not merely a canon of behaviour but a mental and physical type. Nobody in North Bromwich knew what Mr. Fladburn's income was, though it could not have been less than ten or twelve thousand a year; but whether it had been two thousand or twenty, it is doubtful if his mode of life would have differed in the least, for no Fladburn had ever lived within sight of his income. Their lives accorded with the accepted model of Liberal Nonconformity, discouraging, equally, ostentation, luxury and all such coloured graces as were not strictly utilitarian. In matters of conduct or expenditure they relied for guidance on the answer to a single question: "Is it necessary?" They were lives not exactly drab but consciously set in half-tones, and their anxiety not to create an impression of prosperity extended to their clothes (the men's were seedy and the women's dowdy) and to the houses they dwelt in.

The particular house—it was called Chad Grange—into which Bella, after strict enquiries into her character, found herself admitted, had been built by her employer's father in the eighteen-fifties. It was a commodious building, of high-pitched gables roofed with liver-coloured slate, and apart from certain patterned courses of Tinsley's blue bricks, a hall paved with squares of red, cream and black, and an enormous conservatory or fernery shaped like a parrot-cage, had no nonsense about it. Its sash windows were glazed with single panes, and the absence of any divisions gave its exterior an aspect of bleakness and shocked surprise. The furniture was of heavy Victorian mahogany, and the principal rooms were decorated with portraits in oils of Mr. Fladburn's grandfather, his father and various uncles and partners, all bearded and solemn and benevolent and obviously pleased with themselves; so that life at Chad Grange had the general effect—particularly on such solemn occasions as the family's and the servants' assembly for morning and evening prayers—of a board-meeting of prosperous business-men in the mid-nineteenth century.

It was beneath the critical eyes of these gentlemen that Bella interviewed her future employer. At first sight she had mistaken Mrs. Fladburn for her own cook or housekeeper, for she wore a black apron, and the studied severity of her clothes and the absence of jewellery suggested some sort of uniform. She was a tall, thin, ungainly woman with very large hands and feet. Her features were small and shapeless, their expression was severe; and this look of severity was increased by the fact that her hair, of a rather thin and greasy black streaked with grey, was strained back from her forehead and screwed into a knot behind so mercilessly as to make her head appear even smaller than it was. Above the high neckband (for no female Fladburn had ever been known to exhibit a gratuitous square inch of skin) it looked like the head of a rabbit that has been skinned—an impression enhanced by her prominent eyes, which resembled bottled gooseberries floating in water.

In contrast to these unprepossessing details Mrs. Fladburn's voice and manner were kindly and grave. She was known as a "really good woman," a "woman of principle"; and if she hadn't, at the same time, shown herself rather too conscious of this reputation, Bella would have found the Fladburn standard impossibly exacting.

"My husband and I," Mrs. Fladburn said, "are anxious, above all, that you shall be happy here, Miss Small. No human being has any *right* not to be happy. We are extremely simple people, as you will see, and, from the first, we propose to regard you as one of the family. I have purposely not made any enquiries into your religious views . . ."

Bella told her that she was a member of the Church of England.

"I imagined as much," Mrs. Fladburn replied; "but of course we shall not allow that to make any difference. Our own Puritan creed is so wide and so liberal that I am sure you will not find anything in it to offend your principles. A Buddhist or a Confucian or even a Roman Catholic—though I am afraid Roman Catholics are somewhat bigoted—could kneel down and take part in the daily worship in which our whole household, family and domestics, are expected voluntarily to join, without any sense of embarrassment, as you will, I'm sure. We have no concern with forms or ceremonies of any kind, nor do we presume to question other people's convictions. You will have noticed I haven't even enquired what your politics are," she added, with the peculiar wiggle of the bust which, in her case, denoted self-satisfaction.

Bella said that she hadn't any.

"That's a pity," Mrs. Fladburn said kindly. *"We* feel it is the duty of every citizen, and particularly of women, to develop a civic consciousness. You and I are not only individuals, Miss Small, but responsible members of a community, and it is our privilege to use our influence to compel other people to lead lives as serious and sober and orderly—if I may use the words humbly—as our own. We, of course, are not ashamed to call ourselves Liberals, and in our case the word is not merely a political label but the proper description of our state of mind. It isn't our habit to thrust our convictions on anybody or to be dogmatic; but no doubt, in due course, you will be glad of the opportunity of hearing Mr. Fladburn, who had the privilege of helping Mr. Bright and Mr. Cobden personally, explain our position more fully, as I'm sure he will be willing to do. People of our kind, Miss Small, are not in the habit of boasting; but you are probably already aware—from outside sources—of what the name of Fladburn stands for in this community, although none of the family would ever dream of referring to it. Mr. Fladburn's untiring activities in the sphere of social reform, in the City Council and on the Watch Committee, have already left a mark on this generation as his father's did on the one before; and in this house, unpretentious as it is, you will have the privilege—though never, of course, be persuaded, to listen, for your conscience is your own—of hearing men speak (in the simplest and most homely manner) whose names will be reverenced for ever as those of Leaders of Liberal Thought. Both our children have enjoyed this privilege since their infancy. My boy Henry, I'm thankful to say, is following in Mr. Fladburn's footsteps and already devoting a large part of his life to Social Research in Germany, where we have business connections. Mr. Fladburn offered him the chance of going to Cambridge, but he preferred—and I, personally, was proud of him, I'm afraid—to get to grips with life. As for my daughter Prudence, whom we have arranged for you to teach: she is a simple child, with Mr. Fladburn's beautiful nature—I think I can use that word without undue conceit, for Mr. Fladburn is only my second cousin—and I know, Miss Small, that you will think her innocence as precious as I do, and be careful that nothing you might feel like saying in a moment of haste or thoughtlessness, such as all of us have, should give offence to one of these little ones. Now, if you will excuse me, I'm afraid I must return to my papers. You probably realize that I am the Vice-president of the North Bromwich Branch of

the Young Liberals' Association. You will make yourself at home, won't you, and ask me about any difficulties? Our servants and employees are our friends:
Mr. Fladburn considers their self-respect as important
as our own. And we always trust them in the same
way as we expect them to trust us. This house has
no secrets and our minds have no reservations. When
people inside it say what they think, even if we happen
to disagree, we respect them for it. You know your
way to the school-room, don't you? You will find
Prudence there."

Bella found Prudence there. She felt rather
frightened of Prudence's dazzling innocence. Her
charge was a stolid, plump little girl of thirteen with
a very high chest that made her look older. She had
small eyes, the colour of her mother's, and sandy eyelashes for which Bella pitied her at first, though not
for long, because Prudence was spoilt yet sufficiently
cunning and observant to embarrass her and make her
feel awkward without being actually rude. Like all
the Fladburns she continued to suggest a moral
superiority, having breathed, from her birth, the
rarefied air of Liberalism. In other ways she was backward, having been only sketchily educated by a long
series of governesses, and had retained, in spite of
them, her parents' manners of speech. From the first
she patronized Bella as an outsider who ought to consider herself flattered by being allowed to penetrate
this inner circle of Free Calvinism in which

everyone who counted was more or less distantly related to the Fladburns. She had all the stock attitudes of the caste at her command, including that one of superiority masquerading as humility which, to Bella, was so much more irritating than frank conceit. Indeed, she patronized everybody except her father, of whom the whole family spoke with bated breath.

Mr. Fladburn, though he always treated Bella with grave politeness, seemed to her an odd object for his family's blind adoration. He was a little, melancholy man, with a bushy brown beard which he was proud of and stroked continually as if it were a domestic pet. He had a noble brow and a shiny dome of bald scalp pale as candle-wax. His wife coddled him shamelessly, and, in public, hung on his words, though in private, beyond any shadow of doubt, she bullied him. From speaking at board-meetings and on platforms and pulpits Mr. Fladburn had developed a rhetorical turn of speech and a booming voice that seemed out of proportion to any part of him except the beard from which it issued; and the certainty of being gravely listened to, whatever he said, made him ready to speak at length and intolerantly on every conceivable subject. It had also taught him to make use of phrases that begged the question, such as "intoxicant" for every fermented drink, "vested" interests for those of his political opponents, "the devil's picture-books" for playing cards, and "all right-minded people" for members of the Liberal party.

At the moment of Bella's arrival Mr. Fladburn was very much on the top of himself politically, for the Liberals were in power with his idol Mr. Gladstone as Prime Minister, which assured the approach of the Millennium and the final defeat of his false fellow-townsman, Joseph Chamberlain, though the fact that Lord Rosebery had compromised the whole party by winning the Derby with Ladas had shaken his faith in the morals of the House of Lords. Bella heard this grave question debated again and again by the guests who stood up with bowed heads when Mr. Fladburn said grace at the dinner-table. This lapse on the part of the Foreign Secretary was regarded by them as the heaviest blow Liberalism had suffered since the Parnell letter and the Dilke divorce.

They were extremely solemn, those Sunday luncheon-parties. (It was part of the Fladburn tradition to dine in the middle of the day, since "late dinners" washed down with "intoxicants" were the fashion among people who aped the habits of the degenerate aristocracy and the people with "vested interests" who opposed the Home Rule Bill.) Whenever sprightliness entered them, it seemed self-conscious and heavy-footed, discouraged by Mr. Fladburn's outspoken demand: "Is it necessary?"

Indeed, life at Chad Grange, for all its virtuousness and conscientiousness—and the members of the Fladburn caste were undoubtedly virtuous and con-

scientious—gave Bella the feeling of a repression even
more narrow and sterile than that against which she
had rebelled at St. Monica's. These righteous people
were so deeply (and honestly) concerned with ordering and influencing the lives of their humbler neighbours in the direction of sobriety and thrift (and all
the other qualities that made labour in the brass-
founder's trade efficient) that they had completely
lost the faculty of living themselves. Painting,
poetry, music, the theatre, the beauties of nature—to
say nothing of such contemptible frivolities as games
and field-sports—all wilted and withered instantly
on contact with Mr. Fladburn's touchstone.

"Is it necessary?" he asked in his booming voice,
and immediately the shadow of the Social Conscience
fell on a grim world of Watch Committees and Night
Schools and Housing Schemes, of Anti-vaccination
and Anti-vivisection Campaigns, of Reports on the
Physiological Effects of Intoxicants and (*in camera*)
the Total Suppression of Prostitution: on a world,
in short, in which people of all classes behaved and
thought exactly like Mr. and Mrs. Fladburn and their
relations. Even Prudence, a girl of thirteen, was beginning to accept as a matter of course and to take
pride in this natural legacy of Social Responsibility.
Bella was sorry for her and did her best tactfully to
adjust the balance; but the pressure of environment
was already too much for her. No Fladburn, it
seemed, could ever hope to escape it.

VII

ONE Fladburn in fact—and he the chief hope of
the family—had temporarily escaped. A year before
Bella's arrival Henry had been permitted to take up
his abode with an approved evangelical family at
Oberhausen in Rhineland. Mr. Fladburn, in consent-
ing to his son's adventurous flight from one Black
Country to another, had carefully balanced the perils
of contact with continental standards of morality
against the commercial advantages of acquiring the
German language, and (since Germany's imports of
brass-ware were falling) Commerce had tipped the
beam. At the end of April, having acquired not
merely the language but a number of spiritual by-
products, Henry Fladburn came home to Alvaston.

For a long time before his return, the whole Fladburn family together with their visitors (who rarely
mentioned anyone who wasn't a relation) discussed
and anticipated it so eagerly that Bella grew sick of
the sound of the young man's name. So many of the
Fladburn family circle's swans had turned out to be
birds of inferior feather that she had begun to reckon
their probable interest in inverse proportion to the
amount of admiration they provoked. Several weeks
before he was due she had already created for herself

a composite image of what Henry Fladburn would be like, taking here and there a feature, mental or physical, from the family collection: compounding Prudence's slyness and her small pig-like eyes and bleached eyelashes with her mother's big hands and feet, and mixing these with a large dose of Mr. Fladburn—his domed brow, his small stature, his melancholy, booming voice, and the Social Conscience so prominently worn on his sleeve. She had made up her mind that whatever else he might be Henry Fladburn must, almost certainly, be a prig with a deep-rooted prejudice against anyone so unfortunate as to have been born outside the strict caste to which he belonged.

In all this she was somewhat deceived, if not disappointed. Henry Fladburn had failed to breed true to such a degree that, if she had not known Mrs. Fladburn, she might have believed him to be the product of some illicit romance. There was little of the Fladburn about this tall, dark, clean-shaven boy with his shy violet eyes, his deep, quiet voice, his graceful though somewhat languid movements and his sensitive hands. In the presence of his parents and his sister he almost appeared to belong to a different species—a species, indeed, which Bella herself had not yet experienced and therefore found fascinating.

Unlike all the rest of the family he was sparing of speech. In their company he became a listener;

and while he listened there lurked always in those fine, shy eyes of his and in his mouth, which was generous and good-humoured—even coarse in comparison with the tight-lipped severity of theirs—a hint of amusement which (although it was quite admirably controlled) found its grateful fellow in Bella's own quiet reservations. With her he was deliberately less communicative than with the members of his family or his relations. His attitude towards her displayed a studied and formal politeness which was foreign in its origin and therefore the more subtly attractive. Yet whenever he spoke to her—and even more when he did not speak—she guessed that he regarded her with a veiled interest and a curiosity which, indeed, she returned—for, again and again, it seemed to her that they two possessed something in common outside (or, perhaps, opposed to) the family's preoccupations. And when their eyes met, in a quick recognition of things that appealed to the same sense of humour, silence spoke more than speech.

This strange boy—he was only strange to Bella because, thanks to Miss Cash, her experience of the opposite sex had been negligible—began by degrees to occupy a large part of her idle thought. She liked him—the more, perhaps, because she had been prepared to detest him, and because he was a healthy young man of her own age and by no means ill-looking: but more powerful than liking was her curiosity about the private world he had created for himself and kept inviolate amid the Fladburn universe.

Among the family it was understood—his German adventure having been providentially completed without disaster—that Henry should now "settle down" in the business and "take his place." He had brains enough to convince them without much difficulty that he was fulfilling their wishes; but in his heart, Bella guessed—and she alone—he was accepting this dictated destiny with reservations. German music, for instance, of which he had greedily drunk his fill in Düsseldorf, was actually more interesting to him than German Sanitation, and Poetry meant far more to him than Sociology. He was, in fact, a "sport" of the kind which is liable to arise—out of nature's protest, maybe, against unnatural conditions—among the best-regulated industrial families: a creature of strong, repressed sensibility, an artist *manqué*, a romanticist in spite of himself. Out of his liberal allowance, which was part of the family tradition, he had accumulated large quantities of books and music which he enjoyed in secret. Mrs. Fladburn smiled on what she called his extravagance, for although the triviality of the arts was reasonably suspect, general culture (if not precisely "necessary" in the Fladburn sense) might prove a valuable adjunct to political oratory and help Henry at some future time to "influence for good" the taste of the community through the medium of the Municipal Art Gallery or the City Orchestra—always provided that it didn't interfere with his business career. His artistic leanings, in short, were a childish foible to be mildly encouraged if only for the reason that they "kept him at home," thereby protecting him from "spending money uselessly" and acting as a safety-valve against those graver emotional disturbances to which youth—even righteous youth—was unluckily exposed.

From these possible sources of peril she did not exclude Bella's presence in the house. On the eve of Henry's return she had "mentioned the matter" to Mr. Fladburn.

"I am not at all sure," she had said, "that we ought to keep her. Miss Small seems a quiet girl so far as I have been able to observe. But the unfortunate fact remains that she is not unattractive."

Mr. Fladburn diplomatically remarked that he hadn't noticed.

"All the same," Mrs. Fladburn went on, "she suits Prudence much better than the last one or the one before *her*. She has been fairly strictly brought up, and I don't think she's sly, though of course that may easily develop under the exciting influence of Henry's presence. It is the girl I am thinking of: I have no fears whatever of Henry. In matters of that kind he fortunately takes after you, John: he notices nothing."

Mr. Fladburn acknowledged the back-handed compliment.

"But if I thought for one moment that she was likely to distract Henry's mind, either consciously or unconsciously, from the business, I should act without hesitation. I shall get rid of her at once and pay her a month's wages in lieu of notice."

Mr. Fladburn, who disliked on principle paying anything for nothing, became attentive. "Is that necessary?" he asked.

"I hope it will not become necessary, John; but forewarned is forearmed. I shall make it my business to watch Miss Small carefully. And I shall question Prudence occasionally. If she has noticed anything she will certainly tell me."

Mr. Fladburn grunted.

"This spring weather is so unsettling," Mrs. Fladburn sighed.

Indeed it was unsettling. Spring came late to North Bromwich, deterred, perhaps, by the town's enveloping smoke-screen and the cold soil of the midland plateau over which it sprawls. On one side of it only—the south-west—is there a gap in the smoke's black barrage; and through this, at the beginning of May, beneath veils of glancing showers and a high panoply of dazzling cumulus, the green banners advanced to reclaim that beleaguered city. Then the shower-sprinkled asphalt pavements shone like blue rivulets, reflecting the crinkled fans of horse-chestnuts released from their gummy capsules, and trussed buds of pink may and stiff plumes of lilac and pallid sprays of laburnum deepening to gold. And a soft wind, blowing out of Wales, dried the gleaming footpaths

and caught in its passage warm gusts of those vagrant
perfumes which ravished the nostrils of mankind with
a novel fragrance, so that staid business-men discarded
their velvet-collared overcoats and walked to their
work over drifts of fallen bloom with a swinging step
and heads uplifted; and the smooth roads of Alvaston,
which had now become alleys of swaying green, were
scattered with nursemaids wheeling perambulators
and children who ran and bounded like lambs in the
golden-green light; and deaf old gentlemen, trotting
out with walking-sticks and mittens and woollen
comforters to take the sun, would pause at the corners
to sniff the provocative odours of youth and pat
children's chubby faces with bony fingers and chaff
their nursemaids, or stand, out of breath and straining
their ears, to catch the familiar sounds of spring: the
challenges of rival chaffinches, the whistles of blackbirds, and the monotonous clatter of mowing-machines
cutting green grass.

Even the long, grim rectangle of garden at the
back of Chad Grange, where Mr. Fladburn's coach-
man-gardener had begun to "set out" his bands of
potted geraniums with their greenhouse smell, and
lobelias and stiff calceolarias, was pervaded by this
tender delirium. The mown lawn lay outstretched like
a striped ceremonial carpet to the feet of a cherry-
tree's pyramid of bridal white, and before that blossom had tarnished and fallen the tight shelly buds of
of apple-bloom began to show pink. In the ugly

thickets of laurel an incredible number of birds softly
fluted or chuckled or burst into sudden song. At
dawn the whole garden rang with echoes like an empty
room, so that Bella, waking, would lie with closed eyes
and listen, her heart vaguely softened by the sound's
communicable tenderness, and inhale the soft air that
seemed charged with an elixir distilled from this
superabundance of resurgent life. Sometimes, indeed,
her own share in that life stirred too violently to let
her doze again; so she would go to the open window
and kneel with her elbows on the sill, gazing out with
sleep-drowsy eyes on a scene that appeared to be
strangely changed and enriched by dawn's dewy
magic, in which everything save that pellucid torrent
of bird-song seemed hushed and still, as though all
its activity were suspended by some enchantment in the
fixedness of a painting rather than the fluidity of living
things; yet she knew that beneath this appearance
of immobility the tide of sap continued to flow through
each straining petal, each leaf, each tendril, each
aspiring blade, with a rhythm as calm and constant
as that of her own slow heart-beats made audible by
that intensity of silence—until suddenly, perhaps, the
quietude was broken by the brittle noise of a thrush
cracking open a snail-shell on the pebbled path, and
the ripples of sound spreading outward from that tiny
breach in the surface of silence aroused, as they passed,
every sleeping thing into tremulous activity; so that
the spell which lay on them was broken and the

hushed garden instantly awoke, and she, too, awoke to a consciousness of eager life and the desire to pursue it, though whither or how she could not divine.

Henry Fladburn was conscious of a similar emotion, and equally unable to comprehend it or give it shape. Ever since he came home his mind had been prey to a vague discontent. He had returned from Oberhausen with quickened sensibilities, with an appetite for beauty whetted but unappeased, with a new conception of values; and he had found in North Bromwich—and particularly in his own home—a life in which the beauty for which he felt himself starving was considered "unnecessary" if not exactly sinful. On the day when he went back with his father to the firm's works at Winsworth, traversing on his way the black heart of the city, the iron of North Bromwich had entered into his soul; when he returned to Alvaston at night to the virtuous but emotionally sterile preoccupations of his family and their chosen friends, his spirit rebelled against an equal frustration and the weight of an almost equal ugliness. The people with whom he had lived in Germany were no less conscientious; the natural beauties of the Rhineland had been no less smutted by industry than those of Alvaston; yet he knew that his German friends— and he with them—had got more out of life than the Fladburns and their relations dreamed.

His covert rebellion took the shape of a moody restlessness which made his mother suspect a love affair, though his correspondence, carefully scrutinized, showed no signs of one. He took refuge in his books and in the music he had brought with him from Germany: the scores of Wagner's operas (at that time scarcely known in North Bromwich) and the romantic songs of Schubert and Franz and Schumann: all perilous food for a restless mind driven in on itself.

Up till now the piano at Chad Grange had been regarded as an expensive and creditable—if not exactly "necessary"—article of drawing-room furniture on which Prudence, under Bella's tuition, practised the scales and five-finger exercises which would ultimately enable her to play the accompaniments of hymns at "social" gatherings and "Pleasant Sunday Afternoons." This long-suffering instrument became the centre of Henry's imaginative life. His untutored fingers had a certain aptitude for playing; and in the resonant but not very melodious voice he had inherited from his father he would sing to himself the *Lieder* whose nostalgic tunes (and, above all, whose words) brought back to him the sentimental aspects of the life from which he had been torn away. All these affecting songs were saturated with the odours of spring: a tender welter of *Frühlingsträume* and *Frühlingsnächte* and *Frühlingssehnsucht* and *Frühlingsglaube*. Their second prevailing theme was love—*Liebesbotschaft, Liebesleide, Liebesgrüsse, Rastlose Liebe*, with a strong sprinkling of tears of various varieties and a background of Loneliness—

Einsame Träne, Waldeinsamkeit, Feldeinsamkeit or
Einsamkeit pure and simple—and the third a vague
aspiration towards Escape expressed in *Wanderlieder*.
But even these sublimations of his restlessness failed
to relieve it when now, its first shy tenderness past,
spring broke over Alvaston in full voluptuousness;
when the sap which had feebly stirred now rose like
a flood, and cuckoos called and bees began to hum amid
the honey-dripping lime-flowers.

There was a lime-tree that shadowed the lawn at
Chad Grange with pallid fans. Beneath its translucent
shade and enwrapped in its murmur of bees, Bella
sat with Prudence and sewed or gave her perfunctory
lessons. And now, as the days lengthened and the air
was still warm and light when Henry came home from
the works, she could often hear him singing and playing as he sat at the piano by the wide-open drawing-
room window. When she listened she thought of him,
not as a romantic—Romance seemed hardly com-
patible with his being a Fladburn—but as an odd,
lonely soul (which he was) for whom she felt sorry;
as an awkward, ingenuous young man with nice eyes
which could easily look hurt; as, somehow, compared
with herself (though she was three years younger
than he), a childish creature whose stiffness and air
of self-conscious maturity were a little comical. She
felt sorry for him because, in the detachment which
prevented her from ever becoming what Mrs. Fladburn called "one of the family," she realized that he

also was too irregularly shaped to fit into the formal pattern of Fladburn life. He was odd man out at Chad Grange, having nothing in common, so far as she could see, with any other member of the family. "And a thing like his music," she thought, "though it may console him, only isolates him further: it will take him 'into' rather than 'out of' himself—for not a soul in the house except me understands what he's playing. And even if he knew that *I* understood," Bella's thoughts ran on, "he would never dare to speak of it—partly because he's so painfully shy (which is rather nice in him) and partly because if he raised an eyelid his mamma, as he calls her, would be after him."

Sitting there under the lime-tree and listening she resigned herself to idle and melancholy reflections on poor Henry's future. In a year or two, she thought, when his father considered him old enough to be given a seat on the board, he would be expected to marry. Mrs. Fladburn, no doubt, would choose his wife for him from among the daughters of her friends. So long as he married inside their caste, Henry would have some say in the matter. Mrs. Fladburn would choose their house too: an Alvaston house, with laurels in front, a bird-cage conservatory, and a rectangular garden at the back. But by that time the octopus of the Social Conscience would have gripped him; he would have become an embryo committeeman, a compendium of statistics, a young hope of the

Liberal Party. In that life, poor dear, there would be no more time for his music. When he came home at night he would be too tired by his beneficent or profitable labours to think about anything that wasn't "necessary." His wife, being all but a Fladburn herself, would coddle him no doubt and see that he did his duty by the birth-rate. They would duly produce a large family of infant Free Calvinists into whom, from their babyhood, Mrs. Fladburn would instil the family principles of Responsibility towards the Community and Setting an Example and Suppressing most things that other people enjoyed.

"That will be his life," Bella thought, "though he won't really be alive. The poor boy was condemned to imprisonment for life on the day he was born. Thank goodness he gets some enjoyment out of the piano, though he does play so badly and thump so. But his voice is really rather nice at a distance," she thought. "Just a little pathetic. One simply couldn't have the heart to discourage him. What is that song he is singing now?"

It was *Der Lindenbaum* from Schubert's *Winterreise*. Bella knew it well, for that mildly tragic cycle had shared with the ecstasies of Schumann's *Frauenliebe* the chief of Miss Boldmere's affections. Now, as she listened to the sway and rustle of the accompaniment and re-shaped in memory the trivial, mawkish words, the associations of the song carried her back to those early days at St. Monica's which her *Schwärmerei* for Miss Boldmere had made magical. She smiled to remember what an odd, emotional little innocent she must have been.

"Three years ago," she thought, "I took everything so seriously and felt so acutely, whereas now I feel nothing—I grow harder and more cynical every day. That's the Fladburn influence—though I suppose, on the whole, it's much wiser to be hard and cynical: sooner or later life forces one to it, so the sooner the better. I ought really to be thankful that I got over that soft phase so early."

Thus she argued to herself; yet even so, her heart was moved and melted, by memory rather than by beauty. That song embalmed the pot-pourri fragrance of many withered emotions, and the movement and scent of its lime-tree became mingled in imagination with those of the living, murmurous lime under which she sat—so that, in spite of herself, she surrendered to its enchantment; her work dropped to her knees; she no longer heard nor saw. So deeply entranced was she as to be unaware that she was alone (for Prudence had left her), that the song had ended and that Henry Fladburn was coming towards her over the lawn.

When he saw her abstraction he stopped, and his stopping made her aware of him. She recovered herself and blushed.

"Mr. Fladburn, you startled me! I was dreaming."

He was easily rebuffed.

"I'm sorry, Miss Small." He hesitated.

"But please don't run away. It was partly your fault, Mr. Fladburn. Your *Lindenbaum* that set me dreaming."

"My *Lindenbaum*?" he asked eagerly. "Then you know it?"

"Of course. Why shouldn't I?"

"Please forgive me, Miss Small. That was clumsy of me. I somehow took it for granted that nobody here knew anything about things of that kind. They don't, you know. Are you really keen on music? Real music, I mean?"

He was so pathetically elated that she had to let him down lightly.

"Of course I love music," she said, "though I don't know much about it. I'm afraid I'm not really musical. If you ask me questions you'll find I'm terribly ignorant."

"No, I won't believe that. But even if it were true it would make no difference. All that really matters is loving things. Don't you agree with me?"

"Yes, I suppose you're right. But don't ask me too much all the same, or you'll be disappointed."

"On the contrary, I'm thrilled. You don't know what this means to me: the thought that in this house, under this roof, there's actually a person capable of . . . of understanding. Why didn't I know it before?"

G

"Well, why should you? I suppose you took me for granted. Another new governess. After all, one governess is very much like another, isn't she?"

"No, no," he protested. "You're quite different from any of the others. I was stupid not to see it before. Only think what we've missed! You know German?"

"A little. We used to read Schiller and Goethe."

"And Heine? It's Heine who matters most to me. There are poems of Heine's that seem to me more than words. No music can touch them. You know what I mean, what I'm trying to say?" (She could only smile, though she felt more at home with poetry.) "Words like: *Wenn ich in deine Augen seh, So schwindet all mein Leid und Weh* . . . You know it?"

"*Doch wenn ich küsse deinen Mund, So werd ich ganz und gar gesund* . . . Do go on."

"*Wenn ich mich lehn' an deine Brust, Kommt über mich wie Himmelslust.*"

"*Doch wenn du sprichst: 'Ich liebe dich!'* . . ."

Her voice faltered; she stopped, for the words embarrassed her. Ridiculous, she thought.

"Please go on!" he cried. "That's not all . . ."

She continued, obediently: "*So muss ich weinen bitterlich,*" she said softly. Then:

"I'm sorry I spoilt it, Mr. Fladburn."

"But you didn't really, Miss Small. You made it sound more beautiful than ever before. Saying words like those to yourself is never quite the same as hearing them spoken. And your voice. . . . Do you mind if I say how beautiful it is?"

Bella laughed: "Does anyone mind compliments, even when they're not deserved? Will you tell me the time, Mr. Fladburn?"

"Oh, what does time matter?"

"It matters quite a lot to your mother. You ought to know that."

"Well. . . . It's exactly three minutes to seven."

"Oh dear, that will never do! I must go and find Prudence."

"I'll come with you."

"You'd much better not."

"Let me carry your work-basket, anyway."

"I'd rather you didn't. You see I'm not used to being waited on."

But though she refused his help, he insisted on walking by her side. His shyness had vanished; he bubbled over with questions:—Did she remember this song? Had she ever read that poem?—coming so fast, one on top of another, that she could hardly keep pace with them or answer with the degree of intelligence she felt was demanded of her. And all the time as he spoke and as she answered him, Bella's eyes (and half of her mind) were secretly concentrated on the staring sash-windows in which, every moment, she expected to see the threatening shape of Mrs. Fladburn appear. She was thankful, indeed, when the wall of the house concealed them from view.

"Though why I should be frightened of her seeing us, I don't know," she told herself afterwards; "for the poor boy did nothing that anyone could object to, and I almost had to be rude to him as it was."

VIII

FROM her window Bella saw Henry Fladburn slowly walking back towards the shadow of the lime. He was finding the incidents of the last ten minutes (for it was no more) almost as hard to check as those of a dream; yet he reconstructed them, one by one, methodically. At six o'clock he had come home from the works as usual and changed. At a quarter-past six he had sat down at the piano and played for twenty-five minutes. The last song, Schubert's *Lindenbaum*, had reminded him of the lime-tree on the lawn and of a verse that pestered his brain like a whining gnat: *A million emeralds break from the ruby-budded lime.* Had the lime ruby buds—or wasn't there, rather, a ruby spot on the stem of the leaf? And what emeralds were these? He was enough of a Fladburn to like making sure of his facts—yes, even in poetry.

So, with the *Lindenbaum* still possessing his mind, he had walked down the lawn, until, suddenly conscious, he became aware of Miss Small, and stopped. She, too, had been dreaming, her head over her work, till his presence startled her. She had looked up suddenly and blushed, and, for the first time, he had seen her eyes—so deeply grey as to seem black beneath

187

her black eyebrows. And in that moment of surprise
—her lips parted, eyes opened wide—she had ceased
to be the Miss Small of everyday life, Prudence's
latest governess, and instantly become the solution of
his doubts, an appeasement of his hunger, a complete
expression of all secret beauty, the essence of great
music and poetry clarified and made flesh.

Of the validity of this transformation Henry Fladburn was certain; yet even now, passionately believing
in it, he sought confirmation in those material circumstances of the miracle which assured him it was no
dream: in the black-trunked lime whose moving leaves
had dappled her figure and whose scent had enveloped
her; in the chair on which she had sat as she looked
up and smiled at him; in a skein of wool that had
fallen to the grass from her work-basket. He picked
this up eagerly and dropped it again, feeling the action
ridiculous. Now that she had gone, the lawn had an
aching emptiness. He reproached himself that in the
sudden dazzle of beauty newly revealed he hardly
knew what she was like. Only the echo of her voice
remained clear to him, and in her voice one whispered
phrase—*Und wenn du sprichst: 'Ich liebe dich'*—
surely the most magical words, he thought, that it
could have spoken!

But stranger even than the wonder of Bella's
transformation seemed the fact that he had not recognized her utter beauty before; that for more than a
month he had lived beneath the same roof and eaten

at the same table yet hardly looked at her. Now that he was in love with her he could find no explanation for this blindness and nothing but angry regret in thinking of his lost opportunities. It was no use brooding over those, he told himself. Sufficient to him was the splendour of the actual moment and the knowledge that within an hour he would see her again. For, until his hungry eyes saw her, until he could count over again those elusive lovelinesses and catch them and hold them fast, he would never be happy or know peace. "Never . . . never . . ." he told himself, as he hurried upstairs to his bedroom: for he heard, on the doorstep, the sound of his father's footsteps and fled from them, feeling that his rapture might shrivel at the touch of ordinary life.

There, alone, Henry Fladburn contrived to collect his senses. The rigid seriousness of his upbringing and his sheltered life made his body and mind a fit medium for the culture of this sweet virus. He was twenty-six, and yet never before had he fallen in love.

Of these ardours and ecstasies Bella knew nothing. Her body and mind—and for much the same reasons —were as virginal as his; Miss Cash—up till this the strongest influence in her life—had taken pride in preserving them. This is not to say that she was unmoved by that evening's encounter: she had been surprised to find herself blushing when Henry approached her and had been conscious, while they talked, of an intensity in the air and of an inexplicable warmth, like that of an unseen flame. Some remnant of this warmth persisted while, upstairs in her attic, she dressed for supper. It was a room which might have been planned to mortify a woman's pride in her appearance, for the mirror was distorted and so placed that little light reached it. Its inconvenience seemed greater than ever that evening when, for some obscure reason, she felt her hair (the best part of her!) more than usually untidy, and wanted to look her best. The lack of light irritated her so much that she dragged back the curtains and threw up the window-sash as far as it would go, straightway becoming aware, despite her frustration, of a sight which she might possibly have seen yet had never noticed before. At that height her eyes were on a level with the top of the lime-tree whose shape, now lapped and transfused by the rays of the sinking sun, appeared as an airy pyramid of palest gold. And the tree was alive; it simmered: amid the intricacies of its leafy filigree and in the warm air above it, innumerable bees rose and fell and darted and hovered—each golden body and gauzy wing transfigured—so that they seemed like so many dancing particles of light thrown off from a fountain's play.

As she leaned through the window, transported, forgetting her haste and her irritation, Bella heard Henry Fladburn singing to himself in the room below. This time it was a Schumann song called *Widmung*— one of Miss Boldmere's favourites. *"Du meine Seele, du mein Herz*," he sang—and the music, for once, had power to move her: it sounded so happy, so near to her momentary mood.

"Though it's a pity," she thought, "that he isn't looking out of the window like me and seeing how lovely his linden-tree looks at this moment! It may never look like this again," she thought, "and he is the only person in the house who could see what I see."

She was so anxious, indeed, to share her delight that she wondered if she dare call to Henry from above and bring him to his window. "Though even if I did," she told herself, "he probably wouldn't hear me, and someone else—probably Mrs. Fladburn or Prudence—might. And the light's fading, anyway: the tree's not nearly so marvellous now as when first I saw it. All the loveliest things are like that," she reflected, resigning her impulse; and at that moment, to make its abandonment final and renew her panic, the bronze supper-gong suddenly boomed in the hall downstairs. Punctuality was one of the Fladburns' harshest virtues. Even if she looked her worst she must hurry to take her place before grace was said.

All through supper that evening Bella was aware of Henry's interest. His eyes never left her. They made her self-conscious. When Mrs. Fladburn asked her a question it caught her attention napping and covered her with confusion, much to Prudence's delight.

G*

"I'm so sorry, Mrs. Fladburn," Bella said. "I didn't hear you."

"I said you looked flushed this evening, Miss Small," Mrs. Fladburn repeated. "I hope you haven't taken cold sitting out in the garden. You had better ascertain your temperature at once and make sure. And please don't kiss Prudence before you know: she catches everything."

When supper was finished, Mrs. Fladburn loomed over her with a thermometer, and appeared to be disappointed to find her temperature normal.

"Of course, the thermometer may be out of order," she said; "but in any case you had better take some Dover's powder and go to bed at once. After all, you may be sickening for something or other. It's a great inconvenience having anyone ill at the top of the house, particularly on the very eve of poor Prudence's birthday."

Poor Prudence's birthday, it seemed, was the most important fixed feast in the Fladburn calendar. It was solemnized by a drive and picnic on Uffdown Hill, the nearest of the Clents to Alvaston, and involved a mass-migration of Fladburn relations and collaterals setting out for the day in a caravan of hired wagonettes. It marked one of the rare occasions on which Mr. Fladburn condescended to unbend and even to take a dignified part in organized merriment, such as "rounders" or "tip-and-run" amid rural surroundings in which his public reputation for seriousness need not be imperilled.

Henry Fladburn looked forward eagerly to this opportunity of pursuing his attentions to Bella, and Bella, who in the meantime had been delicately evading them, knew this. Ever since their solitary meeting under the lime Henry's glances had followed her; he had kept hovering round her with little flattering attentions which she would have been happy to accept if they had not seemed so dangerously obvious to his mother's eyes. She was by no means in love with Henry. She still thought of him critically as a more or less typical Fladburn as yet undeveloped, another pathetic victim to the repressions of his caste; yet the mere fact of his being pathetic laid her more open to the flattery of his naïve admiration; and her consciousness of the power which she exercised over him (without her troubling to assert it) appealed to her spirit of mischief. If Henry showed signs of breaking loose from the family fold it would be no more than his parents deserved. "And nobody can say it's my fault, if he does," she reflected.

Bella wasn't in love with him; and yet, when she came to think of it, he had far more in common with her than any other soul in North Bromwich: he was young, he was eager, he was lonely; he was sensitive and in tacit rebellion against the taboos that irked her; he had glimmerings of humour that sprang from his knowledge of a wider and more generous life, and more liveliness of mind than the rest of the family put

together. Furthermore, when she came to think of him
—and thoughts of him often invaded the vacuum of
her routine as Prudence's governess—she discovered
that his person was not without charm. He was tall
and strong and healthy; he was as dark as she was
fair, and if his eyes were too serious and always a
little puzzled—as though he wondered how on earth
he had come to be what he was—his mouth, with
its admirable teeth, showed little of the Fladburn
severity, and his deep voice, so indubitably male, had
a timbre that moved her far more than the music he
sang. Even the casual contacts which she shirked so
skilfully made a difference to the atmosphere in
which she lived, made it kinder and softer and, somehow, indefinitely sweeter.

If she admitted the truth, she must have said that
Henry's proximity had added considerably to the interest and excitement of life; that she felt more important, more pleased with herself when he was present and less keenly alive when she knew that he was
away. He was clever, too, in the deftness with which
he suggested, by allusions that were dark to others,
an understanding between them; and this fiction
pleased her if only because it implied a secret, and
because the existence of a secret—even an imaginary
one—gave a spice of desirable wickedness to life in
the Fladburn world. It amused her, again, to watch
the transparent devices by which Henry schemed to
be near her: such as his sudden access of interest in

Prudence's music, which before this (and for the best of reasons) had bored him, and in Prudence's general education, which was no business of his.

That first meeting under the lime-tree had established a precedent. The spell of dry weather held; and now, every evening, hurrying home as early as he could escape from the works at Winsworth, Henry Fladburn was surprised to find Miss Small demurely established beneath the tree's murmurous shadow. Discovering her thus by sheer accident, he considered it his duty (since it was part of the Fladburn code to be kind to dependants) to stand by for a moment and engage her in serious conversation on the subject of her work and of her pupil's progress. If Miss Small should ask him to sit down, it would be impolite to refuse or to show any obvious impatience in her company. There were many subjects, indeed, of a purely artistic or intellectual interest, which it was proper for them to explore because they reflected on her calling. It was a pity that these subjects bored Prudence, for whose benefit they were discussed; but duty was duty, and if the child chose to wander away and leave them alone it wasn't their fault. Unfortunately Prudence's powers of resistance to the boredom she felt were fortified by an unconscious perverseness or, perhaps, by a conscious jealousy of anyone who could claim a larger share of her brother's attention than herself—with the result that she grimly clung to them until the bitter end. And this obstinacy amused Bella

too because of the irritation which poor Henry
obviously felt and the virtuosity with which he tried
to conceal his compliments and express his admiration
in terms which the wretched resolute child found in-
comprehensible.

It was a game, of course, but a game which was
mildly dangerous and therefore fascinating; a game
for two played in a spirit and a setting that suggested
romance: the wide, empty lawn drenched with sunlight; the turbulent birdsong of May, the imminence
of the great golden lime dropping honeyed perfume
and drowsy with the hum of bees. They spoke much
of music, in which Bella was at pains to pretend the
enthusiasm he craved so eagerly, and of poetry, in
which she felt more honestly at home. Sometimes
Henry timidly touched upon topics potentially personal; but whenever these seemed to be verging on
emotional intensity, Bella sagely restored them to the
safer plane of flat generalities discussed with impersonal coldness—so successfully that, except by im-
plication, Henry never made love to her, although
every word he spoke was a confession of love.

In these difficult moments, indeed, Bella evaded
his assaults or turned his position so skilfully that he
never quite knew where he stood; and this uncertainty
combined with a sense of positive frustration only
increased the ardour which it was apparently intended to subdue. Her cruelty—if cruelty it were—
made her more desirable; and the fact that prudence

(or Prudence) compelled her to be cruel entailed a corrective complement of pity or remorse which, while she tormented him, softened her heart towards him. Miss Cash would have suffered if she had known how her influence had unconsciously prejudiced her disciple in favour of the passion she abhorred. Yet so it was. Henry Fladburn was her first opportunity; and in the depths of her heart Bella was eager to love and to be loved.

IX

On the morning of Prudence's birthday the weather changed; the languor of that brief foretaste of summer gave way to a cooler air. A gay breeze from the west lashed the lime-tree; if the bees still clustered in its blossom their humming was drowned in a rustle of blown leaves. Towered banks of cumulus sailed slowly overhead in a crystalline sky that appeared to be unvexed by the lower air's commotion. It was a morning that uplifted the heart and made the blood race as though in anticipation of some inevitable, obscure excitement. So Bella felt, standing in the pantry cutting ham sandwiches, watching the lilacs that tossed and swayed like the plumes of a gay cavalcade, and listening to the wild sweetness of thrushes that sang like stormcocks. She could have sung herself if she had not felt that singing might offend Mrs. Fladburn on an occasion that demanded a special degree of propriety and an exhibition of the military discipline which she habitually displayed and enforced in her public work.

To Mrs. Fladburn a picnic was no casual, light-hearted affair but an event demanding discipline and organization. Every glass, every bottle (of non-intoxicants), every packet of sandwiches had its

proper, unalterable place in the plan of campaign. On
the drive the three hired wagonettes with three red-
faced coachmen stood spaced like a battery on parade.
Even the guests stood at ease with a certain alertness,
awaiting the word of command without which they
dared not mount to their allotted places. When
Henry, who had been restlessly scheming to travel
in the same wagonette as Bella, made an eager move
in its direction, he was called sharply to order and
mercilessly attached to the eldest and richest of his
maternal aunts, a Miss Gubbins who—to judge by her
cylindrical shape and the blankness of her countenance
—had evidently, Bella thought, emerged that morning from a Noah's Ark.

Mr. Fladburn, muffled in "comforters" to the neck
for fear of catching cold, wearing a Panama hat, and
stroking his beard affectionately, was the last to
emerge from the house. Only then, at Mrs. Fladburn's signal, was the procession permitted to
advance. It moved slowly up the Halesby Road;
the very horses, apparently impressed by the gravity
of the occasion, adopted a ceremonial pace. It reached
the level of St. Monica's. From the practising-rooms
Bella heard the discordant tinkle of several pianos.
She thought of Miss Boldmere—Miss Boldmere
eternally immured there, like a recalcitrant nun
bricked-up in a convent-cellar—and shivered to think
of the prison from which she had escaped: out of those
long bleak corridors and classrooms, smelling of ink,

into this delicious day of blue and blowing white under the open sky.

Henry Fladburn's presence contributed to her elation. She could see him wedged into the hindmost seat of the next wagonette gazing sidewards and backwards from time to time to catch a glimpse of her. It was a shame, Bella thought, that his mother had cheated him out of her company. Had Mrs. Fladburn done this on purpose? Had she any idea that Henry was in love? That seemed hardly likely, Bella reflected: the poor boy was so shy that she herself, the object of his passion, could only divine its existence by indirect evidence. Yet she felt glad, that morning, to know that Henry had fallen in love with her. It was right that young men like Henry should fall rashly in love in this season of rising sap and resurgent bloom, when the whole visible world was free and tender and glowing. On a day such as this it seemed foolish not to be natural. So, when Henry gazed anxiously back at her—though heaven knew why he should look anxious—she smiled, and once waved her hand. She felt nearer to him and kinder than ever before. She had a feeling that to-day he would probably try to kiss her, and she wouldn't mind if he did.

The wagonettes climbed to the brow of the Tilton escarpment. Here the hills which were the party's objective appeared to be lifted into the windy sky. At their feet Hayseech smouldered; but even in that pit the wind had its way, blowing the curdled smoke eastward from the chimneys' mouths and leaving them stripped like masts of gigantic shipping. But now the road ran downhill, and that vision of the Black Country sank with it. In the mean little streets of Halesby, bordered with pavements of Tinsley's Blue Bricks, a continuous tinkle of nailers' hammers was heard; and this sound, the undertone of all her childhood, carried Bella's mind back to her first home at Bromsberrow, to the smell of her grandfather's warehouse, and to the untroubled days she had spent in his company watching old Waldron at work. All that part of her life seemed in retrospect incredibly remote and little and unimportant. She found it hard to believe that she, Bella Small, had actually lived it; yet the memory moved her—most of all because she found the figures associated with it pathetic—her own included. All life, that morning, seemed exciting, mysterious and a trifle unreal. Who would ever have dreamed, for instance, that the odd wild little girl who had ridden on her grandfather's shoulder, his beard tickling her legs, and run in and out of the nailers' cottages like an inquisitive kitten, would some day—this day—be jogging along in a grand wagonette and in the company of such distinguished people, one of whom quite clearly was in love with her? To enhance this picture the artist in Bella suppressed all aspects of the Fladburn clan that were open to criticism. It pleased her, for once, to take them at their own valuation, and at their own valuation the Fladburns were extremely important.

But now that the tinkling hearths had been left behind, the road climbed again. They were nearing the base of the hills. Here the road changed its surface of macadam for tawny pebbles; the windswept hedge-rows were brightened by sprays of gorse, and the lane, sinking deep between them, resembled the dry bed of a torrent. Yet, every moment, the air grew cooler and sweeter with the almond odour of gorse, the wild scent of young bracken. It was a thin mountain air, pellucid as spring water, and its heady rarefication lightened Bella's spirit as though a physical weight had been lifted from it. She felt gay and reckless and mischievous, and so sure of herself that the presence of her stately companions failed to intimidate her: they were no longer venerable examples of the new industrial aristocracy, but stiff and slightly ridiculous puppets whose propriety she longed to shock. All but Henry: he, surely, must realise how odd his relations were and long, as she did, to shock them: he, surely, could understand her mad provocative mood.

It was partly the fault of the wind. On the dome of Uffdown it blew half a gale. There, right in the teeth of it, with the Severn plain still as a picture eight hundred feet below, Mrs. Fladburn deployed her forces. While her husband and the more decrepit relations sat solemnly sheltering on the edge of a larch-wood, she watched Bella and Henry and

Prudence unpack the baskets of food and lay the luncheon. This was a comical business, for the wind took part in the game, not merely blowing away Mrs. Fladburn's voice as she shouted her orders but tearing the papers and cloths from their hands. Bella began to laugh; but Mrs. Fladburn was in no mood for laughter. The climax was reached when one basket, containing the eldest and richest aunt's invalid diet, was found to be missing, and Prudence, opening another, discovered three shameless frothy quart bottles of Astill's Entire, the liquid part of the coachmen's luncheon. When Prudence sniffed at them to see what they were, Mrs. Fladburn cried out with as much alarm as though they contained prussic acid. For the moment her conscience was in doubt as to what should be done with them. Left to herself she would certainly have poured them away as an indignant libation to her own grim gods; but Mr. Fladburn, more accustomed to dealing with the working classes, felt that this infringement of the rights of property might be resented.

"If they want their intoxicants, Alice," he said judicially, "they will in all probability come up the hill and fetch them. The exercise will help to counteract the effects; and if they *do* come you can send them down again to fetch Aunt Hester's luncheon."

Mrs. Fladburn was far from satisfied by this advice. For the sake of the party's safety on the homeward journey she felt that the drivers ought to be forcibly protected from the poison which providence had directed into wiser hands. She was still struggling with her conscience and longing to empty the bottles when the driver with the reddest face of all came panting uphill with the missing packet which contained Miss Gubbins's diet. When he saw the beer his eyes glistened.

"Well, that's one good thing anyway, madam," he exclaimed. "To tell you the honest, when Albert said: 'Jim, where's the beer?' it give me a reg'lar turn. You see I thought starting out in a hurry like it might have got left behind at the stables. However, thanks be, here it is, none the worse for the trip by the looks of it. Clear as amber, this four-ale of Astill's. Pure malt and 'ops and no chemicals I don't think! So 'ere's your good 'ealth, ma'am—you and the other ladies and gentlemen!"

He uncorked one of the bottles, took a long swig, touched his forelock and beamed on the company, who received this gesture of friendliness so stonily that Bella felt sorry for him. Mrs. Fladburn, to whom it was addressed, did not deign to reply. Contemptuously leaving the coachman to soak in his degradation she turned and summoned the rest of the party to luncheon.

"If you will all sit down on these rugs," she proclaimed, "Miss Small will hand round the chicken and ham and you, Henry, will pour out the lemonade. Aunt Hester will sit next to you, John: that cushion's for her. Give Aunt Hester your arm, dear, but *do* mind your hat!"

Mrs. Fladburn's voice rose to a scream of warning too late. At that moment the white Panama which, all day, had been balanced on Mr. Fladburn's bald dome as though it hated it, put an end to the unnatural connection. Before she had finished her sentence it was off and bowling away on the wind like a scrap of waste paper.

"Oh, what did I tell you, John?" Mrs. Fladburn screamed. "Henry . . . Quick!"

Bella, too, was after it; but the hat, like a mischievous, animate thing, was too wary for either of them. Caught up on a new gust of wind it rose like a rocketing pheasant and went sailing away out of sight over the brow of the hill. Bella laughed:

"Never mind. I'll fetch it."

"No, don't worry. Please . . . *please!*" Henry cried.

But already she was running, picking her way through the patches of gorse. It was delicious to be racing like a child down the boisterous wind. Where the slope fell away it was hard to keep one's footing: one could only run on and on and hope for the best. She heard Henry's steps thudding behind her, and ran even faster. Mr. Fladburn's hat, losing the wind, floated gracefully down like a parachute in a thicket of dead bracken where, finally, she fell to her knees and triumphantly pounced on it. Henry reached her a moment later, laughing and panting.

"What a rate you went!" he said. "If you'd caught your foot you'ld have come an awful cropper. I was terrified. Thank heaven you didn't!"

Bella, too, was breathless. "Oh dear, what a lovely gallop. I loved it. I felt I wanted to do something quite mad. I wish we didn't have to go back," she sighed. "Let's sit down here a minute. My breath's gone and my hair's all come down. Isn't it heavenly here? So quiet . . ."

Henry looked round anxiously. Beneath the shoulder of the hill their nest was completely hidden from the others' eyes; the high wind, roaring overhead, could not reach them there. He stood, hesitating, gazing at her.

"Why don't you sit down?" Bella said, and her voice seemed part of the quietude. She looked up at him, smiling, but her eyes fell as soon as they were raised. There was a look in his she had never seen before, a look that made her shy and conscious of being alone with him. His silent gaze embarrassed her; she wished he would speak. His face went so pale that for the moment she wondered if he were ill.

"What is it?" she said. "Is anything the matter with you?"

He threw back his head and laughed. "Don't you know what's the matter with me? Don't you know what's been the matter ever since I saw you? Don't

you know how shatteringly lovely you are? Don't
you know how I worship you?" He fell to his knees
beside her and clasped her hands. "Oh, Bella, why
won't you look at me? Why won't you say something?"

He was kissing her hands. It seemed odd that anyone should want to do that. They were not very
clean, and she felt certain they smelt of sandwiches.
If she had known this was going to happen. . . .
But she hadn't quite known, and she was glad, all the
same, it had happened, though even more bewildered
than glad. For in that moment she became aware of
herself, Bella Small, sitting somewhat dishevelled and
breathless in a clearing of bracken and listening, for
the first time in her life, to protestations of love which
surely demanded a setting less casual and more dignified than this. Her silence alarmed him.

"Oh, Bella," he cried, "say something, for God's
sake, my darling!"

And his voice was so shaken and agonized that now
she felt forced to look at him—timidly at first, for this
ardent stranger seemed far more formidable than the
good-looking, remote young man who had lately shown
such a flattering liking for her company. Yet when she
did look, she could only feel kindly towards him,
far more kindly than she had ever felt towards anyone
before. He was no longer remote and superior but
near and humble; and it seemed that his happiness
depended so completely on her mercy that even if she

couldn't honestly confess that she loved him—which was, apparently, what he expected—she really hadn't the heart to say that she didn't. And perhaps she did love him, after all, though in determining this she felt oddly helpless, since all her ideas and standards on the subject were derived from books in which no avowal of grand passion had ever been concerned with anything so ridiculous as the chase of an elderly gentleman's Panama hat. She only knew that in this moment, when her hands lay in his and her eyes, meeting his, found them far less formidable than she had ever imagined, she felt strangely secure and warm and dreamily tender, and perhaps less lonely, than ever before since her childhood.

"But surely you knew, my dearest," Henry was saying. "On that evening under the lime-tree and a hundred times since."

"Well, I suppose I thought you liked me . . ."

"Liked you?"

"Well, 'loved me' if you like. But just knowing that somebody loves you is very different from being told so by their own lips. And you never told me before."

"I've never had a chance."

"And this isn't a real chance either. We've no business to be talking here. They'll be sending to look for us."

"Yes, we'd better go back. I don't mind. Nothing matters now. You love me, Bella?"

She shook her head. "I don't know. I mean, I don't *know* you."

"But you don't mind?"

"How could I mind? I can't stop you, can I?"

"Nothing on God's earth will stop me!"

"Do let's go. We can't stay here talking."

"Very well. Give me your hand and I'll help you. It's terribly steep."

She surrendered her hand, but he did not help her. He preferred to walk by her side. They had climbed half the slope before Bella discovered that they had left Mr. Fladburn's Panama hat behind. It was so ludicrous that they burst out laughing together. Bella liked him when he laughed.

"All right," he said gaily. "I'll go back and fetch the damned thing. You go on and tell them you've seen me still looking for it. That'll be perfectly true."

Bella smiled at this example of the Fladburn conscience's delicacy. As if it mattered to her whether what she said was true or not! But she liked him for calling his father's hat a damned thing. That wasn't Fladburn, anyway. She supposed she was rather in love with him after all.

X

WITHIN a few days she no longer had any doubt of it. In her rich and virgin imagination the seed had only to be sown to germinate and run riot. After all, she was her mother's daughter and her grandmother's grand-daughter: it was against the Tinsley tradition to feel or do anything by halves. Her warm nature was ready for love, and the idea of love (irrespective of its object) once conceived filled and dominated her life to a degree which her lover—in whom passion was tempered by timidity—felt somewhat extravagant. Her immediate response was more than Henry Fladburn had bargained for. He found himself in the position of a prospector who, boring for oil in secret, had struck a "gusher" whose flow he was unable to cope with.

His nature was less generous and narrower than hers in every dimension; and Bella, had her eyes not been dazzled by sudden wonder, might have seen this and been chilled by his hesitations. But Bella was now so blindly in love that his very caution was dear to her, a darling defect in a paragon whose perfection might otherwise have surpassed humanity. There were times, indeed, when her unguarded rashness appalled him.

"Can't you see," he would say, "that we're simply asking for trouble?"

She was all innocent amazement. "As long as we love each other, what on earth does that matter? Sooner or later, if they don't find it out for themselves they'll have to be told."

"But Bella, my darling. It isn't as easy as that. If I happened to be my own master . . ."

"What difference does that make?"

"You don't know my people."

"Oh, don't I indeed!"

"I mean you don't realize how wrapped up they are in tradition. To begin with, they'll all expect me to marry a third cousin and a Free Calvinist."

"Well, I'm afraid I can't be a cousin, but the other part's perfectly simple. I'm quite willing to be converted or whatever you call it if you'll tell me how to begin."

"It's all very well to laugh. It's no joking matter."

"But I'm not joking, Henry darling. I mean just what I say. I'm nothing in particular, and I'd much rather be what you are."

"And that's only one side of it," he went on gloomily. "I'm entirely dependent on them. I haven't a halfpenny of my own."

Bella laughed. "What does money matter?"

"What does *money* matter?" His tone was scandalized. To a Fladburn her question implied a heresy graver than any religious difference. "Well, we shall have to live, shan't we? It's all very well, but you can't live on love."

"I think *I* could live on love," she answered dreamily, "but even if you couldn't we're both of us perfectly capable of earning our living. I'm doing so now. Are you frightened of being poor, darling?"

"Oh, it isn't a matter of being frightened. It's just being reasonable. If you'ld only give things a chance of settling down and working themselves out. You're in such a desperate hurry."

"Of course I'm in a hurry. That's natural, isn't it? I love you."

"Can't two people be normally in love without losing their sense of proportion?"

"Of course they can't, darling. What a horrid idea!"

"Well, if you go on like this you'll simply ruin everything. If you'll leave it to me . . ."

And finally, of course, just because she adored him unconscionably, she did leave it to him, finding an inverted rapture—since her ardour, damped in one way, must find vent in another—in adventurous secrecy. Their meetings and love-making were so strictly limited by his prudence—which she despised in her heart, yet acquiesced in because it was his—that they reached for her a pitch of almost intolerable sweetness. His passion, it seemed, was prepared to dwell on a far less exalted plane than hers. He could pass his days contentedly in the flat routine of the works, pursuing a life that conformed to the standard of Mr. Fladburn's "Is it necessary?", returning at six to enjoy Bella's company in a mood that was nearer to relaxation than to excitement.

But the intensity of Bella's emotions never relaxed. She was possessed and possessive. In the intervals between their meetings her body and mind never lost that glow which the mere sound of his voice or his nearing footfall could instantly fan into a consuming flame which Henry, schooled from his childhood in principles of strict moderation, found quite "unnecessary," and even exacting. The young women of the Fladburn caste held a more balanced view of the place of love in an industrial civilization, as a solace to the tired business man, not as a stimulant. They had been taught that the first maxim in love was "business as usual," that a young man's career must invariably take precedence over his passions, and that the "settlement"—about which Bella knew less than a South Sea Islander—was the most important feature in a marriage contract.

Bella, to Henry's regret, was too old to learn these rudimentary principles; yet the regrets, in his case, were complicated by the fact that he was genuinely in love with her. Even before he met her, his allegiance to the Fladburn tradition had been sapped by the glimmerings of a richer life which he had perceived in Germany. Now Bella's impetuosity shook the divided structure of his life to its foundations. He became a prey to alternations of rashness and fear, of rapture and doubt.

Bella knew no doubts and acquiesced in no reservations. It was her nature to live each moment as though none had gone before and none would follow. When once she had discovered the surprising fact that she had fallen in love it conditioned her whole existence. From that moment her sole purpose in life was to love and to be loved. Therefore much of her life seemed purposeless and exasperating, since the hours when Henry was absent from her were hardly worth numbering, and even in those when he was at home she saw very little of him, for his mother's standards of filial duty were exacting and claimed much of his leisure.

Thus Bella's days resolved themselves into a series of shifts and stratagems for the contrivance of contacts which were so brief and so incomplete as to irritate both of them: touch of hands that momentarily met amid sheets of music; meeting of lips on a darkling stairway or at a half-opened bedroom-door; words whispered in passing; smiles and glances perilously exchanged across the solemn Fladburn dinner-table; swift embraces snatched behind lilac-bushes in the summer garden, where the bee-ravished lime-blossom was beginning to fall.

Hers was a love that, craving much, had to content itself with so little, for by now he had convinced her that their happiness depended on secrecy. Whenever they met Bella felt that inquisitive eyes were set on them: she was thankful that they were, so far, merely inquisitive and not suspicious, though Prudence's interest in their movements and conversation troubled her until she discovered its true explanation, which was that Prudence had lately conceived for her a devotion resembling that which she herself at the same age had felt for Miss Boldmere, and was actually jealous not of Bella but of Henry. Unfortunately, as far as the lovers were concerned, it made little difference whom Prudence was jealous of, or to which of them she clung. The result was the same: the abominable child perpetually shadowing them and intervening with a pertinacity that allowed no escape.

Henry, always playing for time, was prepared to acquiesce in this intervention as an Act of God, but Bella rebelled against it and refused to accept his helplessness. If they couldn't spend a moment alone under the roof which they shared they must meet elsewhere. To this end she revived, as a plausible fiction, her intimacy with Marjorie Astill, the school-friend through whom she had found her place at the Fladburns'. Mrs. Astill would have been only too thrilled if Bella had chosen to conduct a clandestine affair in her house, for she was romantically minded and her own married life had not been distinguished by passion. But on the occasions when Bella informed Mrs. Fladburn she was going to visit her friend, she

never went near her house. She went to meet Henry
Fladburn, usually at dusk and in streets on the
northern side of the Halesby Road which were un-
fashionable and therefore unfrequented by any Fladburn connections.

They became, in fact, these two, just another
anonymous couple amid the hundreds of suburban
lovers who sought happiness in the dark solitude of
Alvaston that summer. Once Arden engreened this
rolling country, and even to-day it has a woodland
quietude, for forest trees still stand in the ample
gardens of bow-windowed Early Victorian houses of
stucco which the Hardware Princes built as a half-
way resting-place between the cottage and the country
seat. There are cedars of Lebanon there and splendid
elms and many old orchards of apple-trees, so that
lovers who walk arm in arm along the discreet pavements overshadowed with weeping laburnum and fans
of horse-chestnut, may hear (if they have ears for
such extraneous things—and why, in heaven's name,
should they?) the whinney of a brown owl ripple
through the night—or even, it is said, a casual
nightingale, or a garden-warbler apeing that peerless
song. Lovers might easily lose themselves in Alvaston
on a June night when the pink hawthorns are out.
The deserted roads do not follow a geometrical pattern, but interlace with long curves and sweeps; the
street-lamps are far between and seem to have been
erected for the bedazzlement of the summer moths

which flutter round them rather than for the direction
of mankind; for most people who live in Alvaston
are not fly-by-nights but solid, respectable folk who
keep early hours; and if, for their own unexceptionable reasons, they should be late abroad, and, returning, find themselves threading a sort of suburban
Venusberg full of low laughter and sighs and (very
occasionally) protests, they sometimes write letters
about "the Scandalous State of the Roads in our
Premier Suburb" to the *North Bromwich Courier* or
to the Watch Committee (of which Mr. Fladburn
was chairman), but more usually and charitably lower
their eyes, reflecting that a population of more than
half a million cooped up in an inadequate number of
three-roomed houses, may be excused for expressing
itself romantically out of doors on a summer night.

That Henry and she were only one amorous couple
among hundreds did not trouble Bella. She had the
faculty of submerging herself in the moment's flow
of emotion to the exclusion of all other sensations.
The mere fact that she had managed to separate
Henry even momentarily from the Fladburn influence
and atmosphere, that she had got him to herself, was
sufficient triumph to make her unconscious of her surroundings. For her these shadowy roads in which
they secretly walked or lingered were pathways
through a private paradise, so that when they emerged
from their dusk into the populous and more brilliantly
lighted reaches of the Halesby Road, over whose

polished wood-pavement the towering three- and four-horsed Tilton buses sailed superbly to and fro like illuminated galleons, she felt the impact of normal life as a brutality.

Before they reached this point they usually separated, for it was extremely unlikely that anyone living in the Halesby Road should not know who Henry was. One evening towards the end of June, at the moment of their parting he became aware that two women on the opposite pavement were interested in them. For a moment they paused and stared, then, having determined on closer inspection, changed their direction, diagonally crossing the road towards the point at which Henry and Bella were standing. The move was so pointed that Henry became alarmed.

"Those people are watching us," he said. "I don't know them, but I believe they know me. Have you any idea who they are? Don't turn round, for God's sake!"

"I don't need to. I know one of them well enough," Bella answered. "She's an old friend of mine."

"I was afraid they knew us. Who is she?"

"Miss Cash."

"What . . . the schoolmistress?"

"Yes."

"I've often heard of her, though I've never seen her before. I doubt if she knows me, thank heaven, and she may not have recognized you. Keep your face turned away. They'll have passed us in another moment." The sound of light, rapid footsteps rose and died away in the distance. "Now they've turned the corner, so that's all right. The girl's rather pretty—a little your type, but younger; and your Miss Cash, I must say, is remarkable: I had a good look at her. She was smiling, but not happily. She has the face of an old woman and yet she walks like a girl."

"Yes, that's true. She's quite ageless. You see she's a vampire. She lives on blood."

"What nonsense you talk!"

"It isn't nonsense. It's true. I know. What awful luck!"

"Awful luck? What do you mean?"

"Her seeing me."

"She probably didn't."

"Oh yes, she did. Miss Cash never misses anything."

"Well, you needn't upset yourself anyway, child. She can't hurt you now."

"But she would if she could. Oh, I do wish this hadn't happened!"

"Now you're simply being ridiculous."

"I'm sorry, darling. I can't help it."

She couldn't. Although she had only seen Miss Cash in the distance and had missed what Henry called her "unhappy" smile, she could not cease from imagining it. She felt something vaguely disquieting in this intrusion of the past into the rapturous present, something sinister in Henry's description of

Miss Cash's companion—"a girl rather of your type, but younger." It reminded her of one of Henry's Schubert songs, *Der Doppelgänger*. As she hovered uneasily on the verge of sleep her morbid fancy suggested that the girl who had walked with Miss Cash was conceivably not flesh and blood but, like the "double" of the song, a wraith of her former self, a vision of ill omen; and when she woke in the middle of the night with a clearer mind she was still haunted, more reasonably, by the memory of Miss Cash's colourless, ageless face with its small, kittenish features and the black eyes that never missed anything. There was nobody in the world whom she would less gladly have admitted to her secret than Miss Cash.

XI

MORNING found her restored to her usual equanimity and ready to laugh at herself for these fantastic forebodings. Summer now approached its perfection, and though the birds, having completed their love-making and hatched their nestlings, sang less tumultuously, the morning had a languid sweetness that softened the heart. It was strangely beautiful, Bella thought, to awake to the consciousness of loving and being loved in an air whose comforting warmth corresponded with her own inward glow. As she dressed she could hear Henry singing in the bathroom below. It was strange that the very fact of his being there, or even existing, made life sweet: sweeter still because she knew he was happy, and her happiness depended on his. Since the early days when she had been jealous of everything that took him away from her her possessive passion had reached a more moderate state. If it was deeper it was also calmer, no longer distressed by petty frustrations or by the urgent fear of time fretting their happiness. From being a jealous enemy time had become their ally. Their love seemed no longer a perilous flare but a steadfast flame which would last as long as they did; and Bella was so young that she knew they would love for ever.

She was so confident of this that when on the
following morning Henry whispered to her that he
could not meet her as usual, she was not distressed.
He was involved, it seemed, in one of those family
councils at which the Fladburn family periodically
"talked things over" and decided, with a seriousness
transcending that of a directors' meeting, just what
was or was not "necessary" in the family's policy.
That evening it seemed clear that the agenda were
important. No less than five Fladburns and Gubbinses,
including the richest and oldest aunt, were invited to
a cold supper, while Bella and Prudence were
dismissed to sup in the schoolroom. There, for a
couple of hours, Bella listened to the drone of voices
that ascended from the dining-room below, feeling
thankful that she was out of it and sorry for poor
Henry who, she knew, found these endless debates
as boring as she did. The discussion continued until
Prudence's bedtime, and half an hour later, when
Bella returned to the schoolroom, it was still droning
on and on. There seemed little chance now that Henry
would even steal one precious moment in which to kiss
her good night.

"I suppose I shall hear all about it to-morrow," she
told herself, and went to bed.

But next morning, though she rose early and walked
in the garden, pretending to look at the dewy rose-
beds but always hoping to catch a glimpse of him,
Henry did not appear. Mr. Fladburn and he, the maid

told her, had breakfasted early and driven into North Bromwich to catch a train. Had they taken any luggage? she asked. Mr. Fladburn hadn't; but Mr. Henry had taken a couple of bags: she had carried them downstairs.

"But he couldn't go away like that," Bella thought, "without letting me know. Perhaps he has left a note in my room." She hurried upstairs, examining first her bedroom and then the schoolroom in vain. Then the breakfast gong boomed and, still hurt and mystified, she went down to the dining-room.

Prudence was there before her, but Mrs. Fladburn, incredibly, came in one minute late. The shrunken breakfast-table, from which Henry's "place" and his father's had been removed, enforced an intimidating intimacy. Even Prudence sat bewildered and mum, and when Bella endeavoured to ease the strained silence by making remarks which, as soon as she spoke, seemed full of the most inappropriate levity, Mrs. Fladburn treated them with a silent aloofness that made them sound even sillier. She could hardly have looked grimmer than she did that morning if Mr. Gladstone had died in the night or John Fladburn and Company called a meeting of creditors. Watching her cautiously nibbling dry toast Bella was shocked to think how unprepossessing Mrs. Fladburn was. She had been too busily engaged in falling in love with Henry to notice her lately; but as she observed her now it seemed that since last she looked at her she

H*

had aged ten years. She was dressed in the whaleboned black satin she had worn on her first encounter,
and a high neckband, supported at regular intervals,
clutched her throat so tightly as to suffuse her face
with purple and make her gooseberry eyes protrude,
while her hair, dragged back from the scalp with an
unusual ferocity, made her face more than ever
resemble that of a rabbit which had been not merely
skinned but strangled. Beneath her plate she had carefully concealed what looked like an envelope. Was
this possibly, Bella wondered, the letter that Henry
had written to her, which had fallen by some mischance
into those bony hands? If it was, she must look out for
trouble.

Mrs. Fladburn's face, however, showed no signs of
a brewing storm. When she had finished her toast she
folded her bony hands serenely upon her flat chest.
It was odd, Bella thought, that a creature so unattract-
ively arid should have collaborated with John Fladburn, who was himself no Adonis, in producing the
man she loved. She felt sorry for Mrs. Fladburn,
who, of course, couldn't help it, but far more sorry
for Henry, whose duty it was to contemplate his
mother without horror or disgust.

These reflections bemused her so deeply that she
failed to notice the signs of impatience and irritation which Henry's mother began to display as she
watched her eating. It was only when Bella had
finished and begun to fold her napkin that Mrs. Flad-

burn broke silence.

"You need not put your serviette back in the ring," she said acidly. "Prudence, go to the schoolroom and wait there. I will come to you later. I wish to speak to Miss Small."

Prudence's pale eyes goggled with surprise: "Shall I go on with my history, Miss Small?"

"You will do what you're told," Mrs. Fladburn broke in. "You will go to the schoolroom and wait for me, and please shut the door after you." She turned upon Bella. "I said I wanted to speak to you, Miss Small, but I find it difficult to choose my words. You have done an unpardonable thing; you have abused the confidence we were foolish enough to repose in you. You have betrayed our trust in the most dishonourable manner. You have behaved abominably."

Her vehemence took Bella's breath away: it was so unexpected. She found herself lamely asking: "In what way, Mrs. Fladburn?"

Mrs. Fladburn bridled. "I am surprised at your asking such a question. Your conscience should answer it. I repeat: you have abused our confidence. You were employed unwisely without any enquiries being made as to your moral character; you were received here as One of the Family, and made free of all the innocent intimacies of our home life. You took advantage of our simplicity, our unworldliness, to embark on a secret intrigue which might have gone even further—I tremble to think how far—if a Certain Person who came to know of it, and who knew your character too, had not considered it her duty to inform us of what was Going On."

As the torrent rolled over her Bella found herself thinking: "Miss Cash! She saw us the other night. How that woman hates me! I must be careful to keep my temper for Henry's sake."

She said: "If you're talking about Miss Cash I'm not surprised. But really, Mrs. Fladburn . . ."

The bony hand waved her aside. "Kindly listen to me: I shall not keep you long. The name of our kind informant is quite immaterial. I am glad, at least, that you have the decency not to go on pretending not to know what I am talking about."

"I suppose you mean me and Henry? If you had said so at first, I should have understood you better. But surely there's nothing so very terrible in that? Don't people . . . is it really discreditable for two people to fall in love? Oughtn't others who wish them well to be glad of it? Isn't it rather wonderful?"

Mrs. Fladburn drew herself up like a hostile cobra. "I will put your question in another way, Miss Small. Is it right, is it honourable for a dependant, a woman who has been admitted to the privilege of living in a house of this kind as an act of charity . . ."

Bella flushed: "Hardly that, Mrs. Fladburn. My wages are not very big, but I do think I've earned them."

"Your wages are what you agreed to accept. That is a business arrangement, and we have duly performed our side of it; but it was *not* part of your contract, I think you must agree, to entangle the son of the house in a clandestine intrigue; it was not part of your contract to deliberately deceive your employers."

Bella held back her indignation—"For poor Henry's sake," she told herself. She said quietly: "Mrs. Fladburn, I don't think you quite understand. Henry and I have discovered that we are in love with each other." (Mrs. Fladburn snorted.) "We didn't want to fall in love; it just came unexpectedly. And when people do fall in love they don't necessarily want to proclaim it to the whole world at once."

"That depends what you mean by 'the world.' In *our* world, Miss Small, people's actions are more above board: the idea of secrecy, of underground scheming is repugnant to us."

"You mean Henry should have told you? Well, *I* didn't stop him, Mrs. Fladburn. He may have wondered how you would take it, and it looks as if he was right. Supposing he had told you he wanted to marry me, what would you have said?"

"I'm surprised at your asking such an impertinent question. You know perfectly well I should have put my foot down immediately. I should have got rid of you at once."

"Then how can you blame him, Mrs. Fladburn?"

"I don't blame him, Miss Small. On the contrary,

I blame myself. I am merely sorry for Henry's simplicity. He has led what I think I may call without boasting a sheltered life. Among the people of our own kind with whom he was likely to associate, simple, high-minded people, precaution would not have been necessary. Mr. Fladburn himself, at Henry's age, was equally guileless." ("He must have been," Bella thought.) "No, I blame myself. It was I, in my thoughtlessness, who exposed him to the lures of an unscrupulous woman . . ."

"You have no right to say that!"

"I had no right to say it until now. Since yesterday, unfortunately, I know rather more about you."

"You believe everything you are told by Miss Cash?"

"Your conduct, unfortunately, confirms everything I have been told."

"My conduct? Even now I don't know what I've done to make you object to me. I wish you'ld tell me."

"I'm not going to discuss the matter. The fact that you've made my son deceitful is quite sufficient. We took you on trust, as I've said. I know very little about you, Miss Small, and I wish I knew less. Let us leave it at that."

"You *can't* leave it at that, Mrs. Fladburn," Bella said. She was thinking: "She can bluster until she's blue in the face, but she can't frighten *me:* she knows that she's beaten. It's a pity we have to offend them;

but that couldn't be helped. We're not children; we know our own minds; if we want to marry—and of course we *shall* marry—she can't stop us. She can send me away, but even that won't make any difference. He's mine more than hers, and she knows it, poor thing, though she daren't admit it. She likes to think that because they're rich and we're poor she can do what she likes with us; but we're two to her one, invulnerable, and if it's fighting she wants we've something far stronger than money or prejudice to fight with. If she'd ever been in love herself, she'ld know this; but of course she hasn't. She married, I suppose, in the cold-blooded Fladburn fashion: it was a marriage of two names, two fortunes, two businesses, not two human beings; and she takes it for granted that Henry is like the rest of them, but that's where she's mistaken." "You can't leave it at that, Mrs. Fladburn," she repeated—and the words now became a challenge. She was so sure of her own power and of the other's impotence that she felt almost sorry for her as she played her last invincible card: "Have you spoken to Henry about this?"

Bella smiled as she spoke; but Mrs. Fladburn did not blench at the fatal question. On the contrary she appeared to take up the challenge with satisfaction as though she had been waiting for it.

"Indeed we have spoken to Henry," she said. "In a matter of this kind, affecting the family, we are not in the habit of making decisions lightly. My husband

and I discussed the situation last night and decided
what would be best. Henry has left North Bromwich
this morning, and will not return until this regrettable
incident is forgotten."

She spoke so ponderously that Bella was forced to
smile.

"Do you really imagine that will make any difference to us, Mrs. Fladburn? Do you really think
he will forget as easily as all that? You don't know
him. You certainly don't know *me*."

"That remains to be seen," Mrs. Fladburn answered
complacently. "I'm afraid you will find you're
mistaken. Henry is not so weak as you think him or
would wish him to be. His father and I talked the
whole matter over with Henry and told him, as sympathetically as we could, what we had decided. Mr.
Fladburn pointed out to him what you both had
evidently overlooked: the fact that he is not in a position to marry without our permission. No doubt you
have thought of him as a rich man's son, a young man
with great expectations . . ."

"The idea never entered my head. I've told you:
I love him."

"That may be as it may be. You have no cause to
be heated, Miss Small. I am not accusing you . . ."

"You're suggesting . . ."

"Far from it. I am merely stating the facts. Mr.
Fladburn is *not* a rich man and never will be. His
generosity and public spirit prevent him from being

so. As for Henry, he hasn't a penny of his own and never will have a penny from any member of his father's family or mine unless he behaves himself as we wish. He was told that plainly."

"And what did he say to it?"

"He said what we expected him to say. He has accepted the position. He was not so deluded as to be incapable of seeing reason. He realized that his father knew best."

"Do you expect me to believe that?"

"I am not in the habit of being disbelieved."

"Perhaps not. But you're lying all the same."

"This is quite outrageous, though I might have expected it."

"Where is Henry?"

"I've no intention of telling you where Henry is."

"You can't put me off so easily as that, Mrs. Fladburn. I won't believe a word you say till I hear it from Henry's own lips. Even then I wouldn't believe it. Do you think you can separate us like this? Of course you don't! You trying to bluff me. I know it."

"He has promised not to have anything more to do with you, and we can trust to his honour."

"His honour! That seems an odd word!"

"Well, he has kept his promise so far. If he had wanted to, he could have seen you this morning before he left. But he didn't." Mrs. Fladburn smiled with serene satisfaction, and Bella knew she had reason to smile, for she had spoken cold truth. Yet she couldn't accept it. "The woman's trying to frighten me," she thought, "and I mustn't be frightened." She managed to smile too.

"That looks bad for me, doesn't it?" she said. "But of course it means nothing." (Did it?) "He can write to me. I know he will write to me. You can't stop his doing that!"

"If he writes to you here when you're gone," Mrs. Fladburn said, "I shall certainly burn his letters; and if you write to him, I shall deal in the same way with yours. I have said all I wish to say," she went on, "and heard more than I wished to hear." From beneath the plate where she had hidden it she produced her envelope. "Here is a cheque," she said, "for your wages up to the end of the month. You will realize that you have forfeited the right to such treatment, but Mr. Fladburn is always unnecessarily generous in these matters. You need not trouble to acknowledge it. Your endorsement will be a sufficient receipt. And now, Miss Small, I shall be obliged if you'll get your things packed as quickly as possible. I have ordered a conveyance to drive round and fetch them and you at ten o'clock, so there's no time to be wasted."

Bella stood with the envelope clenched in her hands. Her first thought was to tear it in pieces and throw the fragments in Mrs. Fladburn's face; but the swelling tumult of anger and haunting doubt and positive humiliation tossed the childish impulse aside. All these

turbulent elements were swamped and confounded
in one wave of hatred and contempt, too long suppressed, for the whole Fladburn system and everything pertaining to it—even Henry himself—
momentarily incarnate in the gaunt woman who calmly
opened the door and stood waiting for her to pass.
The wave rose and broke and blinded her.

"You devil!" she cried. "You damned, mean,
hypocritical devil! You with your cant of freedom
and justice and liberality! If you want your son you
can keep him . . . you're welcome to him. When I
marry, I'll see that I marry a man with a mind of his
own, not a weakling like him. You can tell him I
told you so. He needn't write to me. I'd sooner be
dead than married to any Fladburn, rich or poor. I
thank God I've finished with the whole mean lot of
you, and I hope I may never set eyes on any of you
again. I hope . . ."

But the pressure of angry words failed suddenly;
the wave lost its impulse, fell back and left Bella
stranded—no longer a white-hot fury, but a desolate
child with a broken heart; no longer a proud rebel,
but a little middle-class governess caught out in forbidden flirtation and summarily dismissed. As she put
her hands to her face and broke into tears, the envelope which she had crushed into a ball of moist paper
fell to the floor. Mrs. Fladburn, savouring her victory
with grim satisfaction, picked it up and handed it to
her.

"You had better take this," she said coldly. The clock chimed the quarter. "You have just fifteen minutes to pack in. Mr. Fladburn has paid for the cab. It should not be kept waiting."

XII

Wʜᴇɴ she stepped into the cab which had been waiting for twenty minutes Bella had no more idea of her destination than the cabman himself, whom she recognized as the red-faced driver from the livery-stables who had disgraced himself by drinking Mrs. Fladburn's health in four-ale on the summit of Uffdown, or his horse, which was one of the long-tailed blacks used for funerals. It was only when they had emerged from the laurel thickets of Chad Grange into the road that the driver pulled up, climbed down from his box and asked where she wanted to go.

The question was literally unanswerable: Bella did not want to go anywhere. She only wanted to escape from the Fladburns' house and everything that reminded her of her angry humiliation; but the cabman's red face, suddenly glowing at the window, looked so innocent, so kind, his liquorish voice was so friendly and his manner so richly paternal, that between them they nearly shattered her self-control. Humanity and kindness were more than she could bear at that moment in a world that seemed wholly hateful; yet somehow, for pity of him or of herself, she managed to smile and to ask if he happened to

235

know where the Astills lived.

At the mention of her friend's name the cabman's red face grew redder. The word "Astill" unlocked his heart.

"Mr. Astill's, Miss?" he said. "Mr. Reggie Astill's? Why, I could drive you there blindfold, Miss. Now *that's* a family if you like! Some talk about Bass and Allsopp and Worthington, but give me Astill's! Pure malt and 'ops, Miss! Why, a treat only to smell it, just driving past like. Food and drink in one! And look how they keep their 'orses! Lovely coats! It's the bran that does it, the same as human beings. Astill's for 'Ealth, like the advertisements say. I reckon them Astills 'as done more for North Bromwich than Joe Chamberlain himself! Mr. Reggie Astill's!"—he continued to gloat on the name. "Why, I'm proud to drive anyone there, miss, and that's the honest!"

They swung out into the Halesby Road. At this hour, in the slack water between the flow and ebb of business-traffic, it lay almost empty. In the midst of it that slow cab, jogging westward, seemed to Bella as lonely and unimportant as herself. Not a soul on the pavements troubled to look at it or dreamed of the confusion and misery that it carried. Her departure, in fact, supplied a just anticlimax to the drama in which, up till an hour ago, she had been conscious of playing such a brilliant part. The play was over. The performance would not be repeated. The curtain

had gone down to a cackle of derisive laughter, and
here she was, stripped of her latest shred of illusion,
a naked nonentity, slinking away from the scene of
her failure, not knowing even where she was going
next or for what new part a contemptuous fate would
cast her. Not that it mattered much now . . .

In the midst of this spiritual numbness she became
aware of one of those odd apprehensions in which the
dimension of time appears to lose its validity. She
felt that she had lived through this particular moment
before. How and when? The sensation came, she
discovered, from the smell of stale straw exhaled by
the floor of the cab. In a precisely similar odour,
six years before, she had set out alone from St.
Monica's to attend her grandfather's funeral. It
shocked her to recall this unreal vision of herself as a
self-conscious schoolgirl, rather awed by the solemnity
of the occasion yet even more deeply impressed by the
noticeable part she was about to play in Miss Boldmere's "black." Yet the system of life to which all
those memories belonged had vanished no more completely than the self around which its appearances and
emotions were centred. It was ridiculous to suggest
that that awkward child she remembered—any more
than her next incarnation, Miss Cash's adoring companion—was herself, Bella Small. She was not. Every
so often, it seemed, at irregular and arbitrary intervals, the celestial accountant ruled a red double
line, balanced up one's account and turned a new page.

Life wrote off the bad debts, carrying forward, perhaps, a small credit or debit in the matter of
emotional experience. But, however much one desired
it, there was no turning backward. Wise people had
enough sense to cut their losses and start the new page
with courage, only smiling if they looked back, though
there were times, particularly at first, when it was not
easy to smile.

And here, on the left, stood St. Monica's itself!
From the open windows of practising-rooms the
chromatic scales and arpeggios of Miss Boldmere's
junior pupils tinkled discordantly. There too was
the window of Miss Cash's office where, no doubt, at
this moment she sat, slim, upright, capable, dealing
with the morning drift of letters. There she sat, the
sly villainess of the piece; yet now, as the rumbling
four-wheeler carried her past, Bella no longer regarded Miss Cash with the hatred her treachery had
seemed at first to deserve. Miss Cash, after all, was
no more than a blind instrument of the celestial
accountancy—and not quite so blind as all that! In a
quick revulsion of feeling Bella saw that, but for Miss
Cash, she herself might never have realized until it
was too late the full depth of Henry's meanness and
cowardice: but for Miss Cash she might still be supposing herself in love with that poor, weak thing whom
her foolish imagination had turned into a hero. Miss
Cash knew how flimsy men were; perhaps it was
because she had learnt her own lesson that she had

tried to teach it her pupil; and she, little fool, had laughed at her and despised her for it—but Miss Cash had laughed last!

"Was I ever in love with him?" Bella asked herself. Of course she had been in love with him! Nothing in all her life had equalled the rapture of those stolen embraces, the glow of memory, the ardour of anticipation between them. Even now it moved her even to remember those moments during which, for the first and only time in her life, she had forgotten herself. Now she knew it was safer, far safer not to forget oneself. Never, never again! Yet even as she assured herself that she scorned Henry Fladburn she knew she had loved, and probably still loved, this man whom she despised—that, quite possibly, she would go on loving him as long as she lived. Though her pride revolted against this while her reason rejected him as worthless, some uncontrollable part of her still obstinately ached and yearned for him; and since this feeling could not be countenanced by pride or reason yet was too strong, even now, to be assuaged or stifled, she turned the rebellious force, unconsciously, into another direction. If she were ashamed to love she might hate: the actual nature of the passion made little difference so long as she could find release for the imprisoned emotion which hurt her—which, unless she could free it (she thought), must surely destroy her or drive her mad. So her hatred—or love transmuted—now given a merciful vent flared up within her hurt mind like a blinding flame, so that she saw no more and cared no more where the slow cab carried her than if it had been taking her to the cemetery and she were dead inside it. This wild hatred was not so much for the man who had humbled her as for the Fladburn system of life which had made his treachery possible, and for the stony world in general which permitted so mean a thing as the Fladburn system of life to exist. So the flame rose up and consumed her and burnt itself out until there was nothing left of her, it seemed, but a black cinder. She came to herself—or to all that was left of herself—as the cab slowed down at the drive-gate of Marjorie Astill's house, and she discovered that she was shaking, and clutching a pitiful handkerchief drenched with tears.

"What can I do?" she thought. "What can I do? Nobody must see me like this! It's soaked through, and I haven't another. If I make him drive on for a little I may pull myself together and make myself fit to be seen."

She leaned out of the window and called on the cabman to stop; but it was too late—already the black horse's nose was inside the gateway; and there, to make matters worse, was Marjorie Astill running down the drive to meet her.

"Quick, darling!" she cried in a fluster. "Jump out quickly and run to the telephone. You're wanted immediately. It's important."

Bella's heart gave a leap of gladness. She might

have known it: that devilish woman had lied, after all!

"Who is it?" she gasped. "Henry Fladburn?"

"Henry Fladburn? Good Lord, no. It's Ernest Wilburn, the lawyer, the nice one; you know whom I mean?" Marjorie Astill was still clutching her arm and hurrying her towards the house and talking diffusely and breathlessly as they ran. "He rang up the Fladburns the minute after you'd left, and Mrs. Fladburn told him he'ld probably find you here. When I took up the phone it was the first I'd heard of it. I thought the poor man must be mad! I'd no idea you were coming. Why, Bella darling, you look as if you'd been crying. What on earth has happened? Do tell me: I'm so wildly excited! Quick, in here on the left, darling. The phone's over there on Reggie's desk. I do hope they've not gone and rung off . . ."

Bella took up the telephone receiver. She was thankful to hide her face.

"Hello!" she said, her voice trembling and hardly her own. "Someone wanted to speak to me."

"Is that Miss Small speaking?"

"Yes."

"Will you hold the line, please? Mr. Ernest Wilburn wants you . . . Hello!"—another voice spoke: a pleasant, cultured voice.—"Is that Miss Small? Miss Arabella Small? Ah, that's good. They didn't seem certain at Mr. Fladburn's where I could find you. However, it seems I'm in luck. Look here,

Miss Small, I want to see you on business as soon
as possible. I've an hour to spare. Can I run out to
Mrs. Astill's at once?"

"Are you sure it's me that you want? Isn't there
some mistake?"

The voice laughed. "No, there's no mistake.
You're the person I want. I've important news for
you. Perhaps you don't realize that your grandfather's
dead? No, no, not that grandfather: the other one.
Jasper Mortimer. My business concerns his will under
which you benefit. I'm sorry to rush you like this,
but I've been three days finding you. Do you mind
if I come up at once? Thanks . . . that's awfully
good of you. Au revoir."

Marjorie Astill stood simmering with excitement
at her elbow.

"What is it, Bella? It sounds fearfully exciting."

"I don't know," Bella answered wearily. "It's
about some will. My grandfather's dead."

"I never knew you had one. But then, why should
I? What was his name? Have I ever heard of him?"

"I don't suppose so. His name was Jasper
Mortimer."

"Jasper Mortimer? *Jasper Mortimer?* Why, my
child, what on earth are you talking about? Jasper
Mortimer's Josiah Tinsley & Co. He's a millionaire!
Only to think of it. . . !"

Bella smiled and shook her head helplessly. She
had neither the will nor the power to think.

BOOK THREE

SEQUEL TO CINDERELLA

THE Tinsley heiress, Ernest Wilburn admitted in the Union Club, was a charming young creature. Professional reticence left it at that; but the approval of such an amateur of women as Ernest—half lawyer, half æsthete, half man of fashion, with one elegant spat (as it were) in Mayfair and the other in North Bromwich —added colour to the circumstances of an inheritance that was already sufficiently romantic. Though times weren't as good as they had been, Hayseech, with its vast and various activities, remained one of the major "concerns" of the neighbourhood, and a hundred and forty thousand pounds was a fortune not to be sneezed at, particularly when it happened to be attached to a "charming young creature;" and Ernest Wilburn, his friends slyly suggested, was a lucky devil to have got in, so to speak, on the ground-floor.

From that moment, indeed, the future of Bella Small—henceforth, by deed-poll, Arabella Tinsley— became a topic for talk and some lurid speculation in North Bromwich "Business circles." If she had been unlucky enough to be born ten years later she would doubtless have been photographed and paragraphed in every local newspaper; but the Press, in the mid eighteen-nineties, preserved a decorum and decency which are now forgotten, and Bella's person remained providentially as obscure as ever.

To Dudley, his sardonic brother and partner, Ernest Wilburn was more communicative. The human aspect of his first business interview with Bella had touched an imagination that was reasonably counted too adventurous for his dry calling. Driving up to Reggie Astill's house—precisely the sort of house one might have expected of *any* Astill: a model of expensive bad taste—he had been ushered into a drawing-room of purple and gold in which the heiress awaited him.

"A mere slip of a girl," he told Dudley, "quite pathetically little, she seemed. Nicely dressed, nicely spoken, too—she must have been tolerably well educated, which is rather surprising—and quite astonishingly contained—one might almost say dignified—although she looked as if she'd been crying: she was clutching a ridiculous soaked handkerchief all the time while I talked to her. A pretty girl, too, I should say. Not exactly that, either. Handsome's really the word, though one wouldn't usually apply it to a woman of her size. 'Distinguished' is actually nearer the mark. You remember old Jasper Mortimer in the days when we knew him first, before his hair went white? Well, this child has bred true. She has that exciting combination of fair hair—*cendré*, perhaps, but with a suspicion of red in it—and coal-black eyebrows. Her eyes, as I told you, were rather the worse for wear at the moment. She'd been crying for some good reason. They looked—how shall I put it? —hurt, but not shy in the least, mind you: dark-grey, almost black, and immensely courageous beneath long dark lashes. Vivid colouring: the real pink and white of the Welsh Marches. There's the Mortimer blood again. A firm, sweet little mouth and a devilish determined chin. The child has a will of her own: there's no doubt of that. The whole thing was damned interesting, Dudley. I mean psychologically. She might throw her money away, but she'll never be fooled out of it. Red-hot or stone-cold. There's nothing tepid about her. I must confess, she 'got me'."

"So I gather, my dear Ernest. Another of your swans, I suppose!"

Ernest Wilburn laughed. "Upon my soul, I believe you're right. That's just what she is. So well poised; those black eyes! Yes, I'll give you your 'swan.' She's no goose at all events."

"How did she take the great news?"

"With astonishing composure: not a single feather ruffled! Of course I broke it to her gently. She'd never heard of her grandfather, or at any rate hadn't the least idea of his position or of what his will might mean to her. As far as I can gather, she knew nothing of Jos. Tinsley & Co. except as a name on railway-wagons. I imagine there must have been some kind of a family feud involving her parents, and that the old man softened and thought better of it at the last. I'm glad he did."

I

"I suppose she grasped what it means?"

"Yes, in general terms. I made it quite clear that she was a very considerable heiress and the principal shareholder in the company."

"That must have impressed her."

"If it did, she showed no signs of it."

"The sheer size of the thing must have dazed her."

"I don't think so, honestly. There was obviously something else on her mind: the business over which she'd been crying, perhaps. No, she took it all in; I'm quite positive of that; but whatever I told her just ran off the inside of her mind like . . . like water off a swan's back. As a matter of fact she said very little at first. Just sat and listened."

"You explained the conditions—the changing of name and so on?"

"Yes. She took to that rather kindly. She seemed to like the idea. To tell you the truth, her whole attitude puzzled and fascinated me. It was as if she welcomed the whole business—not, as you might have imagined, as a tremendous reversal of fortune, but as an opportunity—how shall I put it?—of forgetting herself, assuming a new identity, of beginning life over again. A new incarnation, and in a brand-new world. As a matter of fact it was just this that intrigued me so much. A child so attractive, so young, so obviously alive! Why on earth should *she* be longing to make a new start? Again, the most natural thing would have been for her to want, first of all, to parade her good

fortune before the eyes of people—particularly
women!—who knew her before. That's the normal
parvenue's reaction. But not a bit of it! That's
another puzzle."

"You needn't have been puzzled. I can guess what
it means in one: an unhappy love-affair. There's no
other strong motive—except jealousy—in a woman of
her age."

"Well, you may be right. If she hasn't attracted
any admirers so far, I'm ready to bet she'll find plenty
of them before long. A hundred and forty thousand
pounds is a strongish inducement even if she weren't
as attractive as she certainly is."

"Yes, there's trouble ahead for your client. You'll
have your hands full protecting her."

Ernest Wilburn laughed. "Do you know, I believe
you're quite wrong. That's another odd thing. As I
told you before, when I went into the Astills' abominable drawing-room and began to talk business the child
was a pitiful figure, rather soft and bewildered. I
found myself feeling middle-aged and protective and
fatherly."

"Quite natural, though not quite professional."

"But as I went on talking, she changed. I've never
before seen a human being change quite so quickly, so
definitely. All the softness, the pitifulness vanished—
not merely out of her eyes and her mouth but out of
her whole body. It was then that I noticed her extraordinary resemblance to old Jasper Mortimer. And

she gave me that impression, mind you, almost without speaking; though when she *did* speak all her questions were straight to the point: not a single word wasted. I might have been talking to a man with a business intelligence, and a remarkably shrewd one at that. It was like watching molten metal hardening into a mould. In the end she had become as hard as iron, hard and cold. Disconcertingly cold."

"That was rough on you, Ernest, after such a promising start."

"Yet I didn't resent it. On the contrary. It's usually a bore when one's women clients are attractive; but this kind of attractiveness, where one's interests become æsthetic and intellectual at once, are extremely amusing without being dangerous. It's great fun for a bachelor to admire a client æsthetically without falling in love with her. And it'll be a brave man, I give you my word, who dares to fall in love with this one. Miss Arabella Tinsley's a very unapproachable woman; and I saw her become one in fifty-three minutes by an execrable ormolu clock. The young lady may have her fancies, of course. If she does, she'll get her way with them. But the man who takes on that proposition will have my condolences. She's delicious to look at and fascinating to study, but I wouldn't call the job cheap at a quarter of a million. No, thank you!"

"Did you settle anything about the future?"

"More or less. I explained that probate probably wouldn't take long. She proposes to stay on with the

Astill woman—a school-friend, I gather, though they've nothing in common as far as I can see—till the end of the week. Then I've promised to drive her out to Hayseech to make the acquaintance of her aunt and look at the property. They've never met; so the encounter may be amusing. The whole situation's fantastic, of course. Pure Cinderella. That suits me. I've always had a passion for fairy-tales. I look forward to the sequel . . . or sequels."

"It rather looks to me as if you'll have your work cut out. However, the estate will stand it."

"My dear Dudley, I'ld take it on gladly if there wasn't a penny in it."

"I'm quite certain you would," his brother grimly replied. "It seems to me rather in your line."

Again Ernest Wilburn laughed. Though Dudley might sneer at the social facility which had won his brother a reputation for "smartness" and gallantry which was hardly professional, he knew perfectly well that these graces were an asset to the firm. A partner who "specialized" in women and was ready to take the trouble to understand them, was well worth his salt in these regrettably feminist days; and if Ernest had the wits to make himself and his advice indispensable to the Tinsley heiress in the highly unorthodox rôle which suited him, the firm of Wilburn and Wilburn might look forward to substantial pickings.

Yet, oddly enough, for all his expertness in feminine psychology, Ernest Wilburn (though he did not know it) had not penetrated very deeply into Bella Tinsley's. The self-possession which she had managed to exhibit when he unfolded the astonishing details of her inheritance was no more than a mask skilfully improvised for the emergency. Beneath its serene and stony surface the actual Bella remained a pitiable prey to violent and conflicting emotions: pain, anger, humiliation and hot hatred succeeding and sometimes confusing one another in rhythmical waves that tore through her mind like a running surf and broke in its midst so thunderously that (though her lips remained firm and her eyes seemed intent) there were moments in which Ernest Wilburn's pleasant voice—half gravely, half humorously expounding his message—was completely drowned and lost in their surging fury.

Emerging from these intervals of broken or suspended consciousness, in which feeling annihilated thought, Bella gathered, by degrees, the gist of Wilburn's news. It seemed that she, who, the moment before, had been insignificant and almost penniless, had become, by some miracle, rich and a person of consequence. The transformation appeared to her less incredible than unimportant: not so much a poetic reversal of fortune or a vindication of injured humility as an exhibition of gratuitous irony on the part of Fate, who, as usual, had been clumsy if not deliberately mischievous in her timing of events. Only a few hours ago such an accession of fabulous wealth—for this talking in terms of tens of thousands obviously had no relation to reality—might have clarified and triumphantly confirmed her position with regard to Henry Fladburn. Even now it might do so, she told herself bitterly, as far as the Fladburns were concerned. It was she herself, not Henry, who had changed in the interval. Henry was still what he had always been, what she had known him to be (she supposed) yet refused to admit: a poor, nerveless, shadowy creature with no will of his own to whose tepid affections her own vivid imagination, and nothing else, had given the semblance of a grand passion! To-morrow—to-day, if she so wished—she knew she could buy back the love he was supposed to have given her; the whole Fladburn family would leap at the chance and fall over one another in their eagerness to receive her. She might even, she thought, find some satisfaction in returning to the Fladburns the humiliation they had inflicted on herself and watching them crawl to prostrate themselves before her new fortune. Yet the price of this easy satisfaction was not so easy. Henry Fladburn had not merely humiliated her or wounded her self-esteem. He had wounded her eager heart, and the wound still bled. Though she told herself she no longer loved him, even that she despised him, she was still unable to think of him without irrational, unconscionable pain. "I must forget him, I *have* forgotten him," she assured herself; but the ache remained.

She was aware of it, less as of pain than as a sort of central emptiness which made the processes of her conscious mind seem detached and impersonal, while she listened to the facts and figures which Ernest Wilburn, so kindly, so smoothly, so tactfully rehearsed. That detached, superficial part of her was apparently capable of being flattered and stimulated by the deference he showed her, and even of responding to it. The mask, so hurriedly improvised, was capable even of smiles. She saw herself, as Wilburn saw her, regaining the appearance of composure. Her surface, as he observed, achieved above the molten core of misery a texture of cold rigidity. She was even aware of an odd access of dignity, an added distinction, and pleased by the precision with which, to his evident admiration, her mind functioned in dealing with the questions she answered or put to him.

Superficially, at least, she was more surely mistress of herself—not of the old self she knew but of this novel machine—than ever before. There were a number of legal formalities, it seemed, in which she must take her own part, and others which she might safely entrust to him if she wished to save herself trouble. Bella made it quite clear that she had no desire to shirk anything. She would prefer, from the first, to make herself acquainted with every business detail she might reasonably be expected to understand. For the moment, she was able to assure him, she had no need of money. As to the immediate future: she had

no reason—and, for that matter, no desire—to stay
in North Bromwich, and no social ties. She was free,
from that moment, to go where she liked and do what
she wished; though since, as he said, the house at
Hayseech had been left to her, she supposed it was
her obvious duty to try to live in it.

That, of course, was merely her own idea. It was
possible that her aunt, Miss Mortimer, whom she had
never seen, might feel some sentimental attachment
to the place and want to stay there; in which case,
naturally some other arrangement might be made, such
as a joint *ménage*. As a matter of fact she had not the
least idea (nor had Wilburn) how old her Aunt
Harriet was or what she was like. She might easily—
and not unreasonably—resent the manner in which
the bulk of her father's property had been diverted
into her niece's hands. Under these circumstances
Bella readily fell in with Wilburn's tactful suggestion
that the possible awkwardness of a first visit to Hayseech might be softened by his accompanying her. She
was grateful for it, she said, and would be delighted
if he could find time to escort her. She appeared
to be equally—but just as conventionally—delighted
by the skilled delicacy of the compliments with which
he bade her good-bye.

But beneath this extreme virtuosity of outward behaviour—not only in her conduct of the interview with
Wilburn but also when, later, she found herself tormented by the flutterings and exclamations and general

I*

inanity of Marjorie Astill—who, like Wilburn, relished the affair as a fairy-tale in real life and became rapturous at the thought of helping the heroine in a debauch of gorgeously reckless expenditure on frocks and fripperies—Bella's inward thoughts continued, in spite of herself, to revolve round that central emptiness.

Again and again, like bats silently and perpetually circling a subterranean cavern, the same shadowy questions came fluttering past demanding impossible answers: "Why hadn't this tremendous reversal of fortune happened a week ago, or even yesterday? What earthly difference would it have made, in fact, if it had? Why, at least, hadn't Henry scribbled a word to explain himself before he was taken away from her? Had he written a letter, perhaps—and had Mrs. Fladburn suppressed it? If he had written this morning, would he think it necessary to write again to-night? And, in that case, to what address? Would he guess what had happened to her and where she had gone? Why speculate, anyway? After all, what use was a letter—even the loveliest of letters— now that she had lost her faith in him and seen what he really was? Could one ever again love a man whom one's heart had despised? And yet, having once loved, could one ever live without loving? Was there any reason, indeed, for wanting to live?

Round and round the dark questions flew, and, since none could be answered, returned again and again.

They gave her no peace. They still harassed her divided mind when Reg Astill, summoned by telephone, came home early from the brewery and insisted on celebrating the occasion by "cracking a bottle of bubbly" at dinner-time. The pair of well-meaning fools stood up, laughing, to drink to her fortune, and Reg spilt the fizzy wine over his clean white waistcoat. Marjorie Astill had already rung up the box-office and booked three stalls at the Prince's Theatre, where, light-headed with Clicquot, Bella sat through two rollicking acts of George Edwardes's latest musical comedy.

This experience, from which she would gladly have escaped, was perhaps the most fantastically unreal of all. Around her, in the dark auditorium, people tittered or cackled: Reg Astill's horse-laughter in her ear was the loudest of all. On the amber-flooded stage a low comedian capered; a demi-virginal chorus leered and grimaced at invisible males in the stalls; a too-girlish heroine simpered and trilled; a tailor's dummy of a tenor threw back his head to drench the gallery with sentiment, and a gross female (a figure essential to this form of entertainment) cracked jokes which Reg Astill relished as "damned near the knuckle." Yet though this spectacle entranced her companions, it appeared to Bella not merely fatuous (as it was) but vaguely terrifying. The simulacrum of gaiety which those marionettes, with their false hair, their false masks, their false smiles, presented, imposed no illusion on her. She found those bright, jigging tunes, those rhythmical movements, that forced live-liness, those debauches of sentiment, less gay than sinister—not a means of escape from life but rather a poignant mockery of its futility, which the pitiful audience, accepting the stage's illusions as readily as their own, refused, or were unable to perceive, con-tributing unconsciously and equally from their side of the footlights to the unreason of the whole—unless, indeed, it were they who were sane and she who had lost her senses!

As the evening dragged on, in spite of Reg Astill's champagne, she experienced the uncomfortable sensa-tion of solitary sobriety in the midst of a drunken rout. What made it far worse was her hosts' pathetic anxiety to assure themselves that she was enjoying the treat they had provided, and the effort it cost her to convince them both that she was.

"Well, I call that a tip-top show!" Reg Astill de-clared. "That comic chap's every bit as good as Huntley Wright. I've not laughed so much for a twelvemonth. As I always say, there's no earthly need to rush up to town and pay half a guinea to see a good show. These 'number one' companies of George Edwardes's, they take some beating. Not only the principals, mind you. The chorus was stunning. And that tenor or whatever you call it. Don't you think so, Margie?"

"Oh, I thought that last song was lovely. You

might get me the score, Reg. As a matter of fact I enjoyed every minute of it, particularly the dresses; but I'm not sure our Bella did."

"Oh, Marjorie, I simply adored it!" Bella protested.

"Of course she did, Marge. Don't talk rot! And you got us the best seats in the house, old dear. Well, what about a wee night-cap and bye-byes to follow?"

"I caught sight of her face when the lights went up . . ."

"Well, of course the kid's tired. That's natural enough. It's not every day of the week you get sacked from your job—by the way, you must tell us about that, Bella: those blooming Fladburns!—and come into a fortune as well. Here's your good health, my children! I'll bet Bella's all right to-morrow."

"To-morrow . . ." Bella thought. It seemed strange that it was still to-day. "To-morrow I ought to hear from him. He'll guess I've come here. And he couldn't—he couldn't possibly—leave things like this; though whatever he writes it won't make any difference now."

Reg Astill put down his glass and smacked his lips. "Come along! I'm a working man, and I have to be up in the morning. By gad, it's nearly midnight." Marjorie threw her arm about Bella and kissed her boisterously. "Good night, kid. Sleep well!" she said. "They've put a hot-water bottle in your bed. What a day it's been! And what fun! I wouldn't have missed it for anything."

"I shall never sleep," Bella thought, as she slipped into bed and switched off the light. In the darkness all the misery which she had tried to dissimulate returned. She found herself experiencing over and over again, in a version which compressed and distorted the dimensions of time and space, every solitary incident and emotion of the desperate day which had ended: the panic that had seized her when she found that Henry had gone; the alarming breakfast-table; Mrs. Fladburn's vituperations; her own spirited reply; her odd, bemused exodus in the red-faced driver's cab; Wilburn's telephone-call and her incredible interview with him; the dinner she had eaten, the wine she had eagerly drunk, and the phantasmagoria of the Prince's Theatre. At the bewildering rate with which the kaleidoscope changed its pattern, it would be possible, she thought, to re-live one's whole life in a single night. But the process was too tiring—one's wretched brain flared away like a newspaper on fire—so tiring that, even now, she knew she was incapable of thinking; she could do nothing but lie helplessly in the dark and wait till the flames had burnt out, and then, perhaps, fall asleep—though whether sleep could give her release from her pain was another matter.

And finally, though she could not say when, she did fall asleep, and slept dreamlessly from sheer exhaustion, till a sudden metallic shiver of curtain-rings awoke her to consciousness of a strange room with a window oddly misplaced through which sunshine streamed, and a buxom housemaid smilingly dumping a breakfast-tray on her bedside table.

"I oughtn't rightly to have woke you, miss," the maid apologized. "But it's half-past ten, and the mistress thought as you might be hungry. There's a boiled egg and bread and butter and marmalade, and if you want anything else Mrs. Astill says I was to tell you you've only to ring. And I was to say she hopes as you've had a good night."

Bella blinked at the light. At the moment she was still half-asleep, conscious of nothing more than a vague sense of refreshment and well-being.

"Yes . . . I think I've had a good night," she said. "Please thank Mrs. Astill for asking."

"Very good, miss. As I said, if there's anything else . . ."

Bella's senses returned. Of course there was something else.

"Has the post come?"

"Oh yes, miss. Long ago."

"Is there anything for me?"

"No, there's nothing come for you, miss. There's a second delivery later."

But no letter came by the second delivery that day. Nor yet on the morrow, nor on the next day, nor on the day after that, nor on Saturday, which was the day on which it was settled that she should leave the Astills' house for Hayseech.

II

On Saturday afternoon, to the minute punctual, Ernest Wilburn pulled up in his rubber-tyred rallicart at the Astills' front door. His prowess as a "whip" was one of the Regency elegances with which he dazzled bourgeois North Bromwich, and Marjorie Astill, who, in spite of her father-in-law's recent knighthood, had not yet reached the Wilburns' social stratum, was impressed and envious. Bella herself felt excited by the prospect of a drive in such dashing company. During the latter part of the week she had fulfilled her friend's hopes by indulging her fancy at the smartest and most expensive dressmakers' shops. That fancy, indeed, was not so flamboyant as Marjorie's, and was restrained by the social propriety of wearing mourning for her grandfather; but black, as Mrs. Astill reluctantly admitted, was always distinguished, and "became her natural colouring." She had chosen a "costume," as it was called in North Bromwich, of stiff moiré silk. The skirt was ample and looped at the front; it rustled as she walked. The bodice, high at the neck with puffed shoulders, ended in a basque whose expansion emphasized the slenderness of her waist; and a straight-brimmed hat, surmounted by black, shiny foliage and transfixed by three silver pins, was securely poised on the top of her gleaming hair. In spite of her friend's persuasions she had bought no jewellery. The *ensemble*, as Marjorie complained, was unnecessarily severe and a trifle 'old' for her; but Bella knew well that youth gained rather than lost by this studied sobriety, and that the lack of ornament displayed her vivid colouring to greater advantage.

She was pleased with her own appearance that afternoon; convinced that—whatever else it had done to her—the emotional stress of the last week had somehow enhanced her personal dignity; and the expert eyes of Wilburn confirmed the correctness of her taste.

Of so much his sidelong glance of approval assured her as, with a flick of a whip-lash, the sleek equipage turned the corner and went bowling merrily up the gradual incline of the Halesby Road. For the moment his attention appeared to be too deeply engrossed in his driving for speech, unless his silence were no more than a superb exhibition of tact. In either case Bella was thankful for this opportunity of composing her thoughts and adjusting herself to her new clothes and to the astonishing adventure on which, without choice or even volition, her life was so hurriedly embarked.

She found it hard to believe that she, Bella Small— no, not even that—Bella Tinsley, was actually the central figure of this experience; to accept it as a fact that only two months ago a person who, as reason

assured her, was her identical self had been driven over
this self-same road in a slow wagonette on the way
to Prudence Fladburn's birthday picnic. The Halesby
Road, at least, had not changed. She recalled with
incredulous wonder the precise state of mind of the girl
who had sat in the wagonette and timidly, daringly,
waved her hand and smiled at the young man gazing
back at her from the tail of the vehicle in front. She
remembered how that girl had been dressed, how her
heart had fluttered in a delicious anticipation of an
event of supreme importance.

She remembered the delirious happiness of their
return that same evening when the supremely important event had taken place. She remembered and
marvelled at herself—if that *was* herself. But of course
it wasn't. Bella Small, as that girl was called, had
undoubtedly died in an access of rage and agony at the
Fladburns' breakfast-table. Her body had been carried
away, appropriately, in a four-wheeled cab used for
funerals and drawn by a black horse with a long tail.
It had been buried, unknown to herself, in Marjorie
Astill's drawing-room; and the soul to which it belonged, after an incalculable sojourn in a purgatory
of dumb suffering and dark dreams and a torment
of unanswerable questions, had been re-born, attached
to the unfamiliar shape of a wealthy and undeniably
smart young woman of the world, still a trifle bewildered, to be sure, by the metamorphosis, but at this
moment superbly charioting westward over the same

Halesby Road in a conveyance infinitely superior to a hired wagonette and in the admiring, deferential company of a man of fashion.

Transmigration of souls. . . . That was one of the subjects which Bella Small had discussed with Miss Cash. Arabella Tinsley smiled to herself, remembering it. If she could have chosen a name for this new incarnation she would have preferred Arabella Mortimer, which, she felt, would be more in keeping with the identity of this hard, self-possessed young woman, secure in the independence of her wealth and in her contempt for those treacherous emotions which had been her dead self's undoing. Bella Tinsley, she told herself, might be counted more fortunate in beginning life—a life of incalculable spaciousness—immune from romantic illusions but steeled by the ghostly memory of bitter experience. Bella Tinsley, fine in her black moiré silk and her dainty hat, was no *ingénue* prone to be fluttered by flatteries or swayed by sentiment, but the indisputable mistress of herself and her fortune, prepared to take her own part, to twist life to her liking and, if life should prove obstinate, to give as good as she got. There was to be no nonsense, she told herself, about Bella Tinsley. Even Ernest Wilburn, charming and persuasive as he was, must not imagine he could do what he liked with her!

Ernest Wilburn was speaking! "You look very grim, Miss Tinsley."

The use of her new name startled her. She smiled.

"I'm not feeling grim, Mr. Wilburn, I'm enjoying myself."

"I'm delighted to hear it. You don't mind my driving so fast?"

"On the contrary, I love it. This air is delicious."

"It suits you. I mean it becomes you."

"I'm not used to compliments, Mr. Wilburn." Yet she was pleased by the pretty speech, for it confirmed the ideas of herself in which she had been indulging.

"Let us say you look more like yourself," he said.

"How can you possibly know?"

"Well, more as you should look. You're considered a very lucky young woman. When I saw you the other day you certainly didn't look like one. Now, anyone who saw you might guess that you have the world at your feet. I'm conscious, myself, of a little reflected glory."

Bella laughed. "Glory's rather a big word."

Yet she felt, after all, it wasn't a bad one to describe the exalted atmosphere of this expedition, this smooth, rapid movement through that afternoon of high summer in which the face of nature appeared lazily contented and at peace. Their very progress westward seemed a proper symbol for her life's new direction. She was actually turning her back on North Bromwich, the hateful city which had been sole witness of every humiliation she had ever suffered, of every incident inappropriate to her new mood of confidence. She hoped she need never set eyes on it again. Even now——

and it seemed as though they had only just started!—
the last straggling houses of Alvaston had been left
behind. They were nearing the Tilton escarpment.
When she looked back she saw that the city of iron
had vanished. In front stretched an apparently endless
vista of blue hills, lying fold beyond fold, with the
twin domes of the Clents rising blue-black and
threatening in front beneath a sky piled with motionless anvil-shaped clouds that gave warning of thunder,
and the nail-shops of Halesby smouldering at their
feet.

"All the collar-work's finished now," Wilburn told
her. "From this point we drop downward all the way.
It's a great view from this point. Have you ever seen
it before?"

"Once before," she told him, and was enchanted
to find that the memory of that "once" had no more
power to disturb her or make her voice quaver: she
took the question in her stride.

They threaded the gritty outskirts of Halesby.
Though it was Saturday afternoon the nailers' forges
tinkled persistently, and the familiar sulphurous smell
of coke blew into her nostrils. That was the smell of
Bromsberrow: it was pleasant to remember Bromsberrow, or anything in the pre-Cash, pre-Fladburn
days. In the middle of Halesby a slender church
spire arose from a nucleus of black and white cottages
that clung to a cliff like those of an Italian hill-town.
Beneath the cliff wound a muddy brook. Wilburn

pointed to it with his whip: "That's the River Stour."

"Do you call that a river? It looks like a drain," Bella said.

"And that's what it is now. But during the last seventy years it has founded a dozen fortunes: Hackett's, Willis's, Bulgin's—your own. Water-power came first. You should respect the Stour, Miss Tinsley."

"I'll try to. It doesn't *look* romantic, does it?"

He became talkative. "Romance is entirely a matter of imagination. There's nothing romantic, but thinking makes it so. Still, I'm always impressed and excited—always have been—by this green edge of the Black Country. A hundred years ago it must have been one of the loveliest bits of country in England, and even Halesby itself an extraordinarily gracious little town. The church is superb, and so is that seventeenth-century half-timber. It's partly, I suppose, the sharpness of contrast between the green and the black, the old and the new, that gets me. But the new, though I suppose it is hideous, doesn't really offend me. (This ugly extension of Halesby, by the way, is called Mawne.) When I see it I think of the amazing vigour and energy and resource of the fellows who exploited the water-power and dug out the minerals: a remarkable breed, Miss Tinsley, we can't deny it. You and I have the honour of belonging to them, and we ought to be proud of it. Compare what they've done, for example, with what the Pomfrets did. You've never heard of them? Exactly! Why should you have heard of them? Well, the Pomfrets were the big people in this district in Norman times and right through to the eighteenth century. They had the chance of making the best of it for seven hundred years. And what did they do with it? Next to nothing as far as I can see. You don't read their names in history. They just hung on dully, selfishly, unimaginatively where they'd been put, and built one or two passable houses, with slave labour of course, for their own convenience. Here's one of them—or all that is left of it: Old Mawne Hall."

On their right Bella saw two gables of Tudor brick rising above a wall protecting an ancient cherry-orchard. The wall had been strengthened in places with wrought-iron stays where the soil, undermined by the pits, had subsided, and one of the gable-ends of the house had been split from top to bottom in a jagged fracture resembling conventional fork-lightning. Even the trees of the orchard shared in the general air of decay and dilapidation. Though some boughs were fledged with sparse leaf they showed no signs of the fruit which should now be set, while others, already dead, had shed their bark and appeared like bleached bones amid the meagre foliage.

"Quite charming in its way," Wilburn said. "I like those enormous stables. It's the smoke from Willis's colliery that has blasted those cherry-trees. Still, when all's said and done, the Great Mawne Colliery's alive,

while Old Mawne Hall—like the Pomfrets themselves—is stone-dead."

Bella smiled. "It's not easy to make out a convincing case for ugliness."

Wilburn pulled up his horse. "Do you call this
ugly?" he said. "Allow me to introduce you to your
inheritance, Miss Tinsley. There is Hayseech!"

Neither the place nor the moment could have been
better chosen for this revelation. It was the sudden-
ness of the vision that made it so dramatic. He had
brought her, without warning, to the edge of Mawne
Bank, a precipitous bluff at whose base the languid
Stour, finding a voice, swirled turbidly through a deep
dingle or holloway to its confluence with the Lapsley
Brook. On their side of the stream loomed the arid
flank of the Great Mawne Colliery's spoil-heap, a
symmetrical mound with smouldering screes of slack
and cinder; on the other rose the hanging woods which
concealed Mr. Willis's domain; while between, in the
huge angle opened by the divergent lines of these
flanking masses, there lay outspread, at a glance, the
whole sombre sweep of the Hayseech valley, choked
from end to end and from side to side with its
portentous agglomeration of shop-roofs and colliery
head-gear and smoke-stacks and furnaces.

From no other point of view could a spectator so
well have compassed its material immensity. Here
the slope of the Hayseech valley rose to meet, as it
were, the downward-gazing eye, and the area of black-

ened roofs seemed to have been tilted in order that
no square foot of its acreage should be lost. It was
the uniform sooty blackness of the works, perceived
through a quivering haze of steam or hot air which
magnified every shape, that made their bulk so impressive. They were all of one colour, or rather of
none. In the whole of their extent not a blade of
green grass or weed could be seen. It seemed as
though the entire valley had been swept and blackened
by fire until no life was left in it; and the fact that
it was Saturday afternoon, in a slack season of the year,
reinforced this impression. The vast organism lay
silent, suspended, still. Kilns and furnaces were
banked down; in the shops no driving-bands hummed
and writhed; on the pit-headgear no spinning wheel
turned; on the rails no bustling engine shunted or
shrieked; on their cables the laden trolleys had come
to a stop. Hayseech, that tremendous source of
mechanical energy, lay there motionless, at first sight
resembling some fabulous, black-hided monster which
had died in its sleep.

Yet, even beneath that apparent suspension of
activity, an enormous potential of chained energy made
itself felt. There was still life in that giant shape:
life compressed in the tubes of boilers that simmered
above the banked fires; life urgent in the arterial
channels of steel pipes distributing steam; life tingling
in storage-batteries and in the reticulations of live-wire
which, like night-spun gossamer, festooned and

spanned the workshops; life of white-hot gases
flickering in black furnace-bellies—which at the movement of a lever, the opening of a throttle, the turning of a steam-cock, the sliding of a switch, might
flood the gigantic body to its last valve or filament with
the power and speed and thunder of a battle-fleet in
action.

"There is Hayseech," Ernest Wilburn repeated.
"Well, what do you think of it?"

Bella spoke in a whisper. "I hardly know. It's so
big and so quiet."

"Aren't you proud of it?"

"I can't say. It makes me feel small. It rather
frightens me."

"Well, you're not very enormous, are you? Do you
realize that your grandfather made it, from the first
brick to the last?"

For a moment they stood gazing in silence; then
Wilburn said:

"I think we had better move on. Your aunt is expecting us."

Bella was glad when, having descended Mawne
Bank, they reached the holloway where long rows of
cottages, which had been concealed by the fall of the
land, reassured her with a sense of neighbourly
humanity. The rows were not beautiful, having been
built of Tinsley's Blue Brick; yet each house had a strip
of garden in front and behind, and the men who
lounged in their shirt-sleeves, the women who gos-

siped, the children who played, seemed so happily absorbed in their private concerns that they scarcely turned to gape at the strangers' passing. Every block of houses in the rows carried a freestone plaque carved with the date of its erection and the inscription J. T. & Co. On the railway siding beyond the brook stood long trains of empty wagons. The words *Jos. Tinsley & Co.* were painted on each. And here, full in front, rose an enormous triple gateway admitting the railway line, which here crossed the road, and two tracks of wheeled traffic. All three gates were closed, and a number of notice-boards proclaimed that there was no admission except on business by order of Jos. Tinsley & Co.; but at the summons of a bell which Wilburn clanged a man with one leg and a hook for an arm stumped out to demand what they wanted.

"Yo' cau' come this road, gaffer," he declared. "Not Saturdays."

Wilburn explained that they were going to Miss Mortimer's. "And this lady," he said, smiling at Bella, "is Miss Tinsley."

If he had expected her name to make an impression he was disappointed. The word "Tinsley" associated with a human being had no significance to the mutilated gate-keeper who, still surly, dragged open one gate with his hook to let them pass.

"Yo'd ought to 'ave gone the other road," he grumbled. "Yo'd ought to 'ave knowed better than come in this road Saturday."

Now that they had actually entered them the works seemed to Bella to have shrunk to more natural dimensions. There were wide alleys, it seemed, between the black sheds. At close quarters, in spite of its blackness, Hayseech did not appear sinister. The sun had burst out. Several workmen, from whom Wilburn enquired the way, were less surly and more forthcoming than the gatekeeper, though Bella found it difficult to interpret their uncouth dialect. It seemed they must go through the brickill and over the bonk, but that beyond the offices there wasn't no 'oss-road. And indeed, half-way up the hill, the slag-faced road came to an end, so that Wilburn was forced to tie up his horse, and the last lap of their journey took them through sickly shrubberies of laurel which had been planted to separate rather than to screen the house from the works.

And what a house! Bella thought. It stood there isolated on the bank like a toy which some giant's child had abandoned. Its shape had no relation to the site, or to surroundings with which the anæmic pink of its brick-work appeared to be in conflict. Even the Fladburns' Alvaston house, an example of the same school and period, had, at least, the mitigating grace of smooth lawns and well-grown trees; but on Hayseech Bank, perpetually fanned by the works' exhalations, no tree would consent to grow. The house stood as naked as when it was first inhabited, with no sign of age but the stigma of its out-moded style and the leprosy with which acid smoke had ulcerated its stone mullions and blank escutcheons. Bella's heart fell when she contemplated it not merely as an unwelcome possession but as a possible place of abode. It appeared to be not only hideous but also uninhabited. There was a mortal blankness about the front windows: a feeling that nobody ever looked out of them—which seemed natural enough when one reflected how little there was to look at. Yet those window-panes through which Bella peered were free from the soot with which, surely, the proximity of the works must continually defile them, and the curtains of Nottingham lace, symmetrically arranged over loops of brass chain on either side, were of an almost distressing whiteness —as if they had been first bleached and then hermetically sealed within a glazed show-case.

"I'm sure we've made a mistake," Bella whispered. "It's empty. Nobody lives here. I don't think I like it. It makes me feel nervous."

Wilburn laughed. "No, this is the house all right. I've been here once before in your grandfather's time. I'll ring."

The wires of the bell-pull scraped and a distant bell tinkled. A door, opening within, suddenly flooded the hall with light. Through the crude stained-glass of the front door, whose brassy yellow gave the interior an effect not of sunlight but of perpetual fog, Bella saw a tall, angular figure approaching. Its fingers turned a key—"How odd," Bella thought, "that the door should be locked"—then with a curious effect as of clearing fog, the door opened slowly.

"How do you do, Miss Mortimer?" Ernest Wilburn said.

Time had dealt sternly yet not unkindly with Harriet Mortimer. She was now in her forty-fourth year. The lateness of her physical development (as compared with that of Bella's mother who, though five years younger, had reached womanhood when her sister was still a girl) had been balanced by a corresponding contraction at the other end of the scale, resembling in this the habit of some plants whose seasons of flower and fruition are so late, so brief and so unnoticeable as to seem of little account in the organism's life. Such, undoubtedly, had been the natural history of Hattie Mortimer. If she had blossomed at all, the event had passed without notice in the obscurity of Hayseech; the surprising bloom had withered, its perfume had faded, like those of the night-flowering cactus which blooms in darkness and for a single night. Yet if nature might seem to have cheated Harriet in one way it had given her compensations in others. If her body had never known the delights of passion it had escaped its scars: if she had never (as they say) "been young" she need never grow old. Middle age had pointed her physical resemblance to her father. Her hair, like his, had turned that pure white which has no shade of yellow in it; her eyebrows were thick and black, the black and the white combining to clear the depth of her fine hazel eyes. Her upper lip was still darkened with what seemed more like a shadow than a moustache. Her teeth, when she smiled, were white and regular. But it was rarely that Hattie Mortimer smiled—she did not smile now—and the general effect upon Bella at that moment was less that of the distinction which she undoubtedly possessed than of agelessness and of an unusual innocence. If her face had been detached from the rest of her body, which was too angular and too thin for grace, and from her clothes, a black dress of some dull-surfaced stuff with a high, whaleboned neck-band, it might have been taken at first sight for that of a refined old gentleman with an astonishing complexion or of a delicately-featured man of middle age whose hair had gone white prematurely. There was a suggestion of physical unreality, of something having been left out, so that the sound of her voice, which was dry and a little harsh, and the unrefined midland accent with which she spoke, came not only as a surprise but also as an assurance of normality.

"Will you step in, Mr. Wilburn?" she said. "The girl's shopping in Halesby and I was putting the kettle to boil. You've come the wrong way."

She was speaking to Wilburn, but her eyes, those innocent eyes of clear hazel, were fixed all the time upon Bella: fixed so intently that Bella wondered what they saw, and felt herself blushing. Was that scrutiny

hostile, she asked herself, or critical, or merely inquisitive? Did this woman resent her as an interloper
and grudge her her inheritance—she felt she wanted
to explain that it wasn't her fault she had "come into"
Hayseech—or did that glance imply only the envy,
the intolerance, of sere middle age for youth? She
could not tell: those eyes were as inexpressive as an
animal's, as impersonal as clear jasper. "But I mustn't
let her stare me out of countenance," Bella thought,
until, all of a sudden, she was aware of a change so
startling that she might almost have believed she was
gazing at another person. Harriet Mortimer's enig-
matical expressionless face suddenly softened; her lips
smiled; her mouth became beautiful; her impersonal
eyes smiled too—they were gentle with tears. In silence
she held out her arms to Bella; and Bella, who, a
moment before, had felt frozen and uncertain, came to
them without hesitation, warmly returning her kiss.
Her heart, which she had lately assured herself was
impervious to emotion of any kind, opened freely,
generously, unreservedly to welcome this woman's
affection. Was it, perhaps, she asked herself, because
her Aunt Harriet was a woman, because the love which
she feared and distrusted was the love of men? Or was
it rather because in this meeting, after years of solitude among strangers, she was aware, for the first time,
of an association more natural and more homogeneous
than any she had known? This woman who had taken
her to her arms was, after all, of her own blood,

and nearer to her than any other human being she had known since she was a child. It seemed to her that in this embrace she had been discharged of a great loneliness; she was returning—bruised, for all her fine show of courage—to the people and to the place to which she belonged.

When she raised her head Wilburn noticed that her cheeks, though flushed becomingly, were wet with tears. Miss Tinsley, it seemed, was not ashamed of them, for she begged her aunt to lend her a handkerchief. Even to a cut-and-dried family lawyer—as he called himself—this was a touching scene. Incidentally it confirmed what he had guessed already: that his delightful client was not nearly so hard as she seemed.

"I have put you to sleep in your mother's room," Aunt Harriet said as she kissed her good night. The hours after Wilburn's departure had been an odd experience. They had sat on opposite sides of a cold fireplace decorated for the summer with a folded fan of white paper, not in the musty seclusion of the drawing-room—resembling a museum in which specimens of mid-Victorian middle-class taste had been piously preserved—where they had "taken" tea, but in the living-room, equally innocent of ornament in good taste or bad, in which meals were eaten on ordinary occasions. On the left of the fireplace stood an ample upholstered armchair, on the right, another of shiny black oak,

K

straight-backed, with a chintz-covered cushion on the seat. Aunt Harriet sat bolt-upright in this, her hands folded on her lap, rather as though she were posing for her portrait; but when Bella moved to occupy the other, her aunt's cheeks flushed suddenly.

"That is your grandfather's chair," she said, implying, it seemed, that to sit in it so soon after his death would be an act of sacrilege which might inconvenience him if he reappeared—and indeed, when she looked at it, Bella saw that the upholstery was indented as though by the pressure of invisible limbs. "If you will pull up that basket-chair," Aunt Harriet said, "you will find it equally comfortable."

It seemed strange to Bella that they two should be sitting in silence like this on either side of that empty chair and, so illogically, facing the paper fan in the hearth. She had tried at first to conduct a conversation, but Aunt Harriet tacitly declined to take her part in it. Such was her habit: Jasper Mortimer had been habitually a silent man. When he came home from the works in the evening he had looked for his supper. After that was eaten he had put on his spectacles and scanned the morning paper—more particularly the columns which dealt with the North Bromwich metal exchange—until his attention flagged, his head nodded, and he woke with a start which reminded him that it was time to take off his glasses and go to bed.

Harriet had assisted at this quiet ritual nearly every

evening for thirty years. In the ordinary way she had filled in the hours of silence by darning her father's old socks and knitting new ones or even underwear. But now that there was no more need to knit, she just sat in her accustomed chair with folded hands. She did not speak because speaking at this hour was unusual, and silence seemed natural. Was all life at Hayseech to be as blank and inexpressive as this? Bella wondered.

They sat there until the light faded. Then the "girl" who had been said to be shopping in Halesby clumped into the room. Her name, inappropriately, was Helen, and in the ordinary sense of the word she was not a girl but a stunted woman of sixty who had been in service at Hayseech since her mistress's childhood. She had a poking face with a shiny complexion and scanty fair hair of the kind that with age goes toneless rather than grey, wisps of which were dragged into a bun beneath a cap with long streamers. Her small pale blue eyes, with blinking lids that were red-rimmed and lashless, gave her a furtive, inquisitive air. With a taper she lit the three gas-jets of an ornate brass chandelier above the table. In order to turn on the taps she had to climb on a chair. Bella saw her elastic-sided boots beneath a pair of bow-legs, and in the window, now converted into a mirror by the darkness outside, a framed reflection of her somewhat grotesque figure which resembled that of a female in a Hogarth cartoon. When she had lit the three fish-tail burners she proceeded to lay the table, finally announcing that supper was ready.

Aunt Harriet's silence during that meal was even more embarrassing than that which had preceded it. Bella began to wonder if it was a symptom of awkwardness or of positive dislike. Yet those clear hazel eyes, it seemed to her, were not unfriendly. Perhaps, she concluded, it was no more than the habit of a woman so accustomed to solitude as to have lost both the faculty and the desire of expressing herself; and now, reflecting on the negation of life which such solitude implied—a solitude which beginning before Bella herself was born had lasted ever since—she found nothing surprising in this silence or in the inexpressiveness of this face on which neither joy nor suffering had graved its record. She felt, indeed, as though she were the woman of experience and Aunt Harriet the child; and the thought of this cloistral innocence and of a beauty (for she must have been beautiful in her way) which had flowered and faded without anyone—and its possessor least of all—being aware of it, filled her mind with tenderness—an emotion which was new to it—and a desire to be kind.

So that now, when the supper-table had been cleared, and they resumed their silent stations, Bella was not merely no longer puzzled and embarrassed but actually consoled by the quietness that was imposed on her. After all, habitually, people talked far too much and said very little. It wasn't only by talking that human beings came to know and understand one another, as the course of this evening proved; for she was prepared to affirm that her Aunt Harriet and she had begun to share, without speech and in a short space of time, a greater degree of spiritual understanding than she had ever experienced before. This comforting fact was not easy to explain—if it needed explaining—unless there were more elements in a blood-relationship than one took for granted; unless it meant that for the first time in her conscious life (for the human relationships of childhood were mainly instinctive) she found herself in touch with, quite literally, a "kindred" spirit: a spirit which shared a common store of that inherited experience which constituted, perhaps, the unconscious basis of conscious thought and behaviour. After all, they both partook of the inheritance of Jasper Mortimer's black eyebrows. Wasn't it plausible, at least, to suppose that the common inheritance might extend to characteristics deeper and subtler? How else could she account for this intimate sense of rest and security—so different from the appearance of composure which, since her disaster, she had imposed upon herself as a protective colouring—unless, again, Hayseech itself—the place in which her Tinsley forbears had lived for so many centuries, had something to do with it. The effect of these speculations was a little bewildering; for her mind, though romantic, was not naturally inclined to be mystical, and that night she was more tired than she knew. Even so, when Aunt Harriet had kissed her good night and quietly closed the door of her mother's bedroom behind her, she had a feeling that one stage, at least, of her life's journey had been completed, that, in a sense, she had come home.

III

THAT bedroom, in which, twenty-five years before, her mother had spent so many hours of passionate meditation—in which the dream out of which Bella herself had taken flesh, had been born—became the centre round which her new existence revolved. It was simple to the degree of austerity. The light which poured in through its blindless windows revealed the bareness of the white enamelled bedstead and furniture, the bleached cotton bedspread, the walls, innocent of pictures, on whose papering the sprigged roses of eighteen-fifty had lost their colour. Its face was as virginal as that of a nun. It had lain vacant so long that not even the ghost of a memory remained in it, every trace of human permanence had been dusted and swept and scrubbed away by the earnest spring-cleanings of a quarter of a century. It was as empty, Bella thought, as a blank sheet of white paper. And that simile pleased her; for the surface of her life, at that moment, resembled a blank sheet too, all her previous inadequate essays of living having been happily scrapped and forgotten.

Her bedroom's one large window commanded the works. It would be truer to say that the works commanded her window, for they filled its whole frame

with their sombre bulk. During her first night at Hayseech and throughout the following day, which was
Sunday, she had hardly been aware of time; but on
the third morning, in the first grey of dawn, she was
awakened by the bellow of the great bull, or steam-
syren, which summoned the hands of Jos. Tinsley &
Co. to work. From this close range the bull's vibrations invaded her bedroom; they shook the window-
panes and filled it with a sound that was like the buzzing
of a swarm of enormous bees. Bella, waking, jumped
out of bed and hurried to the window to see where
the sound came from. Outside there was nothing visible
but a bank of white summer mist, settling low in the
valley. This dense coverlet hid the works, but through
its upper and thinner layers invisible chimney-stacks
spouted volumes of curdled smoke. When the noise
of the Hayseech bull had subsided she heard the bel-
lowings of others more distant—such as Willis's at
Mawne and Bulgin's and Hackett's at Halesby—and
these melancholy sounds, which were like echoes of the
first, reminded her of descriptions she had read of fog-
bound estuaries where liners groped their way to their
moorings, hooting all the time. Now the light of day
was increasing. The flocculent smoke, which at first
had seemed to lie on the surface of the mist like a scum,
began to combine with it, sinking down of its own
weight of oils and carbon and turning the white vapours
yellow, until the sun, climbing, burst through the
thinned fog, and the mass of the works became mani-

fest, hazily clothed in that characteristic Black Country air which not only appears to have been tinged with soot and sulphur but tastes and smells of them.

By the time that its shape became visible Bella could have no doubt that Hayseech was alive and awake. Wherever she looked she could see a bewildering multiplicity of movement: on the earth human figures hurrying here and there with an obscure purposiveness; high in air wheels of colliery hauling-gear that span round merrily on the network of sidings, engines that snorted and whistled and shunted trucks that collided; over the hillside, above the pit-head, the files of squat trollies creeping insect-like to and fro in contrary motion.

And each of these objects that moved visibly, together with many invisible, contributed its share, considerable or minute, to the composite rumour of the works: to that great surge of perpetual sound which Bella soon came to recognize as the voice of Hayseech. From the distance of her window it was hard to discriminate one sound from another: they were so many, so various in tone and in intensity, and the volume of the whole seemed to vary from day to day, almost from hour to hour, with the set of the wind or subtler conditions of atmosphere; yet it was composed, as a whole, of noises metallic and gaseous: sibilant steam, humming dynamos, throbbing lathes, batteries of clicking or thudding or mightily-thundering hammers; red-hot forgings hissing as they were plunged into cool-

K*

ing-tanks; rumour of rolling-mills that drew from mangled metal shrieks as of pain; stutterings of exhausts, thrummings of fans, profound snorings of furnace-draught; deafening stertor of steam blown off under pressure; screeches of wagon-wheels, clanking of couplings, dull clashes of buffers—all these elements and a hundred more were merged in that volume of ceaseless, insensate sound which resembled, at a distance, nothing more than the tuning-up of a Plutonic orchestra, and yet, strangely enough, had a rhythm, a pulse of its own, as though, like the body of a living organism, it were controlled and vitalized by a single brain and heart.

As she gazed at Hayseech from her window Bella was no longer intimidated but fascinated. After all, this monster was largely her private possession. In this respect Wilburn had fired her imagination. She refused to consider the works as outside her province. If she owned them she wanted to know and to understand them. She told her Aunt Harriet so.

Miss Mortimer was somewhat shocked. Neither she nor Bella's mother had ever been allowed to have anything to do with the works or with anyone in them. They were a purely masculine mystery. Bella laughed. Her Aunt Harriet had yet to learn that the days of purely masculine mysteries were over. Miss Cash's feminist armoury supplied her with arguments. It was a long time now since women had left behind them such modest aspirations as those reflected in *Princess Ida!* No doubt this might be, Aunt Harriet returned. Even so she could find no precedent for this impropriety. Neither Mrs. Willis of Mawne nor Lady Hingston of Stourford had ever, so far as she knew, presumed to invade the great works with which their males were connected.

"But then," Bella said, "they have men to represent them. And I haven't; that's precisely why I want to see things for myself."

"You won't understand them, Bella."

"At least I can try. After all, the works are more or less mine. Who is in charge since grandpa died?"

Aunt Harriet wasn't quite sure. She supposed Mr. Wilkinson.

Next morning, prepared for the adventure in clothes that were as impressive and as unsuitable as they well could be, she picked her way delicately between the heaps of slag and piles of metallic debris and presented herself at the office, a building of staring terra-cotta, which stood on the site of the house where her mother had been born. A weedy young man with adenoids received her. Indeed, all the clerks in the office at Hayseech, whose heads, one by one, popped out to get sight of this unusual visitor, had the blanched look of sprouts or sea-kale forced in a cellar. She enquired confidently for Mr. Wilkinson. The clerk looked shocked. She might with equal propriety, it seemed, have enquired at the gates of heaven for

God the Father. Mr. Wilkinson, it appeared, was not accessible to common folk like herself. It struck her that the clerk imagined she was a typist looking for a job. He was evidently no student of costume.

"Will you tell Mr. Wilkinson Miss Tinsley would like to see him?"

"*What* name?"

"Miss Tinsley."

"All right, miss."

The pale young man hurried away and shortly returned. Mr. Wilkinson would see her in a moment. She was not invited to sit down, so stood, amused by his lack of manners. The office depressed her: it had been built more than thirty years, and had begun to look shabby. The air inside it was foul: it smelt of stale oil and grime and unclean clothes. No wonder the clerks who worked in it had such bad complexions. Even on an oppressive morning like this nobody dreamt of opening a window. They looked, indeed, as if they had never been opened, so deeply were they encrusted and bleared with soot. But perhaps, after all, Bella thought, the clerks were wiser to leave them closed; for the air which blew in from the desert outside whenever the swing-doors opened was parched and dusty and sulphurous and hot as a simoon, and with it there entered all the noises of the works, which, however romantically they might sound at a distance, were certainly a torment at close quarters.

A door at the other end of the office opened. A

man came towards her. He was tall and gaunt, with a pronounced stoop, his figure all angles distorting a suit of shiny blue serge. His face was shrewd and careworn, his brow deeply furrowed beneath scurfy grey hair. His complexion was as colourless as the others', save for his prominent nose, the veins of which seemed to be congested by the pressure of spectacles whose bridge bit into its base. He smiled, and the smile showed good teeth.

"And what can I do for *you?*" he said with a North-country accent.

"I want to see Mr. Wilkinson."

"I am Mr. Wilkinson."

"And I am Miss Tinsley."

"Yes?"

The start was not encouraging.

"I should like to see over the works, if I may."

Mr. Wilkinson pursed his lips. "Well, I suppose that's quite possible. I'll see if I can find somebody to show you round."

Bella was growing angry. "I would rather you came with me yourself, Mr. Wilkinson."

He stared at her in surprise. "Well, really. . . . As a matter of fact . . ."

"I gather that you have been more or less in charge since my grandfather's death?"

"Yes." He laughed, and that laugh was the least unpleasant part of him. "That's exactly why, at the moment, my time's rather precious. Things are a little involved. However . . ." He smiled; and now the smile struck her as charming. "However, I'll take you. Come along."

He addressed her rather as if she were an exacting child whom he had decided to humour. As they stepped out into the works—her works, not his—Bella felt at a disadvantage. He apologized for his incompetence as a guide. "One of my clerks, a fellow named Bailey, usually takes people round. Your grandfather had a strong objection to visitors."

"Which you share, Mr. Wilkinson."

"Which, generally speaking, I share, Miss Tinsley."

"I've not come out of mere curiosity. I'm interested, you know."

"I admire your enterprise. If you could have seen the works ten years ago, when first I came here from the Tyne, the sight would have been—what shall I say?—somewhat more inspiriting. This spot we're on now is the original centre of the works: Tinsley's Brickill, they called it. It was started by your great-grandfather."

"It looks like a crater."

"Aye, the crater of a dead volcano. All the clay they made the blue bricks from was dug out years ago. We have one or two other pockets which keep the kilns going; but this one is now nothing more than a sump for surface water."

"Isn't the water useful?"

"Useful? Water useful?" He ran his hands through his hair. "Water is the bane and terror of my life. Your grandfather and I and the Drainage Commissioners have been fighting water for the last ten years. It's the curse of this coalfield. If we'd closed down these pits—every one of them—over six years ago, Hayseech 'ld be worth twice as much as it is to-day."

"Well, why didn't you close them down then?"

"If you'd known Mr. Mortimer, Miss Tinsley, you wouldn't ask me that question. First of all there was his pride. He was a man who would never own himself beaten, not even by nature. More than that— though this, too, was perhaps another part of his pride —he wasn't going to see his pay-roll go down and the men who had worked for him, father and son, on the bank. Yet oddly enough, you know, even they didn't love him."

"Still, it's rather fine, isn't it?"

"Ay, it's fine enough in one way. Not too fine for the ordinary shareholders, and not too fine for the other departments of the works whose profits have been poured down the drain, as you might say, in pumping. You'll not mind my saying this?"

"I'm not a child, Mr. Wilkinson."

He looked at her, smiling approval. "I can tell you one thing: you're your grandfather's grandchild, Miss Tinsley."

As they moved through the works he gradually lost

the air of resentment with which he had started their
tour. He showed none of that patronizing indulgence
of a man of the world towards a pretty woman which
had sometimes, it must be confessed, offended her
slightly in the attitude of Ernest Wilburn. Perhaps
it was her resemblance to her grandfather which had
wrought this change in him. If that were so, she was
proud of it. But whatever the cause may have been
she was astonished and, somehow, touched by the way
in which this uncouth and unattractive man began to
talk to her, if not as an equal intelligence at least as a
confidante.

It was not only the coal-pits, she learnt, which had
suffered from inundation. Indeed some of the best
seams—the brooch-coal, for example—were already
nearly exhausted and would be better abandoned. The
flooding had also restricted the output of ironstone:
"Not that this," the manager told her, "matters so
much to us to-day as it did. When I came here, Josiah
Tinsley & Co. were best known as producers of
wrought iron. We had twenty furnaces turning out
puddled bar. But wrought iron is going under now—
going under steadily beneath the competition of steel.
Why? I'll tell you the truth: because steel's the better
material for general purposes; because puddling's a
handicraft—machine-puddling's no good—and steel-
making's a mechanical process. Wrought iron's as
helpless against steel as a hand-loom against a power-
loom."

"But can't we make steel?"

"Your grandfather asked himself that. That's why, in the last few years, he sank so much money in the new works in South Wales. I have nothing to do with them. My job is Hayseech. My heart's in Hayseech, Miss Tinsley, if you take my meaning. Let me answer your question. Have you any conception of what the economical unit of a modern steel-plant would cost? The best part of two million pounds! And even if we erected it we should have to bring our materials from far afield. Even the coal we have left isn't suitable for coking. Imagine Hayseech buying coal! No, no, that's impossible. Too late. . . . As we are, the concern as a whole is just holding its own; but that's due more to Mr. Mortimer's personal sacrifices than to itself. If I can keep it going at that pitch, I shall be more than satisfied. But it's a hard furrow I have to plough, I assure you, Miss Tinsley, and the way things are going it's likely to be harder still. Of course miracles happen sometimes . . ."

"Miracles?"

"The American Civil War was one, and the Franco-Prussian another."

"But that's rather dreadful, isn't it?"

"Well . . . they made your grandfather. I wish to God we'd not lost him."

They had reached, at this point of their tour, the company's board-room, where, over the seat which he had occupied as chairman, the portrait of Jasper Mor-

timer presented to him by the Iron and Steel Institute
dominated the empty table. Bella gazed at it. The
painting was no more than a conventional piece of por-
traiture; yet even through this inadequate medium
the personality of that old man asserted itself: beneath the fixed pose his body had the quality of a
steel spring at tension; the dark eyes seemed to
smoulder with a fire which owed nothing to the
painter's skill: a tragic fire, Bella thought, a fire of
frustration. The man was tired and lonely. She said,
suddenly:

"Were you fond of him, Mr. Wilkinson?"

"Fond of him? No, not exactly. He didn't inspire
affection. There were parts of him that I hated:
for one thing, he wasn't just. For another, he was
an unreasoning autocrat, who acted by instinct. He
believed that Hayseech was himself: *L'état, c'est
moi*—which meant that he refused to delegate anything. I'm suffering from that now, and so is Hayseech. The threads fell from his hands in a tangle,
so to speak. I'm still sorting them out—not very
successfully!"

"And I'm wasting your time. You must forgive
me."

He was silent. Bella had a feeling that he might
have assured her there was nothing to forgive. Ernest
Wilburn, in his place, would certainly have been more
polite. She laughed. "Ah—I see that you won't.
Well, that's honest anyway. You realize that I'm not

merely inquisitive? After all I have reasons—material as well as sentimental—for wanting to understand Hayseech, haven't I?"

"Most certainly you have. And I'll help you if I can."

"You've helped me already, although I can't say you've encouraged me."

"Courage isn't a quality in which you appear to be lacking, Miss Tinsley."

Well, that was a sort of compliment: the only one with which she returned from her interview. That morning's adventure had modified her vision of Hayseech. Now an element of pity was added to the enthusiasm and awe with which at first she had regarded it. Gazing down from her window on the works, continually impressed by their simmering activity which, beginning at daybreak, continued till nightfall, and even in darkness made itself felt by volcanic rumblings and sudden flashes that lightened the perpetual tawny glow in the sky, she found it hard to believe that this monstrous concern with whose fortunes her own were linked—this gigantic growth with its roots so deeply implanted in the earth—was, if not exactly moribund, struggling for life.

According to her nature she saw that struggle in a romantic light and made it her own. Above all, the figure of her grandfather had touched her imagination. She was interested in him not so much as the creator of Hayseech but as a remarkable human being

directly responsible for the engaging mysteries of her
own personality. She sought information from her
Aunt Harriet, without much success. Aunt Harriet,
it seemed, knew very little about him; she had
regarded him with veneration and affection, but with
no curiosity. From her Bella turned to a mine of more
payable ore, to the accumulation of documents stored
in the attics of Hayseech, which constituted, in fact, a
complete record of its history from its earliest origins
to the foundation of the series of limited companies
controlled by Jos. Tinsley & Co.

Miss Mortimer regarded her niece's passionate researches as eccentric if not indiscreet or even indelicate.
Her ideas of a woman's sphere had been fixed thirty
years before by the admirable Miss Beagle. She was
shocked rather than elated when Bella discovered the
faded documents relating to the Tinsleys' successful
resistance of the Pomfrets' threatened enclosure, and
the weekly pay-rolls of the "brickill" laboriously kept
in the almost illiterate hand of the first Arabella. She
was Miss Mortimer of Hayseech, a woman of
property, an object of respect and a paragon of
respectability in the small world of Halesby; and no
advantage was to be gained by what she called "ferret-
ing" into the less creditable past. She was unable to
imagine the origin of Bella's enthusiasm: which was
her restlessness, her need of being violently engrossed
in some interest outside the empty leisure of Hayseech. She was still hurt and disorientated, though she

refused to admit it, by the defection of Henry Fladburn.

How empty that leisure was Aunt Harriet had no power to realize. Having never experienced any other condition of life, she was satisfied with it. She was flattered, indeed, by the curiosity and social interest which Bella's romantic succession to the property aroused. People wanted to examine the heiress about whom they had been talking. Invitations poured in from houses which she had respected but only visited rarely on formal occasions. Mrs. Willis of Mawne, even Lady Hingston of Stourford, the baronet's wife, gave "full-dress" dinner-parties in Bella's honour. Miss Mortimer had the impression of being admitted at last, not before the compliment was due, to a social sphere of unique and heady brilliance, and blossomed accordingly.

It is to her credit that she never showed the least sign of jealousy or of envy for the facility with which Bella appeared to shine. The child had the faculty of adapting herself to all kinds of society. She was equally at ease with Walter Willis's mutton-fisted compliments, with his son Edward's shy admiration, and with Sir Joseph Hingston's heavy solemnity. She could hold her own with all of them—even with Lady Hingston, who was the district's nearest approach to a woman of fashion and was generally feared for the uncertainty of her temper and the extravagance of her wit. To meet these unusual social demands Miss

Mortimer equipped herself, under Bella's direction, with two new "costumes," one for afternoons, one for evenings. Though she insisted on their preserving the style of eighteen-seventy, Bella's taste made the most of her aunt's natural dignity. For the first time in her life Miss Mortimer's timidity permitted her to feel herself a person of public importance. She accepted the position shyly and gratefully but with reservations, assuring herself that she knew just what it was worth. It would take more than that to "turn the head" of a daughter of Jasper Mortimer.

Nor, she noted with satisfaction, was Bella's head turned. She, too, was sustaining the family reputation for hardness. Bella and she, in fact, by this time were becoming great friends. It took several months for Aunt Harriet to overcome not only her suspicions of an invader who, although she was her niece, was a stranger, but also the habit of taciturnity which had become second nature. Now, when once the ice of her suppressed thoughts and emotions was thawed, their content overflowed like an alpine torrent in summer. When they were alone together—but only then—she became almost loquacious; and her mind, which at first had seemed to Bella a mere vacuum, discharged itself of a detailed accumulation of memories and a shrewd commentary on the present, leavened always (and this was the quality which amazed her most) by an acute observation and a humour, often sardonic, which took point from the vivid phraseology of her Black Country speech. It was still natural for her to keep silence, to watch with those fine hazel eyes of hers rather than to speak; but when once the floodgates were opened and her fancy given rein, Aunt Harriet became an entertaining companion.

Above all when she spoke of the past: the period about which Bella, naturally, was most curious. She was particularly anxious to learn all she could about her mother and the passionate romance in which her own being had originated. This was the one subject on which, whenever it was broached, Aunt Harriet became distant and frigid and uncommunicative.

"Your mother and I," she said coldly, "had never much in common. Indeed I knew very little about her: all this happened so long ago. Her hair was the same colour as yours, of course, but she hadn't your eyes or eyebrows or your disposition. Nobody would ever have taken her for a Mortimer. In any case it's no use bothering me with questions, Bella, because my memory's shocking. She behaved very badly to your dear grandfather: that's all I can tell you."

"He behaved very harshly to *her*, Aunt Harriet."

"She disobeyed him. He was within his rights. If he was harsh, he was always just."

"Mr. Wilkinson . . ." Bella began, then checked herself: this was hardly fair. Even though Mr. Wilkinson thought differently nothing was to be gained by quoting him. By this time she had guessed why Aunt Harriet protested ignorance on the subject of her sister. It was because it happened to display Jasper Mortimer in an unpleasant light. In a spirit of fanaticism rather than of love she had created an unreal image of him which she worshipped with a hard, blind loyalty. She had immolated her own life—more than forty years of it—in the service of that idol, and was prepared to sacrifice anyone, sister or stranger, who, even through no fault of their own, detracted from its sublimity. Bella had not realized before how devilishly cruel a blind loyalty can be.

She was more fortunate in her investigations with Helen, the bow-legged "girl," whose accounts of her mother's adventure were circumstantial and highly romanticized. Helen, it seemed, had been her sole confidante in the Small affair; had left doors unlocked for her at night, and had even helped her to pack on the day of her disappearance. This vicarious experience of passion was the only one that had ever entered Helen's life. That was why her memory had treasured every detail of it.

"Why, I can see our Miss Bella, bless her heart, miss," she said, "every time that I look at you! I s'ld reckon that yo' and her was just of a size. And sometimes, when yo' speak of a sudden like, it fair gives me a turn: like the dead coming back, as they say! I can see her now, miss, coming into my kitchen one night on the tips of her toes and putting her hand over my mouth to stop me hollering. Then 'er'd croodle down anant my fire, all bivering with cold. 'Ooh, Helen,' she says, 'I'm that clammed, all my bones are frozen. Give me a cup of hot tea, Helen.' You see, miss, I always kep' a teapot on the hob, like. And then she says: 'Helen, come here. Can yo' keep a secret? I know yo' con, but will yo'? Put your 'ead down by me and I'll whisper. Helen,' she says, 'I'm in love!' That was the first I heard on it, Miss Bella, and it's twenty-four years ago. Her'd been going with your father that-was-to-be up by Lapsley Mill!"

So Aunt Harriet spoke of her grandfather and Helen of her mother, each made tender by reminiscence; but of the two it was the memories of her mother which touched Bella more deeply— chiefly, perhaps, because she emerged as a more human figure, more passionate, more fallible, more like herself. Aunt Harriet assured her again and again that she was a Mortimer; but when Helen dredging her cloudy waters of memory dragged up from the past those long inconsequent stories of hers, Bella's eager mind was able to seize on a hundred details which made her cry to herself: "Yes, *I* am like that: that's exactly what I should have said!" convincing herself (as she wished to be convinced) that she was a Tinsley for more reasons than a change of name by deed-poll.

The duality of her nature intrigued and fascinated her. It made her (if that were possible) even more interesting to herself. During this period, indeed, the shape of her life seemed strangely indeterminate, as though its disintegrated fragments had not yet found a new mould. Her interest in the works, in spite of Aunt Harriet's disapproval, remained intense. She had even succeeded in inviting her friend Mr. Wilkinson to supper. Aunt Harriet was profoundly shocked, not because she disliked Mr. Wilkinson or underrated the importance of his position, but because such a thing had never happened before.

"In your dear grandfather's time," she told Bella, "we always kept to ourselves. Nothing could have been more cordial than his relations with his employees, but they never set foot in the drawing-room as long as he lived. The necessary entertaining was always provided in North Bromwich. However, the house is now yours, and I suppose you can do what you like with it."

"I wanted to show Mr. Wilkinson the papers I found in the attic," Bella told her. "I know he'ld be interested."

"I don't see what they have to do with him or he with them," Aunt Harriet replied. "All I venture to hope is that you won't get yourself talked about. But of course you will do as you wish."

After this Mr. Wilkinson became a frequent visitor at the house on Hayseech Bank. There was never between him and Bella (in spite of Aunt Harriet's fears) the least hint of a romantic relationship. They were interested, both of them, in Hayseech; *he* was proud of it and loved it, and Bella was the first person—and perhaps the most appropriate—to whom he felt he could open his heart. He delighted in her swift intelligence and in the quickness with which her untechnical mind sometimes illuminated by chance aspects of his problems which hadn't occurred to him. When her comments missed fire—as they often did— and displayed her ignorance, he was not impatient. It impressed him to see with what determination she had set herself to the impossible and unprofitable task of understanding the various processes in which the works were engaged.

Bella was still interested in these subjects and resolved to master them; but she knew enough now to realize that the prospect which had flattered her imagination on its first contact with the works could never be attained. Hayseech was too big and too unwieldy, too hard, for its present or future to be affected by any thought or action of hers. From being a loose concatenation of mechanical units it had come, thanks to Jasper Mortimer, to resemble a living organism. Under his guidance it had finally reached a superb maturity, after which its bones and articulations had set, as it were: its shape and character could no more be changed or modified (even if he had lived to attempt it) than the term of its natural life could be prolonged or its decline averted.

So now, even when she was impressed by its

inherent power and magnitude—the giant, though
inclined to totter, was still a giant—Bella could never
contemplate Hayseech without a twinge of melancholy. In its own defeat it had defeated her. Apart
from her friendship with Wilkinson, she had formed
no human relation in the works. The anonymous
hordes who checked-in at the triple gates every morning and walked out of them every night had no personal significance for her. Although she supposed it
was her money that fed and clothed them, they hardly
troubled to look at her, and when they did, their faces
appeared to her surly. Wilkinson had often assured
her that she was mistaken in this. Though he himself
was a North Countryman, he admitted a great admiration for these Black Country folk; for their energy,
their adaptability, their humour, their common sense.
But Bella never got near enough to them to appreciate
these qualities. To her they seemed, like herself, mere
adjuncts to the decline of Hayseech: working parasites, but parasites all the same, on that sick body. As
soon as the body died and went cold, they would crawl
away and find another to batten on. She had a feeling
that she herself might be happier if she left it before
it died. When she thought about it too much, the
place got on her nerves.

That was why she experienced such relief in
escaping from the sound and smell of the works into
the Lapsley Valley. It, too, was haunted, of course;
yet frail ghosts were pleasanter company than the

solidly-moribund, and the perfume of a dead romance very different from the smell of corruption. Quite apart from its associations with her mother, with whom she felt an increasing kinship, the valley attracted her: it was beautiful in itself, and the black barrage of Hayseech made it lonely. Since the Fladburn affair she had developed a liking for solitude. Along the upper reaches of the Lapsley Brook, where its waters issued from the brambly thickets of Uffmoor Wold, she found herself able to indulge it, escaping not merely from Hayseech but from herself, and surrendering herself to sensations rather than to thoughts. Her Aunt Harriet found it hard to explain this wandering habit—or, perhaps, to find any explanation but one.

"I've missed you all afternoon, Bella," she would say. "Where on earth have you been?"

"Up the brook to the Mill and then on to the wood. It's delicious there now. The haws are like sealing-wax—you've no idea how brilliant. And the Traveller's Joy . . ."

Aunt Harriet grew uneasy. Lapsley Mill, after all, had unfortunate associations. "Going there all alone! Why, it's not even a beauty-spot. I can't think what you see in it. It's morbid, that's what it is."

Bella laughed; yet she couldn't be quite sure that this anxiety to escape wasn't a little morbid, until she considered the alternative: the static existence which poor Aunt Harriet appeared to accept without ques-

tion. It was far more morbid, surely, to be contented
to live like that: to acquiesce in the limitations,
spiritual as well as physical, by which not only Aunt
Harriet but all the rest of the females of the new
industrial aristocracy—Willises, Hacketts and so on—
preserved their darling illusion of social distinction.
It seemed terrible to her that these people should have
so much money and so little imagination with which
to make use of it; that they should sit idle, or uselessly
busy, year after year in their smug little backwaters
amid the smell and smoke of works, when they had
only to step beyond the smoke-screen to see the full
flood of adventurous life go swirling by in its rich and
various beauty. It was rarely that any of them did this
—as her mother had done.

Thus, little by little, the limitations of Hayseech
which, when first she came there, had been soothing
and not ungrateful to Bella, became, as she recovered
her natural pliancy, increasingly irksome. At Hayseech there was nobody who could understand her restlessness, so she made no confidences. Aunt Harriet,
in any case, would have regarded it as ungrateful if
not impious, while Mr. Wilkinson, grappling with
his grim material problems, would have been
astonished to learn that such things as spiritual
dilemmas existed.

Indeed, their only visitor from the outside world
was Ernest Wilburn, who drove down from time to
time in his dashing turn-out, with matters to be dis-

cussed or papers to be signed. Although for her taste
he was rather too obviously a "ladies' man," Bella
welcomed Wilburn's visits. Though he came there on
business, business was only part of his life. He was
ready, and seemed even relieved, to put it aside at the
first opportunity. He preferred to talk about plays
and music and pictures and scenery, and did so, en-
chantingly. Sometimes he lent her books which would
certainly have shocked Aunt Harriet if she had read
them, and confirmed the suspicions which she attached
to every man who entered the house: that he was
"after" her niece because of her money. But what
softened Bella towards Ernest Wilburn more than all
else was that he appeared to be interested in her as a
human being and took pains to understand her, con-
tributing thus to her understanding of herself.

"I can see you are finding life dull here," he told
her. "This life doesn't suit you."

"Have you heard me complain?" she asked.

"No, I haven't. And that's what I don't like about
it. You ought to complain. And I'm the right person
to complain to, by the way, because I think I understand you. You're too young and too rich and much
too lovely to waste your life and your vivid percep-
tions in a place like this. You ought to be living at top
speed. You ought to be greedy for every kind of experience—as you are, in the bottom of your heart, if
I know anything about you."

"Do go on, Mr. Wilburn."

"Well, aren't you? Of course you are! I should like to speak candidly, brutally. You're wasting your time here. A girl like yourself can't live in this hideous house. I think you're an artist of a sort, though I can't quite say what sort. You were not meant to live without beauty, Miss Tinsley, and the world's chock-full of it. Ah . . ." He sighed. "If *I* were your age and had your opportunities!"

"What do you want me to do?"

"Oh, no, I'm not going to advise you in anything but business. That's too great a responsibility. Just wake up and be yourself. That's all that I beg of you."

"And that's begging the question too, isn't it?"

"Don't stay here too long. There are awful examples. Not that I think for one moment you'll follow them. Why, you never even go to North Bromwich!"

"I don't think I want to. I wasn't particularly happy there, to tell you the truth."

"All the more reason to force yourself to go. That sounds to me morbid."

"Aunt Harriet has told me I'm morbid, for quite a different reason."

"Well, well, I won't argue with you. As a matter of fact I don't think there's the least need to do so. *Au fond*, I'll admit you're an extremely definite person. By the way, there are two things I wanted to remember before I go. First of all, I'm sending a present to you and Miss Mortimer. I'm a director of a company that's making bicycles and is going to make my fortune and perhaps yours as well. A fellow named Pearce has started a factory in Coventry. I've told the works to send you along a couple. They're all the rage. You'll find it great fun, and it'll get you away from Hayseech."

"But that's awfully kind of you . . ."

"Not a bit. It's a subtle form of advertisement. We want all the best people to be seen falling off Pearce's machines. And the other thing's this." He produced from his pocket a parcel. "It was left at the office addressed to you the day before yesterday. Now I think I must go."

He mounted his rallicart and went bowling away: a man of great charm, Bella thought, with something just a little odd about him, though she couldn't say what. She went back into the living-room and opened the mysterious parcel. It contained three clean handkerchiefs marked with her name and a folded sheet of notepaper. When she saw the address on the paper her face coloured. She read:

Chad Grange,
Alvaston,
August 20th, 1894.

Dear Miss Small—or should I say Tinsley?
Here are three handkerchiefs of yours which have come back to us after being lost in the wash. I should

L

*have forwarded them before if I had been certain of
your address. Having only heard to-day that Messrs.
Wilburn are your solicitors, I send them immediately.
We were all naturally delighted to hear and to read of
your great inheritance and to realize what a great
power for well-doing has been put into your hands by
Providence. Dear Prudence has grown so fast since
you left that you would hardly recognize her. She
often speaks of you, and so do we all. Mr. Fladburn,
who keeps fairly well, I am thankful to say, would
like, I am sure, to join with me in sending you every
good wish and wishing you every Blessing,*

I am,
Yours always sincerely,
Alice Fladburn.

*P.S. Dear Henry has now returned from the works
in South Wales. He is getting on splendidly, and
would, I feel sure, wish to be remembered to you if
he knew I was writing.*

Bella read the postscript through twice. Then she
laughed and slowly tore up Mrs. Fladburn's letter.
Aunt Harriet looked up from her work: "What are
you laughing at, Bella?"

"Nothing really. Somebody's sent me three handkerchiefs of mine with an amusing letter. Quite
ridiculous, really."

And she laughed again.

IV

Miss Mortimer was at first inclined to regard Ernest Wilburn's gift of a safety bicycle as a practical joke and one not in the best of taste. Even in Bella's case it seemed an action of doubtful propriety: in her own, at the advanced age of forty-four, it showed a painful lack of respect which wasn't, perhaps, altogether out of keeping with the lawyer's reputation. She had "heard things" about him. He was a man who "went up to London." Wild horses, she declared, should not drag her on to a bicycle. When Bella suggested that such animals, even if procurable, were surely not adapted to the performance of a delicate balancing feat, Aunt Harriet informed her that she had been using a figure of speech. The female cyclist, indeed, was associated in her mind with the costume invented by a Mrs. Amelia Bloomer, whose brief efflorescence had scandalized her governess Miss Beagle thirty years before. Even when Bella explained that the "Lady's Safety" had been invented expressly to avoid such offences to modesty Aunt Harriet could not be convinced. It was not until she heard that not only such local celebrities as Lady Hingston and Mrs. Willis, but even female members of the Royal Family, had fallen victims to this new form of "sport" that she consented to be hoisted on to the machine and fall off it. Even when she had found her balance and been forced to admit that the movement was exhilarating, she continued to regard bicycling as a rather daring frivolity which should only be indulged in with strict privacy.

"I think," she would say, "I will go for a little refreshing spin"—which meant riding to and fro, her skirt hitched up with safety-pins, along the extent of the crushed-slag drive, as far as the gate on the Halesby Road and back again.

"The smooth surface of the public road makes riding much easier," Bella assured her; but in spite of all persuasions Aunt Harriet refused to venture outside. "I don't *think* I should fall off now, Bella," she said, "but if I did, and was forced to reveal my underwear, I should never get over the shame of it." "But everybody . . ." "I know exactly what you're going to say. The fact that everybody wears them has nothing whatever to do with it. I am conscious of a similar anxiety whenever I am compelled to mount an omnibus. You are fortunate to be less sensitive, Bella."

Bella often thought how clever Wilburn had been in divining one of her needs when she set off alone on her new Pearce-Tregaron. Those were the great days of the bicycle in England. The empty roads, still unblackened by tar, had reached the highest perfection of macadamized stone, so that they still seemed part of the land they traversed. The radius of a dog-cart was ten or twelve miles. In that era of tedious transport the country which lay at a greater distance remained mysterious. The coming of the bicycle un-veiled that mystery. It gave wings not merely to the feet but to the imagination and quadrupled the store of natural beauty attainable.

Wilburn's present made Bella free of these novel delights in the most enchanting season of the year: the halcyon days of late September. In the black pit of Hayseech itself the passage of seasons was appreciable only in the increase or diminution of light and warmth. It was not till she had climbed to the crest of the circle of hills which like the lip of a crater enclosed that volcanic area, that she knew how passing sweet the air of the outer world could be. South and west stretched a land of orchards, and this was the season of harvest. Pale yellow, streaked scarlet, dark crimson, the cider-apples lay scattered in dewy grass or, heaped into mounds, already exhaled their vinous perfume. Heavier still and richer on the air hung the scent of the perry-pears lying beneath the noble candelabra of the trees from which they had fallen. Down and down into the warmth of that rich green land, down and down through the pallid gold of the motionless air, Bella drifted in a flight that seemed as ghostly quiet as that of the heavy-winged butterflies that floated or lazily fluttered from heap to heap of bruised fruit.

In this land, it seemed to her, the pulse of life must surely beat more naturally, more steadily, than amid the bricks of North Bromwich or the cinder paths of Hayseech where, even if one were blind to the surrounding ugliness, one's ears must suffer the perpetual assaults of hideous sound. There the visible world was a challenge, or at least an offence. Here its gentle hues and slow curves had a consoling quality; they fell upon her sight without disturbance or even excitement. And the eyes of the people she met on the roads or in the fields appeared to reflect the repose, the placidity of the landscape they gazed on. There was no surliness in those eyes, as in the eyes of the workers at Hayseech, no suspicion, no grudging, no shadow of discontent. And how could they be discontented, she asked herself romantically, living in cottages, each with its garden of old-fashioned flowers and vegetables in rows and laden fruit-trees, in the heart of so sweet a country? Or in those isolated farms of red brick or half-timber whose very fabric a sober prosperity had warmed for hundreds of years, with their neatly-thatched ricks of hay and straw, and long-roofed byres where the cows trailed in for milking, and ponds where white ducks swam and waggled their beaks under water, and kennels where chained dogs basked and yawned in the afternoon sun? Or, for that matter, in those villages whose delightful names, fading on finger-posts, lured one on, even when one was tired, to explore their mystery: Wychbury, Stour-

ford, Hackett's Norton, Chaddesbourne d'Abitot—
each completely satisfying in its orderly, clean composition of church and vicarage and inn and post office,
and, perhaps, a great house with a winding drive hidden discreetly behind spinneys and shrubberies, and
each completely different in feeling as well as in shape
from any of its neighbours.

The North and the Middle of Worcestershire were
full of these tiny individual centres of communal life,
minute knots of a network of lost lanes so deeply scored
in the red marl by the flood-water of successive centuries that no traveller, without climbing the banks,
could guess where they led; lanes that meandered
in circles or sometimes, out of sheer perversity,
changed their mind and turned in their tracks, or came
to a stop without warning in the mire of a farmyard
or on the edge of a cover. This country was one of
small precipitous hills that dived down of a sudden
between dark hedges of holly and ended, as likely as
not, in water-splashes of red gravel or tawny sand
crossing brooks clogged with cresses. No deep waters
worth bridging ran there, save where the brooks
had been dammed to turn water-mills, and in most
of these the wheels had grown mossy-green with disuse; the leats lay choked with silt, the mill-house
windows were broken.

And because every valley was like the next and each
road resembled its fellow, revealing, where hedges
had thinned or been laid or were broken by a gate,

identical vistas of poorish, rolling pasture-land divided into small fields of irregular shape sprayed here and there with gorse-bushes which, ragged by the wind, gave the land the feeling of an elevated plateau, though in fact it lay low; because this whole country-side was so much of a piece that it possessed no land-marks of its own, save certain characteristically-shaped patches of woodland, last remnants of the Mercian Forest, which only fox-hunters knew; because, since it was neither blessed nor cursed with natural riches or obvious beauty, the "improvements" of the industrial era had not yet touched it—for all it was one in which one could hardly blame a stranger on a bicycle for losing his way.

Bella often lost hers. That was one of the reasons why she continued to haunt it. For the most part the country appeared to be uninhabited, and the infrequent signposts gave little help. Such as they were, they tottered with decrepitude and stood bearded with lichen. Bella thought of them as hoary, feeble-minded old men whose directions were hard to follow and generally unreliable. Most of them vaguely indicated the direction of a market-town many miles away such as Worcester or Bromsberrow or Kidderminster—hardly ever of North Bromwich: in their days North Bromwich had not been a place of much consequence. Others boldly announced the name of some village. But when, having taken their word, she came to a place where the road divided again,

the next signpost, in all probability, would substitute
the name of another. Not that it mattered in the least.
All these names, Bella thought, had an entrancing
flavour of their own: some grotesque, some comic,
some beautiful. She would often go miles out of her
way to visit a village because of its name, and, as often
as not, fail to find it.

It was on a signpost even more decrepit than
usual that she first read the name of White Ladies.
An odd name for a village, she thought, but fascinating. Even if it turned out to be disappoint-
ing, she determined to see it. But Fate, or the
irritating habit of signposts, was against her that day.
In a series of successive cross-roads White Ladies was
not mentioned again. She was forced to abandon her
search, but the name continued to haunt her imagination, and it was with a thrill of surprise that a week
later (for after a few days of rain the Indian summer
returned) she encountered it again. This time, she resolved, the elusive village should not escape her, and,
for once, the finger-posts seemed to be more consistent. At three cross-roads, one after another, she was
able to maintain her direction. This seemed too good
to last, and at the fourth she drew blank. She found
an ancient milestone, indeed, but its friable surface
had crumbled, and only the ghost of the word
Worcester remained on it.

Faced with the choice of three roads, she decided
to follow the middle one and trust to luck——

L*

unwisely, it seemed, for within a few yards of the
cross-road the lane which she had chosen began to
degenerate into a grass drive running between hedges
of untrimmed holly darkened, here and there, by
enormous yew-trees whose trunks, soaked by the
recent rainfall, shone blood-red. Wherever it might
lead, this track—it had ceased to be a road—was obviously unfrequented. No wheel-tracks had scored its
smooth surface of rabbit-cropped turf, which, soft as
a carpet of emerald velvet, muffled the sound of her
footsteps. It was certain that no human being had
lately passed that way, for the space between the dark
hedgerows was spanned by spun threads of gossamer
so fine as to be invisible till they caught her face. Over
all hung a silence so profound that she felt it a little
uncanny. There was a moment when, halting to listen
to it, she was moved by a vague sense of panic and
found herself frowning, wanting to turn back. Such
a sensation, she told herself, was unworthy of a
sensible woman. This lost track was perhaps the most
beautiful and decidedly the most mysterious she had
ever followed. It ran so straight, with such an air of
purpose and certainty, that it must surely arrive at
some definite conclusion, as she was assured, a few
moments later, when, although another metalled road
crossed it, the velvety track, after this brief hesitation,
ran on.

From this point, it seemed to her, the flanking
hedges, though still unkempt, assumed greater im-

portance. Though the hollies and yews persisted, they were topped by elms of great age, discreet remnants, it appeared, of an avenue of approach, which gave the long track of green a ceremonial significance. It seemed unlikely now that it should lead to a village, for, in that case, surely its surface would display more signs of use. Perhaps it might lead to a house, she told herself, to a house of some consequence; yet even a road which approached a house should show foot-tracks or wheel-ruts—unless the house were no longer a house in being but one that had fallen to ruin, or perhaps a fire-blackened shell. Fire, she thought, would be a terrible thing, in a place so remote, so secret as this, with no telephone-wires to send out an appeal for help. A house in a place like this might burn till the roof fell in with a crash, and not a soul in the sleeping country-side be the wiser! She shuddered. For the moment a vision of crackling towering flame had possessed her. Wherever the road might lead, this was an air that bred fancies.

And now the slope fell away from her; the track widened; the vista, which had seemed endless, was closed by the velvety blackness of an enormous yew hedge which rose like a wall backed by tall dark woods straight in front of her: a wall broken in the midst by an edifice of pale stone, a gatehouse of classic pro-portions, through whose central arch the green track disappeared to be lost in shadow. Bella approached it, entranced. The sudden appearance filled her with in-

creasing wonder. This building was not a full stop, but
an even more definite note of interrogation propound-
ing the new mysteries. Lovely as it was, she felt, somehow, that it ought not to be there, this fine work of
formal Renaissance art amid those Gothic surroundings, this building of stone in a country of brick and
half-timber. In feeling it recalled the gateway of the
banqueting-house of Whitehall, that chaste work of
Inigo Jones, which, long ago, she and Miss Cash had
examined together; but the stone of this building was
softer and warmer in tone—not blackened by London
smoke but golden with lichen—and the mood of its
composition seemed less severe, being tempered (and
weakened perhaps) by a more Italianate fancy, such as
that of a pupil of Inigo who, having lived through the
wars, had succumbed, in later life, to the blander influence of his fellow-disciple, Webb, or of Wren; for the
curved broken pediment in itself had a sensuous line;
it was supported on Ionic columns instead of pilasters,
and the stone pinnacles and ornaments which flanked
it gave it an air of artifice and restlessness rather than
of repose. The chambers on either side of the gateway were vacant; their windows gaped, like empty
eye-sockets. And indeed, when she came to think of it,
this odd, isolated building, exquisite as it was,
resembled—in nature if not in shape—a bleached
skull: a bony fragment of something which had once
been alive, and had perished not very long since. The
eeriness of its skeletal vacancy fell on her as she

pushed her bicycle under the arch. From its pillars, no doubt, massive gates of wrought iron or bronze had once hung; but no gates hung there now, so why, after all, not pass through?

The drive within the gatehouse lay so sunk in shadow that, though the sun still shone, she fancied it must have gone in. Her progress was more silent than ever. The rabbit-cropped turf had been invaded and vanquished by moss. The heels of her shoes sank into a spongy surface of emerald-green scattered with what looked like gouts of blood, but were actually crushed yewberries spilt by the birds, though no whimper or rustle or snatch of song could be heard. This shadowed alley was so quiet, so heavily oppressed by the height of the black yew-hedges on either hand and the dense wood behind them, that when a squirrel, the first living thing she had heard or seen, bounded over the track in front of her, she started.

She was puzzled. That formal gatehouse, she thought, should properly have commanded the length of a straight vista, a drive, or a broad walk, leading the eye to a stately house of the same period. But this drive (if it was a drive) over which she walked, restricted the eye to a view of its own convolutions. One proceeded blindly and not very happily, losing all sense of direction, through the paths of an overgrown maze, so heavily shadowed by trees as to give the impression of a tunnel—a dank, silent, endless tunnel, she thought, for by now it must surely have led her the best part of five hundred yards.

And then, of a sudden, the trees seemed to fall back on either side, disclosing, with the effect of a fanfare of trumpets breaking through a murmur of muted strings, above, an enormous expanse of white sky, and below, a wide sward of turf, most piercingly green within the woods' dense circlet. And in the midst of the green sward stood a house.

Not the house she had expected. It was neither great, nor formal, nor yet of stone. It lay isolated in the bottom of that shallow depression like a stone that a jeweller displays on its cloth of velvet—like a sombre ruby, she thought, or better, perhaps, a dusky cornelian; for the rays of the sun, now declining, enriched its substance of ancient brick with a rosy transfusion pervading the clay's compact granules of sand in such fashion that every one of them threw back a minute reflex of light, and each face of the building glowed like the facet of a gem until each window facing her became a crucible of fire and the whole insubstantial structure seemed lapped in flame.

It was the ghost of a house, she told herself—but such a warm ghost, such a kindly ghost in comparison with that cold empty gatehouse! And so beautiful, so satisfying not merely in its texture but in its shape! Bella gazed at it solemnly, scarcely breathing, almost as if she felt the sound of a breath might snap some spell and cause her vision to vanish, until the sun slowly sank into layers of cloud. The flaming windows went suddenly blank; the brick was no longer transfused; the house, if it had ceased to be transfigured, became approachable.

She approached it slowly and with the awe that its beauty imposed on her. The sward, too, had lost its enamelled illumination. It had become no more than a short-turfed, tussocky pasture; but the surface of the drive, still discernible, lay velvety with moss. As she drew nearer, the detail of the building defined itself. It was even smaller than she had imagined at first, yet conceived in the grand manner at that period when a novel appreciation of the virtue of light— and perhaps an increasing degree of public safety— had persuaded builders to abate the military severity of the Tudors' gothic glooms by a more ample window-space.

In this building, indeed, the heavy moulded mullions and transoms of the Tudor window had been retained; yet the number of such windows, multiplied by the projection on either flank of octagonal turrets, their glazed faces rising through three storeys from basement to balustrade, and, in the centre, the surmounting pilastered entrance, a rectangular oriel, broke the monotony of what might have been a uniform façade and gave the whole structure the light-ness, the grace, the transparency of an enormous lan-tern. For all its strength, Bella perceived, the character of this house was feminine; it was within the full comprehension of her intelligence and the limits of her taste, which in this art above all others was instructed and sensitive.

Yet if she had known it was beautiful and that its beauty was of the kind to which she was most susceptible, she did not measure the full strength of its particular appeal to her until, coming even nearer, she saw that it was surrounded by a moat of still water. At the front a deep terrace or flagged walk separated the water from the house, which was approached by a narrow bridge; but on either side, where the flanking towers projected, the brickwork rose from foundations submerged beneath the moat's surface, so that reflection prolonged the line of the window mullions downward and gave their aspiring shafts a slenderer grace. Two houses there were, it seemed: one rising into the autumnal air, now bloomed with invisible mist, and another house, under the water, that seemed neither more nor less real. The house of a dream. . . . "The house of *my* dreams," Bella told herself.

It was getting late. Already a milkiness blurred the surface of the moat, making it look like a mirror of steel which has been breathed on. The air of the waterside had a chill in it; but Bella could not bring herself to turn away. She felt that as soon as she reached the curving yew avenue this precious illusion might vanish. Such a moment of sheer beauty might come once, and never again.

"I must be going," she thought. "How beautiful!

If I could possibly peep inside!"

She supposed the place was empty. No smoke aspired from the fluted clusters of chimney. All the windows were closed. She had stood there—how long? Heaven knew!—without being aware of sound or of movement. Supposing that by some miraculous chance the door might not be bolted? She propped her bicycle on the parapet of the moat and drew near. The door was of ponderous oak with wrought-iron furniture. She turned the handle and pushed. The latch grated; the door swung open, revealing a huge flagged hall with a staircase gallery about it; but what impressed her more than the size of this hall or even than its beauty was the illusion that she had stepped out of the falling twilight into the glow of the vanished sunset, into an amber radiance, proceeding, as she soon discovered, from the yellowish panes of the great oriel window above and behind her—into what she could only think of as a luminous dusk: a light powerful enough to enrich the shapes she discerned with an illusion of warmth (she had almost said of kindliness) yet so faint as to show no detail. Once again she found herself saying: "How beautiful! I must be going . . ."

As she turned, reluctantly, she became aware of a pattering sound like the tapping of a stick, and a faint rustle which seemed to proceed from somewhere in the air above her. Looking upward, she saw an obscure figure moving behind the oak newels of the gallery.

Then a ghostly shape appeared at the head of the stairs and descended them rapidly, clinging to the baluster with one hand and hopping from step to step. If she could have run from this apparition Bella would have been inclined to do so, but the limping, witchlike figure was on her before she could stir. It was that of a little, twisted woman, no bigger than a child of twelve. She wore a dress of black cloth, fitting close to her crooked figure, a knitted shawl of black wool, a black net on her hair. Her features were peaked and ancient and birdlike, and she chirped in a thin, birdlike voice:

"What d'ye want, miss? What d'ye want, what d'ye want, what d'ye want?"

"I'm sorry. I tried the handle and the door was open. I just looked inside."

"You've no business looking in other folks' houses, miss. No business. No business." The repetitions were like echoes gradually fading away.

"I'm sorry. I didn't really mean to."

"No business," the creature continued to chirp. "No business, no business."

"I'm afraid you're quite right. I thought the house was empty. I came here by accident. I don't even know what it's called."

"It's called White Ladies, White Ladies." The words trailed away like the wail of a plover.

"Then it wasn't exactly an accident. I was looking for it. I thought it was a village."

"No village, no village. There never has been no village."

"Would you mind telling me whom it belongs to?"

"It belongs to the master, Mr. Pomfret, Mr. Hugo Pomfret, Hugo Pomfret, Esquire."

"But he doesn't live here?"

"Mr. Hugo? He's not lived here for years. Not for years. Lives in Italy, Italy. Lives on the island, the island."

"What a terrible waste that seems! What on earth does he do there?"

"Do there? Do there? What should a gentleman do? He does nothing, nothing."

A vague idea had begun to take shape in Bella's mind.

"I suppose . . ." she began, "you don't happen to know if this house is ever let—with the furniture, I mean?"

"What? White Ladies let furnished? *White Ladies!* Well, what an idea!"

Bella laughed at her horror. "If I came here again, some day," she said, "could you show me over the house?"

The witch shook her head vigorously.

"Never heard such a thing. Not without Mr. Hugo's orders. Not without written orders. Never."

"Well, I'm sorry I troubled you. I hope you'll forgive my impertinence. I didn't exactly mean to come in, you know."

Still muttering, "No business, no business," the small creature hopped round and opened the door with a click of the latch. Outside, dusk enveloped the earth. Only, above the dark line of woods, a single horizontal streak of blood-red light gashed the sky. As she stepped out on to the terrace Bella heard heavy bolts shot viciously behind her. It was now growing dark so rapidly that she did not relish the prospect of her ride home. On the edge of the wood, where the drive emerged from its hedges, she turned once more to look at the house. Its form was now hardly more than a thickening of the darkness till, of a sudden, the mullions of the oriel defined themselves against a faint whitish luminosity. They were lovely even at that distance. Bella supposed that the little lame woman had lit a candle and was limping round the gallery, for the light waned and went out.

"Still, I've found it at last," Bella thought. "My lovely White Ladies."

BOOK FOUR

HEART'S DESIRE

I

RIDING home through the dark that evening Bella
Tinsley was strangely elated. It was as though the
vision of White Ladies—it was thus that she thought
of it, for the whole incident had seemed to transcend
normal physical experience—had contributed the precise reagent or precipitant which had been necessary
to clarify and crystallize her cloudy aspirations. But if
this adventure had the quality of a dream, there was
nothing dreamlike in her reaction to it. During that
rapt journey homeward her unsettled mind, which
ever since the Fladburn disaster had been searching in
vain for something on which it might concentrate its
energy, had discovered, at last, an object and a
direction.

Hayseech, on which her imagination had fastened
first, had failed her. It was too vast and too complicated for her intelligence to embrace; strong in itself,
yet too tragically at the mercy of forces beyond her
control; too grim to be loved; too deficient in beauty
to inspire. In White Ladies, on the contrary, she had
found not only a complete satisfaction for her æsthetic
sense but also an object within the scope of her possessive instinct. Miss Cash had judged her shrewdly
when, years before, she had marked the child's passion

for beauties that could be touched—for material rather than imaginative possession. And here, in the lovely shape of White Ladies, Bella had discovered not merely a beauty of a size which her imagination could grasp immediately but one on which, quite possibly, her fingers might close.

She was in love with White Ladies. She had loved it at first sight with a love far deeper and more satisfying than that which, for want of any other expression of her natural ardour, she had lavished on Henry Fladburn. Human beings, she had learnt to her cost, were variable and fallible. Human beings were capable of treachery and subject to mortality; the woman who gave her heart to a man—to any man— exposed it to the chances of loss and pain, and of what was even more bitter: humiliation. But a love of the kind which now filled her heart was less risky. White Ladies was a possession—she thought of it now as though she already possessed it—which would never "let one down." That unchanging beauty had been created centuries before she was born, and would stand long after she was dead. It offered her not only the rapture of devotion but also security. By the time she reached Hayseech she had determined, whatever it might cost, to make it her own.

Miss Mortimer was puzzled and secretly alarmed by Bella's abstraction that evening, suspicious of a radiance which reminded her of the days when Bella's mother had first fallen in love. The child would not eat her supper. She excused herself with an unnatural, high-pitched gaiety. Her movements were quick and restless; her black eyes glowed. Something had happened, Miss Mortimer felt, which threatened their peace, the tenor of her well-ordered life at Hayseech which had been so happily enriched by Bella's company. Whatever this new interest that had stolen her niece's attention from her might be, she felt sore and jealous and forsaken. Ernest Wilburn, she told herself, was the villain of the piece: Ernest Wilburn with his wildly adventurous ideas and his wretched bicycles! It was he who had introduced these tares of discontent and restlessness (as if his own notorious crop of wild oats were not sufficient!) into the prim garden which she and Bella should be pleased to cultivate with virginal dignity. It came as a heart-chilling confirmation of the rightness of these surmises when Bella, rising suddenly from the supper-table, spoke Wilburn's name.

"I want to send a telephone message to Mr. Wilburn to-morrow morning," she said. "Do you know how early the office opens?"

"I know nothing whatever about telephones," Aunt Harriet answered shortly. "I've never used the things and I never will."

Bella laughed. "My dear Aunt Harriet, you sound cross. What on earth's the matter with you?"

"What's the matter with *you*, Bella, is much more to the point."

"There's nothing the matter with me, darling."

"You're excited to-night. You're as restless as a tiger in a cage. I can't think what's happened to you."

"I am rather excited. And I'm tired. The fresh country air, I expect."

"The fresh air indeed! What's wrong with the air of Hayseech? Your grandfather always maintained the carbon in it was good for the lungs."

"But not exciting, Aunt Harriet."

Miss Mortimer grunted. "Excitement! What d'you want with Wilburn?"

"I want him to come over."

"He'll be coming next week."

"I know. But I want to see him at once."

"Well, your money's your own, I suppose; but *I* call that throwing it away. When your grandfather wished to consult a lawyer, he went to him—*he* didn't waste cash—and I really don't see why you shouldn't do the same. What d'you want to see him about?"

Bella teased her: "Ah, that's a secret. But I promise I'll tell you later, Aunt Harriet, truly."

"I knew there was something. You might just as well have admitted it all along. Well, it's time for bed anyway. Kindly pull the bell for Helen to bring my hot water."

Wilburn drove out to Hayseech on the following afternoon at some inconvenience. Miss Tinsley was a client sufficiently valuable to be humoured; but when he arrived he was surprised to find that she seemed disinclined to talk business. Aunt Harriet, whose curiosity had increased overnight, clung to them like a leech, and for some reason obscure to herself Bella did not wish to mention White Ladies in her presence. Finally, determined but feeling rather guilty, she carried Wilburn away to the office at the works on the pretence of discussing some matter with Mr. Wilkinson.

"Well, what's the great mystery?" Wilburn asked.

"There's no mystery. I merely wanted to see you alone. Do you know a place called White Ladies?"

"White Ladies? Of course. It's near Boscobel. Charles the Second took shelter there after Worcester Fight."

"No, I don't mean that one. There's another in Worcestershire. You go through a village called Chaddesbourne to get to it. It's not easy to find."

"Chaddesbourne d'Abitot. Yes. That belongs to Roger Ombersley, a client of ours. But White Ladies . . " He shook his head.

"It belongs to a man named Pomfret. Hugo Pomfret."

"Now I'm there! I remember, though I've never been near it. That's an odd bit of country."

"Do you happen to know anything about the place? It's a lovely name, isn't it?"

"Nothing whatever. I suppose it must have been a Cistercian house."

"What exactly were the Cistercians? I'm afraid I'm awfully ignorant."

"A branch of the Benedictines. They were called the White Monks. As a matter of fact I'm rather well up in them. One of their biggest guns was an English saint—St. Stephen Harding, the abbot of Citeaux. The White Monks were great fellows: they made Tintern and Rievaulx and Fountains—nearly always their abbeys were built by the side of a stream. And they were great farmers, too. In the thirteenth century they controlled the English wool-trade, and the wool-trade, as you probably know, was the making of England. They were a powerful order. At one time, I believe, they had more than seven hundred houses. Of course they're all ruined now."

"But the White Ladies? What were they?"

"Well, they, I suppose, were the female of the species. I expect they were farmers too. And this place you're talking of must have been one of their nunneries. What makes you so curious about it?"

"Because I want to buy it."

"To *buy* it? My dear young lady!"

"Why not, Mr. Wilburn?"

He laughed. "For no reason in the world. Isn't this rather sudden?"

"I saw it yesterday and I fell in love with it."

"Is it for sale?"

"I don't know. That's exactly what I want you to find out. After all, this is partly your fault, you know. You'll have to admit that you've 'put me off' living at Hayseech."

Wilburn considered her judicially, then nodded his head and smiled: "You're an amazing young woman, Miss Tinsley. Do you know anything about this house—the extent of the estate and so on?"

"Not a thing, I'm afraid. I only know that it's beautiful and that I want it more than anything I've ever wanted before. It doesn't seem too dreadfully big, and it happens to be empty. Can you tell me anything about the owner, this Hugo Pomfret?"

"Very little. I've certainly heard of him. I've a vague idea that he's a middle-aged man, about my own age. He must be a direct descendant of your Pomfrets—the ones we were talking about the other day, who owned Hayseech and Old Mawne Hall and the rest of it. The title's extinct, of course, I think it was an earldom. I remember a letter somebody wrote—who was it? Lady Mary Montagu, I think— to a Countess of Pomfret. I imagine this fellow Hugo must be rather hard up. Otherwise he'ld probably live in his house. They usually do."

"That sounds encouraging. His being hard up, I mean."

Wilburn gazed at her intently for a moment. "Look here," he said, "are you serious about this?"

"More serious than I've ever been about anything in my life, Mr. Wilburn."

"Well, I suppose there's no harm in making enquiries."

"Don't waste too much time over that. I've told you: I want to buy it. I shall have enough money, shan't I?"

"Oh, I don't think there's much doubt about that. If it's for sale, it will probably go cheap. From what I know of the Pomfrets, it's likely to be pretty dilapidated. But you can't buy a Norman estate—or whatever it is—like a packet of pins."

"It's not Norman," Bella assured him gravely. "Not the part I saw at any rate. It's late Tudor, or probably what you'ld call Elizabethan. There's an exquisite oriel, and a moat, and octagonal bays with stone mullions. There's a Caroline gatehouse, too. And there are woods all round it."

"It sounds rather grisly to me. My tastes are not Gothic. As a matter of fact, now that I come to think of it, the Cistercians were like that. They never built their abbeys near towns or villages. The more lonely and savage the country, the better they liked it. Well, there's no accounting for tastes. By the way, I suppose there are some monastic ruins there?"

"I didn't see any. I was only there half an hour."

"Astonishing woman! Well, all right, I'll do what I can."

"And you won't waste time, will you?"

"I'll get on to it at once and let you know as soon as I have anything definite."

"Oh, please, *long* before that!"

"Very well. I'll keep you informed."

"I can hardly live till I hear from you."

"Seriously, you know, I think you should take this matter more calmly, Miss Tinsley."

"Calmly, calmly, Mr. Wilburn?" she cried. "You don't understand. I'm in love."

That very night the Indian Summer ended with a south-westerly gale and a deluge of rain. Day after day on the heels of this first assault other storm-systems followed, pouring the rain they had sucked from the Atlantic on Hayseech like water sluiced from a bucket. Bella thought she had never in her life known rain so voluminous and persistent—probably because she had never before sat idle and watched it falling, as she did now from the window of her little bedroom, looking down on the works—or on as much of them as could be seen through the texture of storms sweeping over them one by one from the inexhaustible south-west. The black sheds seemed to cower beneath the rain; even the noise of the works was muted. It would have been difficult to find in the world, Bella thought, a more melancholy spectacle.

The sight of Hayseech irked her the more because she was forced to admit that she had lost all interest in it save as a means of financing her new infatuation, and the admission shamed her, for it implied that she was fickle and unfair She felt even more conscious of guilt when Mr. Wilkinson came splashing up to the house in his oilskins to tell her how things were going. This abnormal concentrated rainfall, he told her, was a minor disaster. Every drop of surface water which the brooks could not carry would find its way sooner or later into the flooded mines and the isolated underground basins or "pounds" that fed them. Most of the rain that fell from the sky would have to be pumped up again. To balance this ill he was able to give her other more encouraging news. During the last few months the pig-iron industry had been "looking up."

"There's a big call for raw materials just now," he told her, "from the finished-metal trades. They can't wait for supplies from abroad, and we've found a new way of making basic-iron for the Bessemer steel-plants. We're using our own old accumulations of what is called 'tap-cinder' or 'puddler's tap,' which costs us practically nothing—and, if we buy it, we can have all that we want for five bob a ton. Hingstons are erecting new basic-steel works and can take all the 'pig' we can make. It's a bit of a come-down, I know, for Hayseech to be depending on Hingstons; but beggars, they say, can't be choosers, and this amounts to a new line of business. I knew you'ld be excited to hear about this development, Miss Tinsley."

Bella was not in the least excited; yet the enthusiasm that made Mr. Wilkinson's eyes glow behind his rain-fogged spectacles—which, she noticed, were biting deeper than ever into the root of his nose and making the tip more purple—made him so pitiful that she had to affect an interest she didn't feel. When she saw him go splashing away again through the puddles, immune, because of the fire within him, from all the surrounding dank misery, she felt dreadfully sorry for him—simply that, and nothing more. The spectacle of the single-minded, however impressive, has a pathetic aspect. If it came to that, she was as single-minded as he.

The dream of White Ladies continued to haunt her, and the outward effects of that haunting to puzzle Miss Mortimer. There were times when Bella felt it was unkind not to admit Aunt Harriet to her secret; but the dream remained so delicate, so vulnerable, until it should have been fortified by the practical results of Wilburn's enquiries, that she dared not subject it in this tender stage to the ruthless pragmatic materialism of a judgement whose soundness she admitted but refused to accept. And it seemed as if Wilburn's report would never arrive. He had promised to let her know when anything happened. Evidently nothing had happened. She went down to the works and telephoned to his office in North Bromwich. Mr. Wilburn was away in London, they told her, and would not be back before the end of the week. This was monstrous, she thought. Because she was a woman, he wasn't taking her seriously. If he kept her waiting much longer she would consult someone else in his absence. That would teach him that

M

Arabella Tinsley was not to be trifled with! She went home to her bedroom and wrote him a scathing letter. Aunt Harriet saw the envelope, and saw Bella's face clouded with anger. If she could have opened the letter without Bella's knowing she would certainly have done so.

At last Wilburn wrote. Her tart letter had not perturbed him. His visit to London had actually been connected with her business, and some progress had been made. The matter was far too complex to be dealt with on paper. He proposed coming to Hayseech to talk it over to-morrow.

"To-morrow!" Bella fumed. "Why not to-day?"

When Wilburn arrived she received him with imperious impatience. "Tell me everything," she said.

"I'll begin at the beginning. The day after I saw you I put the usual enquiries in hand. Then I went down to White Ladies myself and had a look. I admire your taste: the house is quite exquisite and probably quite uninhabitable. I didn't get inside. If anyone was in charge, they refused to come to the door. I'm not at all sure that the air of desertion doesn't add to its beauty, by the way. Later on I got hold of a neighbouring farmer. The estate is small: approximately eight hundred acres. This man was one of Pomfret's tenants, and decidedly sorry for himself. Tenants usually are; but in this case I think he has grounds for complaint: an absentee landlord who takes all he can get—which isn't very much—and gives

nothing in return. Up till recently the agency has
been in the hands of a fellow who acts for our client,
old Ombersley of Chaddesbourne; but for some
reason—financial, probably—it's recently been handed
to a firm in London. I secured their address and a
good bit of gossip from the tenant.

"Next I made an appointment and ran up to town.
Your extremely rude letter reached me there . . ."

"I was dreadfully impatient, Mr. Wilburn. You
might have guessed that. But please go on!"

"Very well. The agents in London were a firm of
lawyers. Quite unknown to me, and, oddly enough,
Italian: Marx and Verona. Polite ruffians. They told
me that Hugo Pomfret was in Italy."

"I knew that already. The old woman told me. On
an island, she said."

"Yes. The name of the island is Capri, in the Gulf
of Naples. In this horrible weather I rather envy him.
He's been there for ten solid years: never comes back
to England. Shady character, Mr. Hugo Pomfret, I
suspect: it's a shady place. Well, to cut matters short,
I broached our subject to their Mr. Verona. I said that
a client of mine had been looking round for a small
estate in Worcestershire and had heard of White
Ladies. My client, I said, was a person of limited
means, and merely entertained White Ladies as a possibility because he knew that the house was dilapidated
and the land more or less derelict. For those reasons,
I suggested, its value was much impaired. In the open

market it would fetch next to nothing. That was why a private sale, to a buyer interested in the neighbour-hood, might be advantageous. If the price were in keeping with the condition of the estate we might do a deal."

"But, Mr. Wilburn, you know I don't care in the least what the price is!"

"Only too well. But it happens to be my business to protect you."

"And what did they say?"

"Their Mr. Verona was blandly non-committal. He said that he knew Mr. Pomfret was attached to White Ladies by ties of sentiment. It was all, in fact, that remained of a great family property. He could say nothing until he had written to Mr. Pomfret."

"*Written?*"

"I asked him to telegraph at length and at our expense. Reply paid. We drafted a wire together. No doubt he added something on his own. A reply came next day."

"Yes . . ."

"No intention of selling White Ladies, it said. Just that and no more."

"But you didn't leave it at that?"

"No, I told Verona that your interest in the property had increased since first I saw him. I sug-gested his sending another telegram putting the matter in his own way. Between him and myself, as one lawyer to another, I gathered that he wouldn't be averse to getting rid of the business, which is probably more trouble than it's worth. So he wired again. I don't know what he said. The reply was exactly the same: 'No intention of selling White Ladies.' "

"Oh dear, oh dear. . . !   Mr. Wilburn, I'd set my heart on it. Something more must be done."

"Well, I did what I thought you'ld wish me to do— the only thing I could do in face of these two flat refusals to sell. I suggested to Mr. Verona that as he'd admitted his client wasn't any too well off and as the house had been vacant for ten years or more, it would be very much to the advantage of the estate to give us a lease—a long lease. He agreed."

"Of course that isn't the same. I wanted to feel that White Ladies was mine—quite mine, to do what I liked with."

"I know. As a matter of fact I even went so far— most imprudently—as to suggest that in the event of a lease being granted we should be prepared not only to pay a substantial rent—what he called a 'price of affection'—but also to spend a substantial sum on repairing the house and modernizing it . . ."

"I don't want it modernized!"

"Well, putting in bathrooms and so on. Verona appeared to think that Mr. Pomfret might like this idea. He realized it would be very much to his own advantage to deal with one person of substance instead of a number of shaky tenant-farmers. So we drafted a new telegram, much longer and more explicit than

either of the others. We sent it off three days ago.
That's why I've kept you waiting. So far we've had
no reply. Verona doubts if we shall. He's talking
by the book, you see: he knows Hugo Pomfret. It
rather looks as if our persistence had annoyed him.
And there it is! That's how the matter stands."

"Can't we possibly do any more?"

"I honestly don't see how we can."

"Are you sure Mr. Pomfret understood?"

"I couldn't have put things more plainly. No . . .
it really looks as if you will have to abandon your idea.
For the present, anyway. Of course, if the owner
should die . . ."

"I wish some Italian would murder him!"

"That's a proceeding I can't advise. I'm very much
afraid you will have to accept the position."

She could not accept it, she told herself, whatever
he said. When Wilburn had gone she continued to
brood over it. There was always the possibility that
no news might be good news. Hugo Pomfret might
have left Capri before the last telegram arrived;
being a vagrant person, as she gathered, he might
easily be travelling; he might still, as far as that went,
be thinking the matter over; in hot countries men's
minds worked slowly; he was probably thinking the
matter over lazily, deciding exactly how much he
dared ask for a long lease of White Ladies, or what
conditions he might impose; he might even, providentially, have died!

Probabilities counted for little against the fact that a week, then two weeks, then three went by without Wilburn's receiving any reply to his last proposal. He himself thought no more of it. He had spent an extremely profitable week in seconding his charming client's caprice without any results, and the incident was closed.

But for Bella the incident was not closed. Try as she might, she could never succeed in banishing from her mind the vision of White Ladies and her desire to possess it. Several times, in brief intervals of fair weather, she scandalized Aunt Harriet by setting off early in the day on her bicycle and not returning till after raw nightfall. She found it less difficult to discover White Ladies now than to keep away from it, though she preferred to make use of approaches less obvious than that which led through the empty Palladian gatehouse. There were other ways of catching the house, as it were, by surprise without the risk of the trespasser being caught by surprise herself.

On these visits she saw White Ladies in a variety of guises: as a lonely mass of masonry spattered by hailstones or swept by lashing rain; as an odd collection of vanes and smokeless chimney-pots protruding through still mist; as a grey wraith; as a blood-red lantern kindled by frosty sunset. And so deeply were these various visions stamped on her mind that later, when she sat moodily gazing through her window on the bank of fog which, at that season of the year, enveloped Hayseech for days on end, the shape of White Ladies would suddenly appear on the void— like one of those images which a tired retina retains when the bright object which has produced them is no longer there, or, perhaps, like those watery mirages of desert oases which are bred of thirst and fatigue.

No word came from Italy. Bella's hopes hung no longer on the ingenious explanations she had invented to account for Hugo Pomfret's silence. Its cause was more simple: he had evidently treated Wilburn's over-tures with contempt, and torn up his telegram. Winter fell on Hayseech. Before the heat of steam-pipes and engines dissolved it, it was beautiful to see unsullied snow lying on the roofs of the sheds and shops, obliterating, in a night, the soot of half a century. But next morning, when steam-valves were opened and dampers drawn, made short work of that lovely crystalline powder. It slid from the sloping roofs in avalanches, leaving them black and shiny, and fell to the ground, to augment the foul compost of slush mixed with cinder which trampling feet had already transformed into a half-frozen morass. Not even snow could preserve its beauty for long at Hayseech.

Soon the east winds began to blow, making every pore shrink and close and constricting the temples as with a band of contracting iron. It was impossible even to pretend to keep warm in the house on Hay-seech Bank. Aunt Harriet and Helen, although they wore mittens, fell victims to chilblains: they almost welcomed their chilblains as a seasonable phenomenon, like mince-pies or mistletoe. They cowered over the old-fashioned grates—fuel was cheap enough there, thanks be!—in the icy draught which the flames sucked up the chimney. They developed tissicky coughs, the irritation of which drove Bella away from such warmth as there was. She had never realized that house's flagrant offence against every æsthetic rule, until the east wind imprisoned her in it—though even a prison, she reflected, might be better heated, and ugly in a more negative way. But it was the darkness even more than the cold of Hayseech that she found oppressive and stupefying. She was used to dark winters. The North Bromwich winter, in all conscience, was dark enough. But at Hayseech, to the natural deficiency of light there was added the constant inter-position between the house and such rays of bleared sun-shine as might normally have reached it, of a blanket of dank air, semi-opaque (one might almost have said semi-solid). In this blanket every foul exhalation of the Black Country appeared to be concentrated—most of all when the wind moved from the east, combing the sky above North Bromwich and Wednesford and Wolverbury, and piling the smoke-laden air against the base of the hills from which, recoiling, it fell back into the sump of Hayseech.

After Christmas the real pinch of winter began. Bella's weariness began to show itself. Her cheeks lost colour. She felt, herself, that she was beginning to look like those sun-starved clerks in the sooty office at Hayseech—or even like Mr. Wilkinson . . . poor Mr. Wilkinson. Even Aunt Harriet, who was so deeply inured to this sort of hibernation as not to observe it, noticed the change in her. Herself the product of a generation in which consumption was the natural scourge of young womanhood, she became alarmed for Bella.

"I think I shall ask Dr. Martock to examine your chest, Bella," she said. "You needn't mind. He is an elderly married man."

"There's nothing wrong with me," Bella assured her. "What I really want is a change."

"A change? Why, you've only just come here!"

"The long winter is trying. It's much more sunny in the south."

"The winter is *meant* to be trying," Aunt Harriet affirmed, "and the winters we have now are nothing to what they used to be. As for running away from them—I am perfectly certain if God had intended us to be migrants he'ld have given us wings like the swallows."

"After all, Aunt Harriet, most people who can afford it go to the south of France."

"Yes, and die there like flies of pneumonia. I very much doubt if the climate's any better than this—or so much better, anyway, as to balance the unpleasantness of living among jabbering foreigners."

"So if I decide to go south you won't come with me?"

"What would happen to the 'girl'?"

"Helen's nearly sixty, and doesn't look adventurous."

"I could never leave her alone, Bella."

"But you could leave *me* alone? Aunt Harriet, isn't that dangerous?"

"If you ask me to go, I suppose I can't very well refuse you."

"Thank you, darling. I'll go down to the works and telephone to Mr. Wilburn."

"Is this why you sent for him so mysteriously back in October?"

"Well, no. Not exactly. Although, as a matter of fact . . ."

"If that was all, I can't think why you didn't tell me."

Bella telephoned to Wilburn. Next day she went into North Bromwich by train from Mawne Road and visited a ticket-agency. Wilburn knew all about the intricacies of foreign travel. He enjoyed squiring Bella round the town. Now that six months had passed since her grandfather's death she had modified her mourning. She wore a sealskin coat and toque, but the toque had a cardinal feather in it. Wilburn gave her tea at the newly-erected Grand Midland Hotel, which was the last thing in provincial smartness and daring. His prolonged farewells at the station were almost sentimental, and Bella enjoyed pretending to flirt with him. It was a change from life at Hayseech.

"I shan't see you again before May, I suppose," he said. "By that time I may have got over the shock of your first words on the telephone."

"About going to Naples? You surely didn't imagine I was going to confess myself beaten?"

"I don't know any other woman who would have been quite so . . ."

"Why don't you say 'obstinate,' Mr. Wilburn?"

"I was going to say 'tenacious'."

"Which means the same thing, of course, but sounds much more polite. Am I obstinate? Or merely perverse? Or just a bit mad? That's more likely, I think. As I told you before, I'm in love. My chief virtue is constancy."

"Well, who knows? You may get what you want. You could certainly get anything in the world that you wanted out of me. Will you forget I'm your lawyer for a moment and allow me to say how that little cap suits you and how remarkably lovely you are?"

Bella laughed. The train started. In her bag she had two return tickets, first-class, from London to Naples.

II

Miss Harriet Mortimer's crossing of the English Channel in January, 1895 was, to her at least, the most important feat of the kind since that of Captain Webb exactly twenty years earlier. A strong cross-wind was blowing, and the packet rolled heavily, shipping sea after sea. The few daring travellers who had left Dover with the intention of making the passage on deck disappeared below, one by one, until, eventually, Miss Mortimer alone remained to defy wind and spray —not out of boastful hardihood (although she did despise Englishmen who were frightened of weather) but because she had determined, when she left Hayseech, never to be separated from her luggage, consisting of two japanned tin boxes on which she sat, and three mysterious brown-paper parcels, which she insisted on carrying wherever she went.

Neither she nor Bella had ever set foot outside England before; but while Bella, her spirits continually sustained by the hidden purpose of her journey, was ready to enter on it eagerly and even to see fun in its embarrassments, Aunt Harriet's attitude, from the first, was reserved and critical. People had talked to her a lot, on and off, about the continent of Europe. She was being dragged off to inspect it, at short notice, against her will and her better feelings, and had no intention of being carried away by enthusiasm for anything merely because it happened to be strange. The climate, for instance, of France, on whose shores she alighted chilled to the bone and drenched with salt water, impressed her as slightly worse than the one she had left at Dover. The customs-officers at Calais who insisted on examining one of her three parcels were unshaved; they smelt of onion, and behaved with an intensity and an hysterical lack of decorum which explained, to her complete satisfaction, their national débâcle in the Franco-Prussian War; while the food in the first-class buffet would never have been tolerated in the house of an English working-man—the bread, quite apart from its odd shape and texture, had been cut with an oniony knife; the coffee was adulterated with chicory and the butter had no salt in it. It was small wonder that a race which filled its stomach with such strange food should be usually on the verge or in the throes of a revolution!

The French landscape, again, did not so much disappoint her as fulfil her worst suspicions. The unhedged cornfields of the Pas-de-Calais lay streaked with snow-drifts. It was hard to say where snow ended and chalk began. Women laboured in them, with skirts and petticoats trussed up to their knees immodestly. The villages through which the train jolted appeared to her oddly unkempt and unfinished: the

roads had no definite verge or footpath, the cottages
no gardens. As she remarked to Bella: the French
had a lot to learn. And Paris, a nightmare city of
clamorous cobble-stones over which cabmen raced their
fiacres all on the wrong side of the road, pleased her
no better. It was associated in her memory with the
siege of 1870, during which its inhabitants had sustained themselves on rats, a fact which made Miss
Mortimer recoil from the soup at the *Gare de Lyon*,
where she mortified the flesh by making her dinner
of biscuits and soda-water—much to the concern of a
friendly waiter who recognized in her abstinence from
normal diet signs of a type of acid dyspepsia from
which a member of his own family had suffered, and
recommended Eau de Vichy in place of Seltzer.
Though Aunt Harriet could not understand what he
said, she knew she was being discussed, and resented it.

"He's just taking a friendly interest in you," Bella
told her.

"You may call it an interest," Aunt Harriet replied.
"I call it an unpardonable liberty."

"He has noticed," Bella said, "that English middle-
aged ladies are usually dyspeptic. He says peppermint
also is useful."

"And how, pray, does *he* know that I'm English?"
Aunt Harriet answered indignantly. "That's none
of his business. I wish you wouldn't talk to them,
Bella. I know you like showing off your French, but
it's extremely undignified. Impudent fellows like that

should not be encouraged. If you give them an inch, they'll probably take an ell. The way in which all these foreigners gaze in one's eyes is most disconcerting. And why one should travel twelve hours in extreme discomfort for a supper consisting of inferior biscuits and flat soda-water passes my comprehension. Do look the other way. That horrid man with the black beard and the napkin tucked into his collar is staring at you. For goodness' sake let's ask for the bill and get away from this place before he accosts you."

The rocking, roaring night-journey southwards did not improve Miss Mortimer's temper or help to reconcile her to what she regarded as an insane expedition. She still had her brown-paper parcels—two of them propped up her head in place of the pillow which, because she had suspected its cleanliness, she had refused to hire; but the precious japanned tin boxes had been rapt from her in Paris and ruthlessly registered; and the thought that inquisitive foreigners were probably at this moment rifling them in the guard's van and examining her "underlinen" prevented her from sleeping a wink. Her stomach was empty; she was beginning to feel rather sick. When she opened a chink of window, to be prepared for the last emergency, it admitted a hurricane of smuts and sleet. When dawn came, amid Alpine foothills, the faint light showed snow lying deep and still falling. Somehow or other, out of sheer tiredness, she dropped off to sleep, waking, later, to a blaze of white snow-light and the vision of a platform on which a crowd of dispirited emigrants stood freezing in attitudes of misery.

It was Bella who had roused her: Bella, her cheeks flushed with the cold morning air, her eyes bright with excitement.

"Wake up, darling," she cried. "Oh, *do* look at that marvellous uniform! We're actually in Italy!"

Aunt Harriet blinked and looked out. She felt cross and faint with hunger.

"Well, if *this* is Italy," she replied, "I think the less said about it the better."

At Modane Aunt Harriet's japanned trunks, whose keys had been mislaid, were as great an embarrassment as his elephants had been to Hannibal on a similar occasion. At Turin the sun shone. In Rome, next day, it was summer. Miss Mortimer was constrained to put up her umbrella to combat the glare, and annoyed at being forced to part with it when she entered St. Peter's. If her black cloth "costume" was rather too heavy to be comfortable in the sudden heat, it was at least in keeping with the fashion of pilgrims prepared for papal audiences, though she declared that wild horses could not compel her to kiss anybody's toe —*or* ring, for that matter. There were far too many priests, she decided, shuffling all over the place like cockroaches. And churches ought to have pews in them.

On the whole, she found Rome unexpectedly tolerable for a foreign city. She liked the wide squares and
the fountains and the scarlet habits of the German
seminarists; and though the style of the buildings
struck her as generally "fanciful," the immodesty of
some statues regrettable, and the universal consumption of wine in the open by the working classes as a
crying scandal, the hotel in which she and Bella were
lodged while they recovered from the results of their
journey was run, though the tea was made with tepid
water, on more or less English lines. Its drawing-
room was littered with out-of-date copies of the
Illustrated London News, read and re-read by English ladies of Aunt Harriet's own age and station.
What shocked and surprised her most was to discover
that Garibaldi biscuits, to which she had confidently
looked forward as a sure line of retreat in the face of
dietetic enormities, and which she had imagined to
be one of the country's staple products, were,
apparently, unknown in Italy. The manager, an intelligent, obliging man, had never heard of them. Garibaldi, yes indeed, but his *biscotti*, no. If the *signorine*
were making a prolonged stay in Rome he would do
his best to procure this exotic delicacy from England.

The *signorine*, Bella said firmly, were not making
a prolonged stay in Rome. On the contrary, they were
on the point of leaving for Naples to-morrow. Aunt
Harriet was hurt. She reminded Bella that she had
only just unpacked her tin boxes and stowed the con-

tents into drawers. What was the sense of staying only two days in a place which the guidebook insisted it would take at least five to "see" thoroughly? Why, she hadn't as yet even set eyes on the Colosseum, which everybody said was worth seeing, quite apart from the poem. And the world was divided, she had heard, between the people who had seen Rome and those who hadn't.

"We can 'see' Rome on our way home," Bella said. "You know we have tickets to Naples."

"The manager says that Naples is most insanitary, to say nothing of mosquitoes, earthquakes, volcanoes and cholera. He told me not on any account to touch a drop of water there, and the tea, I feel sure, will be awful," Aunt Harriet complained.

"Well, we won't stop there long. The best place to stay in is Capri."

"And where may *that* be, pray?"

"It's an island. Not far from Naples."

"An island. Goodness knows where you'll want to go next!"

Bella smiled. "That's the end of the journey. Let me help you to pack. We're catching an early train."

Miss Mortimer saw little of Naples next day, and that little she abominated. As the train pulled up at the platform it was instantly besieged by a rabble of ruffians, in no way resembling the species of porters to which she was accustomed, who fell upon her and Bella like a pack of hounds rolling over a fox. They poured into the carriage, each possessing himself of whatever article of luggage he could lay his hands on. One grabbed two of Aunt Harriet's brown-paper parcels, another her umbrella; a third and a fourth fought like wolves over Bella's valise, while two more, perceiving Aunt Harriet herself poised in horror on the step, seized her bodily like a couple of centaurs pouncing on an elderly nymph, and tossed her to the platform. In the near distance another section of the pack was engaged in worrying the heavier luggage. Miss Mortimer, recovering her wits in advance of her dignity, saw her japanned tin boxes being seized and separated and hurried away in opposite directions. It appalled her to think that after all the hazards of a thousand miles they should have come to this. She cried: "Bella . . . Bella. . . . For heaven's sake stop them—*stop* them!"

Bella shook her head hopelessly, which was reasonable: in that pandemonium no voice would be heard or heeded. But Bella was laughing: and that was far harder to forgive. A gold-braided official appeared and silenced the yelping pack. Bella spoke to him. He bowed graciously and waved his hand. He looked, Miss Mortimer thought, like an admiral at least, but was, in fact, an hotel-porter touting for tourists. After another burst of music he succeeded in re-assembling the dismembered luggage. They had just time, he intimated, to catch the steamer for Capri, and he would see them aboard. A file of no less than

nine porters trotted silently in front of them along the
length of the platform. The admiral tipped them and
hired three carriages. He himself sat superbly amid
a third of the luggage in the first; the remaining two-
thirds filled the second, while Bella, with Aunt
Harriet, still indignant at the assault on her person,
brought up the rear. They shot out of the station-yard,
all three like competitors in a chariot-race; the cabs
swayed and skidded from side to side, turning corners
on two wheels while sparks flew from the pavement;
under the white-hot sun they went tearing along without heed for life or limb through those teeming,
strepitant streets: through the jangling of church bells,
the jingling of harness, the creaks of revolving wheels,
the agonized cries of carters and shouts of hawkers—
on and on through the bewildering combinations of
uncontrolled noise and colour, of splendour and
misery, which make up the delightful, tawdry, gay,
cynical extravaganza of Neapolitan life.

Suddenly the wide street debouched into an even
wider *piazza*, at which the leading cab swerved to the
left and the others followed. Full in front and below them Bella saw an expanse of glittering sea em-
bosomed in mountains, and in the midst of it—more
like a lovely shape carved out of blue cloud than a
piece of ponderable earth—there lay, or rather
seemed to float dreamily on the waves, an island. This
apparition had the immediate effect of exciting the
admiral, who stood up in his cab and waved his arms,

enthusiastically pointing and bawling back at them: *"Signorine! Signorine! Eccola! L'isola di Capri!"*

"What is that fellow gesticulating and shouting about, I should like to know?" Aunt Harriet asked coldly.

"He says that is the Island of Capri," Bella replied.

"Well, even if it is, I see nothing whatever to be excited about," said Miss Mortimer.

III

THE Island of Capri was then—as it had been in the reign of Tiberius, is now, and ever shall be—unique and immutable in its beauty and in its character. Superficially, it may be described as a jagged fragment of mountain limestone torn away in some geological cataclysm from a seaward spur of the Neapolitan Apennines; five miles long and from one to two wide; for the most part intensively cultivated in the production of oil and of a pernicious wine which a number of men of letters (whom this beverage has robbed of reason and veracity) have made famous.

It is mainly inhabited—though few readers of fiction would believe it—by a numerous, kindly, industrious peasantry, lamentably inbred and continually inbreeding. Add to these fifty priests, who are responsible for the island's strict moral tone, and two or three hundred tradesmen and hotel-keepers, subsisting, as did the Sirens before them (but with less æsthetic qualifications), on the substance of passing foreigners, attracted to that dangerous coast by its legendary magic. Theirs is the function of parasites in a purely artificial world of faked corals, faked tarantellas, faked antiquities, faked emotions and faked romance. Then, finally, and quite unim-

portantly, if the truth be admitted, there is the world
of the "foreign colony"—largely composed of oddities
and indifferent dabblers in the Arts, representing a
small (but mathematically constant) proportion of
chance visitors who, once having slipped through the
Sirens' talons, have become naturalized—or perhaps
artificialized—and remain on the island during the
rest of their lives. They stay there for no precise
reason, it would seem, save the fact that they have
been chosen to do so by some invisible selective
mechanism which sorts all newcomers like a fruit-
grading machine, automatically rejecting the norm of
humanity and only accepting its extremes—the "unco'
guid" as willing as the "unco' bad"—and, once having
accepted them, preserves them tenderly: choice
museum specimens embalmed in blue Mediterranean
air like flies in amber.

In this collection even the types of oddity have been
standardized, and, such is the profusion of nature, the
supply rarely fails. No sooner has the existing
Eccentric Philosopher, Cashiered Guardsman, Epicene
Hellenist, or Well-connected Remittance-man,
vacated his place through drink, drugs, cancer of the
liver, or mere bland old age, than another candidate
for the label pops into his place like a trout which has
been waiting for a favoured "lie" in a stream.

The indigenous population accepts this "foreign"
colony, with its exaggerated vices or virtues or mere
eccentricities, as a natural phenomenon like flies or

mosquitoes in summer or grubs in the olives. Possessed by the odd delusion that the island is theirs, they come and they go—as the boon-companions of Caligula, the pirates of Barbarossa, the bewigged Bourbon courtiers and His Majesty King George the Third's Royal Corsican Regiment have come and gone after them. The true owners of Capri—the tillers of the soil, the treaders of grapes and gatherers of olives, take little heed of them. To these they are just *"forestieri,"* foreigners; and resident foreigners, as everyone knows, whatever their nationality, have always been much of a muchness, divisible by tradition into three precise categories: *ammalati, pazzi* and *disperati*—the sick, the mad and the down-and-out. It must be confessed that, generally speaking, tradition had not erred.

Mr. Hugo Pomfret, although a foreigner, could not be said to conform to any of the three classes. For more than ten years he had enjoyed reasonably good health; his only symptoms of madness were a languid interest in landscape-painting which he indulged out of doors when the weather was neither too hot nor too cold, and an occasional, but hardly serious, bout of drinking; as for finances, he rented his own house, paid the rent fairly regularly, and, by local standards, was not extravagantly in debt. He was not even qualified to fill any recognized position in the museum of foreign oddities; for the only niches to which he might possibly have aspired—those of the Cashiered Guardsman and the Well-connected Remittance-man—had been occupied for years by Major Carl von Stolp and Mr. Reginald Mohun.

Mr. Pomfret, in fact, was so nearly normal as to appear something of an abnormality. In his outward appearance, which he did not neglect, he was not unlike any other middle-aged country gentleman. He was always clean-shaven, but for a large grey moustache which just failed to hide a mouth that was pleasantly humorous but a trifle weak; he had a well-modelled head of the small bony Norman type which suggests feudal architecture, and palish blue eyes which gave an impression of shyness; his figure, originally well-knit and well-proportioned, was beginning to show signs of a certain laxity which was corrected to a certain extent by the severity of his dress—cord riding-breeches, a Norfolk jacket of tweed well strapped-in at the waist, and, invariably, a clean white starched collar with a blue and white-speckled neck-tie.

It was, people supposed, Mr. Pomfret's partiality for starched linen and the expense of laundering it which had induced him to acquire as his housekeeper and mistress the daughter of his laundress, a woman much younger than himself called Carmelina Paturzo, in whose company, for more than eight years, he had been established in a tumble-down cottage, consisting of a bedroom, a studio with a north light, and a kitchen, on the outskirts of the mountain village of Anacapri. Hugo Pomfret's Carmelina was a full-blooded brunette, Greek-featured and black-eyed, with the

sanguine complexion overspread by a purplish bloom
like that of a ripened peach which prevails in those
parts. When Mr. Pomfret acquired her she had possessed not only a straight Greek nose but the poise
and shape of a Tanagra figurine; but the latter, as the
result of richer food and diminished exercise, had
rapidly deteriorated. She had a singularly harsh and
piercing voice and, it was said, a vile temper. A husband of her own race would certainly have beaten her.
In addition to washing his fine linen and starching his
cuffs and collars, Carmelina had borne two children,
quite possibly his.

What Hugo Pomfret did with his time when he
wasn't killing it with painting or Carmelina's society
was something of a mystery. In the mornings, when
the weather permitted, he spent most of it among
the peasants who worked in the vineyards and olive-
groves. He understood and spoke their dialect, which
he had learnt from his mistress, better than polite
Italian. He was knowledgeable and interested in their
work and happy in their company. In the afternoon,
when the mail had arrived by steamer, he read the
Morning Post with as much concentration as he could
achieve within earshot of Carmelina and her children.
At sunset, when the Angelus clanged, he dined heartily
and inexpensively and drank enough of the local wine
to make himself comfortably sleepy before he retired
to his bed in the draughty, whitewashed studio.
Carmelina and the two children slept in the bedroom

on an enormous iron bedstead of the kind called "matrimonial."

It was a routine of life which would surely have been stultifying to any man of taste or education. Hugo Pomfret, possessing a modicum of each, showed no outward signs of resenting it but an increasing disinclination for intercourse with people of his own culture and race. He lived very much to himself, rarely descending from the mountain to Capri. Most members of the English colony knew him by sight, but not one of them intimately. His avoidance of social relations gave equal offence to the two main camps into which it was divided.

The first, under the acknowledged headship of a widow named Mrs. Spettigue, felt the more strongly about him. Mrs. Spettigue, a tall, sallow woman with long teeth and a pendulous lower lip which her enemies said made her resemble a camel, was, by Capri standards, wealthy; the principal pillar of the Anglican Church and guardian of the community's morals. She confessed to a weakness for aristocracy—even of the Neapolitan variety, and on his arrival in Capri she had been greatly taken with Pomfret. She found him "a gentleman by birth" and "well-connected." Having verified those connections in Debrett she was in a position to discuss in public his second cousin, Lord Clun (about whom she had read in the newspapers) and his third cousin, Lord d'Abitot, whom she had actually met when he was ambassador in Rome. She had been able to discover, with some ingenuity, a relationship much more remote with her late husband's family, and to claim him as a connection by marriage of her own, and even addressed him with arch playfulness as "Cousin Hugo." For her, his only defect, in those early days, had been his disinclination to take active sides with her in the bitter schisms which rent the Protestant Community, and his failure to set an example by becoming a Communicant. Pomfret's fall from grace in the matter of Carmelina had been the last straw to break Mrs. Spettigue's back. Though unable to disclaim his relationship—after all, he *was* well-connected—she firmly regretted it; but what she deplored far more than the personal stigma was the fact that Pomfret was English. This irregular union reflected on the National Character.

In the opposite camp the news of Hugo Pomfret's lapse was received with delight, less on its own account than as a resounding smack in the eye for Mrs. Spettigue. The leader of this faction, Mrs. Louisa Robinson, was by profession a painter of enormous allegorical pictures composed of nudes so cunningly postured as to avoid giving offence to any eyes but Mrs. Spettigue's. In her dress she followed the fashion set by Rosa Bonheur; her manners were hearty and expansive and she detested nonsense—particularly thin-blooded nonsense of Mrs. Spettigue's kind; and though in theory she winked at free-love, particularly among artists, she was respectably and not unhappily married to a timid little man whom she pampered, and who spent his whole life in cultivating "real English vegetables." Mrs. Robinson's villa was the centre of Bohemian life in Capri. Her pictures, on account of their resemblance to Old Masters in everything but their strict decency, found a ready market among Midland manufacturers and North Country millers, which enabled her to entertain on what, in Capri, was counted a lavish scale.

No sooner was he rejected by Mrs. Spettigue than Louisa Robinson received her "Cousin Hugo" with open arms; but even in this society, for which his behaviour had qualified him, Pomfret was not a success. Though he might dabble in paint and convenient promiscuity, no power on earth could ever make him a Bohemian. He was, in fact, by nature, a shy, stiff, self-contained gentleman, whom an early widowhood —in youth he had married a woman of his own class and been left with two daughters—an instinctive, fatal indolence, and a series of financial losses, had mysteriously washed up and left high and dry and, for a creature of inactive ambitions, by no means uncomfortable on this island of lotus-eaters. The key to his character was implicit in those riding-breeches, in the starched cuffs, the stiff collars, and the daily *Morning Post*—and in one other passion which, as far as Capri was concerned, remained a fast secret. Among Mrs. Robinson's hearty Bohemians with their jargon of Art, their small scandals and sniggling immoralities, he was even less at home, more ready to wilt and shrivel up into himself than in the rarefied propriety of the circle from which he had been banished. Mrs. Robinson's boisterous satellites decided that he was a snob and no sport. Mrs. Robinson herself found him stupid. By degrees he slipped out of their society and was not regretted, becomng in the end a mere nodding acquaintance whom everybody knew (except the implacable Mrs. Spettigue) and nobody spoke to. His interests grew narrower and narrower without losing their character; his indolence increased; his life became as static and self-contained as that of a hermit-crab in its shell.

He had occupied this odd, isolated position in the island's polity for ten years at the time when Bella Tinsley and Miss Mortimer landed on Capri. Bella had lost no time in making enquiries about him. The proprietor of the Hotel Paturzo, in which they were established, was carefully non-committal in his replies.

Signor Pomfret, of course he knew him. Everyone knew Signor Pomfret. How not? A *bravo signore:* one, in short, who paid his way. He lived up the mountain in Anacapri and rarely descended; but if the signorina wished a message to be conveyed to him, that would be easy. As a matter of fact Signor Pomfret was married to a cousin of his . . ."

"Married. . . ?" Bella repeated.

Paturzo returned a leer. "Well, married—what

was the word?—*morganaticamente* . . . morganatically
married. Miss Tinsley would understand? Miss
Tinsley understood.

"If the signorina desires to see Signor Pomfret,"
Paturzo went on, "I would send a message to Anacapri at once and let him know that two ladies, friends
of his, have arrived."

Bella discouraged his impulse. They were not, she
hurriedly assured him, Mr. Pomfret's friends. This
method of approach did not seem to her tactfully
correct. Signor Paturzo's was scarcely the type of
introduction she desired: the connection being one of
which Mr. Pomfret might not be proud. Now that
she had reached this point in the adventure she felt
less sure of herself.

The next day was Sunday. Miss Mortimer
signalized the fact by appearing at breakfast in a black
satin dress, black kid gloves, and an expression to
match. She appeared to be shocked that Bella had
not done the same.

"Even if we are in Italy, Sunday is Sunday," she
said. "You had better ask Mr. Paturzo, or whatever his name is, what time church begins."

Mr. Paturzo regretted to say that at the moment
there was no Anglican chaplain, the last having left
suddenly as the result of a quarrel between Signora
Robinson and Signora Spettigue, who were both *brave
signore*, he added hurriedly and tactfully. Yes, *signore bravissime*. Both spent a great deal of money and

each burnt at least a *quintale* of wood a day. It was possible that a new chaplain might arrive at any moment.

Aunt Harriet remained unperturbed. It was her habit to go to church on a Sunday morning, and to church she was going. As far as she was concerned *any* church would do. Bella accompanied her to the door of the little cathedral, a dank building which smelt of dirt mingled with incense, and left her alone with her sense of duty in its malodorous gloom. She herself wandered forth to breathe the fresh air of the little *piazza* which lay open towards the sea and commanded, in fact, one of the most spectacular views in Christendom: the blue gulf embraced by the mountainous spine of the Sorrentine Peninsula; the volcano's smoky pennon blown over the white stones of Naples; plumb beneath, at her feet, the fertile levels of Capri, their brown vineyards dotted with whitewashed roofs and straw-screened orange-groves; and beyond these, terrific in its pinnacled magnitude, the incredible limestone bastion of Monte Solaro which concealed the drift of domed cottages called Anacapri.

Bella gazed at this unique spectacle unmoved by its beauty. Another remembered beauty possessed her mind. As she walked to and fro in sunlight, she thought of White Ladies, encircled by its wintry woods, with an absorption so deep that she was unaware of the glances of interest and curiosity which the presence of a young and elegant stranger excited

N

among the members of the foreign colony who shared
her promenade: so engrossed, indeed, that she started
when a hand touched her sleeve. It was Signor
Paturzo's.

"Excuse, *signorina*," he said. "There is Signor Pomfret. He has descended to take his journal. Would
you wish me to make a presentation?"

Bella blushed. "You startled me. Which is he?"

"The signor over there. The one who walks
quickly."

"That is kind of you. Thank you very much. I
will speak to him myself."

"As you wish," said Paturzo.

He bowed and retired. Bella's eyes followed Hugo
Pomfret. He was not, to begin with, in the least what
she had imagined. In a way, less formidable. For
some unaccountable reason she had pictured him as
tall, gaunt and bearded. It seemed an odd proceeding
for a solitary young woman to address herself to a
stranger; yet it was the amusing aspect of the situation and her consciousness of being not unattractive
that gave her courage. She smiled at herself as she
moved across to waylay him. Pomfret, walking
rapidly with downcast eyes, very nearly collided with
her. He looked up, raised his hat, and excused himself
in Italian.

"It was my fault," Bella said. "Pardon me—are
you Mr. Pomfret?"

"Yes. That is my name." He gazed at her suspiciously. He had certainly never seen her before, and he had got out of the habit of speaking. If he could have done so without appearing rude he would have passed on.

"This is unconventional, isn't it?" Bella said— and her smile was charming. "I heard your name mentioned, and I wondered. You see, I come from Worcestershire too. Your name is familiar."

He said: "Yes . . . ?"

"I was wondering if you have anything to do with White Ladies?"

"White Ladies? Of course. I happen to be the owner."

"It is the loveliest thing in the world."

"You think so? It's a charming place. How do you know it?"

"I don't know it really. I saw it first a couple of months ago."

"You're luckier than I am. I've not seen it for more than ten years."

"How can you keep away from it?"

He laughed. "There are a variety of reasons."

"I'm sorry. But you would go if you could?"

"Of course. I'm devoted to the place. I entirely agree with you. It's unique in its way. When I was a boy and my uncle was alive—the man from whom I inherited it—I spent a great deal of time there. I know and love every inch of it. So well"—his tone changed—"that on the whole I prefer not to think of it. However, I'm glad to hear that it's looking as well as ever. Poor White Ladies!"

He laughed awkwardly. His hand went nervously to his hat. Bella saw that he was going to escape. What could she say to detain him? Aunt Harriet, arriving at that moment in her Sabbath array, provided an excuse. Bella snatched at it eagerly.

"Mr. Pomfret, may I introduce you to my aunt? Miss Mortimer . . ."

Hugo Pomfret bowed. Aunt Harriet returned the bow stiffly. Her face was full of anxiety and distress. "I couldn't stay there another minute," she said. "The air was suffocating. There was a dreadful old woman who insisted on crowding up against me though there was plenty of room. She kept scratching herself all the time. I shudder to think why." Aunt Harriet shrugged her shoulders and shivered. "Not another moment. I feel as if I were crawling!"

"My aunt has been to the cathedral, Mr. Pomfret," Bella said gravely.

Pomfret laughed. "I can quite understand how she feels in that case."

"I feel I shall never be happy till I've had a bath," said Miss Mortimer, "if there *is* such a thing on this island."

"In the meantime, Aunt Harriet, wouldn't it be nice if Mr. Pomfret would come to our hotel and have luncheon with us? Three lonely Worcestershire people—or two at any rate? He has lived in Capri for ten years, and could help us a great deal, if he would be so kind."

Miss Mortimer gaped. It seemed to her that her niece must suddenly have taken leave of her senses. Her behaviour, in any case, had been sufficiently unaccountable lately. But to invite a strange man, whom she had met heaven knew how or where, to luncheon! And Hugo Pomfret, on his part, was hardly less astonished. He had not the least desire for the company of this vivid, imperious young woman—of this extremely attractive young woman, he was bound to add: though what had he, at his time of life, to do with attractive young women? He had come down innocently from Anacapri that morning to fetch his daily paper; and here he was, ruthlessly accosted and invited to luncheon in terms which made it impossible for a man to refuse without being positively rude. He felt inclined to be rude. It was with difficulty that his ingrained good manners got the better of him— these and a sudden pathetic realization of his own loneliness which Bella's speaking of White Ladies had perhaps reawakened. It was pleasant too, after so long, to hear and speak one's own language.

"It's years since I've lunched outside my own studio," he said.

"Then all the more reason! Will you join us at half-past twelve?" Bella's smile was radiantly triumphant.

"I shall be delighted," he said.

"In that case, *a rivederci!*"

Paturzo was unable to give his "morganatic" relation many details concerning his guests. Their names
were Mortimer and Tinsley. Nationality, English.
The luggage of the elder lady appeared to be of poor
quality. That of her niece, on the other hand, was
elegant and obviously new. They had also stayed at
an expensive hotel in Rome. Signorina Tinsley had
already enquired for him by name. *Enquired for him?*
That was mysterious. Hugo Pomfret's shyness was
so scared that he nearly turned tail. He might even
have escaped if, at that moment of alarm and hesitation, Bella had not appeared in the hall of the hotel
and taken possession of him and put him, in spite of
his doubts and suspicions, at his ease.

She was frank, she was gay, she was humorous, she
was—it seemed to him—curiously excited. She was
a lady. She was above all—in her quiet voice and
the quick grace of her movements—the completest
of contrasts to Carmelina. Miss Mortimer, on the
other hand—and particularly Miss Mortimer's accent
—puzzled him. But Paturzo's luncheon was a
delicious relief after the monotony of Carmelina's
fare, and Paturzo's wine was excellent. Whatever
designs this strange couple might have on him—and
in the back of his mind the alarm and suspicion remained—Hugo Pomfret was forced to confess that he
was enjoying himself. The food and the wine restored
the social courage which in years of loneliness he had

lost. He found that his disused sub-acid humour was still capable of making Miss Tinsley laugh; and when Miss Tinsley laughed, Miss Tinsley was delicious. They got on so well together that he made up his mind to ask her point-blank, before luncheon was over, what had made her ask Paturzo about him. But by the end of luncheon he had forgotten what he had intended to do.

"It was kind of you to take pity on us," Bella told him.

"On the contrary," he protested. "Didn't you take pity on me?"

"Some day we must come and see your work at your studio."

"Heaven forbid!"

"Well then, when you deign to visit Capri you will come and see us?"

"It's most good of you to suggest it."

It was, Bella thought, a most skilful escape. No sooner had he turned his back than Aunt Harriet began to question her. How had she made this stranger's acquaintance? Why on earth had he come to luncheon? What was it all about?

"His name's Hugo Pomfret," Bella told her, "and he's lived here for years. He knows all about the place and can be useful to us. He's a gentleman. He has nice manners."

"He drank a good deal of wine," said Aunt Harriet severely: "our bottle is practically empty. Who ordered it, I should like to know? Mr. Paturzo assures me the water is perfectly safe here."

"We won't grudge him his bottle of wine, darling. After all, he's a Pomfret."

"What has that to do with it?"

"Well, we *did* steal Hayseech from them, didn't we?"

"That was ages ago. I don't suppose he knows anything about it."

"We'll ask him when he comes to tea."

But Hugo Pomfret did not come to tea. A week passed and Bella saw no more of him. He even sent one of Carmelina's children to the *piazza* to retrieve his *Morning Post*. Bella felt that after what had seemed like a promising start things were going badly. The shy bird had escaped her. In the meantime Mrs. Spettigue had called on them to investigate the possibilities of their admission to Capri Society. She had found Miss Mortimer alone, a superior woman with a regrettable accent and no recognizable connections. In an outpost of civilization such as Capri one could afford to take the broad view of such deficiencies: all that mattered to her were the visitors' morals and associations. Before accepting the two ladies Mrs. Spettigue took pains to assure herself that they were not acquainted with any member of Mrs. Robinson's set.

They knew nobody, Miss Mortimer innocently told her, but a Mr. Pomfret.

"Hugo Pomfret?" Mrs. Spettigue went up in

smoke. No respectable woman could possibly know Hugo Pomfret. Of all the bad characters on the island, he was easily the worst. A man devoid of religion and morals and principles who had, literally, gone native. She thanked heaven she had been "sent" to warn them and to preserve them from contamination. Her words and feelings were so violent that Aunt Harriet was impressed. She communicated the awful news to Bella.

"I knew there was something amiss with that man," she said. "It appears he has married his washerwoman —or rather *not* married her. I noticed at the time that his linen was remarkably clean. This only shows the danger of picking up stray acquaintances in foreign countries. I hope this will teach you a lesson once and for all."

Bella listened submissively: this was a subject on which argument would be a sheer waste of time. On the whole, Mrs. Spettigue's malignant violence prejudiced her in Pomfret's favour, though what he might be or not be was a matter of indifference to her: she was only concerned with him as the owner of White Ladies. She felt a little piqued, too, by the manner in which he had avoided her. Though she had no desire to attract him, she didn't like being "turned down."

It was partly, no doubt, this feeling of pique that determined Bella to pursue the chase into her quarry's own fastness. One day after luncheon, when Aunt

N*

Harriet was safely submerged in her siesta, she hired a *carrozza* and drove up to Anacapri. It was a day of wind blowing in fierce gusts which shook the frail vehicle as though they might carry it away. The streets of the mountain village were deserted. The roar of the blanched olive-groves enveloped it like the sound of the sea. She dismounted in the shabby *piazza* and enquired in a salt-and-tobacco shop where Signor Pomfret lived. The shop smelt of charcoal-fumes; the woman who kept it sat like a sibyl over a brazier; at a table near by, men with calfskin tied round their feet sat playing cards. When Bella spoke, they all stared at her without comprehending her Italian. They shook their heads and jabbered in a harsh dialect. She repeated the word "Pomfret" again and again; and suddenly a small bright-eyed child, who had been knitting with curved needles, appeared to jump at her meaning. In the resulting babel Bella distinguished the name "Carmelina." "Sì, sì . . . Carmelina!" they all cried. The woman of the shop gave directions, and the little girl, abandoning her knitting, wrapped a shawl round her head and invited Bella to follow her.

The streets of the village were narrow and twisting. Bella wondered if she could ever find her way back out of such a maze. At a door in a blank wall faced with crumbling plaster the child stopped and called with a shrill voice. Bella heard the clatter of wooden shoes. Two other children, a boy and a girl, pulled open the door, revealing a courtyard paved with concrete of beaten pumice-stone on which soapy water was lying in milky pools. From a clothes-line, washing flapped fiercely in the wind: black stockings, a tattered petticoat, and three white shirts with starched cuffs.

"The washerwoman . . . of course!" Bella thought.

The squalor of that courtyard oppressed her. It was surrounded by a pergola of disintegrating plaster pillars, over which an ancient vine swarmed like a black snake. The two children ran into the house to announce her. A moment later a woman appeared: a thick-set swarthy woman, with a sanguine fine-featured face and magnificent teeth. Her skirts were tucked up at the waist and her red legs were bare. A fine animal, Bella thought, who must once have been graceful. There was still splendour of a sort in the classic lines of those features and in those smouldering surly eyes. She repeated the word "Pomfret" anxiously. The woman nodded and beckoned her into a vaulted room dense with steam and the smell of soap-suds. She pushed open a door at the end of it and invited Bella to enter.

The second room was obviously a studio. It had an arched window, facing north, with several cracked panes mended with paste and brown paper. On the walls hung a number of crude water-colour drawings and several framed photographs, among which, with a thrill, Bella recognized one of White Ladies. In one corner stood a terra-cotta stove with an ugly tubular flue of rusty iron; in another an easel and a pile of dusty canvases; in a third, on a divan heaped with gaudy blankets, a man lay sleeping.

As she stared at him, he became conscious of her scrutiny and sat up with a start. It was Hugo Pomfret. His face was flushed with sleep (she hoped it was only with sleep) and his eyes blinked at her for an instant as though they did not recognize her. She apologized quickly.

"I'm afraid I've disturbed your *siesta*. Please forgive me."

He rubbed his eyes. "Oh, it's you, is it?" he said, not invitingly.

"Mahomet has come to the Mountain."

He laughed, but his laugh was not pleasant. "I warned you not to, Miss Tinsley. However, since you are here, I suppose you had better sit down."

He was wide awake now. In his white shirt, without a collar, he looked younger, she thought, than when last she had seen him. She was amused to notice him becoming self-conscious.

"If you will wait a moment," he said, "I will try to make myself tidy and get you some tea. My tea is my only luxury."

"Please don't bother," she begged him. "I only want to talk business."

"About what?"

"White Ladies."

He smiled nervously. "Ah . . . I thought as much."

"Do you mind, Mr. Pomfret?"

"What do you want with White Ladies?"

"Quite frankly, I want to buy it."

"I see. That explains a great many things. The offers that reached me were yours?"

"Yes . . . my lawyers'."

"I turned them down."

"Yes. That's why I came here."

"You're a determined young woman."

"So I've been told. Isn't it better to discuss a matter of that kind personally?"

"Not in this case. White Ladies isn't for sale."

"Nor even to let? Our last telegram wasn't answered."

"Nor even to let. Please let me make you some tea. I want some myself."

He went to the door and spoke to the woman brusquely in dialect, then returned.

"This is an odd situation, isn't it? I wish you'ld enlighten me."

Bella told him the story of her first discovery of White Ladies. He listened so sympathetically that the narration was easy. When she spoke of the beauty which had moved her so deeply, he smiled and nodded approvingly. He laughed at the tale of her encounter with the little lame witch.

"So you see," she told him at last, "it was a case of love at first sight. I am alone in the world, Mr. Pomfret. I have a great deal of money and nothing particular to do with it. I was looking, I suppose, for something to satisfy me, something to set my heart on; and the moment I saw White Ladies I knew I'd found it. I'm prepared to pay anything you ask. Why won't you sell it to me?"

He was silent for a moment. It seemed as if her simplicity as well as her intensity had impressed him.

"Has it never occurred to you, Miss Tinsley," he said at last, "that I, too, may conceivably love White Ladies as much as you do?"

"Then, why not live in it?"

He laughed. "That's a rich woman's question. I've told you already: because I can't possibly afford it. If I opened the house for a month I should be liable to rates, and, quite frankly, I couldn't pay them."

The woman Carmelina came in with a tray of tea. Her eyes were jealous and suspicious. She hung about the room, as though anxious to hear what they said even though she did not understand it. The two children peered through the doorway. Pomfret told her to take them away. Squalls were heard from the courtyard. He poured out the tea for Bella with a courtliness which embarrassed her by its obvious contrast with those sordid surroundings. In spite of them the man had a striking natural dignity. He might have been acting as her host, she thought, in the great hall at White Ladies.

"I'm afraid you may feel the cold here," he said. "Of course I am used to it. Won't you wrap this blanket round your knees?"

She assured him that she was quite warm—indeed her face was burning—but he insisted on lighting a fire of olive-twigs. The oily leaves crackled and flared; their sweet scent filled the studio. Outside the wind boomed. It fluttered the brown-paper with which the window was mended. Little draughts swayed the cobwebs on the roof.

"And now," Pomfret said, "since you've told me your story, let me tell you mine. I, too, am alone in the world, and I have no money at all apart from the little which my agent sends me when the expenses of collection from rather bad tenants are paid. That doesn't amount to much. It's enough to keep me in what I call comfort and you would call squalor. I told you the other day White Ladies came to me from my uncle. It was once church property, you know, and is supposed to have a kind of curse on it that prevents it from being inherited in the direct line."

"Is there anything in that?"

"God knows. It usually happens. It happened in my case, and it looks like happening again. I married young . . . and foolishly. I was a soldier in those days. We had two children: both girls. My wife died with the second. That's a long time ago. Both my daughters are grown up and married. My wife's people looked after them: a widower's pretty helpless in a case of that kind. I came out of the army soon after she died. Never had much heart in it. You see I knew White Ladies was coming to me from my uncle. I'd loved the place from a child; it was all I thought of; and as a matter of fact I believe I know more about it than any of my ancestors: not only the history of the house itself but of every blessed thing in it and everybody who's ever been connected with it. Nobody can say, at any rate, that I didn't take the job seriously. All this personal history bores you, I'm afraid . . ."

"Indeed no. Please go on."

"Well, my Uncle Hugo died twelve years ago, and I inherited. I was in Paris, putting in time and pretending to paint. I'm a very bad painter, as you can see for yourself, but I love it. If you don't want to think, there's nothing like painting. I came home for the funeral. I was sorry the old boy had gone, in a way. He'd been kind to me, and was a fine fellow. Of course that was to be the great day of my life. And, of course, it wasn't. My uncle had lost most of his money—and his all wasn't much—in trying to make more for me. He left practically nothing except a house with a roof that needed money spending on it at once. And when we came to look into things we found that this wasn't the worst. The house was mortgaged. He'd actually borrowed money on it.

It wasn't, in fact, really mine after all! You can imagine I felt rather bitter."

"You had reason to feel bitter. It must have been terrible for you."

"The penalty of waiting for dead men's shoes. There was nothing to be done about it. I had an excellent adviser in a friend, a lawyer, who's dead now. I couldn't live at White Ladies: that was quite clear. At a pinch—and it *was* a pinch, mind you— I could just manage to keep up the fire-insurance— that, of course, came first—and to pay the interest on the mortgage. I've actually reduced the principal of the debt by a few pounds every year. (It's amazing how those little sums mount up, by the way.) If I'd taken my friend's advice I should have thrown in my hand and sold White Ladies for what I could get. But I couldn't, you know. The place was the dream of my life. I felt I'ld rather own it and starve and never see it than part with it. And so I cut loose and came here.

"Let me see . . . yes, twelve years ago. I'd been to Capri before and had rather liked the island—this part of it, anyway. For a year or so I lived in an hotel. That's a devastating life. Then I took this cottage and acquired various other things. That woman, Carmelina, who let you in, was one of them. Ten years ago, though you'ld hardly believe it now, she was astonishingly beautiful—pure Greek of the age of Phidias. I was forty years old and a completely normal man. I couldn't afford to marry a woman of my own kind—I was married, in a sense, to White Ladies—and I had an instinctive dislike of casual, promiscuous relationships, so I think Carmelina, on the whole, was a rational solution. There are two children: complete barbarians and aggressively healthy. The good ladies of Capri object to what they call my loose morals—which seems to me an odd way of describing consistent monogamy. I used to resent it. Of course I'm much older now. I'm fifty-one. The things people say have no longer any effect on me. If I live to be eighty I may just manage to pay off my uncle's mortgage and totter home to die at White Ladies." He laughed. "Thirty more years of this. A bright prospect, isn't it, Miss Tinsley?"

Bella shook her head. As he spoke, his words interspersed with shy, quick glances which seemed timidly to probe the extent of her sympathy, she had felt deeply touched by Hugo Pomfret's narration, above all, by the complete candour and naturalness which made it so much of a compliment to herself. While she listened to his voice—the most attractive, perhaps, of his personal attributes apart from the nice physical cleanliness which even Aunt Harriet had noticed—she couldn't help feeling the contrast between this bare draughty studio and the highly civilized graces of White Ladies.

That a man of this kind, well-nurtured, well-bred, should be living this sort of life was an offence against

nature. So much would have been obvious to the first
casual observer who should penetrate the flapping barrage of Carmelina's washing; but in all the world,
Bella reflected, there was probably no person other
than herself who would be able to understand Hugo
Pomfret's attitude with regard to White Ladies, to
sympathize with it and accept its rightness without
reservations. She perceived that this was a passion
even more single-minded than her own, and capable,
alas! of defeating it. Yet, while she approved of his
spirit, she couldn't help feeling, without any bias, she
told herself, from her frustrated desires, the pitifulness of his paradox. That a man sufficiently cultured
and sensitive to appreciate White Ladies should consent to live here like this! That he should be forced
to live here like this because of his devotion to White
Ladies! "What a waste," she thought, "what a waste!
Is there no way out of it?"

Perhaps the habit of solitude had made him sensitive to unspoken thought; perhaps he saw the pity
in her eyes; for suddenly he broke in on the silence
that had followed his question. "You are asking yourself: 'Is it worth it?'" he said. "I believe you are
feeling quite sorry for me. You must be careful. I'm
not used to people being sorry for me. It's much kinder
to treat me for what I am, and say what you think."

He laughed as he spoke; but Bella thought she saw
his lip quiver. It seemed to her that he was on the
verge of further confession. And why not? she

thought. Surely the saddest part of this wilfully isolated life of his must have been its spiritual loneliness: the fact that the things he felt most deeply could never be released in speech to a soul who could understand in the least what he was driving at. It was a privilege, she told herself, to receive his confidence; it was even suitable; for after all, in their identical passion she had more in common with him, perhaps, than anyone living.

"You don't answer," Pomfret went on. "I see you are afraid of hurting me. That's nice of you. But I assure you I'm much tougher than you might think. Why don't you speak?"

"Why should I, Mr. Pomfret? After all, it's no business of mine. When you ask 'Is it worth it?'— meaning your sacrifices—I believe I should answer 'Yes'; but White Ladies, of course, is a subject on which we're both hopelessly unreasonable. The only thing . . . But really, you know . . ."

"Yes. Please go on. Be frank. I've been frank with you, haven't I?"

"Well, don't you ever feel, even as things are, that there's something wrong with . . . with all *this?*"

"With the squalor in which I'm living? That, I think, is the right word. I'll tell you. If anyone had come here a year ago and asked me that question I should have answered 'No' without the least hesitation. Men as indolent by nature as I am, you know,

are extremely adaptable. And there's an odd division
in my life. The part I live here—the purely physical
part: food, drink, exercise, Carmelina—is not awfully
important. The other, the real thing, the life of the
imagination, is wrapped up in my appalling canvases
and, of course, even more in this . . ." He pointed
to the photograph of White Ladies. "But just lately,"
he went on, "my answer would not have been so confident. The first thing that upset me was your lawyer's
telegrams. The wording was clever. 'My client,' he
said—that's you!—'allows me *carte blanche.*' I
answered the first one easily and felt pleased with myself. The second gave me more trouble. I said: '*Retro
Sathanas!*' The third I didn't even trouble to open.
I was taking no chances of temptation. I threw it in
the fire. I suppose the third *was* from your lawyer,
by the way?"

"Yes. We asked for a long lease."

"I'm thankful I didn't open it. Well, those wires
were the first things that upset me—by just devilishly
suggesting the possibilities of another kind of life. I
got over them though, as you know. And then, when
I was beginning to settle back into my . . . sty—yes,
let's call it my sty—*you* came, if you please!"

"I'm sorry . . ." Bella began.

He laughed harshly: "Much good being sorry!
Why couldn't you leave me alone, I wonder. You
came up to me down there on the *piazza* like . . .
what shall I call it? . . . like a breath of the English

spring. You, with your lovely, tantalizing youth and your elegant air: with your suggestions of all the things I want passionately and have missed . . . missed or lost. And because you were lovely, as God knows you are, and I was weak, I allowed you to drag me in to lunch with you and make me gaze at you. (Did I drink too much, by the way? I felt cornered. I had to do something like that to cover my feelings.) But even when I'd got away from that table I couldn't escape from the discontent you'd poisoned me with. That's why I took mighty good care not to come near you again, Miss Tinsley. You've given me a devil of a week, and I can promise you I've wished you farther! And now, just to finish things off, you've followed me up the mountain and hunted me down. However, I don't think it matters much now. I believe we understand each other." Pomfret walked away and stood with his back to her.

"Yes, I believe we understand each other," Bella repeated. "We both want the same thing equally, and neither of us can have it. It's an *impasse*. I'm sorry. There's no way out of it, is there?"

Pomfret made no answer. Then suddenly he turned and faced her.

"You know, there *is* one way out of it," he said. "Would you care to marry me?"

"To *marry* you? Well, really . . . I must admit that had never occurred to me."

And then, of a sudden, Hugo Pomfret burst out

laughing. He controlled himself: "You must forgive me," he said at last. "Could a scene as fantastic as this have happened anywhere in the world but on this mad island?"

IV

ERNEST WILBURN, arriving late at his office in Sackville Row, North Bromwich, on a raw January morning, was greeted by his brother, who handed him a foreign telegram.

"It was addressed to the firm," Dudley said, "but is obviously intended for you."

Ernest Wilburn read: PLEASE COME CAPRI IMMEDIATELY AND PREPARE MARRIAGE SETTLEMENT TINSLEY HOTEL PATURZO. He said: "Well, I'll be damned!"

"I should think you would," said his partner. "Thank heaven I don't have to deal with clients of that kind. It's quite obvious that the poor girl's lost her head and is in a mess, and I suppose you'll have to go and pull her out of it. Of course it might have been worse. From the fact that she mentions a settlement I gather she isn't yet married. Still, I shouldn't lose any time. If you're going at all, the sooner you go the better."

Ernest Wilburn still pondered the message.

"Yes, the sooner the better," he repeated. Then he chuckled to himself.

His brother looked up: "What's the matter?"

"By gad, I believe she's done it!"

"What? Married the man?"

"No. The house."

"What on earth do you mean?"

"I'll tell you when I come back. This Tinsley girl's a strange woman; but if you think that she's lost her head, I believe you're wrong. Her head's screwed on quite as tight as yours or mine. A woman who has lost her head over a love-affair doesn't cable her lawyer and talk about marriage-settlements."

He left London that night and reached Capri by the morning steamer three days later. Bella awaited him on the jetty. When she saw his drab, travel-worn face bobbing up and down under a bowler hat in the small boat crammed with priests and sea-sick peasants, Wilburn seemed to her to have lost much of his former distinction, like a policeman in plain clothes, she thought, or a Life Guardsman in mufti. There was something cruel and disillusioning about this Mediterranean light: the quality which made the Latin so unsentimental. Wilburn waved his hat to her. She had never realized before what a ridiculous invention a bowler hat was. He had recognized her easily from the distance by the vividness of her cheeks and the bright hair coiled under her little black hat. By contrast with the small, dark people on the quay she seemed taller and slighter than he had remembered her; and when, stumbling ashore, he shook hands, he was also aware of a perceptible increase in her personal dignity: she had no longer the air of a *protégée* amenable to advice and direction, but that of an employer who knew her own mind and was prepared to dictate instructions to a subordinate. Her manner towards him was friendly, but faintly patronizing and tinged with mockery. It reminded him, in effect, how decidedly she had wiped his eye over this White Ladies business, while neglecting to consider the means, unavailable to himself, which she had employed. If he resented this, he was forced to admit the efficiency with which, speaking what seemed to be fluent Italian, Bella dealt with the swarms of porters who competed for his luggage, coolly rescuing him from their clutches and establishing him without scathe at her side in a waiting cab.

"I've booked your room at our hotel for a week," she told him briskly. "I think that should be sufficient. Weren't you a little surprised by my telegram?"

"I shall never be surprised at anything you do, Miss Tinsley."

She laughed happily. "I take that as a compliment."

"Why not? I suppose the . . . the fortunate man is Hugo Pomfret?"

"You're quite right. This shows how much easier it is to settle a matter of this kind between principals."

"That depends very much on the principals, doesn't it? I can quite understand any man being anxious to fall in with your wishes in such a romantic affair."

"I don't like the word 'romantic,' Mr. Wilburn."

"You mean it's to be regarded entirely as a business transaction?"

"We are engaged, and have posted notices in the Consulate-General at Naples. We are to be married next week."

"I wish you both every happiness."

"That's kind of you. In the meantime there is a great deal to be done. Mr. Pomfret is no man of business. I think you will have guessed that already. He is not fond of lawyers, and was anxious, in fact, to leave all the arrangements to me. Still, we ought to have everything put into its proper shape, oughtn't we?"

"Undoubtedly. A marriage-settlement is an extremely important instrument. He, too, should be represented."

"He doesn't want to be. The matters on which we have agreed are quite simple. First of all, there's White Ladies. There are two mortgages on the house and estate. I am going to . . . to pay off, or whatever you call it. It will be easy to find money for that, I suppose?"

"It will not be difficult. You can borrow it from the bank, if you wish; or, if you'ld rather, you can realize a block of your ordinary shares in Jos. Tinsley and Co. Not in the market, of course. We shall have to find somebody who's interested. If you pay off the mortgages on White Ladies, I take it you get something in return?"

"Yes. I am to have a life-interest in White Ladies. I don't know if that's the right word. I mean I am to have possession, whatever happens, as long as I'm alive."

"I quite understand. And then?"

"If I should have a son, he must inherit White Ladies as well as all my own property. That's quite easy, isn't it?"

"In the absence of any provision to the contrary in a previous settlement. Wasn't Mr. Pomfret married before?"

"Yes. He has two daughters living; both married. But they're already provided for by the mother's family."

"And no son?"

"No son by that marriage. There is one other matter, Mr. Wilburn, which will have to be dealt with tactfully and confidentially. I want to make some provision at once for a woman, Carmela Paturzo, who has kept house for Mr. Pomfret for ten years, and for her two children. I should like you to buy the house for her and arrange a regular allowance—sufficient to keep her and her children unless she marries . . ."

"Re-marries?"

"No, marries. The children should be supported until they're old enough to earn their own living. I expect you have made arrangements of this kind before?"

"Indeed yes. More than once. You can safely leave that to me. I shall have to consult an Italian lawyer before I can decide what kind of allowance is usual in such cases."

"I want to be generous."

"I will see that you are just, as well."

"Then I think that's all—at any rate, all for the present. If you don't mind, I think you had better console my poor Aunt Harriet. She thinks I'm quite mad. Do *you* think I'm mad, Mr. Wilburn?"

"I have very few data to go on. As a bachelor I regard all marriages as slightly suspect."

Bella laughed: "That's a clever way out of my question," she said.

Wilburn was astonished, as he wrote and told his brother that evening, by his client's extraordinary mixture of worldliness and naïveté, of rigour and tenderness. If in some ways she appeared to him harder, she seemed also capable of more gentleness. There was about her a sort of glow, a mild radiance of the kind which envelops the Madonnas of medieval Annunciations: *Magnificat* and *Nunc Dimittis* in one. "*There is no doubt at all,*" he wrote, "*that this makes her more attractive than ever. At first sight you would jump to the conclusion that she was in love; yet I'm positive she isn't—not in the ordinary sense of the word. Her attitude is a little high-pitched, exalted, and somehow unreal. I should also say dangerous, although there, again, I can't specify what the danger*

*may be. The whole business is awfully odd and fright-
fully interesting. I have promised to stay here till the
wedding is over. She seemed anxious—almost
pathetically—for me to do that. So expect me when
you see me."*

In his impressions of Hugo Pomfret, Wilburn
found himself agreeably surprised. The man didn't
in the least resemble the waster whom he had expected to find. He still looked, quite obviously, a
gentleman: "a gentleman of the eighteen-seventies,"
Wilburn told himself. His costume as well as his
manners belonged to that date, being formal, precise
and curiously "out of the picture." If he had come
a social cropper—as Wilburn supposed, for why,
otherwise, should he be living in Capri?—he had
evidently recovered from its effects a long time ago
and managed to pull himself together. Physically, he
seemed fit and hard and decidedly young for his age.
He possessed, moreover, an astonishing amount of
natural dignity: sufficient to "carry off" a situation
which, to say the least, was equivocal—that of a man
of slender means with a shady reputation (to say
nothing of a mistress) who was about to marry a
woman half his age for her money. *Was* he marrying
Bella Tinsley for her money? The fact that this question proposed itself was the most surprising part of
the whole affair. When he made himself answer it,
Wilburn was forced to confess that he honestly believed Hugo Pomfret to be in love with her. He was

as certain that Pomfret was in love as that Bella was not; and in this, remembering their respective ages, he saw elements of inevitable tragedy.

"If only they'll hurry up and have children," he thought, "the situation may possibly be saved." Yet he disliked the idea of Bella having children by Hugo Pomfret.

The third member of this fantastic trio imposed a greater strain on his tact and discretion than either of the others. Bella had put it mildly when she said that her Aunt Harriet needed consoling. Miss Mortimer was not merely inconsolable but furious. She clung to Wilburn as a drowning woman might cling to a rock in a dark, tumultuous sea. She was glad, she told him, to set eyes on a sane person at last: the first she had seen since the day she had been tricked into leaving Dover. Her hard-worked wild horses would not drag her out of England again. This island of Capri was nothing but a lunatic asylum. Consider only its weather: burning hot one moment and equally icy the next. Consider the price of tea: seven shillings —would any sane person credit it?—seven shillings a pound and undrinkable at that! Consider the fleas in the cathedral and the morals of the inhabitants. The whole island, according to a very superior woman named Spettigue, was nothing less than a cesspool, and this man Hugo Pomfret, who had got hold of Bella, was the lowest of the lot. Not that she needed any telling. She had seen what he was from the very day on which he had scraped acquaintance with Bella on the *piazza* and forced himself on them for lunch. As for Bella—well, ghastly as her present infatuation might be, it might almost, Miss Mortimer supposed, have been expected. There was, she regretted to say, a mad streak in the Tinsley family. It had "come out" once before in Bella's poor mother, and now it had "come out" in her. If Mr. Wilburn could stop it. . . . But, of course, she knew that he couldn't. The girl had gone clean off her head. It was no use talking to her. Whatever you said made no difference. She just smiled and smiled. If she would lose her temper and get thoroughly wild, it might bring her to her senses. But no. She just smiled like an idiot and said: "Yes, Aunt Harriet, do you think so?"

"I'll tell you what, Mr. Wilburn," Miss Mortimer said grimly, "if her poor dear grandpa had been alive there'ld have been none of this nonsense. He'ld have taken the strap to her—I give you my word he would! —and have taught the child sense at the end of it. I tell you, that Pomfret will run through our Bella's money in a couple of years. Mark my words!"

On that point, at any rate, Wilburn was able to reassure her.

"Miss Tinsley," he said, "has a very good business head. If she hadn't, that is why I am here. It's my job to protect her. The settlement I'm making is by no means a one-sided affair. She acquires a life-interest in his property . . ."

"What. . . . You don't say that Pomfret has property?"

"Indeed yes. And I can promise you also he won't touch her money."

"You can't promise anything of the sort, Mr. Wilburn, and you know it. If the poor fool thinks she's in love . . ."

"Do *you* think she's in love, Miss Mortimer?"

"Well, if she isn't. . . . Upon my soul, I begin to think you're another! Is anyone sane on this island? Or have *I* gone cracked too?"

"No, I think we're all right, you and I," Wilburn reassured her. "And, odd though it sounds, I believe there is method in Bella's madness, too."

"Well, I, for one, give it up," Miss Mortimer declared. "The whole thing's beyond me, and I wish to goodness I was back at Hayseech. What's more, let me tell you this: if I could have faced their shouting and waving and thieving and jabbering"—she still smarted under the memory of her handling by the porters at Naples—"I should have packed my traps a week ago and gone straight home. However, that's all right now," she added with satisfaction. "Bella tells me you've kindly offered to escort me back to England the moment this monstrous wedding —if you can call it a wedding—is over."

Wilburn gasped. This was the first he had heard of it. Then he smiled and assured her that nothing would give him greater pleasure.

o

"And, after that, never again!" said Miss Mortimer. "Never again! I must say I find the whole business distressing and sordid from beginning to end."

There were sordid elements in it, Wilburn was forced to admit. Though the marriage-settlement was a straightforward piece of routine—for Pomfret's affairs were in much better order than he had imagined —his dealings with Carmelina, or rather with her family, proved far less easy. Such arrangements, the local lawyer insisted, were much better approached in secret and indirectly, with at least three or four intermediaries between the principals concerned. In this case, unfortunately, the secret could not be kept; and the mild cupidity of Carmelina who, left to herself, would have had very little objection to being "planted" as long as her children were provided for and her own future secure, was fanned into flaming rapacity by her kinsman, Paturzo, who not only took it for granted that all English travellers had money (or how else should they travel?) but also that Bella, as the employer of a private lawyer who lived like a lord, must at least be a millionairess. Hence the dilapidated cottage, which belonged to another member of this predatory family and could have been bought, at any previous moment, for two or three thousand *lire*, became, suddenly, a priceless heirloom which its owner could only be persuaded to part with it for a sum more than ten times its value. At the same moment,

Carmelina's virtue assumed a price which she herself had certainly never put on it. It soon became clear that Pomfret—or Bella—would have to pay through the nose.

The Italian lawyer was not in the least disturbed by this bargaining. If the *signori* would only wait, he assured them, the matter would soon arrange itself. But Bella refused to wait. She had a feeling almost amounting to a superstition in the back of her mind that she couldn't safely assume possession of White Ladies unless she had settled every outstanding indebtedness. She showed also what seemed to Wilburn a curious delicacy in her anxiety that Pomfret, whose business it certainly was, should not be consulted or even become aware of the terms on which it was settled. Once more Wilburn was made aware of the ruthless realism which this young woman combined with her idealistic passion.

"For heaven's sake pay whatever they ask," she said, "and get it over."

"My colleague assures me we needn't," he told her.

"That doesn't matter. Don't you see I want to forget about it?"

Wilburn's colleague threw up his hands in horror at this reckless munificence, and, on the strength of it, trebled his own fees: in his judgement it was only right that fools should pay for their folly. In the end the "plantation" of Carmelina and Pomfret's putative children became an expensive business.

Wilburn's visit dragged on from seven days to a fortnight and then to three weeks. The first gales of March had lashed the blue gulf into a fury of leaden surges when Miss Mortimer finally packed her tin trunks and the party crossed to Naples. The wedding, at the Consulate-General, was a sombre business. Miss Mortimer, present under protest, maintained an attitude of unappeasable grimness. Hugo Pomfret, though studiously polite, was clearly nervous of her. Indeed, the only member of the party who appeared to enjoy the proceedings was Bella. She could not have appeared more radiant, Wilburn thought, if that dingy office had been St. George's, Hanover Square, and the ceremony the culmination of a happy love-affair. When the formalities were completed, in the interval before the departure of the married couple for Rome, Wilburn seized the opportunity of getting the bride to sign the transfer-certificates relating to her sale of two blocks of ordinary shares in Jos. Tinsley & Co. to Walter Willis and Stephen Wilkinson. He noticed the firmness with which she handled the scratchy official pen, and the decision with which she wrote her new designation: Arabella Pomfret. A bold signature, Wilburn thought, and a high-sounding name. As she handed the pen back to him, she said:

"Is that *my* Mr. Wilkinson? Hayseech, I mean."

"Let me see. Yes. Hayseech. That's the man."

"This shows he has faith—and hope, too, doesn't it?"

"What about the other thing?"

Mrs. Pomfret sighed. "Ah well, one can't have everything. Hugo, it's time we were moving."

"Yes, we ought to be moving," Pomfret replied. "Good-bye, Miss Mortimer. Good-bye, Wilburn!"

"Well, there they go. That's all I can say about it," Miss Mortimer declared.

V

THEY made straight for White Ladies, barely halting in Rome and Paris, arriving at Bromsberrow, the nearest main-line station, on a wild March evening. Having usually approached White Ladies by road and from the north, Bella was somewhat shocked to find herself alighting on that familiar platform. She had not set foot on it, indeed, since the day when, eight years before, a callow and self-conscious child, she had returned to St. Monica's after her grandfather's funeral. In the meantime she had imagined that she had said good-bye to everything connected with that part of the world and of her existence: yet here she was, an entirely different person, an elegant young married woman in a sable coat, completing one of those mysterious circles in which, it appeared, life ran.

Bromsberrow Station had not changed in the least. Its platform still had the identical smell of smoke and train-oil and milk-cans. The same porter who on that sombre occasion had carried the little leather bag Miss Boldmere had lent her and condoled with her on Mr. Small's death, now wheeled Mr. Hugo Pomfret's piled trunks and hat-box towards the conveyance which had been ordered for them. Though he observed Bella with curiosity he did not guess who she was; and she was glad of this. It would be a mistake, she thought, to mix the new life with the old. In future, she decided they would use some other station.

She was thankful, again, when the cab turned sharply to the left, avoiding the road which led past Hypatia House to the nailers' cottages and her grand-father's warehouse. In old age, she had heard, it was a recognized trait of human nature to return like a ghost to the familiar haunts of one's childhood. But she was not old: she believed that the most important part of her life was only beginning, had hardly begun, and she was eager to embark on it unhampered by any dead-weight of sentimental memories or regrets. She was even happier when the outskirts of Bromsberrow were left behind and they took to the open country.

Even so, these fugitive reminders of the familiar past made a curious effect on her by emphasizing the strangeness of her unfamiliar present. As they drove in silence through the deep wintry lanes of the clay-land, she could not help wondering at it. She had actually been married for nearly a week to the stranger who sat beside her. He was a pleasant stranger. No-body could have been kinder or more considerate than he in his handling of this unusual situation. He had always been courteous; he had been gentle; he had shown delicacy; he had been wise, no doubt, from his extensive experience of women. He declared that he had fallen in love with her at first sight and that he had never loved any woman in the same way before: two flattering assertions which she was inclined to believe. As a lover she had not found him unpleasant. He said she had renewed his youth, had "made a young man of him"; and though she had to confess that she herself hadn't noticed any change in him—apart from his having shaved his moustache—it was nice of him to give her credit for it. In any case, young or middle-aged, he was not a clumsy lover, and being married had given her an unexpected feeling of bodily fulfilment and content. Yet if she was pleased by the physical effects of this novel submissiveness and by the comfort of mind which arose from having surrendered for the first time in her life to another's will and possession, she was aware, none the less, that something was missing. This marriage—although her husband might think differently—was very different from the marriage of her romantic dreams. Even in moments of complete abandonment it had none of the spiritual rapture which she had momentarily experienced in the arms of Henry Fladburn. However rigorously she might persuade herself otherwise, she knew it was, in essentials, *terre à terre*, devoid of imaginative ardour and of emotional intensity. That defect must be faced. If she had neglected to face it in the beginning, she must do so now: she must recognize it, deal with it, and put it out of her mind, instead of leaving it there as a closed focus of infection which might later poison her existence with vain regret and dissatisfaction. As she had remarked to Wilburn on the day of her wedding, one couldn't have everything, and the emotional deficiencies of her marriage with Pomfret would be made good by the infatuation for White Ladies which had led her to accept this compromise; and the bearing of children would give her passion an even greater validity.

So far she had never questioned the rightness of these presumptions. It was only as they approached White Ladies that afternoon that their rashness began to trouble her. Though a wintry sun shone through the hedgerow elms, the air, after that of Italy, seemed dank and unhomely. Pomfret, seeing her pinched and shivery, wrapped a travelling-rug about her. This attention touched her, because she was not used to such things; but the chill from which she suffered was one of the spirit. Supposing, she asked herself—supposing White Ladies should "let her down"? It was an easy matter for Pomfret, coming back to his ancestral home, to a house whose walls were saturated with the dreams and hopes and sufferings and aspirations of his forefathers. Would its ghosts accept her as readily? Now that she came to consider the matter in cold—and in such cold!—blood, it occurred to her that this house on which she had set her heart was even more of a stranger to her than her husband. She had only set foot in it once, for a few brief moments; and though its beauty, then perceived, had obsessed her with

o*

increasing power ever since, who could say for certain that she was not the victim of hallucination? Perhaps it might not be so beautiful or so satisfying as she had imagined. Perhaps she had accepted the substance of this strange marriage for the sake of a shadow. She sat huddled in her wrappings, a prey to haunting anxiety, her eyes closed for fear of what, in a moment, they might see.

She need not have been anxious. This she knew with a thrill of unique and almost painful ecstasy when, the cab having entered the domain through the lodge-gates that guarded it on the east, Hugo Pomfret's hand clutched her arm suddenly. "Look, Bella!" he said. "My God, that's worth coming some way to see, isn't it?"

She opened her eyes to a dazzle of slanting sun-light that drenched the wide winter-bleached park-land from one wood-verge to another. In the fore-ground, their reedy fringes absorbing and solidifying as it were the sun's pale amber, two curved pools, spring-fed by the water that trickled from the moat, reflected the high March sky; and the channel which joined their twin steely discs was crossed in the midst by an arched balustraded bridge whose ornaments re-called the deserted Palladian gatehouse; a structure which looked at a distance so slender that it hardly seemed fit to bear the weight of their laden carriage.

"Good heavens, how those reed-beds have grown," Hugo Pomfret was saying excitedly. "We must get them cut and dredge the mud. It was here, by the side of the bridge, that I caught my first pike. Look, there goes a mallard!" and his arm went up as though it lifted a gun.

But Bella, though she smiled, acquiescing in his enthusiasm, was not looking at the duck which, with neck outstretched, swerved black across the sky on their left. She was gazing ahead through the arch of the bridge at what that arch, in the artist's mind, had been planned to enclose like a gem set in stone: the shape of the house, White Ladies—the house of her dream made permanent in brick and stone, its flank more perfectly placed, perhaps, in this formal approach than the frontage which she knew already. There it stood, seeming strangely small, she thought, by reason of its classic proportions—small enough, she reflected thankfully, to be grasped and loved in spite of its dignities. It was hers at last—and not only hers but, as never before, alive: for the curtains had been drawn aside from the mullioned windows, and from two fluted clusters of chimney-stacks trails of smoke, rising straight into the still air, announced habitation and warmth.

"And there's the house!" Pomfret cried. He laughed with quiet pleasure. "Twelve years it's been waiting for me—for us, and it feels like yesterday. Nothing changed!"

"Things like that don't change," Bella said. "Are you happy, Hugo?"

"This the happiest day of my life. I can hardly believe it. I can hardly bear it, my dear."

"I'm glad you are happy," she said.

As soon as the cab stopped Hugo Pomfret jumped out and gave her his hand.

Seeing him thus, alert and confident, with a smile of content in his eyes, Bella felt ready to admit that he had, as he boasted, grown younger. During their journey across Europe she had noticed from time to time, when he was tired or his attention flagged, his face clouded with expressions which reminded her of the derelict Hugo Pomfret she had first observed striding to and fro on the *piazza* at Capri, and that other whom she had surprised asleep in his studio. When she saw these shadows return, she had felt sorry for him, realizing how hard it must be to shake off in a moment the habit of more than ten years. There was no need to feel sorry for him now. From the moment when he stepped out of the cab and opened the door of White Ladies for her to enter, she had a conviction that she need never feel anxious for him again. He had become once more the master of himself and his destiny. Already he commanded her liking and her respect. Now, at last, she felt proud of him too.

The great hall was lighter that afternoon than on the day when she had invaded it. Once again the amber tinge in the panes of the oriel gave an effect of mellow sunlight, but the clearer sky illuminated

details which she had missed before. The huge stone-
flagged expanse had lost its mystery. A wood fire
burned brightly on the open hearth. The walls were
warm with the glow of faded tapestries, the rich hues
of old portraits and the glint of arms and armour.
She saw nothing that did not appear to be ancient
and rather shabby: nothing which had not gained by
age and by use a certain softness, a sort of spiritual
patina. Bella had always been sensitive to the feelings of friendliness or hostility that proceeded from
inanimate things and, above all, from houses. This
place had so long been accustomed to being lived in—
and lived in by such a variety of human beings—that
it seemed to accept her, the stranger, without question. It was too old and too wise, too secure in its
individuality, too conscious of human impermanence,
to be much concerned with the quality of its latest inhabitant. Another Pomfret had brought home another
bride who, herself, had become a Pomfret, and that
was enough. As for Hugo, he was completely at home.
There could be no doubt of that. He even appeared
to have drawn from this contact with his proper possessions a new dignity which became them no less
than himself. She was glad that she had been able
to witness this transformation alone and not in the
presence of inquisitive eyes.

"Apparently nobody's heard us arrive," he said. "I
suppose I had better ring."

But even as he spoke Bella heard the tap of the

stick which she had half expected. A door concealed
in the panelling opened, and the figure of the little
black witch came hopping towards them. Hugo turned
to greet her: "So there you are, Miss Penney!" He
teased her. "We've caught you napping."

"Not napping, not napping, Mr. Hugo. Not napping," the shrill voice chirped. "I was upstairs in your
bedroom, upstairs; I heard you; and Thomas has gone
for the luggage."

"This is my wife, Miss Penney."

The little black eyes surveyed Bella. They looked
puzzled, then startled by sudden recognition. They
went through her like gimlets, peering, prying,
malicious. Bella laughed: "You see who I am, Miss
Penney. We've met before."

"Yes, we've met before, Mrs. Pomfret, Mrs. Pomfret. You're welcome, madam. Welcome home to
White Ladies, White Ladies." But her eyes gave
no welcome: they were grudging and, Bella thought,
devilish.

"Miss Penney," Hugo said, "is the guardian angel
of this place. She was housekeeper here to my uncle
when I was a boy, and for twelve years, ever since he
died, she's lived here alone."

"Yes, alone, alone in White Ladies," the little
thing chirped. "You'll be cold, Mr. Hugo. You'll
be wanting some tea . . . some tea. If Mrs. Pomfret wants anything she has only to tell me, to tell
me."

She turned like a tit on a twig and went away tapping her stick.

"The poor old thing's twisted by rheumatism," Hugo said. "She must be over seventy. Oh, much more than that. She looked exactly like this when I was a boy. I've never seen her still for a moment; she's always moving. Isn't it amazing for a crippled woman to have managed a house of this size and kept it, exactly as it always was, for all those years? Of course it's her passion: the only thing in her life. In a way it's more hers than ours. Can't you feel how she loves it?"

"Yes, I can see how she loves it," Bella said—"and hates *me*," she thought. "To tell you the truth, Hugo, she rather gives me the shivers. She isn't quite human, is she?"

"Poor thing, she can't help *that*."

"I don't mean her body. She's like—what can I say?—like a little black spider that lives in a cranny in the oak and watches you with cold insect eyes. I felt that when she caught me prying in here before. She appeared out of nothing. I just heard the tap of her stick."

"What a ridiculous fancy! That just showed what a good guardian she is. She's the soul of loyalty."

"To the house and to you, perhaps."

"Well, dear child, you'll soon get over your feelings, and we shall have to put up with her. She belongs here as much as we do. She's served two generations faithfully, and you couldn't possibly get rid of her at her time of life."

"Yes . . . I suppose we shall have to put up with her. Here comes the tea."

It was brought by the man called Thomas: a little grey creature who might easily have been older than the ageless Miss Penney. He was dressed for his duty in a dark green footman's uniform—though whether it was intended to be green or was merely a black that had lost colour with age, Bella could not determine. All the garments composing it appeared to have been made much too large for him, unless, indeed, it were his body which had shrunk and shrivelled like a walnut in its shell. As a contrast to that of the housekeeper his manner was a relief. He had a small, round head covered by a short crop of wiry white hair which had obviously been clipped in the stables, and timid blue eyes; yet even his hair seemed hardly paler than the skin of his wrinkled face, to which the light that streamed from the oriel gave a yellowish tinge. He moved slowly and breathed heavily—it was evident that the transport of their luggage had tired him—and his pale hands, silently arranging the fluted Queen Anne silver and the green Rockingham tea-cups, trembled as they moved. Hugo Pomfret spoke to him familiarly. It was clear that they were old friends. Before he answered he had the habit of pausing and sighing, as though the sound of human speech were somewhat foreign to him and words must be pondered before they were understood; but when he did speak, his voice, which was unbelievably quiet, and the slow syllables of his Worcestershire speech, gave an effect of simplicity and gentleness which was touching. It would be impossible, Bella thought, to deal harshly with a creature so inoffensive, one whose colouring and texture, she told herself, had become assimilated to that of the threadbare carpets, the worn upholstery, the faded tapestries among which he had lived, one whose very movements disturbed the atmosphere of the hall no more than the passage of a friendly ghost.

"Dinner will be served at eight, as usual, madam," he said, "if that is convenient."

If it had been inconvenient, Bella felt, she could not have altered the hour. If dinner at White Ladies was usually served at eight, that practice must continue: the house must be permitted to dictate the manners of its inhabitants. She consented and thanked him. Then, pausing for a moment, he said:

"The wine, Mr. Hugo. . . I have taken the liberty of bringing up a bottle from one of the bins of claret. Lafite seventy-one, sir. That wine should be in nice condition by now. The port you already know, sir. It's the sixty-four. I'm afraid there's not much of it left."

"You were quite right, Thomas," Hugo told him. "This is a great occasion. I shall expect you to drink my wife's health and mine."

"I shall do so with pleasure, sir. It's a great happiness, if I may say so, for me as well. The house feels quite different already."

"*The house*," Bella thought. "How strange, but how right! It's always the house." When the butler had gone she turned to Hugo and said: "There's still wine in the cellar? That's the last thing I should have expected. I should have thought you'ld have sold it."

He smiled. "No, that wouldn't have seemed right. Everything here is exactly as it was when my uncle died. I've never sold anything. It's just possible that some of the wine may be ullaged. But I doubt it. The cellar belongs to Thomas; he has always gone on with his work, just the same as Miss Penney. The fact that he's been on less than half wages—and she, bless her heart, on none—will have made no difference. Did you notice the silver?"

"I saw it was beautifully kept."

"Thomas's father kept it just as beautifully before him, my uncle has told me. Between them they've kept it polished for a hundred years. It's strange to think of, but I believe the things in this house have always been cherished. When they do die, they die of old age, like the servants." He rose. "The light won't last long. I should like just to have a look round while I can. Will you come with me?"

"Unless you would rather be alone?"

"I should like you to come."

No wonder that poor Thomas had looked exhausted

and that his hands trembled! In each room that they
entered a fire had been lit and the furniture un-
covered; all appeared to be kempt and dustless; none
smelt uninhabited. Hugo led her rapidly from one to
another. On the left of the entrance, a drawing-room
rising sheer from the moat faced west. The full blaze
of the sinking sun illuminated an interior which
seemed oddly bright after the hall's subdued amber;
for here, in some age more greedy for light, the oak
wainscoting had been covered with paint which had
once been white, but now, with impalpable accretions
of dust and wood-smoke, had the soft tone of ivory.
Some feminine fancy, rebellious against feudal
glooms, had had its way with this chamber. All the
oak with which once, no doubt, it had been over-
crowded, had given place to materials more exotic and
delicate—mahogany and satinwood, gilt pine and
lacquer. A heavy chimney-piece of parti-coloured
marbles was flanked by a pair of Soho tapestry hang-
ings, the oak floor partly covered with a French
tapestry carpet of later date, in whose faded threads
the sun which had bleached them refreshed, as it were,
the subdued colour that remained. On the panelled
walls hung many mirrors but few pictures, and the
latter partook of their setting's delicacy. They were
family portraits of women and children in pastel:
a chalky possible Cotes, a pair of more vivid Cosways,
and a group of children by Gardner which in its
luxuriant forms anticipated the graces of Lawrence.

It was above all, as Bella perceived, a woman's room. The pictures, even more than the faded embroideries, set the tone of it. If it were to be painted, she told herself, pastel would be the only appropriate medium for the expression of its luminosity of rose and ivory. She adored it at sight, but Hugo appeared to regard its graces impatiently.

"Come along," he said. "I want you to see the dining-room."

He led the way rapidly, crossing the hall, into a room which in shape—and in nothing else—corresponded with the last. Here the oak of the feudal age had not only persisted but also been blackened by time. The darkening eastern sky made no compromise with a gloom out of which, as she stood with her arm in her husband's, stern faces and high lights of weapons or steel cuirasses appeared to detach themselves from a uniform darkness crowded with a muster of armed men. All the faces of Hugo's ancestors seemed to her grim and sombre and wary: the faces of men with nerves keyed to the exigencies of a dangerous life and the determination to keep their footing —or perhaps their heads. She felt thankful that she had not been mistress of White Ladies in their days.

Out of all that ghostly assembly of painted faces there was only one which appeared to be free from anxiety. It was that of a young man who wore no armour: a clean-shaven face awkwardly set above a ruff and a black-velvet doublet on which rested a medal hung from a silver chain. The portrait was a piece of hurried and slovenly painting, the tapered fingers that grasped the chain conventionalized and devoid of character; yet the features, the smallish round head, the palish blue eyes, and, above all, a suspicion of humour that seemed to lurk in a mouth that was generous but not over-strong, immediately reminded her of Hugo. "If we have a son," she thought, "he might look just like that. It would be nice to have a son who looked happy and could see a joke as he did." She pointed to the picture:

"Who is he?" she asked. "I like that best of all, I think."

"A namesake of mine. Hugo Pomfret. The painting isn't a good one."

"I know. I didn't think of it in that way. He's like what you must have been as a boy. Do tell me about him."

He laughed: "It's a sad story, I fear. The poor fellow got tangled in the fringes of the Gunpowder Plot. He was a Catholic: you see his medal. He got mixed up with the Winters at Huddington—which is not very far from here—and some of the other Catholic gentry, and although he wasn't very important he lost his head. The estate went to a cousin, a Protestant, so that was all right. Being heir, in the direct line, to White Ladies, he should have been more careful. As you know, it's a risky business."

"But surely there's nothing in that story? Isn't it just a matter of chance?"

"It's against the law of averages. That's all I can say."

"If it's true it seems to me dreadful."

"Well, well, there are compensations. If my cousin had lived, you and I wouldn't be here now."

"But supposing . . ."

He cut her short. "Come along, my dear, we must hurry. There's something I want to show you before all the light's gone. This is a magnificent dining-room, isn't it? It's too dark to see the ceiling. When the candles are lit for dinner you'll see the plaster-work's superb."

He took her arm and hurried her from the room. In the great hall no light remained but the amber glow of the oriel. They ascended the shallow-stepped stair-case of uncarpeted oak. From time to time, as they passed it, Hugo pointed to this or that picture which he remembered.

"In a little time," he said, "you'll know them as well as I do. None are very valuable; but each of them has something to do with the house in one way or another. The best bedrooms are all on this floor. Yours, I think, will almost certainly be at the end of the corridor facing east. There's a Chinese wallpaper of birds and tropical fruits in it, and a Queen Anne lacquer bedstead. We'll look at that later. There's no time to lose. This corridor runs the whole length

of the front of the house. When I was a boy I was
scared to death of it. It was so dark and one's feet
echoed so. I used to think ghosts brushed past me.
Children have queer fancies."

"And not only children," Bella thought. It was
odd that he should have spoken of those fears, for,
at that very moment, she had been saying to herself
how thankful she was that Hugo was with her. This
dark corridor had a different atmosphere from the rest
of the house. She felt it as one sometimes became
suddenly aware of stepping into a patch of warm air
or cold on a country road. But her present sensation
was not ghostly; ghosts didn't trouble her. It was
rather a consciousness, instinctive and not derived from
the senses, that some jealous watcher of flesh and
blood followed them. Indeed, once she had felt it
so strongly that she had looked round—and seen
nobody.

"Up here!" Hugo said. He preceded her up a
narrower stairway of stone on which their tread fell
more silently than on the oak-floored corridor. At
the top he halted. "Now prepare yourself for a real
surprise," he told her. "Take my hand, shut your
eyes, and follow me." Bella obeyed. "Now open
your eyes."

Through their closed lids they had been aware of
a change in the intensity of light, but not for the
dazzle which now overwhelmed them. They opened
on what was without doubt the principal glory of

White Ladies: the Long Gallery running from end
to end of the uppermost storey in the building's
western flank. It was the great elevation to which
three flights of stairs had lifted them out of the lower
regions of air, now plunged in shadow, into those
that the sun's last radiance still transfused which
gave this high clerestory its air of pure light and
freedom. Nor only that, for the gallery itself had
a celestial quality that made it seem to belong to sky
rather than earth, being drenched with the light that
streamed from a range of windows uncurtained and
unbroken for more than a hundred and twenty feet by
any partition, and was reinforced by reflection from a
floor and a wainscoting of oak which had been
bleached by the suns of three centuries to a silvery
grey. The whole length of the gallery was empty of
any furniture except a few painted chairs and
settles which the wealth of light had reduced to
the same ashen hue, and a number of glazed cases
of more recent date, museum-furniture containing
muniments and seals and miniatures and military
relics, carefully covered with faded baize to protect
them from the sun.

It was in these, it seemed, rather than in the
gallery's aerial beauty that Hugo was interested.

"All our best things are here," he told her. "They
fascinate me. There's no end to them. Can you
wonder I'm excited? I haven't seen them for so long.
I used to spend half my life here. Look at this, for

instance!"—He opened a case. "It's a free pardon for Roger Pomfret—the grand-nephew of the Hugo you saw downstairs—for the part he took in the Great Rebellion. You see—the pardon is issued by the Parliament of England, but it's sealed with a clumsy imitation of Charles the First's seal. The generals were so busy that they hadn't time to invent another! And here—yes, you'll find this interesting—here's the medal poor Hugo wore in his portrait and carried to the block. I forget what particular saint it is, and now we can't see. The light's going so quickly. Yes, it's practically gone."

He put back the medal and closed the case. As they turned away Bella heard a faint rustle, and saw out of the corner of her eye that some unseen hand was replacing the baize cover that had fallen to the floor. She looked round sharply and found herself gazing into the spiderlike eyes of little Miss Penney, sharp and black as jet and jealous beyond belief. Were those the eyes, she wondered, which had seemed to be watching them? She shivered in spite of herself. Hugo, wondering what had delayed her, turned too.

"Why, Miss Penney," he said. "I'd no idea you were there."

The witch smiled: "I came upstairs, Mr. Hugo, upstairs. I thought you'ld be here. It was the keys, madam, the keys, the keys of your luggage. They were forgotten, forgotten."

"Oh, you needn't worry about them, Miss Penney. I know you're short-handed. I can easily unpack for myself."

Hugo added: "It's the corner room, isn't it, Miss Penney, the one with the Chinese wallpaper?"

"Yes, the Chinese room, the Chinese, Mr. Hugo. The room that the master died in, died in."

Hugo laughed. "That sounds cheerful, doesn't it, Bella? Miss Penney knows all the ghosts here, don't you, Miss Penney?"

"Yes, I know all the ghosts, all the ghosts, Mr. Hugo, *and* they know me."

But this time, Bella thought, the long corridor below seemed far less ghostly.

They dined in some state that evening. However uncanny Miss Penney might be, she was an excellent cook. The table-silver was superb, and Thomas glowed under Hugo's compliments on its condition. Hugo drank a good deal of the seventy-one Lafite and happily recalled with Thomas old fragments of family history. He looked wonderfully at home, Bella thought, sitting there at the head of the huge oak table. She herself was unusually quiet. She felt tired and elated and rather overwhelmed by the strangeness as well as the loveliness of what she had seen. They sat on over the table until they were ready for bed. When, at last, Hugo left her, alone in the lacquer four-poster watching the flicker of firelight illumining the bright birds of the Chinese wallpaper, her mind was a prey to so many emotions that she could not sleep. Lying there, with closed eyes, she prayed to the God of Miss Boldmere, Whom she had almost forgotten, that she might have a son.

BOOK FIVE

POSSESSION

I

BELLA's coming to White Ladies had released a torrent of constructive and reforming energy which positively bewildered poor Hugo, accustomed to the easy ways of Capri, where the next-best-thing satisfies most people and to-morrow (or the day after that) is as good as to-day. In the first weeks of their marriage he had declared that she had made a young man of him: now her "restlessness," as he called it, began to "age" him. Bella resented his word, with some reason. She wasn't restless. Indeed it would have been difficult to discover a purpose more constant than hers. Having become possessed of a thing which she believed to be uniquely beautiful, she was determined to preserve and, if necessary, to enhance that beauty by devoting to it every atom of energy and money she could expend.

To begin with: it was hard for a man like Hugo, whose experiences of housekeeping in Capri had been of the simplest, to conceive the forethought and effort involved in the process of "running" a house of the size of White Ladies smoothly and efficiently. It meant setting in motion not merely a mechanism which had been rusted and corroded by twelve years of disuse, but one whose design was faulty and obso-

lete and, in practical detail, defective. Hugo Pomfret
would have been contented, as he said, to "pig it"—
to live, in effect, the same sort of life as he had lived
in his Capri studio—amid surroundings that, because
of his long exile, were sufficient in themselves to make
him completely happy. He felt there was no hurry
to alter things in any case: what had been good enough
for his forbears was good enough for him.

Bella could not regard the position with such complacency. The difference between their two attitudes
was radical. It was precisely this supineness in the
Pomfret method of looking on life which had allowed
the wealth of Mawne and Hayseech to slip through
their nerveless fingers and had reduced White Ladies
itself to the state of abandonment in which she found
it. She herself was a Tinsley—and even more a
Mortimer, her grandfather's grandchild. It was not
in her nature to leave anything to which she had set
her hand half-done.

She felt it necessary, to begin with, to enlist battalions of servants to deal with the visible and invisible dust and dirt which had accumulated in every
corner and cranny of the rambling house during its
years of emptiness. Even in those days it was not easy
to staff a mansion so utterly isolated from all normal
social intercourse. Only "country" maids would consent to live in it, and country maids she found slug-
gish and inefficient and rough in their treatment of
precious things which were so old that in the mere

process of handling they fell to pieces. These early
domestic difficulties and tragedies were complicated
by the fact that mischievous tongues in the villages
had set rumours running that White Ladies was
haunted. And indeed White Ladies *was* haunted—
not by ghostly influences but by the uncompromising
malice and jealousy of little Miss Penney, who did
all that she could to make every change difficult by
creating obstructions and pitfalls so elusive that only
their distant effects could be felt.

For a long time Hugo felt a vague uneasiness at
the threats to his bachelor peace which emanated from
Bella's endless output of energy. At first he had been
inclined to smile at it tolerantly and even to take a
proprietary pride in it as a quality in which he knew
himself to be lacking, another proof—if that were
needed—of his bride's remarkable nature. Little by
little, however, it began to strain his nerves. They
were taut to a dangerous degree when the subject of
Miss Penney precipitated his first quarrel with Bella.
One still summer evening, when he came in from the
fields under a sky that threatened thunder, she tackled
him.

"I want to talk seriously about Miss Penney," she
said.

"Well, what has Miss Penney done *now?*"

"If I could tell you exactly it would be easier. I
can't. Without doing anything I can lay my finger on
she upsets the whole household. The maids can't do

P

anything without feeling that she's watching them. They hate being haunted like that. She gets on their nerves."

"Then there's something wrong with their nerves. They're a poor-looking lot, I must say."

"They weren't chosen for the front row of the Gaiety chorus, Hugo. With enormous trouble I manage to get hold of a number of decent girls. I try to train them according to my own ideas, and they do their best; but no sooner have I settled what I want done than I find my orders changed. If only the woman would not interfere . . ."

"Probably she thinks that you're interfering."

"Interfering? In my own house?"

"Well, isn't it usually the housekeeper's job to give orders?"

"To see that my orders are performed."

"After all, Bella, she knows a great deal more about running this house than you do. She's lived in it for fifty years and you've only been here three months."

"Well, you can't have two mistresses in a house."

"Of course not. And you can't have two housekeepers."

"She behaves as if everything belonged to her."

"Well, it does, in a sense. At any rate she belongs to the house."

"She's belonged to it far too long. I don't propose to put up with her. I shall get rid of her."

"You'll do nothing of the sort, Bella. You can do what you like with the servants you engage for yourself. Thomas and Miss Penney belong to me, and you'll oblige me by leaving them alone."

He spoke hotly. Bella, looking at him, saw his round, Norman head go obstinate; an angry vein bulged in the middle of his forehead; his neck went red; his face grew lurid and threatening as the thunder-charged sky; his weak mouth showed an ugly curl.

"Can't you leave the place alone?" he almost shouted. "Can't you get this maggot of interfering restlessness out of your head? Why do you *want* to change things? Hasn't White Ladies got on without you for three hundred years?"

His mood was so violent, so foreign to all that she knew of him, that it startled her. Her own spirit flared up to meet his. She wanted to tell him not to shout, not to forget she was his wife and not his mistress; her mind was choked with bitter things crying for speech; but prudence, for a wonder, got the better of her rising passion; like her grandfather she knew by instinct when it paid her to lose her temper and when it did not. She spoke calmly:

"At least you will speak to Miss Penney and tell her that you object to my being obstructed."

"I shall do nothing of the sort," he answered. "The whole thing is sheer moonshine. If Miss Penney offends you it's merely out of excess of devotion. I don't blame you. It's natural, I suppose, for a woman in your condition to have fancies."

"Well, really, Hugo . . ."

But before she could finish her protest he was gone. She saw him pass out of the front door under the oriel and turn the corner. From the window she watched heavy drops of thunder-rain splashing in the moat. The pattern of spreading ringlets fascinated her. Strangely enough, she was no longer angry. It now struck her as comical rather than as outrageous that he should throw his baby—so to speak—in her face. She was beginning to regard him, in fact, as a middle-aged child, occasionally charming, occasionally irrational and petulant. He had given her a share in White Ladies; he was about to give her the son who would wholly possess it. Apart from these functions, which he alone had been qualified to perform, Hugo Pomfret had little standing or significance in her life. In relation to them she respected him, and otherwise, at times, rather liked his companionship. All his actions and thoughts were so beautifully calculable. If they lacked imagination and enterprise they were at least, in comparison with her own, reassuringly stable. The principal defects of his character—and perhaps, after all, they had something to do with his age as well as with the Pomfret blood—were a complacent indolence, an obstinacy which had its roots in weakness rather than in strength, and, above all, an instinctive dislike of facing unpleasant facts. And though she was often impatient with him, she more often pitied him—particularly on such an occasion as this, when she thought of him running away from her through the pelting rain which now lashed the moat unmercifully and rebounded from the flagged terrace like hail. When their son was born, she thanked heaven, he would be Mortimer as well as Pomfret. As the boy grew up, he and she would face all their problems side by side and see them through the same eyes. Though White Ladies could not yet be wholly hers, it would become hers, through him, as soon as he succeeded. As soon, in other words, as her husband died. Poor Hugo! How callous the processes of reason were! Remorse for that cruel speculation quickly assailed her. She assured herself that she would be genuinely sorry to lose Hugo. But she would be much more free. And, in some ways, hardly less lonely.

On the whole, in spite of that loneliness Bella and he were excellent friends. The black witch remained and seemed likely to persist as a source of petty irritation; yet despite her obstructions and Hugo's obstinate failure to stand by his wife, Bella succeeded in her main object, the establishment of a capable household loyal to herself. Miss Penney continued to haunt her, to shadow her, to hover in the background wherever she went; but it was in small things rather than in great that Bella found her attentions a nuisance: in such details as the arrangement of the miniatures in the rose-and-ivory drawing-room. There was, for instance, a Cosway which caught the light in such a way that its peculiar delicacy was lost. One day Bella exchanged it for a far less attractive Cotes. Returning, within an hour, she discovered that ghostly hands had returned the two miniatures to their original positions. At first she found it difficult to believe her own eyes. She wondered if perhaps she had mistaken her intention for a deed, and carefully replaced them. Yet when next she entered the room they were back again! The situation was becoming ridiculous; for, this second time, she knew she had made no mistake. Once more she exchanged the two pictures and, to make certain of the change being permanent, locked the drawing-room door and took the key away with her. But when, later in the day, she unlocked it, she found that the Cotes and the Cosway had changed places again!

The same watchful, jealous, invisible agency persistently rectified or reversed every change her fancy might make in the arrangement of pictures or china or even of movable furniture. Its persistence angered her at first, but as time went on she began to regard it with amusement as the expression of an odd, sub-human intelligence, resembling that of those mischievous poltergeists which manifest themselves in the aimless displacement of small objects—though she knew that in this case the mischief had no ghostly origin and that the purpose was tinged with malice.

One thing was quite certain: on the subject of Miss
Penney, Hugo's obstinacy was quite impervious to
reason. Miss Penney's presence was one of the unalterable conditions of life at White Ladies, and must
be accepted as such. In any case Bella was far too
busy to worry over it. Quite apart from the settlement of the ménage and the cleansing of the house's
interior, which demanded incessant watchfulness because so much of its fabric and furniture appeared to
be insensibly disintegrating and falling to dust out of
sheer old age, there were dozens of other things that
cried for an immediate attention, the need for which
Hugo could not—or would not—appreciate. All
through the long days of her pregnancy she gave them
ungrudgingly every atom of energy she could afford.
It was a blessing, in a way, that she was able to lose
herself in outside interests.

There were the gardens, for instance, or rather
what had once been gardens. On the northern side of
the house, and at some distance from it, walls of
eighteenth-century brick, finely coped with freestone,
enclosed more than three acres of kitchen-garden,
shaped like the letter D. It was doubtful if, even in
Hugo's boyhood, this enclosure had been cultivated;
for the box-bushes which bordered the paths had shot
up into hedges, the wall-fruit had run to riot above
thickets of suckers, and the gooseberry-bushes and
raspberry-canes made thorny jungles beneath which
rabbits which had slipped into the sanctuary through

its broken doors had made their warren. Along the straight arm of the "D" ran a range of vineries, half an acre at least of broken glass roofs which—under the weight of panes pressing downward on timber that had rotted to touchwood for lack of painting—had in some places sagged and in others miserably collapsed in a ruin through which the sprouts of unpruned vines protruded like withies. The desolation of this place challenged Bella. She could not be content till it had been made productive again; until the ragged box-hedges were lowered and trimmed, the dead fruit-trees, which clung to the walls like crucified mummies, replaced and the survivors pruned into bearing; until the last rabbit had been trapped or ferreted out or shot, the broken doors re-hung and the long vinery re-built. The last of these jobs alone cost her more than twelve hundred pounds.

Nearer the house there was even more to be done. Originally, when the moat had first been dug or adapted to embrace the convent, it was unlikely that White Ladies had possessed any pleasure garden. One had been made, she gathered from prints which she discovered in the long gallery, in the late seventeenth century: a formal pleasance of clipped yews with grass-plats and beds of roses and even a maze (she had found the clue to it), a garden whose geometrical shape had conformed to that of the new Elizabethan house. But the doctrine of a return to Nature had frowned on this work of Art, and in the late eighteenth century its flagged paths and symmetrical topiary had been swept away as an offence to the new romantick, the area which it had once graced remaining as wild as need be until some early-Victorian Pomfret, with a few pounds to spare, had reclaimed and reduced it to a meaningless pattern of circular, oval and triangular beds, which, barren in winter, in summer were filled with geraniums and edged with lobelias.

To Bella's mind there was only one thing to be done: to restore the formal garden which matched the house; to relay its flagged paths, to replace not merely the maze and the topiary but even the stonework and balustrades whose position and proportions could be calculated from her prints. Landscape-gardeners were called from London to make measurements and give estimates. They found a client to whom cost was apparently of no moment; one who knew exactly what she wanted and was prepared to pay for it. To lay out the Elizabethan garden of the prints, they told her, was merely a matter of skilled labour. The stonework, of course, would take time and might prove expensive. As to the topiary: the yew was a tree of slow growth in any circumstances and took years to mature before it was ready for the clipping, which was a fine art in itself. If young yews were planted now, or better still in the autumn . . .

"In the autumn?" The mere suggestion of delay was enough to stimulate Bella.

P*

"Can't you find me clipped yews ready grown?" she demanded.

It was just possible, they told her. Full-grown yews were trees which transplanted badly.

"In America they transplant forest-trees."

"After a year or two of preparation. Even then there's a risk of losing them."

"A *risk?* I don't mind taking risks if I get my garden in the end. How soon can you finish it if you use a large gang?"

With intensive work, they said, it might be finished in a couple of months. In all jobs of this kind there was such a thing as an economical unit of labour. If too many men worked together they got in one another's way. Under pressure, they promised to make a start in a couple of days.

By the end of a week White Ladies was swarming with workmen, and the area on the south-west of the house, from which turf had been lifted in rolls that looked like confectionery, became a trampled morass. One gang toiled with picks and shovels loosening the red marl; another wheeled it in barrows over tracks of planks laid in the mud; another, hurrying hither and thither, knocked in pegs and stretched measuring-tapes and set up T-squares, while the foreman "boned" the levels. He was a tall, thin Scotsman, with a broomstick back, oddly wooden and rectangular from his square-topped felt hat and his spade-shaped beard to the toes of his boots. Whatever might happen to him he was not going to be hurried or diverted by as much as an inch from the programme he had mapped out. The slowness of his speech and movements drove Bella wild; he would ponder for half a minute, like a canny witness in the box, before he answered the simplest question; and the rest of the workmen appeared to take their pace from his leisurely beat, so that what should have been a brisk *scherzo* became a slow movement.

Whenever she looked out of the window it seemed to her that the gang had stopped work, not only at the regular times when they were supposed to "knock off," but also at others for which there was no excuse. One day, in the middle of the morning, when she had watched them for at least ten minutes swarming about the foreman's square hat like bees bunched round a queen, she could bear it no longer. Her temper, about that time, was becoming a little ragged, and she felt it would do her good to give the Scotsman a "piece of her mind." As she approached them the gang showed no signs of moving. They stood solemnly grouped round the latest-dug excavation like mourners on the brink of a grave.

"What's the matter, Mr. Duncan?" she asked him. "Has something gone wrong?"

The foreman touched his hat slowly and paused to consider.

"It would seem, my lady," he said—Bella always wished he wouldn't call her "my lady"—"it would seem that we've struck some pairt of a building. There's a sandstone wall and the spring of an airch, and a lot of bones forbye."

"What sort of bones, Mr. Duncan?"

"I canna say preceesely, my lady, but I doubt they'll be human. If there had been a kirk or grave-yard hereabouts . . ."

"Of course there was once a monastery."

"Well, that will explain it."

"May I see?"

The men made way for Bella. She peered into the trench. The spring of the sandstone "airch," as Duncan called it, was plainly visible. A jumble of bones, like driftwood, lay beneath. The man who had been digging looked up.

"The first I knowed, ma'am," he said, "was when I shoved the point of my pick through this skull here. There's two others beside that; and here's a little 'un, what I take to be that of a babby like." He held up an object as big as a half-grown swede-turnip, encrusted with marl. "Aye, and some of these here bones, ma'am, be no bigger nor a lamb's: I reckon they must belong to it." He picked out another fragment and brushed it on his sleeve. "Poor morsel, too!" He shook his head mournfully.

Bella turned away. She was not frightened; she was not consciously moved; yet she felt as though something physically cold had touched her heart, something vaguely connected, though that was surely

ridiculous, with the child she was bearing. This discovery was an unpleasant omen. She didn't believe in
omens. Yet the memory of those minute, pitiful fragments of mortality left her uneasy; it haunted her
until Hugo, who had been prowling round the estate
with a gun, came in late to luncheon.

When she told him what had happened he nodded
eagerly. The discovery excited him: it was an addition to his store of precise knowledge relating to
White Ladies. He showed much more interest in the
wall that had been laid bare than in the progress of
her garden.

"That will give us a clue," he said, "to the lines
of the ground-plan. If we follow that wall we shall
certainly come to an angle that will give us another.
I'll see that they do that. Your garden will be all
the better for deep digging," he told her, "and this
is the only chance we're ever likely to get. Of course
we know that some of the house's foundations are
based on the remains of the convent, and some other
remains were found to the east in my great-grand-
uncle's time. But I'd no idea there had been any
building on the west. It's a bit of good luck being
able to kill two birds with one stone."

From that day forward Hugo worked all day with
the gardener's gang, and the main job hung fire more
than ever. After that one little group of skeletons no
more bones were found, but the plan of a spacious
building began to show itself. It was all very well, and

exceedingly interesting for Hugo; but if the work dragged on in this way they looked like missing the autumn planting-season. There was a question of money too. Not that Hugo worried about that. He had never possessed much and knew nothing about it, as witness the shocking incompetence with which he had handled his own affairs. On the whole, though he teased her about it, he was rather proud of Bella's extravagance, regarding it as one of her personal characteristics, like the contrast between her eyebrows and her hair, her determined, quick movements, and the swiftness with which her mind fastened on the essentials of her desires. In addition to these, he gave her credit for a business acumen and a sense of the value of money which she did not possess and which he himself could certainly never have supplied.

For all that, since her marriage, Bella's money had been pouring into White Ladies like a river that loses itself in sand. Whenever she needed more, she asked Ernest Wilburn for it, as though she took it for granted that the supply was unlimited. He supposed she was "having her fling" and would soon settle down; but now, after six months, her demands grew heavier than ever. He wrote her a cautious letter on the subject. She did not even trouble to answer it. This would never do. It looked as if she were losing her head.

A week later he made a special visit to White Ladies. Bella seemed delighted to see him; it was

evident that the married state suited her; and he
noticed with satisfaction, for more reasons than one,
that she was going to have a child. "That may put the
brake on," he thought, "and make her go easy. It
will settle her mind as well. If this marriage had been
childless there might have been the devil to pay."

She showed him all over White Ladies from the
ground floor to the Long Gallery. He was forced to
admire the way in which already she had the contents
of the house and its history at her finger-tips. Her
instinct had been right: if ever a woman was designed
and qualified to possess it, it was certainly she. When
she had finished showing him the house she tramped
Wilburn off his sedentary legs through the autumn
afternoon. Her energy, in spite of her condition,
appeared inexhaustible. As a bachelor he was appalled
at the idea of anyone having to live in the company
of such a dynamo. He wondered how Hugo Pomfret,
who wasn't dynamic, was standing it, and noticed that,
although she seemed happy enough, she didn't mention his name. Whenever she spoke it was very much
to the point. Her mind was as clear-cut as her
features, her judgement as sharp in its definition as her
colouring; he could see imagination as well as vigour
in everything she said and in the competence with
which she grasped every situation: the same kind of
imaginative competence, he supposed, far-reaching
and ruthless, which had made Jasper Mortimer loom
rather more than life-size against the Black Country

scene. Wherever they went men were working, and in every case Bella appeared to be aware of the stage which the work should have reached at that moment and to envisage its end—even more clearly than those who were working on it. It was easy for Wilburn to see where the money was going.

By the time they had finished their round, he found himself exhausted and fainting for the tea which she gave him in the great hall. Here, again, Bella displayed her appropriateness to her new surroundings. As she sat at her tea-table, glowing with health and enthusiasm, so self-possessed, so deft in her handling of the Queen Anne silver, she gave him the impression of having been born and having lived at White Ladies all her life. At this point she did speak of Hugo, kindly, almost affectionately. She had hoped he would have been home for tea, but his movements were always uncertain; he was perfectly contented walking up partridges over the prickly stubbles with a dog and a gun, and had no sense of time. Bella's presence, Wilburn felt, gave the great hall an extraordinarily homely feeling; a sense of being lived in, and lived in happily. Only once was he aware of any disquieting sensation, when suddenly, lifting the cup to his lips, he felt certain that a third person was watching them from above. He put down the cup and looked up, instinctively, at the staircase-gallery, and could have sworn that he saw a shadow move as he did so. Bella smiled.

"What is it?" she asked.

"A ridiculous fancy. I thought I saw something move up there."

"Oh no, it's not fancy. That's Hugo's pet, Miss Penney. She watches everyone and everything. She's a witch. I'm getting quite used to her."

When they had finished their tea Wilburn broached the business that had brought him. "You know, you *are* going it!" he said.

"Overtiring myself? You don't know how strong I am!"

"No, spending too much. You're living above your income, and that's putting it mildly: you're digging pretty deeply into your capital."

"Well, it's all going into White Ladies. Don't you call that a capital investment?"

"Investment is hardly the word. By the end of this year, at this rate, you'll have spent twenty thousand pounds. And the money's gone. If you sold the estate at the end of it you'ld find that its value had not been appreciably increased."

"But I'm not going to sell White Ladies, dear Mr. Wilburn."

"Are you getting the return that the capital represents—fifteen hundred a year? Investments are supposed to pay interest, you know."

"Doesn't the money all come from my shares in Hayseech. Do you consider them an investment?"

"Most certainly."

"But Hayseech only paid two per cent last year," she replied triumphantly, "and this year, unless I'm mistaken, they'll pass their dividend."

Wilburn laughed. "If you put it like that, of course you're unanswerable. But Hayseech has a future, we hope . . ."

"And White Ladies none? The future of White Ladies is *my* future. I'm afraid I shock you. My argument may be bad in finance and perhaps in reason, but it's good in—what shall I call it?—it's good in life."

"May I beg you to be careful—a little more careful, anyway?"

"Yes, of course you may; and I'll bear what you say in mind. But I think I shall want at least five thousand pounds more by the end of the year." She smiled. "Will you allow me that?"

"Reluctantly. It means selling more stock at a most inopportune moment. In a way you're quite right when you feel discontented with the Tinsley results. Are you particularly anxious to retain your interest in Hayseech? For sentimental reasons, I mean?"

"I have no sentiment whatever for Hayseech. All my feelings bind me to . . . this."

"Well, you can't go on living on your capital for ever, can you? Nor on hopes, for that matter. If you'll allow me to do so, I should like to talk the matter over with our brokers, Magnus & Levison. I'm not at all sure that if an opportunity of selling arrived, we mightn't do better with your money than leaving it there. May I do that?"

"Of course. You know that I trust you implicitly."

"It's nice of you to say so. And it's nice, too, to see you looking so well and happy. Tell Pomfret I'm sorry I missed him, will you? I'll look you up again in a couple of months."

"Yes, do. It's been delightful to see you. When next you come here you may find an heir to White Ladies."

"Let's hope so," said Wilburn.

II

BELLA had what they called "a bad time." It lasted, in fact, for more than twenty hours, and ended with an anæsthetic. Emerging from the mist of chloroform into silence and a subdued candle-light—for during the interval of unconsciousness darkness had fallen— she became aware of a faint sibilance, like that of steam or air escaping from a tap, which resolved itself, as her fogged senses grew clearer, into a whispered conversation. The sound irritated her. If she had been asleep it would have been unnecessary: since she was awake, it was impolite. She disliked to hear servants whispering round corners like that, because it meant they were ashamed of what they were saying. The sensation of annoyance brought her nearer to herself. It seemed she had awakened from sleep, horribly tired, a little nauseated and feeling as though her body had been crushed and bruised. She was in her own lacquer bed in the Chinese room. Between her gummed eyelids she could see in flickers of firelight fantastic thickets of bamboos and frayed plantain leaves and the plumage of tropical birds. At her bedside a wax night-light shone palely, or so she supposed; she was too tired and too heavily bruised to turn and make sure. (If they would only stop whispering!) Then, suddenly, she was wide awake. All the horrors of that endless, relentless agony returned to her. Her child was born. It was over. She could hardly believe it. She called feebly. The whispering stopped; was renewed. She called again, more loudly. The nurse hurried to her side and looked down at her with what Bella thought was a silly self-satisfied smile.

"You were sleeping beautifully," she said. "Would you like a little drink . . . just a sip?"

"Tell me about the baby," Bella said. "Is he all right?"

"You've no need to worry about the baby, Mrs. Pomfret. *You*'re the person who matters. Let me see to your pillows. My word, what a muddle you've made of them! Then just have a nice little sip and go to sleep again."

She spoke in the cooing, consolatory voice which is supposed to be appropriate to children and invalids.

"Put your arms round my neck," she said, arranging the pillows. "Now that's lovely. You'll be ever so comfy. Think of nothing and go to sleep."

But Bella was not to be soothed or evaded.

"I asked you a question," she said crossly. "Is the baby all right?"

"Oh, don't trouble your head about *that*," the nurse replied.

"Please tell me. I want to know."

"Well, you had a shocking bad time, Mrs. Pomfret. You should be thankful you're through it. It was you or the baby, you see. And of course we had to think of you first."

"You mean that the baby's . . . dead?"

"Dr. Boyd couldn't possibly save the poor mite. He did all he could; but the poor little thing . . . Well, you must be brave about it. It's a good thing really, as doctor says, that she didn't live."

"*She?* You mean it was a girl?"

"Yes, a beautiful little girl. But don't think about it now."

Bella said: "A girl . . . I was sure it was a boy. If it was a girl I don't really mind. My mouth is so dry. Please give me something to drink."

During her convalescence people were extraordinarily kind to her, Bella thought, and lavish with their wasted sympathies. Her body recovered more quickly than any of them had imagined. She had, as the doctor said, a fine constitution. The fortnight's inactivity did her good. It was actually the first rest she had known since the day when her imagination was impregnated with the idea of White Ladies. No surroundings could have made a more delightful scene for a convalescence than the Chinese room, with the frosty January sun pouring in every morning through the octagonal bay-window. In that bitter, bright weather the best place to be in was bed. At tea-time, when Hugo came in to the warmth of her fire-lit

room, he would tell her his own story of the day's
small happenings: how the garden-work, which still
dragged on, was progressing; how the meet of the
Woodland Stourton at Chaddesbourne had been can-
celled because of the frost; how he had picked up a
brace of woodcock close to the ice-bound pools, or seen
the track of a badger in new-fallen snow.

Ten inches of ice on the moat! he told her gravely
one evening. Whenever the moat was frozen Hugo
grew uneasy. The disaster he dreaded most for White
Ladies was fire, and, indeed, not unreasonably. One
could imagine what a blaze its tinder-dry floors and
panelling would make. The only innovation on which
he had insisted when they first came to live there had
been the provision of an expensive and elaborate fire-
fighting plant: a big manual engine with a length of
hose sufficient to reach the twin pools; axes, helmets,
fire-escapes, chemical fire-extinguishers: material
enough to equip the fire-brigade of a fair-sized village.
In those early days she had often awakened to hear
him moving at night, getting up again before he had
fallen asleep to steal downstairs and make sure that
guards had been left in front of the fires, and hearth-
rugs turned back out of the range of a spitting ember.
Since the new engine had come and the hydrants had
been laid this fear had haunted him less; but whenever, as now, it froze hard, he grew restless and
anxious, always sleeping with the key of the engine-
house under his pillow ready for an emergency.

Ten inches of ice on the moat, he told her, shivering. His twelve years in a southern climate had made him peculiarly sensitive to cold. But winter was unable to penetrate that warm bedroom where, as soon as the lamps with their rosy shades were lit, Bella could almost imagine herself in the midst of the luxuriant jungle with which the Chinese wall-paper surrounded her. When she was alone in firelight, she had noticed, it came alive; the pointed leaves of the bamboo-canes shivered as the light of the fire flickered over them, each wayward spurt of flame illumining some new patch of colour, so that the brilliant birds seemed to flutter from spray to spray amid the intricacies of writhing vines and thickets of foliage.

These patterns, so richly and variously conceived, were a background for the restlessness of a mind which, when once the shock and fatigue of her fruitless adventure were over, could never be still. This was the first time since her marriage that she had really had time to think, to take stock of herself and of her position. In spite of her loss, she told herself, this year had not been wasted. She had accomplished as much as might reasonably have been expected—perhaps even more. The house was "in hand." By the beginning of spring, the gardens, too, should be finished. These were affairs in which she had insisted on asserting a personal taste; but there were others, and many others, in which she expected Hugo, in spite of his natural indolence, to take his part. Between

them, she told herself, they must deal with the
neglected estate. Bad tenants—they were mostly bad
tenants, she gathered—must be got rid of and replaced
by others more carefully chosen. One farm at least
must be taken over as a source of supply for the house,
re-equipped and maintained according to the best and
latest methods of agriculture. Then the woodland belt
must be dealt with: dead timber felled and cleared and
new trees planted—hardwood trees which would come
to maturity when their son—a son was the central part
of the next year's programme—reached middle manhood. (Hugo gaped when he saw her coverlet strewn
with agricultural treatises and books on forestry which
the obliging Wilburn, at a moment's notice, had sent
her.) Then the land of the whole estate must be re-
conditioned, re-limed, re-drained; farm-buildings and
farmhouses modernized, barns and byres re-roofed—
not with the damnable corrugated sheeting which was
invading the countryside, but with the ruddy tiles
which were proper to the Worcestershire landscape.
And roads must be salved from the quagmires into
which winter turned them by new cores of macadam
and calculated cambers and adequate drainage.

She was approaching the problems of White Ladies
in much the same spirit and with the same boundless
hope as Jasper Mortimer, forty years since, had
addressed himself to those of Hayseech. She was,
though she did not know it, turning into a new channel
the vital energy that had once flowed through the old.

As to that energy itself, there could be no question: as to its material resources some doubts might be felt. Ernest Wilburn had suggested as much when, a few months ago, he had begged her to be careful, and his doubts were later innocently re-echoed by Aunt Harriet who, as soon as she heard of the loss of Bella's baby, had decided to sink her differences with her niece and her instinctive dislike of Hugo, and had driven over to White Ladies, with one tin box, to stay.

Hayseech, Bella gathered from her, was in a melancholy state, which she attributed not to the slump in the heavy industries which had overtaken the whole district, but to the fact that the works were no longer in her father's control.

"Anyone with half an eye," Aunt Harriet said, "can see that they're at sixes and sevens. That poor Mr. Wilkinson of yours is an honest man, though not very polite or presentable. Of course, he has too many masters, and Hayseech had been used to one. You can tell the difference by the curtains," she went on, mysteriously. "The last pair Helen put up has stayed clean for three months—there's hardly a speck on them, and the works are so quiet at night she says she can't get to sleep. However, as your grandfather always says—I mean 'said'—the iron trade's like that. Up and down. And as soon as it's 'up,' Hayseech always comes out on the top."

Bella determined that as soon as she was "up and about" she would go over to Hayseech and look into

matters for herself. If her imagination was no longer
stirred by the works, they were still of supreme
importance to her materially: since the beauty of
White Ladies itself drew sustenance from that smoky
source.

"When Aunt Harriet wants to go home," she
thought, "I'll drive her over, and take the opportunity of having a talk with Mr. Wilkinson. In any
case he'll tell me candidly just how things are. If the
directors are worrying him and he wants anything done
at the next General Meeting, I can give him my support as the largest shareholder. He had better make
use of me while he has the chance," she told herself,
"for if I sell out of Jos. Tinsley & Co., as Ernest
Wilburn is half suggesting, he'll have no votes to back
him, poor man."

It seemed odd that while the prospect of abandoning
her interests in Hayseech did not prick her conscience,
the idea of deserting "poor Mr. Wilkinson" did. It
was more than a year since she had seen him, and yet,
in the crowded interval, she had often thought of him
as a lonely and never very attractive gladiator grimly
fighting for his life, or for that of Hayseech, in the
sulphurous haze. She thought kindly of him, she supposed, just because he had been honest with her to the
degree of rudeness; because her relation with him
was the only one in her life which had been completely
devoid of any artificiality.

"I wonder what he would think of White Ladies?"

she asked herself. "If he told me the truth—and I'm sure he *would* tell me the truth—he'ld probably say that he much preferred Hayseech. I'll certainly take the opportunity of seeing him, and helping him if I can, when Aunt Harriet goes home."

Miss Mortimer, however, having once come to White Ladies, showed no signs of moving. She derived from a generation in which the week-end was unknown: when people paid visits they stayed for at least a month. The sheer size of White Ladies impressed her. As she innocently remarked, she would never have thought it of Hugo Pomfret, whom she had regarded from the first as a cunning adventurer. Hugo himself, with his unfailing tact, made her feel at home. Even if he had not been in love with Bella, as he still was, he was a man of his word: when he made a bargain he stuck to it, and Miss Mortimer, though something of an oddity, was part of his bargain with Bella. Aunt Harriet, on her side, was astonished to find that Bella was happy and not, as she had expected, repenting of her hasty marriage. She was even forced to admit to herself that Bella had improved. All her languor, her apparent lack of direction, had vanished. In her broad grasp of affairs, in her direction of this complicated organism, Bella was showing herself a genuine Mortimer, not so much her mother's child as Jasper's granddaughter.

In the matter of housekeeping, a craft in which she considered herself an expert, Miss Mortimer permitted herself graver doubts as to Bella's efficiency. She was convinced that the "bevy" of servants, as she called them, were "tumbling over each other" and "eating their heads off"; that sugar and tea were being smuggled out of the house in quantities that would "feed a regiment"; that the "back" was constantly infested with hordes of "followers"; that the cook was "thick as thieves" with the butcher and grocer, and "making hay while the sun shone" out of the surplus dripping, and that Miss Penney, whom she detested at sight and described as "that black insect," was "feathering her nest." Indeed, Bella had the greatest difficulty in preventing Aunt Harriet from invading the kitchen in person, turning out corners and store-cupboards, inspecting the contents of bit-buckets, pushing in dampers, and teaching the expensive and highly-qualified cook her business.

Apart from this passion for interference in one direction, Bella was glad when Aunt Harriet stayed on at White Ladies. Hugo, fond of her and admiring as he might be, was no great company for her. His interests were primarily those of a country gentleman, an out-of-door man who was never so completely happy as when he was prowling about his own lands alone with a dog and a gun in all sorts of weather. When he came in at dusk, he was generally drugged with fresh air and exercise which, if it had hardened and tautened his sinews, did not make for liveliness. It was a comfort for Bella to have another woman in

the house, particularly such a woman as Miss
Mortimer, who, in spite of her starched conventionality and her habit of speaking in *clichés*, possessed, in
fact, a rich dower of sound instinct and common sense.

Her visit to Italy, which she still, in memory, resented, had, strangely enough, made her attitude
towards life much less rigid. She no longer—though
wild horses (as she certainly would have said) could
not have compelled her to admit it—considered Hayseech the spring and centre of the universe. She no
longer accepted chilblains and fireless bedrooms and
an atmosphere mainly composed of fog, smuts and
sulphur, as normal, beneficent and necessary elements
in human existence. She was not, as she confessed, "as
young as she had been," and she enjoyed the more
kindly climate of the Severn basin, perpetually bathed
in a wash of Atlantic air which stopped short of Hayseech, no less than the inner warmth and comfort of
White Ladies. She was even sensitive—and in this she
astonished Bella—to the beauty and grace, no less
than the stateliness, of these novel surroundings. She
knew nothing whatever about architecture or painting
or furniture or tapestries; yet the neighbourhood of
beauties of this kind awakened her curiosity and mildly
excited her; it almost seemed as though there must
always have been in the pragmatic Mortimer strain
a hidden artistic vein, allied, perhaps, to that brooding imagination which, in Jasper, had seen from far
Shropshire hills the Black Country's fiery reflex, and

drawn from that tawny glare the dream which his genius later transmuted into the black magnificence of Hayseech.

Even physically, Bella found Aunt Harriet not "out of the picture." In her formal dress, which never transgressed the canons of her own period, no less than in the distinction of her bearing and her handsome features, she conformed to the setting of White Ladies with less effort than Bella herself. As to dignity, she could hold her own in the company of most of the Pomfret family portraits—not those soft pretty Cosways and Gardners with their *Petit Trianon* graces, but the great Caroline and Augustan ladies who, with straight backs and firm lips and fine eyes, seemed a match for the armed cavaliers and portly periwigged gentlemen whose beds and boards they had honoured in marriage.

Bella was aware of this most of all when, during the spring, the belated "county" came to White Ladies to call and to condole with her on her misfortune in losing her first-born. All over that rolling country of red marl there lay scattered isolated villages. Every village possessed its dilapidated church, its vicarage, and its half-timbered manor-house. Many of the manor-houses had long since fallen on evil days; the families who built them had died out, and their landed estates had been split or fallen bodily into the hands of more vigorous neighbours; but in a number of them which survived there still persisted the remnant of a

disintegrating stock. The names which these people
bore had meant little in the past, and in the present
meant nothing whatever outside their own narrow
society, though, among themselves, they felt extremely
proud of them. They were most of them old and poor
—far too poor to escape (even if they had wished to
escape) from the rigours of the winter climate; so,
when autumn was over, they shut themselves up in
dark half-timbered houses and hibernated like dormice,
only emerging in their old-fashioned conveyances to
take the air and begin life again when the hedgerows
began to burgeon and the lanes, which were like ruts
in the red clay, became passable.

They appeared, Bella thought, these shabby,
dignified old ladies, these Abberleys and Ombersleys,
in their lace dolmans, their moth-eaten sealskin tippets
and their bonnets trimmed with faded artificial flowers,
like insects cautiously crawling out of worm-eaten
timber. They were shrewd and sharp-eyed and critical:
for White Ladies, though greater in degree, was a
house which belonged to the same category as their
own; they knew something of its history, and were
ready to resent any change in it, particularly those
changes for which, rumour had told them, Hugo Pomfret's new wife was responsible. They entered the
great hall with a proprietary air; they sat down obviously fearing the worst. Their suspicions embarrassed
Bella; but Aunt Harriet, oddly enough, felt no embarrassment. Bella's callers appeared to enjoy her com-

pany, and she theirs. Apart from slight differences
of accent they spoke the same language. They
belonged, in fact, to the same period and shared the
precise type of manners and culture (or lack of it)
to which Miss Mortimer had learned to conform under
the tuition of her old governess, Miss Beagle, who,
herself, might have emanated from a mid-Worcester-
shire manor-house. When they returned to their
winter-quarters the Miss Abberleys and Ombersleys
declared that though Hugo Pomfret's new wife
seemed a little awkward and newfangled, her aunt,
Miss Mortimer, was an exceedingly well-bred woman.
After all, they remembered, Mortimer had once been
a mighty name.

Among the procession of callers Bella was thankful
to find there were very few Pomfrets. The first of
the name to arrive was the rector of Wychbury, a
dense, courtly, red-faced, fox-hunting parson, second
cousin to Hugo. He brought with him the elder of
Hugo's two daughters by his first marriage, a woman
of Bella's own age. Eleanor Pomfret, four years
before, had made a "good" marriage to George
Hingston, the son and heir of the Wolverbury ironmaster to whose house, Stourford Castle, Bella and
Aunt Harriet had already been invited from Hayseech
in the days before she had even heard of White Ladies.
Bella was acutely interested in Eleanor Hingston and
slightly uncomfortable with her—not so much because
she was her step-daughter—though that *did* seem

Q

strange—as because she recognized in her and her children (she had twins, a boy and a girl) potential rivals in the ultimate possession of White Ladies. Not that Eleanor Hingston showed the least interest in it, or, for that matter, in anything else. She had a lifeless physical perfection, as cold as that of the precious stones with which her husband had decorated her, a wan, beautiful smile, and lovely, but equally lifeless grey eyes. She greeted Hugo, with whose features, when one came to examine them, her own had much in common, with a stranger's remoteness.

"How she must hate him for having married me and me for having married him!" Bella thought.

But she judged hastily: no emotion so positive as hate warmed that marble placidity. Aunt Harriet, more shrewd in her judgement, was nearer the mark.

"That young woman," she said when Eleanor Hingston had gone, "is simply unhappy. And no wonder! She ought to have known better than to marry a son of Joe Hingston."

She regarded the whole Hingston family with dislike and contempt, not because she knew them, but because the great works at Wolverbury had always been rivals of Hayseech, and because Sir Joseph had leapt at the baronetcy which Jasper Mortimer had refused.

"I don't think that poor thing will trouble you much, Bella," she added confidently. "Before she's finished—and you mark my words!—she'll have a peck of trouble of her own. I wonder what your other step-daughter's like."

She continued to wonder; for Hugo's younger daughter, Sibell, still lived near her grandparents in Shropshire and showed no signs of wishing to renew her father's acquaintance.

Summer came, and Miss Mortimer continued to put off her return to Hayseech. She had good reasons for staying on at White Ladies now, for Bella was expecting a second child in November, and Aunt Harriet, though naturally and properly ignorant of such matters, felt convinced that if she had been present Bella would not have lost the first. Bella herself was inclined to treat her condition with more respect. In that first year, after all, she had made such imprudent calls on her energy; there had seemed to be so many things crying out to be done, and such an excited sense of urgency in the doing of them, that she had not taken the rest which she owed to herself or permitted herself a moment of relaxation. This time she would be wiser—for her son's sake. It was true that a hundred matters on which she had set her heart remained undone; scarcely one of the plans which she had made as she lay scheming in the Chinese bedroom had begun to take shape, and Hugo, on whom she had counted for help, seemed in no hurry to begin them.

Bella was resigning herself, in fact, though she did not know it, not so much to the dictates of prudence as to the influence of White Ladies; acquiescing in the inertia of a tradition of living that discouraged all eager activity, all restlessness (that was Hugo's word) by a mute insistence on its own slow continuity. When, in moods of impatience, she accused her husband of vegetating, the criticism implied no slur, for the process of invisible ripening by which White Ladies had attained its inimitable mellowness had far less resemblance to the growth of short-lived humanity than to that of a tree, increasing its stature twig by twig and its girth ring by ring in obedience to the external influence of seasons and the movement of heavenly bodies rather than to the behests of human wills. Even the works that her energy had planned during the previous year had left little mark on it. The great house appeared to accept them without enthusiasm, to assimilate them without effort, to absorb them into its own immutable placidity with an indifference which suggested that it was neither better nor worse for them.

She was coming round, gradually, to Hugo's way of thinking—to the way in which generations of Pomfrets had thought. However benevolently or mischievously she tampered with White Ladies, White Ladies would still go on, slowly moving, with each atom of dust that fell from its wood and brick and stone, to an ultimate dissolution which would certainly not, she told herself gratefully, come in her time. And meanwhile, in the delicious suspension of these months of waiting for the birth of her son, and above all in this season of early summer, when the sweet mowing-grass in the park made a shelter for corncrakes and above the green acres cuckoos flew calling from one woodland verge to another, when white jasmine and old-fashioned roses pervaded the air with their vagrant perfume, and the house stood brooding, as it were, over its own warm beauty reflected in the mirror of the moat—in these lavender dawns and blue twilights and golden noon-days, there was surely beauty enough and more than enough to assuage the most hungry heart. She could understand now why the Pomfrets had never worried, why they had never done anything of importance in the great world.

So the days slipped by, and the weeks. August thunderstorms breaking brimmed the moat and the twin pools. They laid Hugo's acres of wheat and drenched the parkland, but did not revive its verdure. September came. Three months more! Bella thought. The late plums on the garden walls drooped, heavy with fruit. In the orchards laden apple-boughs sagged to the grass. The burden of fruitfulness weighed on the world. Bella, too, felt its heaviness. For more than five months she had scarcely stirred from under the shadow of White Ladies. Her old restlessness returned, and was now less easily borne. This vegetative existence was getting on her nerves. She felt an acute desire to escape from herself and from her long brooding—even to escape from White Ladies. She felt tempted to do something outrageous and perilous, if only that she might prove to herself that she was alive, that she was herself, Bella Pomfret, not merely a patient animal waiting for the day of parturition.

III

The opportunity for "breaking out"—as she called it to herself—arrived at the beginning of October, in the shape of a letter addressed to Aunt Harriet from the offices of Jos. Tinsley & Co.

The directors had decided, she learned, to invite their manager, Mr. Wilkinson, to join the board, and in order that he might have the advantage of living "on the spot," the company was prepared to make her an offer for the freehold of the house known as Hayseech Bank which had been left to her by the late Chairman. If Miss Mortimer should feel inclined to sell the house, the board would be glad to know what value she placed on it before the date of their next meeting on October the twentieth.

Bella was less surprised than Aunt Harriet by the contents of this letter. At the last general meeting, on Wilburn's advice, she had strengthened Wilkinson's position by arming him with all the votes at her command. The company had obviously suffered from divided counsels and uncertain direction, and Wilkinson, it had seemed to them both, was the most suitable person to take control.

Yet Hayseech Bank was the only home Aunt Harriet had known in her forty-five years, and though

she had shown no signs of returning to it for the last
nine months, the mere prospect of selling it offended
her possessive instinct and awakened her dormant
affections.

"You've been perfectly happy at White Ladies,"
Bella told her.

"That's all very well; but it's your house, not mine,
and I don't like remaining on anybody's hands like
a poor relation."

"There's no question of that. We love having you,
both of us. Why not stay on through the winter, till
this business of mine is over? And then, if you like,
we'll try to find some small house in the district. All
ours are farms or labourers' cottages; but we'll ask
Mr. Ombersley or Mr. Loach, the Vicar of Chaddesbourne, to look out for one."

Miss Mortimer still shook her head. There was the
question of the "girl," who was Black Country born
and bred and wouldn't be happy anywhere else. Bella
suggested pensioning her. Aunt Harriet was shocked:
this was only another example of Bella's "big ideas."

"If your whole life's going to be governed by
Helen's prejudices," Bella said, "I give you up."

Miss Mortimer was obstinate. Even if she allowed
herself to be persuaded out of some of her earlier
objections to selling Hayseech Bank, there remained
another on which there could be no argument. This
was not a matter of sentiment but of loyalty. Her
father had built the house and had been devoted to it.

What would *he* think, she asked, if he saw it in the hands of a stranger?

At this Bella lost her patience. "I know perfectly well from what you've told me yourself," she said, "that my grandfather never cared twopence for anything outside the works. Hayseech Bank was the house he slept in and read his paper in, and even when he was in it his thoughts weren't there. If you talked about being loyal to the works for his sake I could understand you. That's just what you're asked to be now. The company wants Hayseech Bank. Why, if my grandfather had been alive he'ld have given it to them!"

In the end, reluctantly persuaded by this argument, and still something of a martyr, Aunt Harriet consented to sell. There was no question of her "giving." Her price, Bella noticed with amusement, was, like that of Hugo's old studio, a "price of affection." She was quite prepared, in fact, for the company to question it; but apparently they were in a hurry and prepared to pay for the convenience. Miss Mortimer's terms were accepted, and she was asked, as a favour, to remove her belongings immediately.

This was Bella's chance of escape. Much to the anxiety of Hugo, who dreaded another catastrophe, she insisted on accompanying Aunt Harriet to Hayseech.

It was a strange, a ghostly experience to find herself once again in her mother's bare, white bedroom;

Q*

to hear, once again, the perpetual rumour of the works; to gaze down upon the acres of black roofs under the same sombre sky. Though the size of Hayseech was as impressive as ever, Bella knew at once that during the last eighteen months a change had come over it. The note of the works, that synthesis of blended sounds, so constant that an ear habituated to it could detect the least variation in its composition, had altered not merely in pitch but in volume. The plutonic orchestra had been cut down to suit a lighter programme. One no longer heard its instruments of percussion: the cymbal-clashes of buffers, the rhythmical beat of hammers.

To the eye no less than to the ear, it was evident that the nature of the works' activities had changed. Though the spidery headgear still towered above the pitheads, the wheels spun round no more, the cages no longer shot down the shafts or came to rest at the top; the little black trollies which once had crawled like slow beetles over the hillside stood motionless in dejected clumps, as though some malignant hand had sprinkled them with insecticide; on the network of metals the shunting-engines no longer bustled hither and thither with nervous shrieks. From a distance Bella had the impression—and could not get it out of her mind—that the Hayseech which she now saw resembled an old oak in the park which Hugo and she had condemned to the axe a few days before. "It's finished," Hugo had said. "Don't you see, it's

dying downward from the top? If the timber's to be
of any use it must be felled while the sap still runs."
And Hayseech was like that, Bella thought: still vast,
still alive, but dying downward from the top, twig
by twig, branch by branch. Less alive, she thought,
in spite of its relative youth, than White Ladies. No
doubt Mr. Wilkinson would soon tell her the worst.

On their second evening at Hayseech he called,
formally. Bella found him marooned by Helen in the
musty drawing-room. She rescued him, and brought
him in to the inadequate living-room fire. Aunt
Harriet was busy sorting linen upstairs, so they had
the cold room to themselves. Mr. Wilkinson's appearance surprised Bella. At first sight she would hardly
have known him. Like Hayseech, he had changed:
but, unlike Hayseech, for the better. Before her
marriage, she supposed, she had noticed him more as
an employee than as a man; and the man whom she
now discovered was by no means unpleasing. He
looked quite ten years younger (and this was her first
surprise) than Hugo. From what she remembered of
him he appeared to have "smartened" enormously.
His blue serge suit fitted him; his linen was speck-
less, his trousers had been pressed. His face was clean-
shaven; his spectacles fitted his nose, and the grey eyes
which surveyed her through them, with manifest
approval, looked lively and confident. She noticed, for
the first time, the vigour and capability of his sinewy
well-kept hands, which were not, like Hugo's, the

hands of an idler. Because of these changes she noticed his north-country accent less. She judged him, in short, a man of strong personality in the prime of life, newly conscious and confident of his powers, and strengthened by the very weight of the position he held and the responsibilities he carried. It was a position, Bella reflected, which he partly owed to herself —though that he would probably find it convenient to forget.

Wilkinson did not, in fact, forget it. In his first words he thanked her for the support she had given him, admitting that, without her, he could never have had his way.

"Now I know where I am," he told her. "Before, I didn't. When I took over, the works were being run without any considered policy. To tell you the truth—though for heaven's sake don't let Miss Mortimer know I said so—at the time of his death your grandfather's grip was failing. Nothing remained but his pride and his obstinacy; and both, as the other directors knew, were beginning to prove expensive. They knew he'd been wrong, as I told them a hundred times, but the prestige of his name weighed so heavily with them that they were terrified of abandoning anything he had begun. The result was confusion."

"And now?"

"Well, now that's all changed. The great thing is, they trust me. You yourself were good enough to

set them the example. And without flattering myself,
I'm certain they're right to do so. I've had nearly
three years of Hades getting things straight; but now
that I've persuaded them to cut their losses, they *are*
straight, thank God. When I get settled in this house
—on the spot, so to speak—my control will be even
tighter."

"And our dividends larger?"

He laughed. "You're in too great a hurry. Don't
forget I'm a shareholder too, in my own small way.
We shall pay something this year. If I had my own
way, Mrs. Pomfret, I should apply for a reduction of
capital. This, of course, is strictly in confidence. When
you consider how much we've deliberately reduced the
size of our undertaking, that's only reasonable."

"What, exactly, have you done?"

"Well, thank goodness, we've abandoned the coal-
mines. The pumping-charges which your grandfather
insisted on shouldering himself were dragging us
down. Now the pits are closed, and the water can do
its worst. It has become the business of the Drainage
Commissioners, and I wish them joy of it. In a year
or so, if you ask my opinion, there'll be no coal raised
in this district on our side of the Great Bentley Fault.
That's an enormous relief to begin with; and, in other
ways, I'm insisting on cutting our coat according to
our cloth. Up to now we've been busy using up our
accumulations of tap-cinder. Basic steel's come to stay,
and all round us we have handy supplies of puddler's

tap left over by concerns that went down under in the
Big Depression. And trade's looking up. The glass
rises slowly and steadily. The Jameson Raid has
settled things in South Africa; gold's beginning to flow
again. Consols stand at a hundred and thirteen, and
the new Companies Act makes industrial investors less
nervous. Every little bit helps—even things like this
cycle-trade boom."

"And the future? The more distant future?"

"Don't ask me about that. Of one thing you may
be quite certain. The great integrated concerns, like
Hayseech as it was in your grandfather's time, are
finished. Thanks to drastic surgery, there's no depart-
ment in Hayseech at this moment which isn't modestly
paying its way. The old heavy industries of the Black
Country are dead and buried; but the district's not
ruined by any means. If new, lighter industries come
to it—as the cycle-trade's come already and the motor-
trade may come—they'll all be in need of steel, and
Hayseech can supply the basic iron from which steel
is made. I'm afraid all this talk of mine has been
horribly technical . . ."

"Not at all. I've been interested in every word
of it."

Bella had been interested less, in fact, in the words
he spoke than in the enthusiasm with which they were
spoken. It was a long time, she thought, since she had
encountered anyone so bravely alive—which was
natural enough, since White Ladies implicitly dis-

couraged that kind of lambent vitality, and the least
contact with it would have been antipathetic to poor
Hugo. It was a symptom, she saw, of her nature's
odd duality that while one part of her—the part which
now glowed in response to Wilkinson's ardour—
assuredly belonged to this more strenuous world which
found joy in making things rather than in preserving
them, the other must hanker eternally for the grace
and mellowness of White Ladies, so near in space, so
remote in spirit. For the moment, if only because
she found Wilkinson's self and his fervour so likeable
and, in a way, so pathetic, she was happy to identify
herself with his aspirations. Yet she knew, all the
time, that the two interests were incompatible; that
though she might temporarily dally with either, a firm
choice must be made. And the choice, when it came
to a decision, was not hers to make. It was dictated by
her child: the unborn heir to White Ladies.

"I hope I shall see you again before you go," Mr.
Wilkinson said. "I know I've talked too much, but
you're the best listener in the world. I only wish
you would come here more often."

Bella smiled. "My lines have fallen in a different
place—such a very different place!—and my life
there absorbs me. I can't serve two masters, Mr.
Wilkinson."

"Well, perhaps you'll sometimes think of us in the
smoke of Hayseech."

"I shall often think of you."

But she knew, when they had said good-bye and she watched his vigorous figure disappearing rapidly down the "bank," that she would not often think of him or even of Hayseech. She liked him; she admired him; she was sorry for him. Yet his presence vaguely distressed her, as did the sight of Hayseech: both accused her, perhaps, of a disloyalty as yet unconfessed; both were more happily avoided—like a friend betrayed or a creditor unsatisfied. The longer she stayed at Hayseech, the more firmly was she convinced that only by snapping the threads which still bound her to it could her restless soul find equilibrium. Swift decisions, heroic cleavages had always appealed to her native impatience. When, next morning, she packed up the box which contained all the early documents relating to Hayseech and addressed it to Wilkinson, she felt not merely relieved but exhilarated.

Aunt Harriet, catching her in the act, disapproved of it violently.

"After all," she maintained, "they're no business of his. Why, there are even your poor dear grandmother's private account-books!"

"The wage-sheets of the 'brickill,' Aunt Harriet? Surely you're not ashamed of *them?* They belong to the history of Hayseech, and Hayseech is no longer ours. It belongs to the company—even this house is theirs—and if anyone in the world has a right to them and is likely to appreciate them it's Mr. Wilkinson."

Miss Mortimer refused to admit it. Even if Hayseech belonged to the company, she said reproachfully,
the name of the company was still Jos. Tinsley & Co.
and Bella was a Tinsley. Hugo Pomfret was proud
enough of his family archives, and the Pomfrets,
heaven knew, had never created anything half so
startling as Hayseech. "Besides, even if it *does* belong
to the company," she said finally, "when you come
down to brass tacks or rock bottom or whatever they
call it, doesn't the company mostly belong to you?"

Bella smiled. "Do you know, Aunt Harriet," she
said, "I sometimes wonder if anything ever really
belongs to anyone—except, perhaps, their own souls.
And that's very uncommon, too."

Miss Mortimer sniffed. Her conception of the
meaning of property was much simpler than that.
"The truth of the matter is," she said, "you do far
too much of this 'wondering.' When your baby's born
—and I wish to goodness it was—you may be able to
see that black is black and white's white. As it is I'm
quite certain that half the time you don't know what
you're doing!"

But Bella did know what she was doing. That afternoon, abandoning the dismantled house in which her
Aunt Harriet and Helen floundered waist-deep in
packing-cases like marine monsters stranded among
rocks by an ebbing tide, she drove to the station at
Mawne Road, caught a train to North Bromwich, and
presented herself at Ernest Wilburn's office.

Wilburn was surprised and delighted to see her.
It was some months since they had met. Sitting there,
with his leather-topped office table between them,
Bella was astonished and rather shocked to notice how
greatly he had changed. He was still urbane; he was
still, undeniably, charming; yet his smartness as well
as his charm, it seemed to her, were a thought overdone. They were both of them surface qualities, and,
beneath that surface, she was conscious of a certain
slackening—she hesitated to call it a degeneration—of
fibre. In that first glance, he seemed to her a man
whose natural leanings towards luxury and easy
elegance were beginning to get the better of him. He
was a little bit too well-fed, too well-dressed, too well-
pleased with himself. In spite of her confidence in him
she found herself comparing him, to his disadvantage,
with Wilkinson, in whom, as it seemed to her, a change
of the opposite kind had been taking place. Why was
it, she asked herself, that whenever she considered a
man's quality, she must always compare him with the
one who had last occupied her thoughts? Why, looking at Wilkinson, had she immediately compared him
with Hugo? Why, looking at Wilburn, did she now
compare him with Wilkinson? Perhaps, as Aunt
Harriet had suggested, she did too much of "this wondering." On second thoughts she felt bound to admit
that Wilburn's shrewd eyes were giving her the best
of his attention.

As indeed they were. Wilburn, too, at that moment,

was considering his client carefully. He, too, was a little shocked, but for different reasons. The Bella on whom he now concentrated his wits was as different from the imperious creature who had swept him off his feet in Capri as she was from that ardent child whose eager reactions he had watched with amusement and sympathy and protective tenderness on the day when first he had driven her out from North Bromwich to Hayseech. She was no longer a child; she was not even an exalted bride. In the three years of their acquaintance she had aged beyond calculation. To his taste she was no less attractive—on the contrary, she was much more so; yet, looking at her now for the first time, he would have guessed her a woman of thirty from whose nature, no less than from her features, the softness of youth had vanished, a woman to whom the word "handsome" had just become applicable. It was fortunate for him that he had reached—and not passed—the age when he preferred handsome women to pretty ones.

When he suggested giving her tea, Bella refused. She had come there on business, and was not disposed to waste time over small-talk or compliments. Her gravity gave Ernest Wilburn a twinge of alarm. Did it imply domestic difficulties? With a marriage of that kind, one never knew.

"I've come to talk about money, Mr. Wilburn," Bella said.

Wilburn thought: "Well, thank heaven it's not a

divorce!" He said: "What? Some new extravagance? I thought you'd taken my advice."

"It's because I've been pondering on your advice that I want to talk to you. I've just come from Hayseech. I've been helping Aunt Harriet to 'move.' "

"Was that altogether prudent?"

Bella laughed. "Have you ever known me prudent, Mr. Wilburn? Well, I'm going to be prudent now, for the first time in my life. At Hayseech I had a long talk with Mr. Wilkinson."

Wilburn nodded. "Sound fellow. I like him. He's pulling the place round."

"Yes . . . as far as it can be pulled round."

"That sounds rather gloomy. Hasn't he faith in it?"

"Enormously. Rather pathetically. And I haven't. That's the trouble."

"Well?"

"I've been thinking over what you said to me last autumn. I believe you were right. I want to get out of Jos. Tinsley & Co., Mr. Wilburn. If I don't now, I believe it will be too late. It wouldn't be right for me to pass on what Mr. Wilkinson told me in confidence. He's pleased with what he has done, and I think he has every right to be; but the future of Hayseech, whatever it may be, is not a big future."

"It's a fairly solid one, you know; and things generally are looking up. Don't misunderstand me. If I seem to be arguing against you, it's only because I want you to see there are two sides to the question."

"I've never in my life been able to do that, Mr. Wilburn."

"Well, in some ways that's an engaging quality. Please go on. You want to get rather a longer run for your money, I take it; even though you have rather a smaller degree of security. Is that it?"

"No, it isn't that in the least, as a matter of fact. Would you blame me if it were?"

"No. . . . Not altogether. But if it isn't that, what is it?"

"If I told you exactly what I felt I doubt if you'ld understand me. There's no reason why you should; so you needn't. I just feel that, as things are, my life is rather divided. Hayseech is too strong for me to be comfortable; and Aunt Harriet's coming to live at White Ladies or near it seems to give me an opportunity—an excuse, if you like, for . . . escaping."

"You mean, seriously, you want to get rid of all your holding in the company, your controlling interest?"

"Yes, that's what I mean. Of course you think I'm a fool."

"I think that's going a little too far, Mrs. Pomfret. Have you spoken to your husband?"

"Hugo knows nothing whatever about money. We never discuss my affairs."

"I think you might."

Bella shook her head. "I don't want to. Of course, Mr. Wilburn, if you disapprove so completely . . ."

"I don't disapprove completely. You know more

about some things than I do. If Jos. Tinsley & Co. are in for a reconstruction . . ."

"Oh, I didn't say *that*."

"No, you were quite unusually prudent. In moderation, I think, as I said before, your attitude is sound. We are, certainly, in for a modest industrial boom, in which people with foresight will make a lot of money. Take those cycle shares I bought you. You've done very well out of them. And now that the red flag is done with, there may even be money in motorcars. The same people, Pearce & Tregaron, are raising new capital. Then there's gold. Now that the Jameson business is settled, the people who dropped money in the last boom will crowd back into that market. Only . . ."

"Yes, Mr. Wilburn?"

"Only . . . I wonder if you realize the effect your withdrawal—your immediate and total withdrawal from Jos. Tinsley & Co.—would have on Hayseech? If you came out of it impetuously, as you suggest, you would hurt your own interests. The position of their stock is none too good as it is, and mass selling of that kind would simply send it toppling. It would embarrass your friend Mr. Wilkinson terribly, too."

"I don't want to hurt *him*."

"If you did what you're suggesting, you'ld probably ruin him as well as yourself. And Hayseech wouldn't be the first reasonably sound concern that has been ruined by fear, Mrs. Pomfret."

"Yes, I think I see what you mean. But I feel just the same."

"You still want to get out of Hayseech. Very well. I'll see what can be done about it. It will have to be done with tact, and very gradually. Being impatient won't help you. Do realize that."

"I'm prepared to leave the matter entirely in your hands."

"And I'm deeply touched by your confidence. I'll go into the whole thing discreetly with Magnus and Levison, and I'll write to you or come and see you. White Ladies is looking as lovely as ever?"

"It always looks lovely. But it dislikes Hayseech."

Wilburn laughed: "I suppose it has never forgiven Hayseech its prosperity. But that's hardly reasonable either. Without Hayseech, White Ladies would never have had you. Are you sure you won't let me give you some tea?"

"Thank you so much. I must get back to my poor Aunt Harriet."

"She'll be shocked at your plans, by the way."

"I'm afraid she will. However . . ."

At the door, Wilburn said: "You remember John Fladburn, your late employer?"

"Of course."

"Well, now he's 'late' in the fullest sense of the word. He died last week and has left a quarter of a million. It all goes to the son. I forget if he was at home in your day. The mother's a terror; but Henry is quite a nice fellow. Did you come across him at all?"

"Oh yes. I came across him. I remember him well."

Next day, in advance of the Hayseech furniture, which was to be stored in the stables, Miss Mortimer and Mrs. Pomfret returned to White Ladies. Two days later Bella's child was born, prematurely. The doctor attributed this to her rashness in moving her aunt's heavy furniture. But the child was healthy and lived. Perhaps, after all, there had been a miscalculation. The baby's head was fledged with a fair down, and there was already a suggestion of black eyebrows. Although Hugo could not find the name in the Pomfret records, his son was christened Jasper.

IV

Now, at last, Bella Pomfret knew the meaning of happiness. For the first time since she had set eyes on White Ladies she had a right to relax. Lying there, in the Chinese bedroom, with her son beside her, she was able to feel that time no longer threatened her with its incalculable spites; that after all her struggles she had performed the most important of the tasks at which she had been aiming. Before this, she had submitted to the inertia of White Ladies unwillingly and with a doubtful conscience, with a fretful anxiety that occasionally took the shape of guilt. Now, she felt able to smile at those qualms. The sense of uncertainty and of hurry was over. The continuity for which she hankered had been made certain. A vista of life, long, calm, uneventful, lay stretched before her, reaching forward into the future, indefinite but secure, of her son's youth and manhood, to the time when, between them, as long as she lived, the possession of the beauty of White Ladies should be quietly enjoyed: a vista which, indeed, resembled the view which her idle eyes now embraced from the windows of the Chinese bedroom—the wide sweep of green parkland, undisturbed by the invitations of mountainous distances, serene, self-sufficient within its girdle of dark woods.

Hugo had once complained of her gadding restlessness; but now, it seemed to her, she was far more tranquil than he. Perhaps this appearance was partly an effect of contrast; but the fact remained that he was much less transported by the birth of an heir than herself. He was, of course, immensely relieved; for though his passion had lost, as was natural to his age, its first intensity, he admired his wife and was fond of her. But when once the baby was duly born, he did seem to take it less as a miracle than as a matter of course. It wasn't, after all, she reflected, his first achievement of the kind, though he might have shown a little more enthusiasm, if only to please her. Enthusiasm, unfortunately, was not a typical Pomfret emotion, nor yet an emotion associated with advancing years; and Hugo, Bella observed now that she lay there and had time to look at him, was beginning to show his age. It was possible that the strain and excitement of marrying a wife so much younger than himself had contributed to this—possible also (for all she knew) that this early decline of vitality was a characteristic of the enfeebled Pomfret stock. Yet, whatever the explanation might be, Hugo had aged considerably since she met him. He had the physical and mental characteristics of a man of sixty who had settled down into a rut and resented the least divergence from it. He was no longer particular about his appearance. His face was shadowed. He was inclined to be fussy and, occasionally, short-tempered. Trifling annoyances worried him unduly and made him querulous. Bella bore with this gently, and with a patience that she herself found astonishing. Abnegations of this kind, after all, were part of her bargain. However troublesome she might find him in small things, in the larger, she was ready to admit, the balance was all on her side.

And if Hugo was unappreciative of her part in their joint achievement, the baby assuredly had his full share of adulation. Aunt Harriet, in particular, made as much fuss of him and displayed as much care and anxiety as if he were her own. In her case the possession of Jasper made a compensation and a salve for the loss of Hayseech, over which, otherwise, she would certainly have brooded. She regarded this baby not as the heir to White Ladies but as the vehicle of the Mortimer strain. The mere fact that the down on his scalp was fair, with a tinge of red in it, and that his eyebrows showed signs of becoming black, was sufficient to enrapture her. That Hugo's hair, before it went grey, had also been reddish was beside the point.

"From the moment nurse washed him," she declared, "I knew he was a genuine Mortimer and his grandfather's grandson. If you had dared to call him anything but Jasper, Bella, I should never have forgiven you! This has relieved me of all uncertainty," she added gravely: "next time Mr. Wilburn comes here I shall look forward to making my will."

Her great-nephew became the central preoccupation of Aunt Harriet's life, and filled it with the autumnal joy of a vicarious maternity. For all practical purposes short of having borne him the child was hers. A sense of unique responsibility engrossed her. She was critical, in fact, not only of his nurse, whose every movement she watched with the solicitude of an anxious hen, but of Bella herself, whom she considered as sadly lacking in seriousness. She even insisted on seeing the baby fed, and was convinced that but for obvious accidents of age and state she could have performed Bella's natural function far more efficiently. During the hours when the baby slept she was usually missing and to be found sitting pathetically beside the cradle with the beatified smile of a faded madonna. She grudged every moment when the child was not under her eyes, and was continually apprehensive of minute disasters which, she firmly believed, no care in the world but her own could avert.

Hugo Pomfret laughed at her, and Bella, though she felt touched, often smilingly teased her.

"When baby's a little older," she told her, "we shall have to do something about it. You'll spoil the poor child to death."

"What nonsense! I'm only doing my duty," Miss Mortimer answered seriously—implying that if she didn't nobody else would.

As a matter of fact every living soul in White Ladies spoiled him. Even the gardeners stopped the moving perambulator and lifted his veil to gaze, nodding their heads slowly with approval, at the sleeping child's face. Old Thomas, who grew, with each year, more shaky than ever, was almost as critical as Miss Mortimer of his admirable nurse, whom he regarded as too young and too "flighty" for her sublime office. He even reminded Hugo that he ought to start putting down port and claret for "Master Jasper," in bottles which his own frail hands would never uncork.

But the most eager and the most inquisitive of the child's many protectors was little Miss Penney. Whenever for a moment the nurse or Aunt Harriet relaxed their vigilance, the little black witch would materialize and stand greedily watching the child with her gimlet eyes. When he was taken out in his perambulator she continued to watch his progress from her high window tucked away like a spider's nest in the south-east turret.

Of all these admirations Miss Penney's was the only one which Bella resented. Apart from their mutual dislike, which time and Hugo's immutable obstinacy on the subject had increased, she hated Miss Penney's attentions to her unconscious son. She felt—and probably not without reason—that Miss Penney regarded the child not as a human being, minute and lovable, but as nothing more than a material part of White Ladies, the object, as were the pictures, the relics, the muniments, of a fierce, possessive jealousy. Bella could hardly blame Miss Penney for that. Her own attitude, indeed, apart from her natural tenderness towards the child she had borne, towards a small being whose helplessness must have appealed in any case to her protective instinct, was admittedly coloured by a kindred feeling: for her, too, the ideas of her baby and of White Ladies were interconnected in a way that made her passion for each enhance her love for the other. But what she most strongly—if vaguely—resented in Miss Penney's haunting was not so much her possessiveness as the physical propinquity of an influence which she knew to be hostile to herself and instinctively felt to be ill-omened: the equivalent in everyday life of a "bad fairy's" uninvited presence at a fairy-tale christening. Miss Penney was the only black blot, the only grotesque and sinister element in the scene of beauty and peace on which her son had opened his eyes.

And indeed, apart from this one ugly shape, what a store of calm beauty this baby of hers seemed destined to enjoy! Out of her new serenity Bella watched the procession of seasons, each contributing, like a shepherd king, its peculiar gifts, each endowing White Ladies with some subtle loveliness of its own. As yet Jasper, kicking in his perambulator and blandly gazing upward out of indifferent eyes (they were blue-black and, Miss Mortimer said, exactly like his great-grandfather's), would, no doubt, have been equally contented with any other world. And yet, Bella felt, if environment had any virtue, surely the child must unconsciously absorb (like an animal the cells of whose skin mysteriously manufacture a pigment to match its surroundings) the essential colour of White Ladies; surely a mind which had been assailed from its first glimmering of perception by the smells and the shapes and the hues of a particular place must find itself saturated, when consciousness at length emerged, with that place's spirit, and regard it as the unquestionable norm of human condition? That was how she wanted her baby, as soon as he should be capable of thought, to think of White Ladies; she wanted him to feel not so much that it belonged to him as that he belonged to it and was part of it, as the cell is part of the organism. Bella had no reason to doubt the validity of her theory. As Jasper grew, becoming each day, as Miss Mortimer triumphantly observed, more and more like his great-grandfather, he did actually seem to fit into his native surroundings, to belong to them and to be accepted by them with an unconscious ease and a naturalness which his mother, for all her jealous love of them, could never attain.

Those first years of Jasper's babyhood were, beyond question, the happiest Bella had ever known. The smoothness with which this self-sufficient life flowed over and past her made her almost insensible to its passage. There seemed no reason why that slow seasonal rhythm should ever be broken; and indeed the event which finally broke it was outside all reason.

On the eve of her son's third birthday hostilities

broke out in South Africa. Bella, isolated from affairs,
regarded the Boer ultimatum and the following
declaration of war as matters of no importance to herself apart from their possible effect on the gold-mining
shares into which Wilburn had put a large part of the
money which had come from his sale of her holding
in Jos. Tinsley & Co., and as to that, Wilburn hurriedly reassured her, she need feel no alarm. This
campaign, he wrote, was in the nature of a punitive expedition to assure and to protect the industry in which
she was interested. In any case it would all be over
in a couple of months at the most. Miss Mortimer,
who, because her father had done so, read the *Daily
Telegraph,* and Hugo, who stood by the *Morning
Post,* were equally indignant at President Kruger's
insolence and convinced that General Buller would
soon teach him the lesson for which he had been asking. Miss Mortimer, in particular, showed a highly
bellicose spirit. She remembered, perhaps, how Hayseech had benefited by the war of 1870.

Two months passed, and still the Boers had not
learnt their lesson. On the contrary it seemed that
in the matter of tactics they had something to teach.
The "Black Week" of mid-December showed the
British generals in an even less favourable light. Miss
Mortimer was flabbergasted, and declared "she would
never have thought it of them." Wild horses would
not compel her to believe that the Boers had fought
fairly. How could English sportsmen be expected to

deal with dum-dum bullets? Hugo Pomfret grew
more deeply concerned. After all, for a short time
in his early days, he had been a professional soldier.
A number of his former friends and comrades-in-arms
were in command of regiments, and several of them
had been killed or wounded. He became restless, frequenting the County Club in search of military gossip.
Even in his own remote corner of Worcestershire the
din of war reached him. Miles Ombersley, the son
of old Roger Ombersley of Chaddesbourne, was out
with the cavalry under French. Gilbert Cashel, the
master of the Woodland Stourton, had volunteered,
and Ralph Hingston, Sir Joseph's heir, had joined a
newly-raised corps, the Imperial Yeomanry. Of course
Hugo himself was a middle-aged man; but then, so
was Cashel. Any fellow who had actually served in
a cavalry regiment and understood horses could make
himself useful in some way or other whatever his age
might be. It was the plain duty of every member of
the caste which he had deserted and later rejoined
to serve his country.

At the beginning of the week before Christmas
Hugo announced his decision. In Worcester, that day,
he had visited the Yeomanry Depot and offered his
services. It seemed probable, in view of his previous
experience, that they would give him a subaltern's commission; even if they didn't he was perfectly ready
to enlist as a trooper. They didn't, in these days, he
said, waste much time over training. Within a fort-

R

night, in all probability, he would have sailed for
South Africa.

Hugo made this announcement at dinner, having
drunk the best part of a bottle of the dwindling Lafite
which he reserved for sublime occasions. His face
was flushed and the big vein bulged in his forehead;
but his tone was casual, and the terms of his announcement a triumph of understatement.

"It's extremely doubtful if I shall see any fighting,"
he said. "The campaign will probably be over before
I get there. But one never knows. In any case Thomas
will look after you."

Miss Mortimer received the news ardently. She
felt proud and awed and elated. In spite of his sly
habit of teasing her, she and Hugo were quite good
friends. She had respected him previously because
he was Jasper's father; but now, at one step, he had
become a figure fit to satisfy her craving for military
romance, a vehicle for her own heroic sentiments. This,
she said, was what, in similar circumstances, her father
would have done. She was sure that Bella, who had
not spoken, felt as proud as she did.

Was she proud? Bella wondered, assenting. Perhaps "proud" was hardly the right word. She was
certainly not surprised. In the back of her mind (she
knew the workings of Hugo's so well!) she had felt
certain that he would feel bound to enlist sooner or
later. She had looked forward to the event without
dread, but with a shade of pity, for, in a way, she

was fond of him. He was certainly too old—in body if not in years—to be fit for campaigning: for all the good he would do, Her Majesty the Queen might easily have spared his services. It was a shame, too, she thought, that this ageing, amiable man, who after such long vicissitudes and sacrifice had at last re-established himself in the orderly life to which he had been bred, should be snatched away from it at the moment when he had earned the right to enjoy it. And yet on the other hand—as the stern Pomfret faces and armoured figures whose portraits dominated the oak-panelled walls attested—he could certainly have done nothing else. To fight for one's country was part of the tradition of White Ladies. To die for one's country, if need be. She didn't want Hugo to die. His presence had become part of her life; his com-pany, and in a limited sense his guidance, would be necessary to Jasper; she still hoped—she had been hoping in vain for three years—that they would have another child. No, she didn't, though she declared enthusiastically that she did, feel nearly so proud as Aunt Harriet: only anxious that Hugo, who needed so much protection, shouldn't suffer unduly; and anxious, for her own part, to do her whole duty by him. Her duty by White Ladies. That was what it really came to.

And she couldn't, in any case, blame Hugo for feel-ing a little heroic, as in spite of his gallant nonchalance he obviously did. Her first duty, as she conceived it, was to give him all the support and all the happiness she could until the day of his departure. She had a feeling that he expected this as a right; but was prepared to devote herself to him of her own free will.

Thus it came about that during the short time before he sailed—the machine moved so quickly when once it was set in motion that they had only eight days together—she abandoned the baby to Aunt Harriet's willing care and scarcely left Hugo's side. There was even, on his part, a quick recrudescence of passion which had for her the effect of an Indian summer, a last flicker of warmth, coloured, vaguely languorous, and always haunted by a sense of brevity and impermanence. They seemed nearer to one another, indeed, and kinder and gentler than at any time since the evening when they had first arrived at White Ladies and walked through the house entranced, hand in hand. Bella was aware, perhaps more than ever before, of the absolute identity of their interests, remorsefully surprised by his taste and his wisdom, which, in the pride of her youth and her money, she had failed to appreciate and scorned to use.

During the daytime they walked together for miles and miles over the wintry fields and through the bare woods, discussing the plans which it would be her duty to pursue during his absence. Up till now Bella had never fully realized what a delightful companion Hugo could be in the open air, how deeply his mind was saturated with country lore, how much, in his slow, unobtrusive way, he had already achieved in forestry and in the betterment of his lands, how much more easily than herself he was able to understand the manners and reticences of country-folk and to be understood by them, how genuinely, as it seemed, his tenants and work-people loved him. It pleased her to hear him dropping into a dialect that awoke echoes of her childhood, recalling to her the speech of the nailers in the warehouse at Bromsberrow. She was glad to think that Hugo and herself belonged to the same "country," not merely by birth but by breed—for hadn't the Tinsleys and the Pomfrets started wrangling over Hayseech over a hundred years ago?

When they came home to White Ladies at night they continued to discuss estate business in the library where Hugo kept his papers and his plans. They leant over his desk, side by side, examining the large-scale maps of the estate on which he had pencilled in the delicious field-names: Marscall, Holy Ground, Hillaries, Long Leasowe, Packman's Innings, Hungry Harbour . . . In those late sessions she discovered a new and a delightful Hugo whom, through no fault of his, she had neglected to find before. In her passion for the house she had overlooked his devotion to the land that surrounded it: an older, an even more elemental piety.

"I'm afraid you'll have to let lots of things slide,"

he told her. "But don't trouble your head about that. As I'm always trying to tell you, this place resents hurry."

"I shall let nothing slide," she assured him. "I shall remember everything you've told me, and when you come back I shall give you an account of my stewardship."

When you come back. . . . The words, so often repeated, had always a hollow sound. As she spoke them, both knew that they took a great deal for granted; yet they never shirked using them. Hugo knew, by hereditary instinct, as it were, how a Pomfret should go to the wars. He was thorough in his forethought, giving her precise instructions as to where his will might be found, handing over to her the labelled keys of various safes and that of the fire-engine shed.

Early in January, 1900, he sailed from Southampton. Bella did not go down to the harbour to see him off—rather to the disgust of her patriotic Aunt Harriet, in whose eyes, since he went into uniform, Hugo had become a hero.

"If I had thought for one moment you weren't going with him," she said, "I should most certainly have gone to Southampton myself. Just to think that poor Hugo was probably the only man on that transport who hadn't a soul to wave to him from the quayside. If you had any heart you'ld have taken Jasper down with you, and made him wave too. As I've told you a hundred times, Bella, there's something hard about you."

Bella wasn't hard—at any rate not in this case. She knew better than Miss Mortimer how deeply her husband disliked displays of sentiment. They had said good-bye and he had kissed her exactly as if he were going to Worcester to serve on the Grand Jury at the assize. But she missed Hugo's company far more than she could ever have imagined, and more, no doubt, because of the curious intimacy of their last week together. By way of atonement for her lack of appreciation she devoted herself with studied conscientiousness to his legacy of duties. They kept her so busy, indeed, that time slipped by insensibly. Spring came; then a wet, green summer. By the end of May Mafeking was relieved; President Kruger had fled from Pretoria; as Wilburn wrote enthusiastically, the Rand mines were safe and the war was as good as over. Hugo, it seemed, had succumbed to the usual fate of "dug-outs"; he was marooned with a small detachment in a block-house in the Orange Free State, and immune—but for the bad luck of some sudden raid by De Wet—from all possible danger.

Even Aunt Harriet began to regard him as less heroic. When the newspapers arrived they no longer anxiously scanned the casualty-lists, until suddenly a new terror came: the outbreak of typhoid in the camps and hospitals at Bloemfontein. That was a danger more deadly and less heroic than the flying bullet, as they realised when they heard that Ralph Hingston, the baronet's younger son, was dead. For the first time since Hugo's departure Bella felt uneasy. People assured her that young people were more subject to infection than the middle-aged. That was one consolation; and yet she couldn't help asking herself what it would mean to her if Hugo caught the disease and died.

In absence and in retrospect she felt more kindly to her husband and far more sorry for him. Until their marriage, she admitted, poor Hugo had not had much of a life; he deserved a better end to it than dying like a sick fly in the middle of Africa. Time and distance combined to soften her judgement, so that she remembered less his positive defects—his indolence, his elderly fussiness—than his native virtues. When he came home, she resolved—if he ever came home— she would identify herself far more closely than before with his masculine interests and compel her woman's mind to understand them, partly for his sake but partly also because they must ultimately become the dominant interests of her son.

Of her only son. . . . Immediately after Hugo's departure she had been flattered for a while by the hope that she might have another; but that hope had soon vanished, and she knew that she had better make the best of the child she had: and indeed, as often as she could snatch him away from Aunt Harriet's possessive adoration, Jasper was beginning to compete with White Ladies itself in his claims on her life.

The child had now reached an enchanting age. He was nearly five. Whatever impression the beauty of White Ladies might have made on his mind, there was no doubt that its pure air and abundance of light had done much for his body. He was sturdy and tall for his age. Miss Mortimer—on heaven knows what grounds of comparison—declared him to be exceptionally intelligent. But Miss Mortimer's judgement was prone to bias. She continued to maintain, with equal emphasis, that he was a typical Mortimer, though, as Bella knew, he was a Pomfret if ever there was one. Of course she knew the Pomfret characteristics more intimately than Aunt Harriet—all those little movements and mannerisms and looks in which, again and again, she recognised a likeness to Hugo. But even apart from these finer shades of resemblance the child was his father's. The texture of his hair was neither Tinsley nor Mortimer. His eyebrows, on whose original blackness Aunt Harriet had banked so heavily, now grew to resemble in shape even more than in colour the eyebrows of the Jacobean Hugo Pomfret who had gone to the scaffold after the Gunpowder Plot. Whenever Bella saw his picture in the dining-room she was struck by an increasing likeness. Aunt Harriet stoutly denied it; but there it was: the same smallish round head; the same palish blue eyes; the same generous but not over-strong mouth (though

R*

how should a child's mouth be strong?) with its suspicion of lurking humour; and, more startling than all else—for she had always regarded this part of the portrait as a piece of weak, stylized painting—Jasper's baby fingers resembled, even in relative length, the painted fingers which grasped the silver chain, being, in fact, no more like Hugo's fingers than hers. Aunt Harriet was furious when Bella called her attention to this detail and declared the likeness purely imaginary, but Bella, to satisfy herself, confirmed it by measurement. The second finger, in each case, was short compared with the normal.

This discovery pleased her as much as she knew it would please Hugo. He answered enthusiastically, only hoping that in Jasper's future history wouldn't repeat itself. On the whole, in spite of Aunt Harriet, she was glad that her child had bred physically true to the Pomfret type and resembled Hugo more than herself. Jasper belonged none the less to her, yet all the more to White Ladies. From what the nurse told her, this likeness had already been noticed by little Miss Penney who, according to the same authority, would never "let the child be." "And what's more, Master Jasper likes her—the horrid little creature," the nurse whispered. "That's the thing that beats me, madam!"

Was Jasper a Pomfret in nature as well as in body? Bella wondered. It was too early to say for certain. In most things, she persuaded herself with something of Miss Mortimer's casuistry, he was much more like herself: it was to encourage this tendency that she became more and more anxious to isolate him from outside influences—and particularly Miss Penney's. Even so, she was forced to confess that in some others he was astonishingly like Hugo: in the quickness of his temper, in an odd combination of shyness and obstinacy with a complete and terrifying disregard of danger. In the end she admitted that she was the last person in the world to decide what the child's nature really was. She loved him, fiercely, possessively, increasingly, and that was enough. She was proud of his health, his strength, his beauty. When Hugo came home she knew he would be proud of him too.

But when would Hugo come home? He had been away for more than two years. The long war had dragged on to the Peace of Vereeniging. Jasper had passed his seventh birthday. Hugo's letters became querulous. He was still kicking his heels in the Orange Free State. It seemed as if the military authorities had forgotten his existence. Then, suddenly, a cable arrived from Capetown. He had actually sailed.

This time Bella went down to Plymouth to meet him and took Jasper with her. She was anxious not to be alone. For some odd reason she had the feeling that she was going to meet a stranger, and that the presence of the child would make the encounter easier. They had a great time together; for this was the first

long railway journey Jasper had ever taken. He had
never seen the sea; and his first glimpse of it, palely
washing the red sandstone cliffs between Starcross and
Dawlish, was almost as exciting for her as it was for
him. They put up at an hotel on the Hoe. She told
him all about Drake and showed him the smoking
grey monsters lying in the Hamoaze. Out at sea, they
heard the booming of guns at target-practice. Jasper
coaxed her into letting him have lobster for dinner,
and was sick in the night. The sight of his pale little
face and dank hair frightened her, for that very week
the King had been operated on for a new and prevalent
disease called appendicitis. She wished she had left
Jasper at home, and wondered whether she oughtn't
to send for a doctor; but after he had explained for
the hundredth time that it wasn't the lobster which
had upset him but merely the excitement of seeing the
sea, he fell asleep, and woke next morning slightly
chastened but as active as ever, skipping all over the
place, while she dressed, in his sailor suit.

By the time they came down to the coffee-room for
breakfast—why was it called coffee-room? he wanted
to know—Jasper had acquired a brand-new appetite
which he attributed to the sea-air, and fancied a grilled
fresh herring. This was rather rich, Bella thought;
and the waiter, whom Jasper had told of his last
night's catastrophe, agreed with her, explaining with
a wink that most naval gentlemen preferred whiting
at breakfast. Jasper hoped that the whiting was as

fresh as the herring, though the bill of fare didn't say so. He wanted fish, he explained, because his home was so far from the sea, and the waiter agreed that there was nothing better or more tasty of a morning.

At the table near them sat a number of hearty young men whom, from what she heard, Bella supposed to be naval officers. They all appeared to be very much interested in Jasper's conversation, and often looked round in his direction. One, in particular, looked as if he wanted to smile, and in a few moments Bella knew quite well that it was herself that he was interested in. She lowered her eyes, so as not to appear encouraging, but was flattered to think that at her mature age—she was now thirty-two, and even thirty had felt oldish to her—she was still sufficiently attractive to make young men take notice of her. On their way out from breakfast this officer happened to find himself walking at Jasper's side and asked him in a very deep voice what ship he was in. Jasper showed him the ribbon of his sailor-cap, which said: H.M.S. *Terrible*. "Well now, isn't that odd?" the young man said, "I'm in the *Terrible* too, but I don't know your face." He laughed and spoke to Bella: "Your son and I are shipmates. Is your husband an N.O.?"

No, she told him, her husband was a soldier, and expected at Plymouth that morning on one of the South African transports; he'd been away for three years. She liked people admiring her and taking notice of Jasper.

"How ripping for both of you!" the young man said, just a little enviously. "I expect he'll find his son grown. Well, good luck to all three of you."

He saluted and left them. The hall-porter hurried up. "The ship's in the Sound, madam," he said, "and the tenders will come into Millbay. I should advise you to go down pretty soon."

Bella thanked him. Everybody in the hotel showed the same friendliness. She supposed they were used to conducting romantic reunions. All the world seemed deliciously gay on this soft June morning. Jasper went jigging along by her side down the ramp which fell from the Hoe to Millbay. Other people were waiting already on the quay. There was an ambulance, too, and a stretcher-party. Jasper kept her busy with questions until the first tender came swinging in to shore. It was crowded with figures in khaki. Some of them waved their helmets. She tried hard to pick out Hugo's figure, and once smiled and pointed in mistake at an officer who looked like him. The tender's contents emptied slowly, like khaki sand running out of the neck of an hour-glass. Last of all came the stretcher-cases, carried shoulder-high down the gangway. But no Hugo. . . . The quay emptied, too.

An officer with a red-cross brassard, who had been staring at her for some time, advanced and saluted.

"Excuse me," he said, "do you happen to be Mrs. Pomfret?"

Bella answered "Yes," eagerly.

He said: "I have a message from your husband. He's not very well, and would like you to come aboard."

"Oh, I do hope it's nothing serious. Do you know what's the matter with him?"

"I'm afraid I can't tell you," the officer said. "I was just told to ask you to come."

"My little boy's with me . . ."

"Oh, of course he must come as well. *I'll* look after him," he added enthusiastically.

They all took to Jasper, she thought. He, of course, was enraptured. As soon as they were on board the tender the officer took him off to look at the engines, and did not return with him until they were nearly alongside the transport. He told Jasper he must salute the quarter-deck at the head of the ladder, where he handed both of them over to a major who was apparently expecting her.

"You might look after this gallant fellow, Reed," he said, "while I take Mrs. Pomfret along to see the colonel. You don't happen to know Colonel Jaques, by the way?" he enquired.

Bella said that she didn't. He led her to a cabin which had the look of an orderly-room where an elderly, red-faced man, with a heavy moustache like Lord Kitchener's, received her. His manner was awkward too. None of these soldiers, it seemed to her, were half as jolly as her young sailor.

"I'm sorry to have given you all this trouble, Mrs. Pomfret," he said. "Your husband was taken ill suddenly—let me see—the day before yesterday."

"Seriously ill?"

"Yes, rather seriously. In fact, very seriously. You are a soldier's wife, Mrs. Pomfret . . ."

"He's in danger?"

"I'm sorry to say so. He had a stroke. He was unconscious from the first. He . . . I'm afraid he never recovered consciousness . . . until the end."

"The end?"

"I'm afraid so. Your husband died last night."

V

EVERYBODY at Plymouth, from the General Officer Commanding to the hall-porter in the hotel, went out of their way to be kind to Bella, a courageous and pretty woman in distress; and Ernest Wilburn, for whom she telegraphed at once, proved as tactful and capable as ever. It was he who had the inspiration of bringing Miss Mortimer down with him to look after Jasper who, in spite of the sympathies and sorrowful head-shakings with which he was surrounded, was thoroughly enjoying his first visit to the seaside and had made up his mind that he was going to be a sailor. Bella, remembering her own first encounter with death at Bromsberrow, felt anxious that the child should be spared any reflection of its grimness; so Aunt Harriet was instructed to take him on to Torquay and keep him playing on the sands till the funeral was over. Miss Mortimer accepted this charge as a duty, but rather resented being "done out of" the ceremony. After all, her nephew-in-law—however much she had disliked him at first—was her own private hero.

They buried Hugo near the sculptured tombs of his ancestors at Sheriff's Bayton, three miles to the west of White Ladies. It was not until the cortège had left the house that Bella realized, for the first time, the significance of that grass-grown drive curving between yew-hedges and under the arch of the Palladian gate-way by which she had originally approached the house. It was the funerary road of state which the Pomfrets used on their way to their last resting-place. That, perhaps, was why it had always struck her as melancholy. She rode, heavily veiled, in the first carriage with Ernest Wilburn and Hugo's family lawyer, a Mr. Chafey from Worcester. In the second came Thomas and Miss Penney and Shelton, the game-keeper; in two others the gardeners and the tenants whom Wilburn had selected to act as bearers. A sad and quite unimpressive little procession.

At the church gates, to her surprise, a large number of mourners were gathered. All the Abberleys and Ombersleys who were capable of movement had crawled out of their half-timbered manor-houses to pay a last tribute to one whose name, at least, they respected. Mr. Pomfret, of Wychbury, Hugo's second cousin, boomed the burial service, taking pre-cedence over the vicar of Sheriff's Bayton, but not sharing his fee. He looked, in his surplice, like a hunting-man in fancy-dress. When the ceremony was over he removed this disguise and accompanied Bella to her carriage. He was sorry that she had not thought fit to bring Jasper to the funeral.

"I hope you will make arrangements in good time," he said, "to send him to school. Poor Hugo was the only member of the family who missed going to Eton." He spoke as though all Hugo's eccentricities—including his marriage—had been due to this lamentable omission. "If you like," he went on, "I will write to the headmaster myself."

Bella thanked him and said that she hadn't as yet made any plans. Jasper was only seven.

"You ought to be thinking about it, all the same," Mr. Pomfret anxiously persisted.

They drove homewards in solemn silence. The day was superb; a green Worcestershire June at its best: cuckoos calling continually over miles of warm, motionless air drenched with scents of meadow-sweet and mowing-grass in flower. Bella was thinking of Hugo—not so much of the Hugo with whom she had lived at White Ladies as of the one she had seen, for a moment only, in the improvised mortuary aboard the transport at Plymouth: a spare, elderly, grizzled man, his skin scorched and shrunk by the African sun, his features stamped, more in death than ever before, with the pride and distinction of race. She was glad to think, at least, that the last twelve years of his life had matched the dignity of those features; but even now, when it was over, she found it difficult to believe that he had been her husband and the father of her two children. It seemed no more remarkable that he was dead than that he had ever lived. It was the strangeness of life rather than the solemnity of death and burial that impressed her.

The carriage rolled over the grassy track with silent wheels. She raised her eyes, and saw before her the empty Palladian gatehouse. It seemed to her as beautiful as when she had first seen it, but no longer sinister. The thought that it had been neglected pricked her conscience. She noticed that the glass in the windows had been broken and that part of the stone ornament was missing. Whenever she had spoken to Hugo about it he had put her off. Now nobody could put her off, she reflected. She was her own mistress. "I must have this seen to at once," she told herself.

When they reached White Ladies the lawyers left her to busy themselves with Hugo's will. There was little remarkable in it, Wilburn told her later. The marriage-settlement had already disposed of all matters of importance. Hugo had practically no money to leave. White Ladies, as they had arranged, would be hers as long as she lived, in trust for Jasper. The only alteration in the will he had made at Naples was a codicil added a few months after their marriage in which he requested his beloved wife, Arabella Pomfret, not to dismiss from their employment at White Ladies his two faithful servants, Emily Penney and Walter Thomas: a provision which, Wilburn remarked, seemed reasonable enough.

Bella flushed with annoyance when she heard of it.

"Thomas is a dear old man," she said, "though he's dreadfully incompetent; but that woman Penney, I may tell you, is the bane of my life. Hugo was

ridiculously obstinate about her. Am I forced to keep
her?"

"You're not forced to do anything. You're merely
requested."

"Couldn't I pension her off? I'ld gladly do anything to get rid of the sight of her."

"From what you tell me I should guess that she
knows all about your husband's request—in which
case it would be imprudent as well as unusual . . ."

"That was rather shabby of Hugo. He knew how
I felt about her."

"All the same, it might look rather odd . . ."

"Then I suppose I shall have to do what he asks."

"I think you should."

So, to Bella's resentment, the black witch remained
to haunt White Ladies. From the look of sly triumph
in her eyes Bella divined that Wilburn had guessed
rightly when he said that she knew of the codicil.
After all, Bella told herself, it was as well for her
own peace of mind that she had decided to accede
to Hugo's request. In some ways she felt more
responsible to him now he was dead than when he
was alive. Then, though she had invariably sought
his advice in matters relating to White Ladies,
he had usually submitted his judgement to her
stronger will. Now her determinations lacked the
support of his approval, and even though that
approval had been dictated by her, she felt the lack
of it, and was less sure of herself than ever before.

The management of the estate was, of itself, no small
addition to her responsibilities. She had not, she discovered, Hugo's inbred, instinctive capacity for dealing with men. Her mind moved too quickly, and she
was prone to act too impetuously, to suit the leisurely
life of the land. She found herself making abrupt
decisions and swiftly repenting them. She would
never, she confessed, have imagined that she would
miss Hugo so much.

Add to this that for at least three years after his
death all her plans were thwarted and her movements
crippled by the weight of death-duties, which Hugo,
inheriting White Ladies twenty years earlier, had
been spared. It was fortunate for her, indeed, that
the results of the speculative investments into which
Wilburn was gradually diverting her interest in Hayseech had justified the risks he had allowed her to
take. The reduction of Jos. Tinsley & Co.'s capital,
which Wilkinson had foreshadowed, had taken place;
but even this sacrifice had not been sufficient to restore
the firm's waning fortunes. The war had added surprisingly little to its resources, and now the burdens
resulting from the war remained to be borne. When
the Liberals swept the country in 1906, the future
of landed proprietors began to look blacker than ever.

Bella was beginning to feel her age. By all standards of reason she knew that this feeling was
ridiculous. After all, in spite of the grey streaks in
her hair, she was only thirty-six. She came of a long-

lived stock, and at this age she had surely a right to think that the best part of her life lay before her. Yet thirty-six was in sight of forty; and forty seemed dreadfully old!

It was the loneliness of existence at White Ladies, she told herself, that inclined her to brood over such things, its monotonous smoothness that allowed time to slide by insensibly like some deep, swift river on whose surface its placid beauty, immutably mirrored, gave a treacherous illusion of suspension, of unchanging life. Yet, for all that, life changed; one grew old perpetually without knowing it, while, in a bemused detachment, one watched other people growing old.

Aunt Harriet, for instance. Of course Aunt Harriet must now be nearing sixty. Women who went grey as early as she, enjoyed the blessed compensation of looking exactly the same for the best part of their lives. It was only during the last year or so that her looks had toppled over, as one might say, on to the downward slope, that her throat had become wrinkled, her eyes sunken, her cheeks furrowed, in a way that made her resemble more than ever the portrait of Jasper Mortimer in the board-room at Hayseech. And with this physical change there had come a change of spirit which showed itself in the inclination of her mind to drift back, whenever the exigencies of the present relaxed, into memories of old faces and places and trivial forgotten incidents.

It dwelt so completely in the past that Bella was
hardly surprised when, at last, she announced her intention of recalling her old maid Helen from her sub-
sidized retirement and renting a little house on the
Halesby side of Hayseech.

"I am extremely fond of White Ladies," she said,
"and I've been very happy here. As a matter of fact
I think the last ten years have been the happiest of
my life. But much as I love it, I don't really belong
here, Bella. At a certain age, as your grandfather
always said, people tend to go back automatically to
the place they were born in. If he had lived, I'm
inclined to think he would have bought an estate in
Shropshire. Just before he died, I remember him saying that if he could find the spare time he would like
to make a driving-tour in that direction. And now
with the convenience of these dreadful motor-cars and
the telephone, I shan't really be out of touch with
you when I'm settled in Halesby. I shall ring you
up frequently and run over quite often to see you.
And of course I shall have Jasper to stay with me.
It's only right that he should know where his great-
grandfather lived."

So Miss Mortimer packed her old japanned trunk
and returned to Halesby.

It was not only the ageing of the people about
her—such as poor dear Thomas, who was really becoming quite impossibly decrepit—that made Bella
feel older than she was. There were other inevitable

reminders—notably the attitude of Jasper's tutors.
Jasper was now nearly eleven. In another year or
so he would be going to Eton. Bella had submitted
thus far to the guidance of the Vicar of Wychbury
and to the family tradition; but, rather than part with
him before it was absolutely necessary, she had
rejected Mr. Pomfret's plan of sending him first to
Cheam, preferring to entrust his preparatory education to a series of young men just down from Oxford
or Cambridge whom his future housemaster at Eton
recommended for the post. They were, on the whole,
she was ready to admit, very nice young men; and
one of them—his name was Sheriff—resembled,
oddly enough, in his appearance and in his tastes, her
first love, Henry Fladburn. They were frank and
bright and enthusiastic; they had all the self-confidence of youth. Bella was glad of their company—
it seemed right to have a man about the house—and
even grew fond of them in a motherly, or perhaps
a sisterly, way. There was never, with any of them,
the least suggestion of a romantic attachment; yet
often she found herself wondering why there wasn't.
Though they treated her with a charming friendliness, confiding to her their small troubles and aspirations, and even their love-affairs, it was clear that
they regarded her not only with the respect that was
owing to their employer but also with an emotional
remoteness due to the difference in their age. She
didn't want any of them—not even Mr. Sheriff—to

fall in love with her; it might have been extremely awkward if they had; but she did think, at least, they might have thought of her as an attractive and desirable woman—as they obviously didn't.

Was she, in fact, she asked herself, no longer attractive or desirable? Only four years ago, in the hotel at Plymouth, that nice-looking naval officer had quite certainly been attracted by her. Externally, she assured herself, she was not greatly changed since then. Could it be true that a woman such as herself, whom men had made much of, had suddenly ceased to inspire any emotion but respect—that this part of her life, which had begun so disastrously with Henry and culminated, without any excess of romantic rapture, in her marriage of convenience to a middle-aged man, was now finished for good and all? She had no desire to re-marry—her single-minded devotion to White Ladies precluded the idea—but the reflection was none the less melancholy.

Two years later, Jasper's going to Eton left her even more lonely. She now felt so bereft and useless that she realized she must really do something to drag herself forcibly out of the brooding habit into which she had gradually sunk. Her financial circumstances had at last recovered from the strain of the death-duties. Ernest Wilburn's management of her affairs, if not always prudent, had proved highly successful. For the first time after many years she had money to spend and felt justified in spending it. It would be unfair to Jasper, she told herself, to resign herself to an inactive and premature middle age. She owed it to him to hold the place to which the possession of White Ladies entitled her in the social life of the county.

Advised by Wilburn, and to Jasper's delight, she bought a motor-car, and began to visit not only the various Abberleys and Ombersleys buried in their half-timbered manors, but the neighbouring great houses such as Stourford Castle and Stoke Priory. The mere fact of emerging into contact with a more lively existence stimulated her. She regained her old energy. Her spirit craved again for the ruthless activity which was its natural expression; and that activity, naturally enough, must be concentrated on White Ladies.

She began to put into practice some of the numerous plans which lethargy and lack of funds had compelled her to postpone. Once more Wilburn tried in vain to moderate her extravagance. This was an age in which country-house life, the conditions of which had hardly been changed in that part of the world since the mid-nineteenth century, was beginning to demand new standards of convenience and comfort. In his stucco-battlemented castle Joseph Hingston showed her, with pride, the most modern electric-lighting plant and a novel system of steam-heating. At Stourford, as might have been expected, the light-fittings and radiators looked extremely vulgar; it would have been impious, she felt, for all their convenience, to inflict such monstrosities on White Ladies; but at Stoke Priory, the old seat of the D'Abitots, lately (and rather noisily) purchased by a reputed millionaire named Griffith Tregaron, she saw similar schemes for heating and lighting adapted in perfect taste to the style of an Adam mansion. Bella eagerly enquired and obtained from the Tregarons the name of the architect who had handled the matter so tactfully, and invited him down to White Ladies to make an inspection and give his advice.

He was a young and ambitious man named Roger Courtenay who, by the charm of his manner, the lavishness of his estimates, and a number of advantageous family connections, had rapidly acquired what is known as an "exclusive" practice. He made it quite clear by the tone of his letters and the scale of his fee and expenses that he was not disposed to undertake any work that did not immediately appeal to his artistic sense.

These hesitations did not trouble Bella. She was confident that as soon as he set eyes on White Ladies he must realize what an exquisite work he had been invited to inspect; and indeed, when he saw it, to Bella's delight, he was enraptured. She was equally pleased when she perceived, from his manner towards her, that his æsthetic appreciation extended to her own person.

"But why haven't I ever heard of White

Ladies?" he asked. "Why has nobody written about
it? It's a gem of the very first water! There isn't a
flaw in it! Such lightness and grace combined with
such dignity. It isn't too big; and no fools of
architects, thank heaven, have ever tampered with
it. For God's sake don't ever let them, my dear
Mrs. Pomfret! If X. . . ."—and he mentioned
a famous name—"set his hand on it, I should
never forgive you. It's a perfect example of my
favourite period—the time when the grimness of
Tudor Gothic first began to unfreeze under the influence of a warm breeze from the south. You know
what I mean? I needn't have asked. I can see you
do."

He took unusual pains to find out what she thought
before he asked any questions. Together they explored
the whole house, from the great hall to the long
gallery. In his knowledge of the period Bella could
see for herself he was no bluffer. It flattered her
to find his eyes noticing with approval her own small
alterations and additions. He was enchanted, particularly, with the topiary garden, and astonished that
she had designed it.

"If I may say so," he told her, "you have the most
impeccable taste as well as . . ."

Courtenay left it at that; but the conclusion of the
sentence was obvious.

It was a long time, Bella thought, since she had
met such a charming person. He showed a cultured

appreciation of all elegant things, including, to the
extent of a whole bottle, the *Steinberger Kabinet*
which Thomas presented in perfect condition at
dinner. They sat long at the table afterwards in
silvery candlelight. His manner was so easy that
Bella found herself unconsciously speaking of things
which she had never discussed with anyone before. They talked about Hugo, the odd circumstances
of her marriage; they discussed Jasper's future.
Courtenay happened to be an old Etonian.

"Is he anything like you?" he asked. The tone
of the question implied a compliment.

"Not in the least bit," she told him. "On the
contrary he grows more like the boy in that picture
every year."

She pointed to Hugo Pomfret, the Gunpowder
Conspirator, whose portrait regarded them from its
frame with pale blue eyes. It was a charming picture,
he agreed, and rather pathetic. Had she noticed the
hands—the odd shortness of the second finger? Indeed yes, she told him, Jasper's hands had the same
peculiarity.

"After two hundred years. . . . It's just things like
that which make life so mysterious, so exciting. Don't
you agree with me?"

She agreed with him passionately. After breakfast
to-morrow, they decided, he and the surveyor he had
brought with him would examine the house in detail.
She preceded him up the stairs towards the first floor,

carrying her candle. He remained in the hall, admiring.

"Stand just where you are," he called from below. "Yes, that is quite perfect. Do you know, Mrs. Pomfret, this house demands candlelight. If we decide to put in electricity we shall have to be terribly careful. I'm not at all sure . . ."

"Can't you get round it somehow or other?" Bella asked regretfully. "I'd quite set my heart on it. Lamps and candles are so inconvenient."

He laughed. "Well, we'll see about that tomorrow," he said. "Good night, and thank you so much for this privilege."

Courtenay spent the whole of the next morning with his man taking measurements of the house. At luncheon Bella found him preoccupied. She felt she was not maintaining her success. When they had finished and he had complimented her on her coffee, he said:

"I'm afraid I've some rather bad news for you."

"What kind of bad news?"

"Well, as a matter of fact, it's rather a good thing for you that I came here and discovered it. There's dry rot in the roof."

"What *is* dry rot?"

"It's a fungoid disease . . ."

"Yes, I know. But what does it mean?"

"I'm afraid it means a new roof. All the timbers are gone. It's a mercy that the whole thing hasn't already collapsed and fallen. Sheet-lead's pretty heavy."

"And that's going to be costly?"

"Horribly."

"How much?"

He spoke vaguely in thousands: he was a very expensive architect. "The point is that whatever it costs it ought to be done at once if you're to save the house."

"In that case we must do it, Mr. Courtenay. Will you see to it and start on it immediately?"

"I must say I admire your pluck."

"I love White Ladies. In a way it will be easier, won't it? to combine the repairing of the roof . . ."

"It's much more than a repair."

". . . well, the replacement of the roof . . . with the other work."

"Yes, that's perfectly true. It will help us in building the new flue for your central-heating, the upper part of it anyway. But if you think of doing it all together, it's going to run you in for a deuce of a lot of money; and I warn you there won't be much to see for it. However, I'll do as you say. I shall leave my man behind to complete the survey. As soon as he's finished I'll get out estimates. It might possibly be cheaper to modify the construction of the roof."

"I want nothing altered."

Courtenay laughed. "Very well, nothing shall be altered."

"And at the same time," Bella said, "you'll get on with the other plans too?"

"There's no hurry for those just yet. The roof's going to take six months."

"You don't know me: I'm always in a hurry."

As soon as he had gone Bella ordered the car and drove into North Bromwich to see Wilburn. She told him what Courtenay had said was necessary and how much it was likely to cost. Wilburn listened sceptically.

"In an affair of that magnitude," he said, "I think you had much better ask for a second opinion. Courtenay may be exaggerating. These fashionable fellows often have big ideas."

Bella refused the cautious suggestion. She liked Courtenay, she said, and trusted him.

"Very well," Wilburn said. "I suppose the next thing is, you'll want me to find the money."

"The money's there, isn't it? And it's mine."

He laughed. "Yes, it's there all right. And it's yours. Of course you shall have it. But it isn't always easy to sell at short notice—or wise, for that matter."

"I'm afraid that can't be helped. He says the roof's positively dangerous; so I shall be glad if you'll see about finding the money immediately."

Wilburn said that he would—ungraciously, Bella thought. That day, for the first time since she had known him, his manner struck her as evasive. She drove back to White Ladies a little cross with him.

s

She disliked being treated as an irresponsible child even by so old a friend as Wilburn. Her money, she repeated to herself, was her own. If she chose to realize capital at a loss, it was no business of his, and she had no intention of being bullied by him. He had behaved almost as if her request embarrassed him, as if he were playing for time. A fleeting suspicion flashed through her mind and troubled it. Was it possible that Wilburn had been using her money for some purpose of his own? Even the shadow of such a doubt seemed unworthy of her, and made her ashamed. She had trusted him as a loyal friend and adviser for more than fifteen years. It would show a poor sort of loyalty on her part if she allowed a mere momentary change in his manner to undermine her trust.

In less than a week Courtenay came down to White Ladies again. The complete survey revealed a grave state of affairs. To make even a passable job of the mischief and to prevent its spreading, the whole roof must come down.

"Well, we can't spoil the ship for a ha'p'orth of tar," Bella said.

It was not, alas! a question of ha'p'orths but of thousands, he told her. He agreed that while the whole house was in a mess it might be just as well to get on with her other plans for heating and lighting. If she decided to go through with them the contractors could start work immediately. She might rest assured that he would be careful to protect her interests. She might even, if she liked, go away from White Ladies while the work was being done and leave everything in his hands; for the noise and the dust would make the house quite uninhabitable.

"I would much rather stay here," Bella told him. "When work's being done I prefer to see it for myself."

She was delighted, in fact, to find in watching the builders' activities a new interest and a new outlet for her energy. It would have been a lapse of duty, in any case, to have left such a storehouse of treasures— less precious in themselves than in their personal significance—at the mercy of strangers. The work dragged on, as usual, much longer than the contractor had expected. White Ladies was "uninhabitable," as Courtenay had put it, for the best part of a year, during which, through one modification of his plans after another, the estimate which had made Wilburn blink was exceeded by nearly a third. The money, however, was always forthcoming when Bella demanded it, and the promptness with which it was paid made her more than ever ashamed of her momentary suspicions of Wilburn's probity.

She enjoyed those twelve months of confusion more in some ways than any year since her marriage. There was always, in the back of her mind, a satisfactory consciousness of things being done and, before her, a vision of White Ladies emerging from the turmoil in a state of increased solidity and convenience without any sacrifice of beauty. Whatever it might cost her, the property which she handed on to Jasper should be better in every respect than when she had received it from Hugo.

Jasper, too, when he came home from Eton, enjoyed the building and shared her interest. His first year at school had improved him enormously, and rid him of the childishness of a boy brought up at home. He was tall for his age but not weedy; and if the bias of his growing mind was not intellectual it showed, at least, a practical quality which was not unwelcome in a Pomfret—as though that attenuated strain had benefited from an infusion of more vigorous blood. After all, Bella told herself, the possession of White Ladies, his main purpose in life, was not one which need make any heavy demands on the intellect. What Jasper needed was specialized knowledge and taste of a kind in which she made it her business to interest and instruct him—and not unfruitfully, for, from the first, he showed something of Hugo's appreciation for the beauties of his own inheritance, its history, its associations.

In addition to this he began to show Hugo's love and practical aptitude for all things relating to the land. Bella found no need to encourage his interest in husbandry and agriculture; he tended towards them instinctively, as though they were in his blood. As a horseman he had a natural seat and admirable hands. He had the observant eye of a born field-naturalist, an ear quick to notice and remember the faintest bird-song, and an uncanny insight into the movements and habits of wild creatures which filled Bella, who was not country-bred, with despair for herself and with admiration for him. His chief friend at White Ladies—apart from old Thomas, who still loyally doddered on, and Miss Penney, for whom he still showed what was to Bella an irritating, unnatural affection—was Shelton, the keeper, who taught him (if that were needed) to shoot and to trap and to ferret. Whenever he could, he went hunting with Mr. Pomfret, who was ready at any moment to spend hour after hour with anyone who could talk about Eton. Mr. Pomfret, too, happily abandoning his clerical kit for a grey flannel suit and a selection of sporting neckwear which included the Free Foresters, the M.C.C., and the I Zingari ties, escorted him to the Worcestershire County Cricket ground, where the brilliant era of the Foster brothers was drawing to a close. And when cricket could not be played or watched, Mr. Pomfret drove him, in his shaky two-cylinder *De Dion* to Lesswardine on the upper Teme, where, on the water of another distant cousin named Delahaye, Jasper learned to cast a floating Blue Up-right over the nose of a rising trout.

These accomplishments, so easily acquired, were enough to convince the Vicar of Wychbury that his cousin's extremely odd marriage had not (as he had feared) played the deuce with the Pomfret blood. What thrilled Bella far more was the boy's increasing resemblance to the portrait of Hugo Pomfret in the dining-room. She rejoiced in this for the sake of White Ladies: that is to say, for her own sake, finding also, in Jasper's quick temper, in his fearlessness, and in a tendency to indolence (which, otherwise, she might have deplored) further evidence of his conformity to the Pomfret type; though, indeed, what touched her even more deeply was his affection for herself and his comradeship, which, together, made up a more satisfying human relationship than any she had known or might hope to know. If she had been asked at this time to decide which she loved the more, her son or White Ladies, she would have found it difficult to answer. And indeed the question was unanswerable. For her they were one and indivisible.

One of the most surprising effects of this unmixed happiness was the recovery of her youth and of her beauty, both of which had seemed at one time to be leaving her. What made her conscious of the second of these more than all else was the regular visits of Roger Courtenay to inspect the contractor's work. She looked forward to these with an eagerness which was not sentimental. It was the quickness of his mind, she told herself, and the similarity of its texture to that of her own, which made his visits so welcome. Though there had never been any hint of a romantic relation between them (and, for that matter, he was happily married) the mere fact of his admiration was stimulating, and put her on good terms with herself as well as with him. Even if he had not been personally attractive, she would have been disposed to like his company because of his love for White Ladies. It was, as he had declared from the first, his ideal house. During his week-end visits, he had spent most of his spare time in making, for his own satisfaction, not only a plan of the house but also a series of drawings and photographs of every detail in its carving and panelling and stonework and plaster. Some of her happiest moments were spent in watching him at work, his deft pencil committing to paper records of the utmost delicacy. She would sit there by the hour, idly listening, while Courtenay told her of his work and of the exciting fashionable world which he frequented in London, its comedy and its scandal. His stories made her feel countrified, though she had no desire to feel anything else.

"I wonder that you don't find it dull, coming down here," she told him.

"Dull? In this perfect place, and in such perfect company? How dare you suggest such a thing?"

She laughed, pleased by his compliment.

"Do you know," he said, seriously, "I believe this is the happiest house I have ever set foot in?"

Bella sighed. "Well, heaven knows *I*'m happy," she said.

VI

It took more than a year in all to finish the work on White Ladies. There were many other things waiting to be done, but the rebuilding of the whole roof, the wiring and the plumbing (to say nothing of the furnaces, the generating-plant and the batteries) had proved to be so much more costly than even Courtenay had imagined, that Bella dared not ask Wilburn to find her another penny.

Apart from its putting an end to her architect's professional visits—and they were such good friends now that he had promised to come down and see her from time to time—the completion of the work, the beginning of which had excited her, came as a relief to Bella. It had fulfilled its chief function, which was to drag her out of the rut of middle age into which she had been slipping. Courtenay's friendship, to say nothing of his admiration, had helped to set her on her feet again and restored her self-confidence. She felt and looked younger now, in her fortieth year, than at thirty-five; and now that he had done his part, she was happily able, if she had so wished, to dispense with his help.

She had discovered a new friend: Jasper was "growing up." By the time he was fifteen he was no longer a child to be shielded and cosseted—his Aunt Harriet had been partly responsible for his childishness—but a companion with whom, even more than with Hugo, she could share her hopes, her plans, her preoccupations, in unguarded intimacy. She was thankful now that she had resisted Mr. Pomfret's persuasions to send him to a preparatory school. Those early years of tutelage, in which his whole being had been cunningly saturated, as it were, with the atmosphere of White Ladies, had laid the foundation of what looked like becoming an absorbing passion, the intensity of which his exile at school increased. It was a joy to her to see this passion developing; to note the wistful nostalgia with which his letters from Eton were tinged; to share the joy and excitement with which he returned to the beloved spot.

Even apart from this common devotion her relation with her son was becoming a sheer delight. Affection until now had played a small part in her life. Only once, and then with disastrous effects, had she given the whole of her heart to another human being. Now she knew the luxury of giving it again, without a vestige of fear or caution, and the mere act of giving brought its own blessedness, curiously lightening her spirits and softening the cicatrix of that old wound and the self-protective callousness she had instinctively assumed. Under the influence of her love for Jasper she found, with secret delight, her whole attitude towards life, particularly the lives of others,

s*

becoming gentler and more generous. She was recovering, in middle age, and to her own happy surprise, the ingenuousness of her girlhood, looking
forward to Jasper's coming with the eager rapture
of a young girl in love.

The most delicious of all these holidays came in
the summer of the Coronation, when the school
authorities added a week to the usual period. It
was a season of great heat and abundant sunshine, so rainless that, for the first time since
the lawns had been laid, the ground-plan of the convent walls showed itself on the turf of her topiary
garden. It was a summer of lazy delights; even the
border rivers ran dry, and Mr. Pomfret, keen fisher-
man that he was, intoned with a personal wistfulness
the Church's set prayers for rain. Unlured by more
distant attractions, Jasper was happy enough to spend
all his time with her. For seven weeks they surrendered themselves completely to the serenity of
White Ladies drowsing in its green basin and screened
from the outer world's intrusion by its girdle of woods,
drowsy too in their summer silence. It was a life of
pure physical peace and relaxation, in which the house
imposed on their human restlessness its own spirit of
timeless beauty.

Fifty yards from the eastern front a huge tulip-
tree shadowed the sward with indented fans. Here,
sheltered from the sun, they spent many hours: Bella
busy with the tapestry which she was making to re-

place the worn *petit-point* upholstery of the rose-and-ivory drawing-room, sewing only in intervals of calm meditation, for the fine work, she had noticed of late, tried her eyes, and she still rebelled against spectacles; Jasper stretched on a rug at her feet, his cricket-shirt open at the neck, pretending to read (for no book could hold his attention for long) but more often gazing through the imbricate greenness of the tulip-tree that towered overhead into a blue dimmed with heat, like love-in-the-mist. When Bella laid down her work on her lap, he would become aware of her, rolling over with a grass in his regular but rather square teeth and gazing up at her through narrowed eyelids. And Bella, returning his gaze, and thinking how strong and young and slim he was, and how he was hers, would smile slowly, serenely, her black eyes softened by love; and then, perhaps, their indefinite silent communion of lazy thought tautened to speech; he would tell her of something that had come into his vacant mind while he lay there, like a strayed cloud crossing the blue; some grave, boyish plan he had conceived for his next half at Eton, or something he wanted to tell Shelton about the pheasants he was rearing in pens by Nineveh Wood. But however trivial what he said might be, Bella gave it her solemn consideration and approval. All their life, in those days, was made up of pleasant, unanxious, trivial things; such was the normal tenor of White Ladies. After which she would return to her tapestry and he

to his book and both of them to the same soothing
silence, until, a little later, perhaps, they would see
the shrunken figure of old Thomas, his white head
brilliant in the sun, limping over the lawn with a tray
of tea-things and followed by the footman who carried
a folding table. The strawberries had been nearly over
before Jasper came home; but there were plenty of
late raspberries with cool Jersey cream from the
dairy; the sun-ripened peaches from the walled
garden were wonderful that year, and Jasper, by
nature a fruit-eating animal, enjoyed them most of
all.

When tea was over they naturally felt much less
lazy. That was the best time for talk—an hour in
which thought flowed more clearly, and every sense
grew more alive; in which, as they quietly spoke or
laughed together, Bella watched the huge shadow of
the house diagonally creeping over the lawn, absorbing, as it slowly advanced, expanses of golden air, and
bringing to life the flower-beds whose colours had
previously been submerged under the flood of white
light—even releasing (or so it seemed to her) their
perfume, which now moved through the cooling air
in soft breaths that to her fancy resembled sighs of
content.

But of these serene hours the most perfect of all,
to her mind, came later, when dinner was over, and
together they walked with slow steps arm in arm along
the flagged terrace facing the moat. At this time, when

the sky was still pale with the ghost of day, or faint
starlight, or fluid flickers of summer-lightning which
the day's heat had bred, the shape of White Ladies
attained an unearthly beauty, the pale mullions of the
bays and of the oriel which rose straight to the
balustrade, dissociating themselves from the darker
mass of brickwork. There the walls of the house and
the flags of the terrace still radiated the warmth
they had absorbed from the sun, and the night-
scented stocks which grew in the crevices exhaled a
perfume which matched, in its appeal to a different
sense, the nightingale's vanished song. This was no
time for speech, but for a silence richer than speech.
Sometimes they would stop, of one accord, in their
walk, to lean over the parapet of the moat and gaze
down on its surface which darkness had cleared, and
see there the house's inverted image imprisoned deep
in a matrix of crystalline jet, so still that only the
zig-zag flight of a bat, reflected, destroyed the illusion
of substance. Sometimes, straying over the bridge
into the harvest owl-light, they would suddenly turn
to see the mass of White Ladies illuminated like a
great lantern of stone which Courtenay's electric plant
filled with unwonted light.

Only one circumstance marred the entranced
placidity of this period: the death of old Thomas. He
died in his sleep, as gently as he had lived, just a week
before Jasper returned to Eton. Jasper himself, no
less than his mother, felt the loss keenly. It was his

first sensible contact with death. At the time of his father's he had been too young to realize it. Though Bella would have preferred him to stay behind, he insisted on following the old man to his grave in the churchyard at Sheriff's Bayton. They drove there together along the grass-grown yew avenue. Bella consoled herself by thinking that mortality in this guise, so quiet, so near to the orderly processes of nature, had lost every element of grimness. Jasper was no longer a child, and this burial, after all, had no deeper tragedy in it than that of a favourite dog or a bird. Thomas had been so old and so shaky for years that death seemed no more than a logical extension of his innocent life.

Driving back from the churchyard she found herself suddenly conscious of the fact that the Palladian gatehouse was still unrepaired, and this threw back her mind to the occasion on which she had last noticed it, driving home, with Wilburn and Mr. Chafey, from Hugo's funeral. The memory took her by surprise; it made her realize, with a shock, how relentlessly time had flowed on since that day. More than eight years had passed since last she had driven through that gateway. More than eight years. . . .

"How life slips away from one!" she thought. "Oh, why can't we stop it?"

The reflection astonished and awed her so much that, this time, the thought that the gateway should be repaired did not enter her mind again. And the solemnity of the occasion, thank heaven! didn't weigh upon Jasper. Life at school was becoming far too full and exciting to allow his thoughts to linger over poor old Thomas. He had promised to spend his last night but one with Aunt Harriet at Halesby, and grudged the time which duty compelled him to waste. Bella drove over with him, rather than miss an hour of his company.

Miss Mortimer's new home, Witley Lodge, was a small late-Regency house with a certain staid dignity which suited its owner and, oddly enough, did not seem out of tune with her Victorian mahogany. It had a prim little garden, and a lawn shadowed by damson-trees from which one looked west to the domes of Pen Beacon and Uffdown. On the east rising ground hid the chimney-stacks of Hayseech, and Bella was glad not to be reminded of them, for her defection was still on her conscience.

At supper, however, Mr. Wilkinson appeared. Since her return to Halesby Aunt Harriet and he had become great friends. He was fascinated by her likeness—which, in her sixty-second year, was what people called "quite ridiculous"—to old Jasper Mortimer. She was old enough now not to feel the visits of a bachelor "improper," and always delighted to talk on the subject which most interested him: the origins and history of Hayseech.

Bella, meeting James Wilkinson again after such a long interval, was surprised to find how little he had changed, and this little for the better. His manner reflected the importance he had gradually acquired as the head of Jos. Tinsley & Co. All over the Black Country and even in North Bromwich people treated him with respect, as Jasper Mortimer's successor and a peer of the other big ironmasters, Hingstons, Hacketts and Willises. Physically, too, Bella noticed, he was wearing remarkably well. Now that he paid, of necessity, more attention to his personal appearance, most people, she thought, would call him a good-looking man. His carriage was more erect; he had changed his steel spectacles for gold, and no longer wore these constantly, for the normal long-sight of middle age had corrected his myopia. The ragged moustache which Bella disliked had gone, revealing a firm, kind, wisely humorous mouth; and his strong iron-grey hair, which had not thinned in the least, gave his features a kind of rugged hand-someness. But what gave Bella even more pleasure than these physical improvements was the wholly delightful relationship, half gallant and half pro-tective, which he had established with Miss Mortimer.

When supper was over, he spoke to Bella of Hay-seech. Trade, he said, had been shocking; but certain new industries—the motor-car trade, for instance—had kept things going. He himself had been deeply interested in a variety of the new compounds in which steel was combined with certain heavy metals—molybdenum, tungsten and vanadium—which in-

creased its hardness without diminishing its flexibility.
All these experiments had been made possible by the
use of the electric furnace. Walter Willis of Mawne
had a man named Stafford working on titanium. He,
too, had a number of bright young metallurgists continually engaged in research, and the results were
promising. One encouraging thing, and he counted a
lot on it, was a considerable renewal of orders from
the Admiralty, which seemed likely to continue now
that Germany was definitely embarked on a ship-
building race.

"If you would like to bring your son to Hayseech
to-morrow," he said rather wistfully, "I could show
you a number of things in which you'ld certainly be
interested."

Bella said that they had to go back to White Ladies,
and that she was sorry. She was not really sorry,
though she liked Mr. Wilkinson better that evening
than ever before. "Jasper hasn't the least mechanical
bent," she told him. "That's curious, isn't it? He
loves driving a motor-car, but he knows nothing whatever about its mechanism. We shall drive to Eton
together, and then, alas! I shall have to look for a
butler. Do you know, Mr. Wilkinson, you've never
yet been to see me at White Ladies? That's rather
unkind of you. I think you would like it, though the
only thing in your line I can tempt you with is a new
electrical plant of which we're exceedingly proud."

He laughed. "I don't need any tempting to come

and see you, Mrs. Pomfret," he said.

The old Mr. Wilkinson, she reflected, would certainly never have ventured on such a compliment. But it flattered her, none the less. And she wanted him to see White Ladies. If he saw White Ladies he would perhaps understand that her behaviour towards Hayseech had not been quite so mean as she felt it.

Next day she drove Jasper over the Cotswolds and back to Eton. White Ladies seemed terribly empty without him and without poor old Thomas. In the matter of finding a new butler, her luck was out. The first she engaged was slovenly; the second one drank. There was an awful moment when, summoned by a message from Miss Penney and accompanied by Shelton the keeper and an awe-stricken under-gardener, she descended to the cellar to find him picturesquely reclining in a thicket of empty port-bottles. And the third, after four smooth months, created a scandal, believing, apparently, that his privileges included the *droit du seigneur*.

Her final selection for the post, whose name was Beaver, appeared with the most unexceptionable references from Stoke Priory, which the Tregarons, after a spectacular bankruptcy, had lately sold. Mr. Beaver's manners and demeanour were almost too good to be true; but she was assured that he was trustworthy and understood silver and wine. His deportment was so superb that Bella, in private, re-christened him Sir Willoughby Patterne. He entered the room

with the air of an operatic tenor. One waited for him
to put his hand on his heart and break into song.
Still, although she and Jasper laughed at him and
even mimicked him, Mr. Beaver, apart from an irritating assumption of omniscience, was a well-trained
butler, a highly respectable man, and, on the whole,
satisfactory. The other men-servants did not find him
comical and accepted his discipline; the women were
awed by him. All except little Miss Penney, who
from the first took a violent dislike to him—so
that, after months of invisibility, she emerged from
her nest in the tower and demanded an interview
with Bella. Never in her life had Bella seen the
little black creature's eyes more concerned, more
malignant.

"If you keep that man Beaver, Mrs. Pomfret," she
chirped, "you'll regret it, regret it. He's bad for
White Ladies, I tell you. He's bad for White Ladies,
White Ladies. He's dangerous, dangerous!"

"Dangerous? That's an odd word, Miss Penney!"
Bella smiled at her heat and her venom. "I don't
know what you mean."

"You'll know what I mean soon enough. Get rid
of him, rid of him! He may not be bad for you, for
you, but he's bad for White Ladies. Get rid of him,
while there's time, while there's time!"

She turned and went limping away, still shaking
her head. The black twisted figure went more slowly
now than of yore; like a decrepit black spider, Bella

thought, too old almost to crawl, yet still wickedly venomous.

"Turn him out while there's time, while there's time!" she repeated.

Her shrill voice died away, but she still shook her head and muttered: "While there's time, while there's time. . . ."

Bella felt oddly disquieted, though not deeply impressed, by her vehemence. The mere fact that Miss Penney spoke so mysteriously and malignantly about him was sufficient of itself to prejudice her in the butler's favour. When she tactfully questioned Mr. Beaver, she discovered that Miss Penney's dislike of him was reciprocated. That was all to the good, she decided. It was just as well to have someone of authority in the house who happened, through self-interest, to be on her side. She had suffered too often from Miss Penney's subversive machinations against herself not to welcome an ally.

When Jasper came home at Christmas she told him jokingly what had happened.

"I know, mother," he said. "The old lady's been at me, too. It's a bee in her bonnet and nothing can stop it buzzing. She's like that, you know. She takes violent likes and dislikes. I think, sometimes, she doesn't like you, though, of course, she wouldn't dare to say so to me. She's very old, isn't she? A little bit dotty, but quite harmless. I should have been sorry, on the whole, if you had got rid of Mr. Beaver.

He's comically stupid sometimes, but he's always amusing."

"And he does his work well," Bella agreed. "He's been awfully good, for instance about the central heating. He keeps the heat down, as Mr. Courtenay told us we must for the sake of the panelling. So far I've not seen a crack anywhere, and it has made an enormous difference to the comfort of the house in weather like this. On the landings we used to shiver."

That summer was far wetter than the last. The rivers kept their level, refreshed by spate after spate. Jasper spent the best part of his holidays in Mr. Pomfret's company, fishing the Teme. During the last half he had decided that he would never make much of a cricketer, and was not sorry, for sport had always appealed to him more than ball-games. His cousin had infected him with the virus of dry-fly fishing, which is one of the most potent on earth. He was never so happy at White Ladies as when he was trying flies or practising fancy casts on the lawn. It was a nuisance, he said, that he had to drive fifty miles to get any decent fishing.

"But next summer," he told her, "I'm going to see a lot more of you. I've a marvellous new plan. I've been talking it over with the vicar and Shelton, and they both agree with me that there's quite enough current in the pools by the bridge for us to put down rainbows."

"Rainbows, darling?"

"Yes, rainbow trout. They come from America. Awfully sporting fish and free risers. I shall put down a lot of yearlings this autumn and one or two hundred sizeable fish that will be all right next summer. There's only one difficulty, really."

"And what's that?"

"The coarse fish and the pike. Pike are deadly, of course, and the pools are full of them."

"What a pity!"

"Oh, I think we can deal with them. First of all Shelton will net all he can—several times, to make sure. Then he'll dredge as much mud from the bottom as he can. Then he'll bomb the bottom with dynamite. I should have done it myself this week if I hadn't been keen to get a last chance of catching a decent grayling. But Shelton knows just what's wanted."

"I do hope to goodness he won't blow himself up."

"Oh, no. He'll be careful. He's a splendid man, Shelton. He'll open the sluices and let out the water as soon as he's netted the pools. Then he'll dredge and he'll bomb. In the meantime, if you don't mind, I'll order the rainbows from a fish-farm. I've got the address. They'll be rather expensive; but, after all, it will improve the property. You won't mind if they cost rather a lot?"

"Not a bit, if you really want it."

"Oh, I'm absolutely dead nuts on it. That's awfully decent of you, darling."

When Jasper had gone back to Eton, Shelton started on the work. Bella went down and watched him. It was fascinating to see the great draughts of fish: the huge pike, mottled green, with their wolfish, snapping jaws, the spined perch and the silver roach with their fins coloured like bright blood. She thought idly how her grandfather, old Mr. Small, would have loved this spectacle. Those days of late September were brilliant; but as soon as the red sun had set frost came into the air. Rime whitened the lawns at morning. October came in with a bitter spell of east wind. It penetrated the bones of the house. Heaped wood fires gave no warmth. Bella felt thankful that Courtenay had put in his radiators, which at least took the chill from the air. These long periods of east wind, not unusual at that time of the year, had the effect of making the landscape of White Ladies depressing. The grey skies deadened colour. The grass in the park seemed to fade; the beeches and elms lost their autumn brilliance; White Ladies itself looked oddly colourless and desolate and unfriendly—even more desolate, Bella thought, now that the moat had been drained, lacking the upward reflection of light from its girdle of water.

In such bitter weather there was no temptation to go out of doors. She sat in the relative warmth and lightness of the rose-and-ivory drawing-room, sewing, reading, or writing her usual long letters to Jasper. Far away, in the park, she could hear the dull detonations of Shelton's dynamite. He was blasting the empty pools methodically. The sound reminded her of the gunfire she had heard from far out at sea when she went to Plymouth to meet Hugo.

It was cold, Mr. Beaver found, in the butler's pantry. Mr. Beaver, though comfortably covered with fat, disliked cold intensely. Even the works of his favourite author, Nat Gould, could not charm away his discomfort. He felt the top of the radiator and found it lukewarm. No wonder he felt chilly! He rang for the second footman.

"What d'you think you're doing with this 'eat, I should like to know?" Mr. Beaver asked. "The rads are stone-cold."

It wasn't entirely his fault, the footman explained. He had reminded Mr. Beaver a week ago to order more coke, and the coke hadn't come. He was trying to economize until it did.

"Economize?" Mr. Beaver growled. "What d'you mean, economize, in a house like this? If the heat goes down it's *me* that'll have to stand the racket, not you, my lad! Don't you understand that at your age?"

The footman was sorry; but what could he do without coke?

"Coke? Coke? What have you done with your brains, if you ever had any? You run along double-quick and shovel on coal, and plenty of it, before the whole lot of us catch our deaths of this blasted east wind!"

At dinner that night Bella was conscious of a pleasant warmth. She remarked to Beaver that she thought the wind must have dropped.

"No, it isn't that, ma'am," Mr. Beaver replied. "On the contrary, it's blowing fiercer than ever. From the south, I think. No, to tell you the truth, ma'am, I'm sorry to say it's that young fellow Harris. Inexperienced. He let the heat down, I'm afraid. He's a willing lad, ma'am, but brains, common sense . . . These young men that come into service nowadays, they don't even use what they've got—and that's not saying much. Will you take your coffee in the hall, ma'am?"

"No, thank you. I don't think I'll have any coffee. Last night the wind kept me awake. You'll be careful to see that Harris doesn't stoke too much, won't you? It's so bad for the panelling."

Mr. Beaver smiled knowingly. "Trust me, ma'am."

He was a willing lad, Jim Harris. This was his first place, and he had no intention of losing it. So he brought in barrow after barrow of coal to the stoke-hole and shovelled it into the furnace. It was the Brooch coal, the hottest and fiercest in South Staffordshire. It burned far quicker than coke—so quickly that Jim Harris had to go on feeding the fire for fear it should sink and Mr. Beaver's radiator go cold. He shovelled and shovelled. The furnace was an insatiable monster. Its red throat swallowed all he could give it, for the dampers were open. Tongues of flame leapt up the flue with a roaring sound like hoarse laughter. By midnight, that flue, in all its length, was like a white-hot blow-pipe thrust into a mass of tinder. And the mass of tinder was White Ladies. . . .

Bella had gone to bed early. The wakeful hours of last night had made her feel drowsy. At three o'clock in the morning she woke with a start. Somebody was in the room. She sat up in bed and saw her maid running towards her.

"Get up, madam, quick. Here's your dressing-gown. The house is on fire. Cook, she smelt it first, and told me to come and wake you. I don't know how I got here. The landing is full of smoke. Put this towel over your mouth, madam. Dear, dear. . . . There's no time to lose."

Bella jumped out of bed. Her mind acted automatically. Under her pillow, following Hugo's example, she had always kept the key of the shed that housed the fire-engine. It was there now, thank goodness! The only thing that mattered! She clutched it hurriedly. The maid was sobbing hysterically and wringing her hands.

In the passage smoke caught Bella's throat and choked her in spite of the damp towel. It was rising in clouds from the great hall, and barred their way to the main staircase. No flame was visible; but she could hear a deep ominous sound, like a tiger purring. By this time the maid had come to the end of her nerves. Bella dragged her in the opposite direction towards the back stairs. As they ran, the smoke seemed to pursue them, and now there was heat in it, like the breath from a tiger's throat. Another blast rose to meet them from the gullet of the narrow back-stair-way. Scrambling blindly down this she collided at the foot with Mr. Beaver. He was dressed in a very short night-shirt and helplessly carried an unlit candle. "Thank God you're safe, ma'am!" he gasped.

Bella thrust the key into his hand. "Run quickly," she said, "and get out the fire-engine!" She thanked heaven that she had remembered it.

But she had not remembered that the moat and the pools were dry. . . .

At the front of the house flame-lit figures in shirt-sleeves were already shouting and hurrying to and fro. Jim Harris had found enough wits to run and wake the gardeners and Gibbs, the chauffeur. Gibbs had quickly taken command. Without waiting for the key he had made them break in the door of the engine-shed to find helmets to protect their heads and axes for battering-in windows. He had even remembered to turn off the current at the switchboard. Not that this mattered now: he knew that nobody on earth could fight this fire without water. The best they could do was to salvage pictures and furniture, and that was not easy. The great hall had already become a red-hot furnace through which the draught of wind blew like a blast. Some fool, trying in vain to enter, had forced open the door and left it. The draught of the fire and the wind together were so strong that it took the strength and weight of three men to close it. Behind it, the wainscoting was alight from floor to ceiling; tongues of eager flame licked its surface on which the oiled canvas of pictures and the tissue of tapestry flared away as they caught like paper and crackled with a sound of whip-cord cracking in the air. Jets of furious flame could be seen through the panes of the oriel.

Nobody could live in the heat of that central furnace; but, on either side of it, the two rooms which ended in the bays were still dark. With their axes the men shattered the windows between the stone mullions and crawled inside, bringing out blindly whatever they could lay their hands on: pictures and tapestries torn from the walls, books, plate and cutlery, candlesticks, glass and china. They flung these out wildly, impeding each other in the smoke, neither knowing nor caring whether they fell on the flags of the terrace or into the mud of the moat. The chauffeur was shouting, trying to put some order into the work.

"Try to get some of the furniture out, boys," he cried; but the spaces between the stone mullions were too narrow for that until, falling upon them with axes, they hacked some of them down—and by this time the heat was too fierce and the smoke too throttling, and the men who dared to swarm through the breach were driven back again. Even the terrace in front of the house was now untenable. The great windows spat splinters of glass and rained molten lead. And by now the noise of fire was no longer that of a tiger purring but of an express-train roaring through the night; a hoarse, terrible sound. Little by little, Gibbs and his helpers were forced to give ground, retreating beyond the moat; and even there the heat scorched them. "It's no good, no good, lads," he gasped. "We've got to give in."

He staggered away from them out of the radius of fierce heat with his hands to his eyes, not merely exhausted but broken. He threw himself on the grass. His only desire was for water to bathe his eyes, to slake his throat, to cool his blistered hands. When he opened his eyes, still dazzled with the glare, he became conscious of the figure of a woman standing over him. It was his mistress, he saw; and the sight of her snapped the last thread of control. He burst into tears.

"We did all we could, ma'am," he cried. "We did all we could."

Bella gazed down pitifully at his working face. The light in the sky was so strong that she could see the white runnels of sweat that streaked it; she could smell his singed hair and clothes. She wanted to cry herself, but was too numbed and too cold to cry. She bent over him tenderly.

"Yes, I know you did all you could, Gibbs," she said. "You did wonderfully well. I do hope you're not hurt . . ."

"Not hurt . . . only done to the world, madam. If that moat hadn't been dry . . ."

A small crowd had gathered round them. During the last hour, aroused by the light in the sky, drawn towards it out of the darkness like moths, people had been hurrying to White Ladies from the surrounding villages. They stood in a gaping, whispering circle gazing at them; and Gibbs, suddenly becoming aware of them, was stung by this exhibition of curiosity. He leapt to his feet.

"What the hell d'you think you're doing?" he cried angrily. "Staring at a lady like that! Get out of it, quick, or I'll make you!"

He advanced on them threateningly, a wild figure, waving his arms. The group scattered, retreated. Gibbs, returning to Bella, apologized. "I'm sorry I spoke like that, ma'am. My nerves are all gone." His voice softened. "I don't like to see you standing like this, ma'am. You'll be starved with cold in this bitter wind. I'd much rather you'ld come to my cottage. You know, if it comes to that, it doesn't do any good standing here."

Bella smiled at his thoughtfulness, gratefully.

"I know it's no good, Gibbs. I can't help that. I've got to stay here till the end. As a matter of fact you're more likely to catch cold than I am. Go and get an overcoat. Don't stay with me. I'm much better alone."

He could see that she meant what she said.

"Very good, ma'am," he said. "If there's anything I can do . . ."

"No, there's nothing you can do for me, thank you."

He left her reluctantly. Five minutes later he returned with a rug from the garage which he wrapped round her shoulders. Bella thanked him with a smile.

By this time the crowd in front of White Ladies had increased. Fire brigades from Bromsberrow and Wychbury and Worcester had come galloping up with engines and ladders. They hung about, helplessly watching, in uniformed groups. The flames shone on their brazen helmets. Bella stood in the middle of the lawn alone. Nobody knew who she was, or, if they did, nobody dared to come near her. The wind now blew a gale from the south-west, inciting the flames to new fury. Already the bedrooms of the first floor were ablaze. The smoke blew away on the wind; every mullioned window shone blood-red till the small panes splintered, till the lead of the casements began to run, and high tongues of flame, bursting through them, leapt out and were blown back again into the fiery caverns behind. Then, suddenly, above the roar and crackle of the fire, there came a monstrous rending sound which made the crowd gasp. The first floor had fallen.

Now the empty shell of White Ladies was one white-hot oven above which the upper floors must surely shrivel like paper. It was a matter of minutes before the roof would go. Bella thought of the sun-bleached panelling of the long gallery, of the cases of family relics and muniments which Hugo had treasured. What did they matter now? Why, the flames had reached them already. Their bright tongues were licking the balustrade. Beyond it the new roof must be swimming with molten lead.

Gazing, fascinated, yet scarcely seeing, for the long concentration of light had almost blinded her, she became aware of a movement in the watching crowd. A shiver stirred it. Men and women were crying and pointing. They stretched their hands upward, pointing to the roof where, against the red sky, the newels of the balustrade made a ribbon of lace. Up there, on the molten roof, there was something moving, some living thing, swiftly scurrying hither and thither: a little black shape that skipped and waved its arms like the legs of an insect. Bella heard people crying: "It's a woman. . . . My God, it's a woman. . . . An old woman!" Their upturned faces were pale with horror. Some put their hands to their eyes, others stared, their mouths twisted with terror. Then the little black figure threw up its arms and collapsed, like a spider shrivelled to nothing on a red-hot plate.

A shuddering sigh broke from the crowd. One

woman screamed; but the sound of her scream was drowned in a roar like the thunder of landslide or avalanche. The roof of White Ladies cracked and fell in. From the chasm into which it had fallen a fountain of sparks leapt into the sky and was whirled away. Bella Pomfret, still gazing, watched it, motionless: a figure of stone.

BOOK SIX

REPARATION

I

WHITE LADIES burned like a bonfire for eight hours
and smouldered for three days until an inch of rain
quenched it. If she had been left to herself Bella
would have stood over it until it was cold. Just after
daylight, however, the Vicar of Wychbury and Mrs.
Pomfret arrived on the scene, the news of the fire
brigade's call to White Ladies having reached him with
his first cup of tea. He found Bella still standing on
the lawn, wrapped up in her motor-rug. Spectators
had been drifting in all through the night, anxious
to see the spectacle of the great fire before it was out.
All the space in front of the house was trampled like
a fair-ground, with folk gaping and chattering and
girls giggling as they walked to and fro arm in arm.
Nobody in the moving crowd had taken any notice of
Bella or even wondered who she was until the vicar
saw the desolate figure with the blanched set face and
hurried up to take care of her.

He was a stupid man but kindly; and, in this case,
although he had always been rather chary of Bella as
of everybody else connected with the lesser breeds
who inhabited the Black Country, the fact that she
temporarily owned White Ladies (or what was left
of it) and that her name was Pomfret, inspired him

with a sense of family duty. He took her by the arm,
unresisting, and led her to his motor-car, where his
wife took charge of her. Bella was so cold, so null,
so stonily silent, that they had fears for her reason.
They wrapped her up warmly in all the rugs they
could find, drove her to Wychbury, put her to bed,
sent hurriedly for the doctor, and confidently awaited
the worst.

The worst wasn't so bad, Dr. Boyd consoled them,
as they expected. They needn't, as the vicar suggested,
send a wire to Jasper at Eton. Mrs. Pomfret was
suffering from shock and from exposure to cold. It
was the shock, even more than the cold, which caused
those long bouts of shivering in which she lay
violently shaken from head to foot with chattering
teeth. Bella's obstinate silence need give them no
cause to fear for her sanity. She was silent because
she couldn't trust herself to speak. She had spoken to
him a few words which showed she was in full and
painful possession of her senses; but the less she was
tempted to speak, on the whole, the better. As her
body was chilled and exhausted, so her mind was
bruised, crushed, almost obliterated. She said all she
wanted was rest (he agreed) and, above all, darkness:
the fire still danced in her eyes. What she actually
needed, the best medicine of all, was sleep. That was
why he had given her a powerful sedative of bromide
and chloral. Let them help him by keeping the house
as quiet as possible.   Hot-water-bottles; warm

blankets; darkness; silence; complete isolation. This
was all his prescription. And, for goodness' sake, he
added, no emotional sympathy; no fuss. Having
attended Bella in two confinements, he thought he
understood her temperament. She was a woman of
enormous courage and spirit, but essentially lonely.
Not being used to sympathy, she was far better without
it. Left to herself, she was mentally brave and
physically strong enough to come through.

The vicar's wife obeyed these instructions
reluctantly. She considered herself an expert in the
difficult art of visiting the sick. Nursing the heroine—
or at least the central figure—of the fire at White
Ladies was a task to which she had looked forward as
conferring, by proxy, interest and distinction on herself. She wanted to know—and even more to tell
other people—exactly what had happened, to appear
as the unique source of inside information; and Dr.
Boyd's rigid ruling deprived her of this privilege to
which she felt she had a right. It seemed a shame to
have a fire, so to speak, in the family, and to be "done
out of" the excitement and credit attached to it. In
this case, it appeared, she could only shine as the
guardian of mysteries.

When the doctor returned in the evening, Bella
was asleep. The sedative, combined with the patient's
utter exhaustion, had done its work. Next morning
he came again, and still Bella slept. The vicar's wife
grew anxious. If she could have had her own way

she would have wakened her to feed her. A glass of hot milk with an egg in it; a cup of strong broth; a few teaspoonfuls of calf's-foot jelly faintly flavoured with sherry? Dr. Boyd turned down all her suggestions. Sleep. . . . Nothing but sleep. If Bella slept for thirty-six hours (it was now twenty-four!) she would be all the better for it.

And that evening, when he stole into the room on tiptoe, she was awake. Boyd found her not only awake but also strangely composed. What torments, what stresses, what conflicts had racked and strained and divided her mind during that day and a half of numb oblivion, she herself knew no more than he. All she knew was, that out of blind darkness she had somehow emerged into a state of mind which was tragically empty, yet which, in spite of the tragedy and because of its emptiness—because, at least, it was no longer choked with the awful confusion in the midst of which consciousness had left her—seemed prepared to receive a new order of thoughts deliberately, clearly, coldly adapted to her new condition of living. Though still physically crushed and shaken, she felt her mind possessed by an inspiriting vigour and clarity which transcended the effects of her loss so completely that Boyd's tactful and kindly condolences, although she appreciated them, seemed somehow unnecessary. She was living already, had he only known it, not in the dreadful immediate past nor in her invalid present, but in a future towards which, without a single backward glance, her eager mind had shot forward.

It was natural enough, Boyd thought, that she should instinctively shy at the mention of anything that too poignantly recalled that nightmare experience. What he admired—but couldn't understand, for it seemed unnatural—was the business-like, the almost indelicate way in which she cut short his delicate attempts at sympathy.

"Yes, thanks to your draught I've slept very well," she told him. "Of course I feel horribly weak—almost as if I had had a baby—but I'm quite myself, doctor: you needn't worry about me. After all, there's nothing physically wrong with me, is there?"

"Well," he hedged, "of course you've been through a tremendous strain. It's your duty to yourself to keep quiet. I'm inclined to think you'ld be none the worse for another dose . . . a mild sedative."

"Do my nerves need soothing? My hand's steady enough. Look at it! My heart's steady, too."

He laughed. "You're a remarkable woman, as I believe I've told you before."

"When can I get up?"

"I should stay here a day or two if I were you, Mrs. Pomfret."

"If you were yourself, you mean. If you were me, you certainly wouldn't."

"Well, there is such a thing as prudence."

"There's such a thing as time, too. I've no time to

T*

lose. I must go home to-morrow."

"I'm afraid you hardly realize . . ."

". . . that I haven't a home? Oh, yes, Dr. Boyd, I do. I shall get them to give me a couple of rooms at Shelton's cottage. They can spare them, they have no children. I've thought all that out since I woke, half an hour ago. I shall be perfectly comfortable there. My maid will look after me. And it's very convenient. It's only five minutes' walk from the front door of White Ladies."

"For the moment, I'm sure, the less you think or see of White Ladies the better. I'd much rather you went away somewhere."

"Went away? What on earth do you mean?"

"It will only depress you."

"I can't be more depressed than I have been. The sooner I get to work the less depressed I shall feel."

"Get to work? I don't quite understand . . ."

"You don't understand? Why, doctor, what do you take me for? Don't you realize that I'm going to start rebuilding White Ladies?"

If he had heard those words on the lips of a normal patient, he told himself later, he would have thought her delirious. Arabella Pomfret, as he admitted, was not a normal patient, nor was she delirious. He owed it, none the less, to his professional conscience to be firm and to resist her domination.

"Well, we'll talk about that to-morrow evening," he said. "In the meantime you'll take the dose I send you. You'll behave like a reasonable human being and get another night's sleep. Will you promise me that?"

"Yes, I'll promise you that. But I won't promise anything else, because I hate breaking promises."

To make sure of quieting her he deliberately compounded a draught that would certainly keep her drowsy for the next twenty-four hours; but when he reached the vicarage next evening, prepared to find her more reasonable, Mrs. Pomfret was gone.

"I did all I could with her," the vicar's wife pleaded pathetically—she herself was disappointed to lose such a topically interesting guest. "Indeed, never in my life have I known such a wilful creature. When I sent up her breakfast this morning she was wide awake. I can't understand it: I gave her your draught myself. After that she insisted—you know how strong she is, doctor!—positively insisted on borrowing some clothes and getting up Then she telephoned to the chauffeur at White Ladies to bring her the car; and by half-past twelve—I *implored* her to stay for luncheon at least—she was off to North Bromwich. It's no use blaming *me*. One might as well have tried to stop an avalanche! She said she was going to see her lawyer, Mr. Wilburn, about something connected with fire insurance, and buy some more clothes. And she's going to sleep in the keeper's cottage at White Ladies. She said if you wanted to see her you could find her there; but if I were you, doctor, I should simply wash my hands of her."

Dr. Boyd pursed his lips. "Did she tell you what she was going to do—that she was determined to re-build White Ladies?"

The vicar's wife gasped: "Rebuild White Ladies? But it's gutted from cellar to roof—the most ghastly ruin! In that case all I can say is the woman's stark mad!"

"Rather a splendid madness, don't you think?" Dr. Boyd suggested.

"Well, if I were that poor boy I shouldn't think it any too splendid," Mrs. Pomfret replied emphatically.

Bella, meanwhile, had long since finished her inter-view with Wilburn. She had driven straight to his office and burst in on him before the clerk could announce her, unrecognizable in old Mrs. Pomfret's clothes, which, though admirably suited to a country vicar's wife, standing five feet ten and a half in her flat-heeled buttoned boots, were the last he would ever have expected Bella to wear. The odd thing was that she seemed completely unconscious of this fan-tastic apparel, which fitted her nowhere either in shape or in style: and when a pretty middle-aged woman became unconscious of her clothes, Wilburn thought, there must be something gravely wrong! He hadn't, as it happened, heard anything of the fire at White Ladies, having only returned ten minutes before from one of those mysterious and regular visits to London which North Bromwich found so suspicious.

"Thank heaven you escaped," he exclaimed. "That's the first thing that matters. If I'd known I should have hurried down to find you at once. And you look none the worse for it, though, of course, you must have suffered terribly. I'm quite sure you ought to be in bed at this minute."

"So is poor Dr. Boyd, and I dare say you're both of you right. But whether you're right or wrong makes no difference to me. I had to come and see you as soon as I felt I could move. I should have made myself worse if I'd waited for you to come to me. Tell me quickly: the insurance is all right?"

"All right?"

"I mean: the premium is paid up to date, the risk is covered?"

"Heavens, yes! We do things like that automatically."

"Please forgive my asking. You know how one worries. I've been haunted all the time by the bare possibility of some slip, some oversight. And the company's a sound one?"

"Sound as Lloyd's. You need have no fear about that. They'll pay to a penny."

"We're heavily insured?"

"Appropriately. Just after your marriage, if you remember, I insisted on your having a new valuation made in detail."

"Yes, that was magnificent of you. You don't

remember the figure, do you?"

"Somewhere round about ninety thousand pounds."

"I'm stupid about money. Are you sure that will be enough?"

"Enough for what?"

"For rebuilding White Ladies, of course. For putting back everything as it was."

"My dear Mrs. Pomfret! What a rate you go! There'll be hundreds of things to consider before we begin to think of that."

"I can only think of one thing at a time. That's the way I'm made. After all, nothing else is really important, is it?"

He knew well enough it was no use arguing with her when once an idea became fixed in her mind. It would do her no harm, it might even keep up her spirits, to play with the idea of rebuilding White Ladies out of hand. Even so, he felt it his duty to her as his client to warn her, in time, that the position was not quite so simple as that. The rebuilding of White Ladies, he agreed, was a tempting ideal. It was insured for a very large sum; but such figures were arrived at roughly, empirically. One could not say, offhand, just how far that sum would go. And apart from that, he explained, there were other considerations: as, for instance, whether it would be prudent or fair to the estate, particularly in hard times like the present, to sink such a huge sum of money in an investment (that was hardly the word for it) which would give back so little. Ninety thousand pounds, he reminded her, represented an income of more than four thousand a year; and four thousand a year was a heavyish rent—rates would bring it to five—to pay for one's house in these days. After all, she was not the only person concerned. The house would some day be Jasper's. If anything happened to Jasper it would pass on her death to her late husband's grandson. Eleanor Hingston's boy had died of appendicitis; but the younger girl, Sibell, had a son just going to Eton, and he was the heir presumptive. No doubt Sibell— what was her name?—Sibell Powys would consider she had a right to some say in the matter. . . .

Up till this point Wilburn felt an increasing conviction that his client was not even listening to him. At the last suggestion she suddenly became attentive.

"Has this woman, Mrs. Powys, any legal right to a say in the matter?" she asked.

"Probably not," Wilburn cautiously replied. "No, I think your position's quite clear. During your lifetime—or rather until Jasper comes of age—you're the sole trustee. The fact remains that people in that position usually do consult the interests of their successors. Jasper himself, for instance . . ."

"He's a child; he will think as I do."

". . . and even this Mrs. Powys. Through her son, she's naturally concerned."

"Even so, the will gives me a free hand with this money?" Bella persisted.

Wilburn hesitated. "Yes, as far as the law goes, your hands are free."

"In that case I shall do what I like with it. I shall rebuild White Ladies."

"Well, all in good time. . . . You can think of it, anyway."

Bella shook her head: "I *have* thought of it, Mr. Wilburn. I was thinking of it while I watched White Ladies burning. I'm afraid you and most other people may find it difficult to understand. But Hugo would have understood, and so will Jasper. Don't imagine for a moment that it's just a caprice on my part. This is a trust, as you say; and I take the trust as seriously as my husband did. You never knew Hugo—nobody knew him, I suppose, except me. You don't realize the sacrifices he made, how he gave up everything, to the verge of starvation, simply to keep up this very insurance policy that we've been talking about. If he'd wanted to raise money he could have sold pictures or pieces of furniture. There were enough valuables at White Ladies to have kept him in comfort all those years. But he didn't. He never sold a single thing. When we came back from Capri together, he had his reward. And I had mine, too. His pleasure was the most beautiful thing I've ever seen— or rather, felt: one saw nothing—he was the kind of man who disliked showing any emotion. No. . . . If Hugo were living to-day I know exactly what he'ld do. I shall stick to our bargain. I'm not going to let him down, and I'm not going to let down White Ladies."

Wilburn smiled and shook his head. There was nothing more to say. But he was a sensitive man, and the sight of Bella Pomfret (for she had risen as she spoke) with her death-white face, in her ungainly borrowed clothes, touched his imagination more than her words moved his reason. She was wrong, that reason told him, utterly wrong; her decision, he knew, implied a wilful injustice; but in spite of this, he could not help admiring her—not merely as a woman, for the passion with which she spoke made her pallid face strangely young and beautiful, but as the living incarnation of an ideal, fallacious, perhaps, but not the less exalted.

"I shall write to the insurance company," he said, "and put in our claim at once. I shall tell them not to bother you more than is necessary. As soon as I hear from them I'll come down to White Ladies and meet their assessors. Do go gently, for your own sake, as well as mine. You probably don't realize how great a shock you have suffered. Where shall I find you?"

"For the next few days I shall be at the keeper's cottage. After that, I shall have to consider. In all probability I shall make some arrangements with Stephens at the Home Farm. It's a charming old house, and I shall probably settle down there and put in the pictures and furniture and things that were saved. It's only a short walk from the house, and I shall have to be on the spot while the work's going on. By the way, I'm afraid I may want quite a lot of money. I haven't a rag in the world, and I shall have to buy a certain amount of furniture. Will that be quite all right? May I overdraw?"

"Yes. I'll see to that. I may have to sell some shares for you, though it's not a good time."

"It never is, is it?"

He laughed. "As a matter of fact it's less good than usual. However, one or two of our rash investments are looking up. And Hayseech, by the way, looks like coming to life again. I'm glad, for your sake, that we didn't entirely clear out of that. Your friend Wilkinson's no fool. It seems he's invented a new steel. Big Admiralty orders coming along. Armour-piercing shells."

"Well. . . . Good-bye. I suppose I must go and get some respectable clothes. I can't face life in these. That will make me feel more like myself."

"You are always yourself," Wilburn said. "That's the way in which you are different from every other woman I know."

When she reached Shelton's cottage the world was white with moonlight. The dense cloud which had veiled the sky on the night of the fire had been blown away in the wind that had fanned it, and that wind had fallen. It seemed odd, settling down in the Sheltons' little front room, which was infested with the gamekeeper's family photographs and specimens

of seaside china, and smelt faintly of naphthaline.
Even more than its spaciousness, she missed the smell
of White Ladies, that peculiar aroma of bees-wax and
dry wood and pot-pourri which was as individual as
that of a human skin. Her maid was waiting for her,
and had prepared a simple meal. Bella was so hungry
after two days of starvation that she ate the plain food
eagerly. Her invalid palate found its clean savour
delicious, and Shelton had drawn a jug of Worcestershire cider with a sub-acid, mealy taste. A wood-fire
burned gaily in the grate. She hated the crackle of
burning wood now.

When she had eaten and drunk, she felt her
strength miraculously restored. That only showed
how Dr. Boyd had misjudged her reserves of energy.
Her brain had by now emerged from the last mists of
his well-meant medication. It was almost too bright
and active for comfort, every thought that passed
through it buoyed up by inexplicable hope. She felt
that she would never sleep—and particularly in a
strange bed—if she gave these thoughts rein. Her
restlessness would not allow her to sit still; so she
decided that a walk in the still night-air would be
the best thing to calm her. When she called for her
coat, her maid was alarmed:

"Surely you're not going out in the cold, madam?"

It was not really cold, Bella said; the air was so
still. "I shall only go out for a minute or two," she
told her.

But when once she had left Shelton's cottage, the still air was so sweet with its odour of fallen leaves, and the moonlight so gentle, that she felt no wish to turn back. She stepped away from the road. The grass under her feet was already crisp with hoar-frost. Within its circlet of shadowy woods the park's rimed surface appeared saturated with cold lunar radiance. Bella walked on and on, inhaling the crystalline air, until she had reached a point from which she knew the house was visible. Here she paused. Although she believed she was mistress of herself, as her freedom from fatigue at the end of this wearing day surely proved, she still doubted if it was fair to subject her nerves to so brutal a test as the sudden sight of what was left of White Ladies. Yet the very fact that she doubted became a challenge to her courage which she feared yet dared not refuse. Advancing a little farther into the open with averted eyes, she halted and looked. . . .

She need neither have feared, nor doubted. Even though a spectacle of horror had confronted her, the magic of that wintry moonlight might have softened it. But the ruin of White Ladies, as she beheld it now, was by no means horrible; it did not even appear to be a ruin. Rising sheer from the glimmering expanse of rimed grassland drenched in moonshine, like a solitary rock emerging from a frozen lake, the dark bulk of the house presented its familiar, beloved shape. Even the silhouette of the crowning balustrade stood out intact, like a lacing of stone, against its background of powder-blue sky; the fire-blackened shafts of the mullions, whitened by moonlight, still delicately defined the conformation of bays and oriel; what she seemed to see was not the ghost of a house nor even its skeleton, but rather a form possessed of that perfect serenity which she had beheld only once in her life, aboard the transport at Plymouth, the serenity of death. And the death of a house, she triumphantly told herself, was not, like the death of a living organism, irrevocable, since the quality one thought of as life, in its case, depended not on a vitality inherent in its structure which time or catastrophe could annihilate, but on the spirit breathed into its dry shell by living and loving humanity. A dead house—and the appearance of White Ladies, as now she saw it, seemed nearer to sleep than to death—was assuredly capable of complete resurrection, of reviving through the influx of new life which might be provided as long as a living Pomfret remained to love it. Already, as she gazed at it, her lively imagination seemed to have begun that pious process of resurrection; already the still, cold shape appeared to respond to the warmth of its caress. When a shiver warned her that it was unwise to prolong her contemplation, she returned to Shelton's cottage with a buoyant step and a heart exalted with inexplicable hope.

II

NEXT morning, to her great joy, there came a letter from Jasper.

Darling Mother, (he wrote)

My tutor sent for me this morning. He had read about White Ladies in the paper and said he was anxious to let me know what had happened at once before I read about it myself and began to imagine things. He told me right away that you had escaped and were all right, and that, after all, darling, is all that really matters to me. What a terrible, terrible time you must have had. I wish I were with you; but T.V. says, quite wisely I'm sure, that if you wanted me you'ld send for me. Of course you would, wouldn't you? And if you do want me, he says, I can go to White Ladies at a moment's notice. As you haven't sent, I suppose the papers have exaggerated. They generally do, don't they? I'm dreadfully sick to think that Shelton having drained off the pools and the moat may have made things worse; but, after all, who on earth could have imagined that anything like this would happen? And, as I say, and T.V. agrees, the one thing that matters is that you weren't hurt, though you must have been terribly frightened. Please send me a wire at once to say that you're really all right, and please promise, if you want me the least little bit, that you'll send for me, my poor little darling. I suppose lots of houses have been burnt down before and built up again, and places like White Ladies are always properly insured, T.V. says, so there's nothing to worry about except the awful strain, of course. I expect by the time you get this I shall have had a long letter from you telling me everything. I can hardly wait till I hear from you. My tutor was awfully sympathetic. I told Gervase Powys about it too, and he was thrilled.

Love and hundreds of kisses, darling, from

Your loving son,

Jasper.

P.S. It was dreadful about poor little Penney. I suppose it couldn't be helped and was instantaneous. She must have been terribly old anyway. You will wire, for certain, if you want me. And as soon as the pools are full, you won't let Shelton forget about those rainbows, will you?

Bella sent him a long wire—she felt guilty when she thought of him expecting a letter in vain—telling him that everything was well and that there was no need for him to come home. At the moment, indeed, his coming would have been an embarrassment. As it was, she had turned the Sheltons out of their best bedroom, and they had no other to spare. She gave Shelton his message about the pools and the trout. A slow smile of amusement spread over his bearded face.

"Them there trout? Well, that's like Mr. Jasper, isn't it, ma'am?"

During the morning she went round to inspect the Home Farm and assess its possibilities. It was a snug red-brick house with rounded gables at either end and delightful proportions which betrayed, Bella thought, the fancy of the architect who had designed the bridge and the gatehouse. With a few unimportant modifications, she decided, it would make her a charming home, just big enough for Jasper and herself, during the rebuilding of White Ladies. Roger Courtenay, who was arriving that afternoon, would soon see to that.

Courtenay, in fact, was delighted with it and wondered why she had never shown it him before. It was a little gem in its own way, he said: a seed-pearl compared with the diadem of White Ladies. With intensive work—and he would see to it as soon as it was empty—it might be ready for habitation by the time Jasper came home for Christmas. Having dealt with the farm they proceeded to inspect White Ladies. It was a drenching day, and the ruins, at close quarters, had lost the appearance of deathly serenity which distance and moonlight had given them. Bella saw, for the first time, the huge breaches which had been hacked in the lower windows of the bays to get out the furniture, the solidified pools of molten lead in which fragments of shattered glass were embedded, the vast heaps of charred beams that still steamed in the rain. The drifts of ashes, knee-deep, from which, like gigantic bones in a funeral pyre, these unconsumed fragments protruded, still held heat; they could feel the hot fumes that rose from them on their faces. Courtenay refused to allow her to step inside the building, not only because, as likely as not, their feet might sink through grey ash to live cinder, but also for fear of the debris, lightly suspended, which at the shock of the least movement in the air or even of their own weight might come crashing down on their heads at any moment.

When he saw the appalling extent of the damage his face grew grave. Bella watched it eagerly. Its weight fell on her and crushed her spirits. The incessant rain added, she felt, to the sense of desolation. If he had seen White Ladies as she had the night before, transfigured by moonlight, he might have felt less discouraged. This cruel, depressing light of a leaden day exaggerated the appearance of damage in the opposite direction. What his eyes saw now was not merely the still serenity of death but mutilation, corruption.

She was happier when, soaked to the skin and no longer weighed down by the actuality of that desolate spectacle, they returned to the lamp-lit snugness of Shelton's cottage.

"Well, what do you think of it?" she asked him, timidly.

He sighed. "I hardly know what to think of it. I've never seen a more hopeless sight, a house more completely gutted. I can't possibly express a hundredth part of what I feel for you. The thought of all that unique beauty reduced to ashes—all the lovely detail obliterated and lost for ever! It's the grim problem of human death all over again: what to do with the pitiful remains. If only, when things die, they could just disappear!"

"But White Ladies isn't dead," Bella answered eagerly.

He shook his head.

"If only you could have seen it last night!" she insisted. "It's not fair to have seen it as we saw it to-day."

"Isn't it really much fairer?"

"But the walls are still standing? The shape of the house is the same?"

"Yes, the walls are still standing . . ."

"And surely," she urged, "that gives us something to begin with?"

"Something. Not very much. I can't tell you— nobody can tell you—what effect that terrific heat has had on the stone, the bricks, the mortar. We don't know exactly what happens, but they lose their nature. Under strain they may crumble. We shall see when we begin to demolish . . ."

"To *demolish?*" she cried. "But, my dear, what on earth are you talking about?"

"I mean that if you should decide to build a new house we ought really, if we can, to use some of the old materials."

"A new house? But that's out of the question. I'm going to re-build White Ladies."

"Have you any idea what that means? Financially?"

"None at all. That's what you have to tell me. The sooner I know, the better."

"Of course, I can't tell you off-hand. It would take me six months to calculate. Even then the figure couldn't be even approximate, and the mere cost of calculation would be tremendous."

"The house was insured."

"Of course. Do you know for how much?"

"Pretty heavily. I think it was something like a hundred thousand."

"I could build you a delightful house for a third of that sum."

"I don't want a new house, my dear Roger. I want White Ladies. And I'm going to have White Ladies, whatever you may say. If I spend my last penny as well as the insurance money in rebuilding it I shall have my White Ladies!"

Impelled by the violence of her feeling, she rose as she spoke and stood gazing at him defiantly. Roger Courtenay was staggered by the spiritual potency of the figure that faced him in the lamplight: this frail woman of forty-two, beautiful still, as he told himself, with her thin cheeks flushed and her black eyes blazing at him under her greying hair. He was moved and momentarily inspired by the ardour she radiated. His own more tepid imagination caught fire from the flame in hers.

"If it were possible . . ." he began. She broke in on him:

"Possible? How can you use such a word? How can you dare to hesitate? Haven't we records—your drawings, your photographs—of every single, every minutest detail? Didn't we spend hours and hours, four years ago, making this possible? We didn't know what we were doing then; but don't you realise that it was a sheer act of Providence? Don't you see how fate's played into our hands . . . how the whole thing's been made easy for us? If it takes you three years—six years, what on earth does that matter? Call it five. Then the house will be ready for Jasper on the day he inherits. We've just time. Can't you see how beautifully everything works out? Though we've no time to spare. Will you send down somebody to-morrow?"

"First of all the insurance company's assessors will have to inspect."

"But what does that matter? You know I shall never be happy unless I can see for myself—I'm like that, I'm afraid—that something is being done."

By the time Jasper came home, two days before Christmas, things were being done with a vengeance. The assessors had been down and met Ernest Wilburn. Even if the insurance company had not been of the most reputable, the state of White Ladies was not a matter for argument. Bella's claim was admitted in full and the money paid into Wilburn's hands. In the meantime, Courtenay had got to work as he had promised. The preparation of plans and quantity-surveys and estimates for the new White Ladies was naturally a lengthy business in which the pace could not be forced to satisfy Bella's impatience; but the work of clearing the debris was put into the hands of local contractors almost as soon as the ashes grew cold. It was a grim sight: the grey figures of the labourers perpetually shovelling, straining with crowbars to move the fallen joists, or hacking with picks at the conglomerate of fused metal and plaster. A dangerous job, too: within a month three men had been injured by falling wreckage. Yet the work of clearing went steadily on: a string of carts slowly moving over the drawbridge—because of the moat there was no other means of approach—carrying away to a mountainous dump in the middle of the woods load after load of fine grey powder, that uniform dust to which the multitudinous beauties of White Ladies had fallen. When a wind arose the dust spilt or blew away from the carts, so that the track which they followed became a grey trail, and the grass of the park, too, was powdered with a death-pale bloom. But the work of clearing went on.

At the Home Farm, too, builders were busy. Bella had been anxious to put it in shape before Jasper came home. This was an emergency after Courtenay's heart, for the house's degraded graces needed no more than a touch here and there to restore them. In six weeks the accretions of dark paint had been stripped from its panelling, two bathrooms cunningly contrived, and a barn converted into quarters for servants. The two principal rooms at the front of the house were delightful, their fine proportions giving a pleasant illusion of spaciousness and their large windows an abundance of light. The heavy black dining-room furniture which had been saved from White Ladies would not go into either of them, so Bella bought a new set in pale modern oak which, with curtains of blue and white Morris print, gave the new dining-room a cheerful air. Into the other, the pine and satinwood chairs and settees and the delicate pastels of her old rose-and-ivory drawing-room found their places as naturally as though they had always been there; and both rooms were small enough to keep warm in the bitter weather.

Jasper found the Home Farm great fun as a change from the grandeurs of White Ladies. Everything seemed small and intimate and homely, and life was a kind of picnic. Bella was happy when he came home, not only because she loved him but also because his company took her out of herself. She had got into the way of brooding over the ruins and haunting them, watching the ashen figures of the labourers at their exasperatingly leisurely work, and the slow carts crawling along to the dump with their creaking axles. If she could have had her way she would have trebled the number of labourers and carted the debris away at a gallop; and Jasper's presence, by distracting her attention, made the work seem to move faster.

Even so, though his life was naturally full of trivial interests with which she pretended to sympathize, she managed, when they were alone, to bring back their talk again and again to the subject that obsessed her. She felt that in her own defence she was bound to do this; for she knew that although Wilburn—and Courtenay, for more obvious reasons—humoured her passion, there were a number of people, including the Pomfrets of Wychbury, who regarded her ambitious designs as foolish, if not as evidence of an unbalanced reason. When she discussed them with Jasper she always spoke as an advocate, deliberately pleading, instilling into his pliable mind by patient reiteration her own fixed idea, reinforcing her arguments by appeals to his love for her and his respect for his father's memory and for the Pomfret tradition, arming him at every vulnerable point against the arguments of others. Jasper only remembered his father vaguely. Now, in their long evenings together, Bella tried to give Hugo's shadow substance, investing his figure with a strength and dignity which he had certainly never possessed, insisting continually on his devotion to White Ladies and the sacrifices he had been willing to make for it.

"We must take him as our example, darling," she said. "Whatever it may cost us we must do what he would have done. When he made me trustee for you it meant, literally, that he trusted me—just as I shall trust you when the trust is handed on."

And, partly because he loved her, and partly because from his boyhood she had taught him to believe that the possession and care of White Ladies must be the central privilege and duty of his life, she found she could persuade him to share her enthusiasm so far as he was able.

By the middle of January, when he was due to return to Eton, most of the debris had actually been cleared from the shell of White Ladies, and the insecure fragments of timber and masonry removed. On his last day at home they went down as usual to inspect the work and, for the first time since the fire, Bella set foot in the space which had once been the great hall. From this point the huge ruin presented a spectacle of mournful majesty. The destruction of the oak staircase and gallery had doubled the size of the hall, but the lack of the upper floors diminished the appearance of this by turning the whole central segment of the house into one high rectangular chamber on whose smoke-blackened walls, resembling the sides of a monstrous flue, the hearths and chimney-faces of bedroom fireplaces protruded illogically. The impression of vast height in this shaft of brick, towering higher than a cathedral-nave, was enhanced by a relative narrowness which made the four walls appear to lean dangerously inward; and the space that their broken edges enclosed was roofed by a luminous plaque of chill January sky, its thin blue made more brilliant by the shadow beyond which it was seen. Standing there in the bottom of the pit, Bella was conscious of a strange awe resembling that of a traveller who finds himself alone in some desolate temple lost in tangles of jungle or islanded in desert sands. She had always thought of White Ladies as of a size within the grasp of her imagination. Now the magnitude of the stark ruin overwhelmed it, and, even more than its magnitude, its silence. For the first time in her life she felt White Ladies alien and unfriendly. Almost frightening. She clutched Jasper's arm for reassurance. He, too, had stood spell-bound.

"I'd no idea the house was as high as that," he said. "I don't mind betting you could see the stars from down here long before it was dark."

"Well, we won't wait to prove that anyway," Bella said with an uneasy laugh. She shivered. "It's getting cold, darling. Let's have a brisk walk. When you come home at Easter perhaps the roof will be on."

"Yes, that *will* be fun," he said, doubtfully.

When he had gone and she had no more company

to distract her mind, the work, which she had thought was on the point of moving at last, seemed more than ever to hang fire. Her impatience embarrassed Courtenay. Never before, though he thought he knew her by now, had he found her so difficult and exacting. It seemed useless to explain that even in its pre-liminaries a job such as this could not be put in hand with the assurance he felt in "converting" a cottage. There was an enormous number of technical details to be worked out: mathematical calculations of strains and stresses and tests of the standing remains. He himself had been working like a slave on them. Considering her purse, he had even been contemplating a number of modifications of the original plan which would not merely save money but add to the new building's convenience. This was their opportunity. If they failed to seize it they might regret their haste later.

"*Modifications!*" For the first time since he had known her, Bella lost her temper. "I don't want any modifications," she declared, "so for heaven's sake don't waste your time over them. You have plans, you have sketches and photographs; the whole thing's perfectly simple. At this rate we shall all be in our graves before White Ladies is finished."

Was she losing her nerve? he wondered. He had known her exacting, imperious, ruthless, before—but never, before, excitable. Her composure, indeed, had been one of the qualities he had most admired in her. How old was she? Forty-three or forty-four, he

supposed. It was a time of life at which women clients
were apt to be difficult; but the job was too valuable
in itself, and he knew his woman too well, for him to
take any risks of forgoing it.

Was she losing her nerve, in fact? Was there,
somewhere in the back of her mind, a lurking idea
that unless she made haste some indefinite hostile
influence might overtake her? Was this impalpable,
unformulated threat the cause of her restlessness?

Bella refused to ask herself these questions, though
she knew, in her heart, that her urgency had some
hidden source. And then, suddenly, in the middle of
Lent, the threats to her peace took shape. One morning she received a letter written in a hand unknown
to her. She opened it and read:

Dear Mrs. Pomfret,

*I have just heard from my boy Gervase, who is
at Eton with your son, Jasper, what my husband and
I consider most alarming news. Jasper had told him
that you are actually contemplating rebuilding White
Ladies. I hesitate to bother you with this letter, but
of course you will realize that the matter concerns us
intimately. We shall both of us be delighted to hear
that the rumour is not true, or at least, exaggerated.
Will you be good enough to let us know?*

Yours sincerely,
Sibell Powys.

Bella answered immediately:

Dear Mrs. Powys,
It is perfectly true that I am about to rebuild White Ladies, as your father would have wished.
Yours sincerely,
Arabella Pomfret.

When she had posted her letter she wondered if it would not have been wiser to consult Wilburn before she wrote it. Even though the next week brought no reply from Hugo's daughter or her husband, the matter continued to worry her. She drove into North Bromwich and showed the two letters to Wilburn. He read them both, and re-read them, then handed them back to her.

"Well?" he said.

"Was my answer all right?"

"You couldn't have put what you wanted to say any better."

"Had she any right to ask me that question?"

"Of course, if she wanted to."

"But is it any business of hers?"

"In a sense, very much so. Her son is the heir presumptive."

"Of course I know that. But my position is perfectly clear, isn't it?"

"Your legal position is perfectly clear. It couldn't be clearer."

"Then how *dare* they . . . ? I suppose I really shouldn't have answered."

"That would have been rather bad-mannered."

"I considered her letter insolent."

"It's a little bit brusque, perhaps; but no doubt she felt strongly."

"She's no right to feel strongly."

"You can't control people's feelings."

"What does this mean, anyway?"

"From all my experience I should say the barometer's set for a first-class family quarrel. If you get any more letters you'd better hand them to me. I'll deal with them."

Bella thanked him and drove back to White Ladies still vaguely uneasy but reassured.

A week later the Powys family returned to the attack. This time Hugo's daughter was less guarded.

Dear Mrs. Pomfret, (she wrote)

We have received your letter of March 2nd, and are shocked beyond words by its contents. As the parents of a possible beneficiary under my father's will, my husband and I are appalled by the high-handed way in which you are proposing to deal with his estate. My husband suggests that before we proceed to apply for an injunction restraining you from your present action we might meet and discuss the matter, thus avoiding the unpleasantness of washing the family linen in public. We shall be glad to come

*to White Ladies on any day and at any time you like
to name.*

> *Yours truly,*
> *Sibell Powys.*

Bella sent on this letter to Wilburn. He acknowledged it briefly. It was foolish, he said, for laymen
to make vague threats of bringing an action which
certainly wouldn't lie. He proposed to answer the
Powyses' letter, telling them that if they had anything more to say on the subject they had better communicate with him.

There the matter appeared to rest. When next he
saw her, Wilburn assured her that any reputable
lawyer whom the Powyses might choose to consult
would certainly confirm the opinion he had already
given her. All lawyers, of course, were not equally
reputable; but her position was perfectly clear. All
she need do was to lie low.

And in the meantime the work at White Ladies
advanced. The first of a series of contracts had been
signed. Courtenay had accepted the tender of the
London firm which had dealt with the roof before.
They were sound people, he said, and already
acquainted with local conditions. It gave Bella a feeling of security to see the faces of foremen with whom
she was familiar. They touched their caps to her, and
seemed glad to be back at their old lodgings in
Chaddesbourne. Within a short time the bulk of

White Ladies could only be seen, like a ship on the slips, through thickets of scaffolding. The workmen cooked their food over wood fires in the broken grates. Smoke rose through the chimneys into the still morning air; the sight of it seemed to Bella a first sign of returning life. All day wagons and lorries came grinding over the road from Worcester with their loads of lime and sand and cement and timber; all day a sound of hammering echoed from the greening woods.

One afternoon, when Bella returned to the farm, exhausted and elated, from watching the progress of the work, Mr. Beaver, who was now re-established, announced a visitor. It was a lady, he said, who would not give her name. Mr. Beaver, as Bella was aware, knew a 'lady' when he saw one.

In the drawing-room a woman rather younger than herself awaited her. Bella knew at a glance who she was. There was no mistaking that round head, those rather close, pale-blue eyes, that weak, obstinate, yet somehow not unattractive mouth. This was Hugo's daughter. Bella took the wind from her sails by saying at once: "You are Mrs. Powys? How d'you do? Let me ring for some tea."

She did so. Mrs. Powys replied severely that she didn't want any.

"But I do," Bella laughed. "I'm dying for it. So I'm afraid you will have to watch me unless you change your mind."

She took off her hat and sat down. Beaver appeared with the tea-tray.

"Are you sure you won't have some?" Bella pleaded.

Sibell Powys shook her head firmly.

"I have come against my husband's wishes," she said, "to make a last appeal to you. I feel that you must be as anxious as we are to avoid any public unpleasantness. . . ."

"Of course I am," Bella agreed. "But what sort of public unpleasantness?"

"You know that as well as I do, Mrs. Pomfret. As the result of this terrible fire, in which you had all our sympathy, my late father's estate has benefited by a large payment of money from the insurance company."

" 'Benefited' seems hardly the right word. A large sum has certainly been paid."

"As you know, my husband and I are interested, indirectly, in my father's estate."

"Much more interested in the estate than you were in your father. But please go on."

"You are throwing that money away, Mrs. Pomfret, wilfully throwing it away!"

"Not at all. I'm devoting it to the object for which it was intended."

"It's all very well to say that. A hundred years ago that might have been true. But to-day. . . . You know perfectly well that a great house like White Ladies is a burden rather than an advantage."

"The burden is mine, in any case, surely. *You* won't have to bear it."

"My son may have to bear it."

Bella smiled: "That is, naturally, a prospect which I prefer not to contemplate. From my point of view it isn't . . . shall I say . . . pleasant."

"Pleasant or unpleasant, it's my duty to contemplate it," Mrs. Powys replied. "We're all of us human and mortal. I have my son to consider."

"I, too, have a son. And my son, I must remind you, comes first."

"You're doing him the worst turn a mother could do him."

"Surely that is for me to decide."

"Hasn't he any say in it?"

"Indeed yes. He agrees with me, fortunately."

"He's too young to agree!" Mrs. Powys wailed. "Can't you see you're ruining my father's estate, just to satisfy your own fancy, your vanity? Can't you see how unfair it is?"

Bella shook her head. "I'm sorry. I'm afraid I can't follow you. There is one aspect of the affair that you entirely neglect to consider: your father's wishes. You never knew him as I did. I'm bound to admit that wasn't entirely your fault. During the years he was abroad you couldn't. But when he came home, when he married me. . . . Even then neither you nor your husband ever took the trouble to know him. Never wrote to him, never visited him, never showed

U*

the least sign of interest in him. As I've said before, you are merely interested in his property. I did know your father; I knew the very bottom of his heart: and I know that what I'm doing to-day is exactly what he would have done. That is one thing. This is another: you have no right to speak of White Ladies as if I had no personal claim on it. When I married your father the house was falling to pieces. The very roof was rotten; the whole place was ready to collapse. I poured money into it, my own money—thousands and thousands of pounds—far more money than your father's ancestors had spent on it in four generations. I saved White Ladies. Quite possibly—though I hope it won't be so—I saved it for your son. And now that it's been destroyed, I'm proposing to save it again. If you think this wretched insurance money is going to rebuild it entirely you're very much mistaken. On the whole, don't you think you ought to be grateful to me?"

Mrs. Powys threw up her hands in despair: "If you want to know, I think you're stark, staring mad. Or, if you're not mad, you're wicked . . . wicked!" she cried.

There was little more to be said; and Bella, at least, had no intention of saying it. Mrs. Powys, with indignant tears in her eyes, retired. Bella, shakily, finished her tea. She had a triumphant feeling that she had heard her last of the Powyses. After all, if Wilburn's opinion was correct—and he had dis-

suaded her from wasting money on obtaining counsel's
—her position was secure. The only person in the
world who could shake it was Jasper. And Jasper, as
she had been able to boast, saw eye to eye with her.

Even if she had doubted this, the certainty was
confirmed when he came home after Easter. He was
in great spirits and ready to share her attention to the
work, although less interested in this than in the fact
that the March Brown was "up" and that his precious
"rainbows" were rising even more freely than he had
expected. Bella was particularly grateful, at that
moment, for anything that might keep him at home
and away from the influence of Hugo's cousin at
Wychbury, from whose frostiness she had gathered
that he shared the Powyses'prejudices. She encouraged
Jasper as much as she could to fish the twin pools and
forget about the Teme, which wasn't an "early" river.
Strictly speaking, he told her gravely, they oughtn't to
be fished, since the spawning-season of "rainbows"
differed from that of brown trout. There was no harm,
however, in catching them and putting them back—
just to see how they were growing. He did this after
the manner of a child who digs up newly-planted
seeds. Though he was now in his seventeenth year,
Jasper was oddly childish in many things. Hugo had
told her that it was in the nature of the Pomfrets to
develop late and suddenly, so she didn't worry. For
some reasons, indeed, it was better that he should be
childish.

Now the work moved more rapidly. At last progress could be seen. By midsummer the new roof was in place and workmen were busy on the joists of the lower floors. For these, following a more modern practice, Courtenay had decided on the use of steel girders. It gave Bella a thrill of strange excitement to discover the words *Jos. Tinsley and Co., Hayseech* stamped on the metal. It pleased her to think that something of Hayseech, something that but for her ancestors' resistance to the old Pomfrets would never have been made there, was now, by sheer chance, being incorporated in the tissue of the Pomfrets' White Ladies and adding to its strength—though later, when she came to think of it, she realized that most of this work was, in fact, sustained by the wealth which the Tinsleys, inspired by her grandfather's genius, had drawn from the Pomfrets' land, and that the Hayseech girders were no more than a graphic example of this romantic revenge of time.

As for money—there was no doubt that the new work swallowed it insatiably. Every month the contractors presented a certificate for huge payments, vouched for by Courtenay. She hardly dared look at them before she handed them on to Wilburn, who, as he told her, continued to make the insurance money "move" by bold yet careful investment. Indeed she was thankful to know he was keeping it "moving," for the mere structural work on White Ladies, which was not even half-done, had already made a big hole in her ninety thousand, and the replacement of details, as Courtenay had warned her, would prove far more expensive. He had warned her of this from the first, and she had taken his warning, though it was not until now that she had grasped its full significance. None the less, she refused to let his plans be modified. *In for a penny, in for a pound.* That was Jasper Mortimer's attitude.

So the summer days lengthened and the new White Ladies took shape. Bella was so busily watching it that she could not even find time to spend the Fourth of June with Jasper at Eton. He came home at the end of July. She drove to meet him at Worcester. He seemed moodier and more silent than usual. That was the effect, she supposed, of the abominable Eton climate. A week in the clean Worcestershire air would soon put him right. There was certainly nothing wrong with his appetite. After tea she proposed that they should walk down together to see the work. He consented, she thought, reluctantly. She showed him the new roof and pointed to the name of *Jos. Tinsley and Co.* stamped on the steel girders; but he seemed, for once, unable to share her enthusiasm. It was clear that there was something on his mind, that mind which had always been so clear to her. She suspected some boyish trouble: a bad report, the worry of some small, ridiculous debt. Or perhaps—who knew?—he imagined he had fallen in love.

All that evening, with small effect, she tried to

arouse him from his gloom with little forced gaieties. At last, when she could stand being puzzled no longer, she asked him point-blank what was the matter.

At first he hedged. It was unlike Jasper to hedge. She laughed and kissed him. "You can't put me off like that, darling. Something's worrying you. What is it? You can be sure I shall understand."

"I wish I could understand, Mother," he said, ruefully. Then the story came out.

He had been unhappy, he told her, ever since the Winchester match: "You remember," he said, "I wanted you to come, but you said you couldn't. Well, it was pretty rotten, being alone on a day like that when everybody's people come down, so I joined up with Gervase Powys and his father and mother for tea. It was decent of them to ask me."

Bella nodded. "Ah . . . now I see!"

"What d'you see?" he enquired suspiciously.

"Nothing, darling. Go on."

"Well, after tea, when we were walking round Agar's Plough, Major Powys—that's Gervase's father—began to talk to me rather seriously. He talked about all this work we're doing, rebuilding White Ladies. Awfully nicely, I must say. He didn't say anything against you. Of course he knew that he couldn't. But he was really anxious—not for himself or Gervase, but for me."

"That was nice of him, darling."

"Don't laugh at me, Mother. It's really no laughing matter. I'm deadly serious."

"Well, why was he anxious for you?"

"He put it like this, quite reasonably. He said: here was this money that came from the insurance people, this ninety thousand pounds or whatever it is. He said, was it wise to put it all back in White Ladies? Wouldn't it be more reasonable to invest it in what they call gilt-edged securities or something? Or to build a moderate-sized house—nobody wants a great big one in these days—and invest the remainder? You see, supposing we spent thirty thousand pounds on a house, and that's quite enough, it would leave sixty thousand, wouldn't it?"

"Sixty thousand exactly, Jasper."

"But, honestly, Mother! Sixty thousand pounds! He said that meant three thousand a year. Well, you could do an awful lot with three thousand a year. You could take a grouse-moor or a deer-forest or a salmon river. I should love a beat on the Dee. Or . . . well, there's almost nothing you couldn't get for it."

"But you wouldn't have White Ladies, darling."

"Well. . . . After all, does it matter so much as all that? In comparison, I mean?"

"Oh, Jasper, it used to matter. It mattered to your father. It matters frightfully to me."

He remained gloomily silent, then sighed:

"You know, Mother," he said, "I sometimes think you're a little . . . unbalanced about White Ladies."

"Did Major Powys say that?"

"Not exactly, in so many words."

"But he implied it? And you let him imply it?"

"After all he'd said, it *did* look a little queer. And money's money, isn't it?"

"Yes. The root of all evil. And White Ladies is White Ladies." She took him in her arms. "Jasper, darling, don't look so tragically obstinate! Now listen to me. There are one or two things you've forgotten. First of all that you're your father's son: Jasper Pomfret of White Ladies. That ought to mean something to you. And the next thing is this: that your darling mother isn't exactly a pauper. If the insurance money we got for White Ladies were all we possessed —and it *is* all that Gervase would possess if anything happened to you, though of course nothing will—it would be a different matter. But we can spend every penny of that, darling, and still be comfortably off. I'm going to spend it: make no mistake about that. I'm your father's sole trustee, and nothing that Gervase's father or anyone else cares to say will make any difference to me. But that doesn't mean that your life's going to be ruined or anything like that. If you want a beat on the Dee, why, of course you shall have it. Not just yet—later on, I mean, when White Ladies is finished. You can have your grouse-moor as well, if it comes to that. But you mustn't mistrust me. That's the one thing I couldn't bear. After all, you're the only thing I have in the world of my very own.

Will you promise to trust me?"

"Why, of course I trust you, Mother," he said. "When you put it like that the whole thing's different, isn't it? Major Powys spoke as though we hadn't another penny."

"We haven't . . . for him or Gervase. For ourselves, thank heaven, we've plenty. Are you happier now?"

As she kissed him, laughing, she knew he was happy. But she was not. She knew now exactly how much—or how little—White Ladies meant to him.

III

For the moment Bella supposed she could congratulate herself on a victory. It was not, she had to confess, a spiritual triumph. Jasper had renewed his easily-shaken allegiance, not through any inward conviction, but in return for a bribe. Only to think that a Pomfret—and her son and Hugo's at that—should need a bribe to stiffen his loyalty to White Ladies! All the more reason for pressing on while the going was good enough. Those Powyses were no fools— Sibell's husband had not taken long to find the weak spot in Jasper's armour—nor were they likely to accept their defeat as final. It was a waste of time worrying over their next move, she told herself. Whatever it might be, the proper reply lay less in arguments, persuasions, or appeals to sentiment, than in confronting them (and also Jasper, alas!) with the new White Ladies as an accomplished fact.

And during that autumn, thanks to her urgency and Courtenay's help, the ruin did actually appear to show signs of returning life. The great hall had been repaved; the staircase was rising; the girders from Hayseech which sustained the first floor were hidden by lath and plaster; new battalions of workmen— plumbers, glaziers, painters—swarmed in to augment the forces of the masons whose heaped debris had added a desolation of its own to the fire's vast wreckage.

By the beginning of the year the great central oriel was re-glazed. This was a piece of work to which Courtenay gave particular care. That soft light, resembling mild sunshine, with which its ancient panes mellowed the hall, had been the first thing a stranger noticed on entering White Ladies. He had been anxious, if it were possible, to retain this effect, and had succeeded by carefully preserving from the first every fragment of the original glass which could be sifted and saved from the drifts of ashes in which its fused fragments lay hidden. He displayed the result to Bella with pride. Inside the hall, indeed, the efforts of his piety had astonishingly recaptured the lighting for which he had striven. From outside Bella was shocked by an effect which struck her as vaguely sinister. "When the glass is put in," Courtenay had told her, "you'll be astonished to see what a difference it makes. You'll feel just as if the house had suddenly come alive." But that wasn't what happened. When first she saw the glass gleaming in the oriel, it was just as if a dead man had opened his eyes. Or one eye—which made it far worse. White Ladies was still dead. No doubt, when the rest of the windows were glazed, this oddly macabre impression would vanish. The sooner the better! The glaziers, she noticed thankfully, were already at work on the western bay.

It was the faithful reproduction of detail, as Courtenay explained, which took so much time. It was this, too, that cost money. During the year and a quarter which had passed with such agonizing slowness since the date of the fire, she (or Wilburn, for her) had been handing out cheques on Courtenay's vouchers for several thousand pounds a month. Bella was thankful, at least, that this one side of the business need not worry her. The insurance money was there and ready to be paid. Though there seemed little enough to show for the gigantic expenditure, there was plenty more waiting—and, as she hoped, increasing— to meet any new demands as they came along. After all, as Courtenay had told her, and as she had seen for herself when she put in the electric light and the heating-plant, it was always the invisible ground-work that seemed to cost most. If it should be necessary— and Courtenay had warned her it might be necessary —she was prepared to spend a large part of her private fortune as well. As she had reassured Jasper, she was not a poor woman. When the prospect of this expenditure frightened her, as it sometimes did, she reminded herself of Hugo's bitter sacrifices and took new courage.

After all, the only thing which could really have discouraged her would have been another threat of defection on Jasper's part. And that, she thanked heaven, was no longer likely to appear. The Powyses,

it seemed so far, had accepted their defeat. During
the Christmas holidays she was careful from time to
time to dangle the bribe she had already offered him
before Jasper's eyes, encouraging him to expect that
as soon as the house was finished she would be ready to
perform her part of the bargain; and though he didn't
respond to the suggestion quite so eagerly as she could
have wished, remaining, in spite of his acceptance of
the situation, a little wary and detached (she had
almost said sulky), she was still able to persuade herself that she had him in hand; and at Easter, she told
herself, when the fishing-season had begun, he would
be even easier to handle.

In February, after his return to Eton, she received
a shock.

Courtenay, as usual, had sent her his monthly
certificate; Bella, as usual, had passed the certificate
on to Wilburn; but the contractors did not, as usual,
return her their receipt. They wrote instead, through
Courtenay, a letter informing her that the sum for
which he had given his certificate had not yet been
paid.

This was evidently an oversight, and so much out
of keeping with Wilburn's business-like methods that
Bella could only suppose that her letter to him had
gone astray. In the ordinary way she would have
telephoned to him that morning, but the day was so
brilliant that she felt tempted to drive into North
Bromwich and see him in person. She would take

the opportunity, she decided, of calling at Halesby on the way back, and having tea with Aunt Harriet, whom she had lately neglected. During the last year poor Miss Mortimer had been almost immobilized by rheumatism, which she attributed not to the dank Black Country air but to the damp which had risen from the moat and penetrated her bones during her sojourn at White Ladies. This was just the right day, Bella thought, with its hint of spring in the air, to warm and cheer her.

For herself, she found it a delicious change to turn her back, for once in a while, on White Ladies and its tense preoccupations, to forsake the green plains, so static and silent, for the keener upland air and bustling activity of North Bromwich. Years ago, even after her marriage, she had sometimes felt chary of entering the city by the Halesby Road, a thoroughfare still haunted by the disquieting memory of two personal debacles: the odd years she had spent at St. Monica's, and the Fladburn incident. Now those wounds were so fully healed that the sight of the Halesby Road did not awake in their scars the least memory of suffering. She experienced in traversing it that agreeable emotion, actually enhanced by a vague but not unpleasing melancholy, which clings to all places in which one has lived—and even suffered—in youth.

"When I was young," she thought, "I felt everything much more keenly than I do now. I suppose that is one of the compensations of age, or of middle age. When one grows really old one simply doesn't feel at all. That's a mercy . . . unless it's a tragedy. I wonder which?"

Gibbs drove slowly into the city. Down the middle of the Halesby Road electric trams had taken the place of the old four-horse Tilton buses. Motors stuttered and hooted everywhere in increasing numbers. Bella was glad to think she got in "on the ground floor" to Pearce-Tregarons. As they turned into Sackville Row, the Art Gallery clock boomed the hour. Newsboys were shouting, and people stood reading a special edition of the *Courier*. Racing or football, she supposed.

The car pulled up at the door of Wilburn's office. She told Gibbs to wait, and mounted the familiar steps. *Wilburn, Wilburn & Wilburn*. What a ridiculous name the firm had! She rang at the door, and a moon-faced clerk, whom she knew already, opened it to her; but this time, instead of letting her enter as usual, he stood in her way.

"Is Mr. Wilburn in?" she enquired.

"Mr. Dudley's engaged, madam. Or rather I have strict orders to say he can't see anybody."

"I don't want Mr. Dudley. I've come to see Mr. Ernest."

The man blinked at her oddly. His face worked as he tried to answer her; his lips trembled; he spoke in a whisper.

"Mr. Ernest's dead, madam."

"Dead?"

"Yes, madam. It's a terrible business. I'm afraid he shot himself. We're all of us—well, I hardly know how to put it. We don't know what it means yet. It only happened this morning. I have no more idea what it's all about than you. But there may be something in the paper. There's a special edition of the *Courier* come out. I can hear the paper-boys shouting. If you would like to leave a message for Mr. Dudley, of course I'll pass it on to him; but just now, I'm afraid . . ."

"No, indeed. I wouldn't dream of disturbing him. This is too dreadful."

"It's a mystery to all of us."

It was not to be a mystery for long. As she left the office Bella succeeded in buying a paper. That told her little more than she knew already. Ernest Wilburn, it seemed, had got up that morning and dressed for the city as usual. His man, wondering at his delay in coming to breakfast, had gone up-stairs to see if anything was wrong. As he tapped at the door, he had heard a sharp report followed by a thud, and had entered to find his master lying on the floor with a bullet through his head. He had telephoned at once for the police and for Dudley Wilburn. The police had arrived and taken the body to the mortuary. Dudley Wilburn would make no statement of any kind to the Press; but the tragedy,

the *Courier* said, had created a "profound and disturbing impression in North Bromwich business circles."
It was known that Ernest Wilburn had been heavily
involved in a number of commercial failures—notably
the bankruptcy of the Sedgebury Main Colliery Company—and in the recent wild fluctuations of the rubber
market. There was a feeling, the *Courier* hinted, that
this tragic affair might be connected in some way with
financial embarrassments. An inquest would be held
to-morrow.

Financial embarrassments. . . . The words sounded
terribly indefinite. Not only the remainder of the
sum the insurance company had paid her, but also the
bulk of her private fortune, had been placed, with
complete confidence, in Ernest Wilburn's hands. He
had been hit by the Sedgebury Main Colliery disaster.
She knew that already. Her own holding in the company, he had assured her laughingly, was small. He
would make up the loss, he had told her, in some
other way. In what way? *In the recent wild fluctuations of the rubber market?* Had he used the money
which belonged to White Ladies—her own money
didn't matter so much—in his rash speculations? One
was always reading of things like that in the papers.
"*Mr. So-and-so, Solicitor, struck off the rolls for
having made use of a client's money . . . mis-
appropriation of trust funds.*" But Ernest Wilburn,
she told herself passionately, wasn't that sort of
solicitor. He was a gentleman; he was her friend.

Other doubts presented themselves: the rumours which she had heard and loyally denied of his being "mixed up" with some actress or other. That explained, people said, his mysterious visits to London. After all, why shouldn't the poor man have an affair with an actress? He was unmarried; and no actress, surely, could be as expensive as all that!

"No, that isn't enough," she told herself. "An affair of that kind might quite possibly turn his head, but it wouldn't ruin him." Yet, even as she reassured herself thus, a new doubt took shape. Didn't the fact of his losing his head in this manner imply a general instability which might have extended in other directions? She recalled, her memory sharpened by this threat (so far, thank heaven, it was only a threat!) of disaster, several recent occasions on which Wilburn's manner had appeared evasive. Nobody, indeed, whom she hadn't trusted blindly, could have put her off so easily. His mocking confidence had always put her to shame. Yet now, thinking backward, she also began to remember things in Wilburn less definite than these evasions: subtler symptoms, which she had noticed but loyally disregarded, of a gradual physical deterioration; a growing inclination to take things less seriously; an impatience which at times approached irritability; an air of being harassed, and barely interested in her enthusiasms; a tendency to avoid talking business if he possibly could, as though the mere mention of it wakened

some haunting anxiety which he realized but refused
to admit. Had he seen himself, through all these
months, all these years, moving steadily, inevitably,
towards this bloody, humiliating end?

It was all very well asking these questions. The
only person who could answer them (supposing he
were still a "person") now lay covered with a rubber
sheet on a slab in the white-tiled North Bromwich
City Mortuary. They could not be answered now,
it appeared, until the complicated tangles in which
Wilburn had finally found himself, like a bluebottle
floundering in a spider's web, should be unravelled by
the Official Receiver. The state of his affairs, she
guessed, must have been pretty desperate; for, two
days later, when the coroner's jury had brought in
their charitable verdict of temporary insanity ("not
so temporary as all that!" people said) Dudley
Wilburn closed his office and called in his creditors.

Meanwhile, at White Ladies, Bella was at her wits'
end. Immediately on her return from North
Bromwich she had summoned Courtenay, who hurried
down next day wondering what new caprice he
might be expected to deal with. When Bella told him
as much as she knew, he looked grave. Perhaps,
among other things, he was thinking of his own fees.

"What we ought to do, I suppose," he said, "is to
close down the work."

"To close down the work?" Bella cried.

"Well, at least suspend it."

"How can the contractors suspend it at a moment's notice like that?"

"Let's put it differently: How can we expect them to go on when my last month's certificate remains unpaid?"

"I refuse to believe we're in such a bad way as that, Roger."

"And I hope to goodness you're right. But we don't *know*, do we? We can't; and until we do, we haven't exactly the right to go on spending at our present rate. When I say 'let's suspend the work,' I mean that we're hopeful. I shall put it to the contractors that this is a temporary hitch, and suggest that they leave all their heavy plant on the spot to save themselves—or us—the expense of bringing it back again."

Bella could not accept this. "Do you know," she said, "I've a feeling, a fancy if you prefer to call it so, that if once the work on White Ladies is stopped it will never begin again. In my case that means a lot. All my life I've backed my fancies. You may laugh at me, but it's really no laughing matter. However mad you may think me, we *can't* stop; we've got to go on."

"And the money that's owing?"

"I must raise it somehow or other. I can borrow on the security of the land."

"Are you so sure?"

"I can find out, I suppose. After all, quite apart

from that, I have a certain amount of property of my own—the remainder of my shares in my grandfather's company for example—which poor Ernest Wilburn can't possibly have touched."

"I like your 'poor Ernest Wilburn!'"

"Well, you see, I was fond of him. He was a good friend to me."

"That remains to be seen. If he had charge of all your affairs, I suppose these shares were in his hands as well as the rest?"

"I'm not sure. You see I left everything to him."

"Well, the sooner you *are* sure, the better. What shall I tell the contractors?"

"Please ask them to go on. I'll see that they have their arrears. You can promise that for me."

Dudley Wilburn, it appeared, was still unapproachable. He was hardly, in any case, the person to approach. Bella hurried into Worcester and consulted Mr. Chafey, the Pomfrets' family solicitor, the neat, shrivelled, formal little man whom she had last seen at Hugo's funeral. She found Mr. Chafey coldly sympathetic but faintly aggrieved: if her business affairs had been placed in his hands, as they should have been, nothing of this kind could possibly have happened. Dudley Wilburn, he said, had always been regarded as a man of high principles. He had never liked Ernest, and never concealed his dislike. However, since Mrs. Pomfret had finally recovered her senses, he would do what he could for her. He agreed that it was unlikely that Ernest could have touched the remainder of her shares in Hayseech. As to the insurance money, which she had apparently thrown into his hands without any vestige of precaution, he was bound to say that he felt much less optimistic. Rumour said that the Wilburn failure was likely to run into hundreds of thousands. Rumour, of course, was a lying jade; but there was no smoke without fire. Bella expected him to talk about "rolling stones" and "stitches in time."

"In the meantime I must have the money I owe the contractors," she told him.

Mr. Chafey's thin, lashless eyelids blinked. "Of course you will stop the work?"

"What has that to do with it?" Bella demanded. "I'm merely asking you to borrow some money for me on adequate security."

Mr. Chafey sighed. "I'll see what can be done," he said. "In the meantime I take it you'ld like me to represent you at the creditors' meeting next Tuesday? After that we may know rather better how we stand."

"I should prefer to go with you and hear how I stand for myself. If you'll fix a time, I'll come in the car and call for you."

She had three days to wait. On the second she received an anxious letter from Jasper. He had read in the newspaper about the Wilburn disaster, and hoped to goodness it wasn't going to hit them. Bella dashed off a hurried reply, begging him not to worry. If her movements were going to be hampered by Jasper's doubts as well as Courtenay's, life would become more difficult than ever. On the following Tuesday she drove into North Bromwich with Chafey. The meeting was a dismal affair. Dudley Wilburn, or rather the grey ghost of him, explained, with tears in his unemotional eyes, the firm's position. All was not lost, he assured his creditors. Such business as had rested in his own hands was in perfect order. As long as breath remained in his body, he told them passionately, he would devote himself to satisfying the clients whom his brother had betrayed. It was no use attempting to disguise the utter confusion of Ernest's affairs. Certain sums which had been entrusted to him, including fifty thousand pounds in cash, the property of the Pomfret Estate, had completely disappeared. That, so far as he could ascertain at present, was the heaviest item; but the total, he feared, would mount up to more than a hundred thousand. He could say nothing more than that he accepted complete responsibility for his brother's debts, his brother's (the poor man shuddered) appalling defalcations. He placed himself unreservedly in his creditors' hands.

One or two of the creditors spoke, some with sympathy, others with violent and fruitless indignation. Those who sympathized least had lost least. Bella watched and listened. Around her she saw a number of people whom she recognized, and some others whom she found tantalizing because she could not place them. Among these she noticed, at some distance, a middle-aged man with a high forehead and iron-grey hair brushed back tightly over his temples. It was the shape of that bald forehead which seemed so familiar to her, though she could see little else; for his head was bent over his notes and his features were hidden. As she puzzled her brains to think who it could be, she heard Mr. Chafey clear his throat and begin to speak.

He was representing, he said, the lady who was in the unfortunate position of being the largest creditor. It would be his ultimate business to investigate ruthlessly the manner in which the enormous sum mentioned by Dudley Wilburn had disappeared. What concerned him even more at the moment was what had happened to the numerous other securities with which his client had entrusted—he had been going to say Ernest Wilburn, but, after the statement they had heard, he would say "the firm." He had been instructed by his client to obtain possession, at the earliest possible moment, of all share certificates and other documents belonging to her. He realized, of course, that in the existing confusion, and given that the estate would certainly be put into the hands of the Official Receiver, these documents might not be immediately available. All his client desired at the moment was an assurance from Dudley Wilburn that

these various securities had not been involved together
with the rest. His client was naturally more than a
little anxious. If Mr. Wilburn could give him the
least indication. . . .

Dudley Wilburn rose heavily.

"I'm thankful to be able to tell you," he said,
"that, so far as I can see at present—and you'll realize,
of course, that I'm not in a position to commit myself
any more definitely—the securities to which you have
referred are intact. I can't specify with any exactness
what amount of money they represent. There are a
large number of shares in various rubber and motor-
manufacturing companies, the value of which, of
course, fluctuates violently from day to day. As you
know already from my circular letter, it was largely
speculations in rubber that led to my brother's difficulties; but apart from these questionable investments,
of which, for all I know, your client may have
approved, I have in my charge, and will hand over
to you as soon as I can, a very large block of ordinary
shares in Jos. Tinsley & Co., representing, I think,
approximately one-third of the stock which my brother
took charge of for her on the death of Mr. Jasper
Mortimer. Whatever else may have been lost, I can
assure you that is quite safe."

Mr. Chafey said "Thank you," and nodded at Bella
approvingly. She was thinking: "One-third. . . .
That means fifty thousand pounds. Just about as much
as the insurance money that's vanished. And besides

w

that," she thought, "there are the shares in motors and rubber. Rubber's dangerous, I know; but the Pearce-Tregarons are all right. He told me he was going to make up what he'd lost. He said that some of our 'rash investments' were looking up. And the Hayseech shares: I remember his saying he was glad he had kept them: something about a new steel. Perhaps, after all, things won't be so bad as we've thought. Motors steady; rubber rising; Hayseech. . . . If only I knew! If only I could feel that I had, say, a hundred thousand. Then I could go on with White Ladies and trust to luck!"

The meeting was over. Mr. Chafey was saying good-bye. He had business in North Bromwich, he said, and would not avail himself of her kind offer of a lift back to Worcester.

"You'll see about that money for the contractors at once? Three thousand will cover it."

He assented, bowed stiffly, and left her. An odd, dry little man, Bella thought. If Ernest had been as precise and arid . . . poor Ernest! She rose and found herself in the midst of the dissolving throng.

Moving slowly towards the doorway, she found herself standing beside the man she had noticed but failed to recognize. His eyes were still downcast; but as she brushed against him he looked up and saw who she was. He raised his hat clumsily.

"Mrs. Pomfret . . . Bella . . ." he said.

She gasped. "Henry! Mr. Fladburn! Is it

actually you? I've been wondering all the afternoon who you were. I was certain I knew you."

He laughed. "I knew you at once—the moment I set eyes on you."

"You've changed, of course, Henry."

"Alas! You've not changed a bit."

"Dear, dear, how I wish that was true! So you're in this dreadful business?"

"Very mildly in it. I had much better luck than you, I'm afraid. I can't say how sorry . . ." He stopped.

"Well, I don't think it's quite so bad as we imagined at first."

"Fifty thousand? That's bad enough, surely? Are you going straight home?"

"I intended to go straight home. Can I give you a lift? Do you still live at Chad Grange?"

"Oh, no. I sold that house long ago. My mother lived there till she died. I'm living in Warwickshire. I've a charming house. Early Georgian red brick. Not at all spectacular, but quite large enough for a bachelor."

"So you're not married, Henry?"

"No, Bella, I never married."

"How odd! I always thought of you somehow as married."

"Did you think of me? That was nice of you."

"Of course I thought of you."

When they reached the pavement he seemed loth to

say good-bye. It was not difficult now, in spite of his glasses and grey hair, to recognize her old lover. He was still shy, still repressed, as when she had known him first. After all, considering what had happened between them, he had some reason to be shy of her.

"It's strange seeing you again after all these years, Henry," she said. "Strange, and rather nice. I should love to have a talk some day about those old times."

"Why shouldn't we have a talk now?" he said. "Won't you come and have tea with me somewhere?"

"I should like nothing better," she said. "I'm dreadfully tired. The strain of this business, you know . . ."

"It's hardly to be wondered at. What about the Grand Midland? That's reasonably quiet."

"Yes, that will do beautifully. It's quite near, isn't it? My car can wait."

She told Gibbs to follow them, and together they walked along Sackville Row. She remembered how, once, Henry Fladburn had felt ashamed—or was it frightened?—to be seen in public with her. He looked much nicer as a middle-aged man than as a boy. Most people looked nicer, really, in middle age, though youth didn't know this. At the Grand Midland, it seemed, Henry Fladburn was a person of consequence. The hall-porter saluted, and the manager bowed to him. That came, she supposed, of having inherited a quarter of a million. It seemed odd, all the same. His father, she reflected, would have refused to set foot inside licensed premises. Henry, at least, had escaped inheriting the family fanaticism.

"If you don't mind," he said, "I'll leave a message at the desk, so that the works can telephone me here if I should be wanted."

She watched him speaking to the clerk at the desk. He was tall, well-made, by North Bromwich standards well-dressed, with a blue-black velvet collar to his overcoat. By other standards, to which she was now more accustomed, he was typically middle-class and provincial, and perhaps none the worse for that: North Bromwich folk had found something to justify their suspicions of Ernest Wilburn's London vagaries. When he had given his message and turned round and came smiling towards her, she could see in his features a great deal of the old Henry Fladburn—though how she could ever have been in love with him (and so terribly in love!) she couldn't imagine.

They had tea downstairs in a basement of mock-Moorish arches and divans and Benares brass called the "Turkish Lounge." A few years before, it had been the "last thing" in North Bromwich; but now it was growing shabby, and smelt mostly of stale tobacco. The China tea, however, tasted pleasant and refreshed her.

"Yes . . . I should like to talk over 'old times'," Henry said.

Bella wished he wouldn't call them that. It was an odd thing, anyway, that he should want to talk of a period out of which, she felt, he hadn't emerged too creditably.

"No. Let's talk about the present," she said. "That's much more interesting. You're in business still?"

"Yes. Mine's a life-sentence, I'm afraid. I succeeded my father in the chair."

"He left a great deal of money, I believe?"

"A good deal. I don't know that I'm any the happier for it. The business is interesting. The brass-trade is so adaptable. Some new outlet always appears. Now the motor-trade's helping us."

Bella remembered how fiercely he had rebelled against the idea of joining the business. She said: "And your music?"

His face lit up quickly. "I'm as fond of music as ever. I've had a good deal to do with the City Orchestra. You were keen on music, too, Bella."

"No, not really. I only pretended to be at the time when I imagined I was in love with you."

"Oh, Bella. . . ."

"Women do things like that. You don't know much about women, do you? Why did you never marry, Henry? Isn't it a pity? With all that money?"

He was silent for a moment. "*Is* it a pity? I don't know. I suppose I've not married because"—he laughed nervously—"because I lost the only woman I was ever in love with."

"That wasn't her fault, Henry."

"No, indeed. I realize that. You'll probably think I'm flattering myself if I tell you now that it wasn't entirely my fault either. But it wasn't, you know, Bella. I was horribly weak: I admit. But weakness —that sort of weakness—is a defect, not a fault. I'm not trying to defend myself . . ."

"Whatever you call it, the effect was precisely the same."

"I know that. And still I wonder if you've ever realized the tremendous pressure of a family . . ."

"I know all about families. I'm dealing with one now."

". . . the pressure of the *sort* of family in which I was brought up? The genuine, hide-bound, tight-laced, old-fashioned Free Calvinist family? The kind of family that talks things over and decides on them in solemn council? My father and mother continued to do so as long as they lived. Thank God, I've escaped from all that! But do you know, Bella, even now I sometimes feel conscious of their criticism? I hardly dare whisper it to you: I'm no longer a Liberal; I'm actually a Tariff Reformer! With foreign competition what it is, I jolly well have to be."

A page-boy went past whining dismally: "Mr. Fladburn . . . Mr. Fladburn . . ."

Henry jumped up hurriedly.

"I'm afraid that's my telephone-call. You'll wait for me, won't you?"

Bella, left to herself, was thinking: "How curious

this is! I suppose he was really in love with me as
he says, and as I was in love with him. He's quite
nice, too: much nicer than he was, though in some
ways he's exactly the same and even more pathetic.
He's kind and he's gentle and he's lonely—too dreadfully lonely, though I suppose he's quite used to being
lonely by now. And he's rich. . . . He's probably
one of the richest men in North Bromwich."

She sighed to herself, reflecting on Henry's riches,
and shook her head slowly.

"If I chose," she thought, "I could make Henry
marry me. His money would rebuild White
Ladies without any trouble. He'ld be loyal and
decent. I know I could make him happy. If I married
him I could tell all the Pomfrets and Powyses to go
to hell. But Jasper. . . . What about Jasper? And
what about myself? I don't love him: it would be
ridiculous to pretend that I could ever love him. He
would be thankful for any sort of affection I liked to
give him. In all probability he'ld imagine it was the
real thing. But it wouldn't be anything like real; it
would all be a fraud. Though he never need know,
I should have married him for his money; and that
isn't good enough. No . . . if ever I marry again,
I shall marry for love—which means I shall certainly
never marry poor Henry."

Henry Fladburn returned. He was in such a great
hurry to join her that he slipped in a fold of the
Turkey carpet and nearly fell. ("That shows the poor

dear's middle-aged," Bella thought compassionately.) She saw that his face was flushed with boyish excitement. He spoke breathlessly:

"I'm sorry I left you so long, Bella. Important business. The Admiralty's given us a new contract for twelve-inch shell-cases. They're increasing their orders. I suppose it's the German Navy." Bella rose to her feet. His face fell: "You're not going? Why, we've scarcely begun . . ."

"I'm rather tired, Henry. The days are so short, and I hate driving back in the dark."

"Well, I mustn't be selfish," he said, "though I wish you could stay just a little longer. You don't know what a tremendous pleasure this chance encounter has been to me. At the meeting I kept asking myself if I dared speak to you; and now . . . well, I find you're just the same as you always were!"

Bella smiled and shook her head. "No, no. . . . Very different. I'm a widow of forty-four with a grown-up son—nearly."

"Would you mind . . ." He hesitated. "Would you mind if I drove over one day to see you at White Ladies?"

She was touched by his eagerness: an eagerness so childlike that it seemed a shame to hurt him. But her mind was made up.

"I don't think you'd better come, Henry. Broken friendships like ours. . . . Well, somehow they won't stand repairing. Much better not come."

w*

"Very well. I'll do just as you wish."

"Good-bye, Henry dear, and thank you for the tea. I'm glad you did speak to me."

It was strange, but seemed natural, that she found him kissing her good-bye. A less passionate kiss could hardly have been imagined.

"Won't you change your mind, Bella?" he pleaded. She shook her head. On the drive home, in the dark, figures danced in her mind like sparks in a furnace. She stopped the car at a post-office in Alvaston and sent Courtenay a telegram.

EVERYTHING SATISFACTORILY SETTLED. PLEASE ORDER RESUMPTION OF WORK AND COME DOWN AS SOON AS POSSIBLE.

IV

Courtenay came down at the end of the week. He seemed almost as much pleased as Bella herself to get the work moving again, but disappointed to find that even now her financial position was none too clear.

"I think we should really try to get more definite figures from your Mr. Chafey," he said.

But Bella's Mr. Chafey was a man by nature averse from committing himself, and he made no attempt, as Wilburn had done, to suit his paces to Bella's impatience. Worcester was not, thank heaven, his manner implied, North Bromwich, but a Cathedral City in which legal affairs were still conducted with dignity and decorum; and lawyers in Worcester, representatives of old family businesses, must not be expected to countenance the slap-dash methods of practice unfortunately current elsewhere. Every share-certificate retrieved from Wilburn's safe must be checked, re-checked and authenticated, by comparison with entries in the books of the companies concerned, before it could be considered to exist; and even when its existence had been grudgingly admitted, each document was still regarded, in Mr. Chafey's office, with the gravest suspicion. With suspicions, indeed, which, in the case of a good many of Ernest Wilburn's so-called investments, were not unfounded. Towards the end of his life, it seemed, he had gambled wildly, taking profits whenever he could, but not even troubling to cut his losses in time when his luck had failed him. A large part of Bella's holdings in rubber and base-metal shares, though impressive in quantity and variety, turned out to be worth very little. Her interest in Jos. Tinsley & Co. remained, in fact, the most solid and profitable part of her possessions. When, finally, an approximate figure was dragged from Mr. Chafey's reluctant lips, it appeared that her capital resources, simultaneously realized, might amount, with good luck, to some eighty thousand pounds—rather more than half her original inheritance.

"You mean I can count on at least four thousand a year?" Bella said.

"Four thousand a year? Why, that would mean five per cent!" Mr. Chafey hated the idea of any-one's "counting" on anything, and the mere mention of any percentage higher than three and a half made him shudder. "In any case, Mrs. Pomfret," he said, "you must not look to us for advice on financial matters. I am a lawyer. Unlike the late Mr. Wilburn, I confine myself to my business. If you *did* ask my opinion—and please understand I take no responsi-bility whatever—I should urge you to get out of these highly speculative investments as soon as possible, and put every penny—I repeat, every penny—into Consols."

"And live on just over two thousand a year, Mr. Chafey? At that rate, how on earth shall I ever finish White Ladies?"

Courtenay proved more sympathetic. He had grown fond of Bella, and the artist in him respected her romantic passion—quite apart from the fact that work, at the moment, was scarce. They talked over the whole problem of finishing White Ladies in the light of Mr. Chafey's new figures.

"It's quite clear we shall have to moderate our ambitions," he said.

"Why can't something startling happen, Roger? A boom in rubber or copper?"

"Booms and slumps never come when you want them. Let's get down to brass tacks. First of all we must obviously finish glazing all the windows to keep out the damp. That, luckily, is three parts done; and upstairs I'm not going to be over-critical about details —matching the tone of glass and so on. After the windows are all glazed, I think we ought to consider the features we can most easily discard. There's the Long Gallery, for instance."

"The Long Gallery? My dear Roger, Hugo thought it quite the loveliest thing in the house!"

"It was lovely, I admit. But it isn't really essential. Nobody lived in it; nobody went there unless they particularly wanted to see it or to examine the muniments. And now there aren't any muniments . . ."

Bella shook her head. "Isn't it awful to have no money?"

"Awful indeed! But by no means uncommon. There are actually people who wouldn't regard the possession of eighty thousand pounds as complete destitution. But where were we? The Long Gallery, of course. Now that we've decided we can do without that, we have the chance of eliminating a staircase, don't you see? and saving quite a lot. This means that we can concentrate most of our energies where they're wanted: on the first floor. Now, speaking as a hostess, tell me the least number of bedrooms . . ."

Bella listened to him and watched him, while calmly, logically, ruthlessly as a surgeon's scalpel, his pencil outlined on the plan of White Ladies the changes he suggested. They were, in fact, the very modifications he had already proposed and she had rejected. They were skilfully contrived and entirely reasonable. They would make White Ladies, she was forced to confess, more comfortable, more convenient and less expensive to "run" than ever before. But the interior which he planned was not the interior of White Ladies.

"You see," he ended triumphantly, "I've given you everything you need. You have kept the exterior of the house with its lovely proportions; you have kept the Great Hall, which was the next best thing about it; you have kept the two principal rooms on the ground floor—and, in addition to keeping these, you have gained what practically amounts to a moderate-sized modern house."

Bella laughed, rather bitterly. "I like your word 'gained.' You don't mention the losses."

"Let's forget them."

"No, I can't quite do that. Tell me this, at least, Roger: supposing, at some future time, I should find myself better off, would the things you're proposing make it difficult for me to return to the original plan?"

"No, I don't think they would. In fact I'm sure they wouldn't. All the same I'm certain you'll never want to return to it."

"So certain as all that? Would you like to bet on it?"

"Heavens, no! I retract. With a woman like you there are no such things as certainties. That's intended as a compliment, of course."

"I took it as a compliment. And supposing . . . supposing I'm weak enough to accept your new plan, do you think, with what's left of my money, I can carry it out?"

"I think, to begin with, you'll have to draw on your capital. Let's say ten—no, say twelve thousand pounds. After that, if you put by a third of your income every year, we ought to be able to go on quietly and steadily to the end."

"And how long will that take? Jasper's over seventeen. He'll be coming of age in rather more than three years. Would the house be finished by then?"

"It should be habitable by then for you two at any rate. You won't need to crowd it with furniture. 'Finished' is rather an elastic word. No house is ever 'finished'."

"White Ladies was."

"Yes, that was the beauty of it. However. . . . Shall we adopt these new plans as they stand?"

"I'm afraid beggars can't be choosers."

"In this case I'm satisfied that the beggar has chosen wisely. Nobody but you will notice any difference, you know."

Bella shook her head. "I suppose not. Let us get to work."

The old plans were duly scrapped and new contracts signed. Bella was surprised, in spite of herself, at the relief (it was almost a physical sensation) of dealing with work planned on a less ambitious scale. Quite apart from the expenditure of money it represented, the material magnitude of that Herculean labour, into which, unconsciously, she had infused every available atom of her own tense spirit, had become oppressive. It was as though a flagging runner in a long-distance race suddenly discovered himself within sight of the tape and in possession of his "second wind." The hard tension in her mind relaxed. She felt young and confident and gay.

Spring's ravishing return reinforced this gaiety. It

was, perhaps, the most lovely of all the springs Bella had seen at White Ladies. Never since those remote days at Alvaston which her meeting with Henry Flad-burn had poignantly recalled had she felt herself so richly aware of the earth's quiet rapture or so near to it. The sleeplessness which had troubled her van-ished; it was a daily delight to awake refreshed, to breathe the sweet air, to listen to the torrent of bird-song, to feel, in her own eager pulses, the warmth of the spring's communicable fire. She looked forward more happily than ever to Jasper's return at Easter. During the last year or two, she realized, her preoccupations must have made her poor company for him; and indeed, though the Powys incident was closed, it had left a faint tinge of awkwardness in their relation—an awkwardness which, now that she had the heart and the energy, she determined to dispel.

Even on the platform at Worcester Jasper was aware of the change in her. It was the most delight-ful of meetings, and his spirits, so largely dependent on hers, swiftly rose to their level in response. He seemed, naturally, eager to talk about the Wilburn disaster. It had been a hard blow, she admitted, though things might have been worse. She parried his persistent questions. "Don't let's talk about that on this perfect afternoon," she begged him. "Let's simply forget about it. To-morrow, when you're properly settled in, I'll tell you everything."

"Is it true," he asked, "that the insurance money is all gone?"

"Who told you it was gone, Jasper?"

He hesitated. "Well . . . Gervase Powys said something about it."

"So I supposed. Whatever he said, you may take it for granted that he doesn't know."

"But there *was* something in it?"

"Something . . . yes. But it's none of his business. Only look at that bush of blackthorn! Isn't it too lovely? Shelton asked me to tell you he'd seen a lot of—what were they?—March Browns, on the pools."

As they approached White Ladies they drove into a cloud of dust churned up by a lorry moving slowly in front of them.

"Use your klaxon and try to pass him, darling," she said. "The driver's probably asleep, and this dust is disgusting. Ah, he's heard you, thank goodness."

The lorry swerved on to the grass verge at the side of the lane. Jasper passed it with little more than an inch to spare. He grumbled: "These blessed fellows imagine the road belongs to them. What is he doing in this lane anyway? It doesn't lead anywhere."

"He's probably going to White Ladies."

"White Ladies!" he cried, decelerating so suddenly that the unchecked momentum almost threw her forward. "What can he be going to White Ladies for? You've stopped the work, haven't you?"

"We stopped it a couple of months ago. Now we've begun again."

"*Begun again?* Mother!"

"My dear child, do look where you're driving!"

"But, Mother. . . . You couldn't possibly begin again. Not now."

"Well, I couldn't leave things as they were, darling, could I?" she sighed.

"But you never told me. I think that was rotten of you."

"I can't tell you everything, Jasper."

"But *that* . . ." he cried. "Well, I really *do* think . . ."

"Even so you needn't entertain Gibbs with a family quarrel. We'll talk about everything later."

He made her no answer. When they dismounted from the car at the farm his face was like thunder. Bella had never seen him quite so angry before. She noticed a big vein, like Hugo's, bulging in the middle of his forehead. She realized too, for the first time, that he was no longer a boy but a man.

He left her without a word and went up to his room to wash his hands. She also tidied her windblown, dusty hair, and ordered tea. She sat down, watching the oily flicker of a blue spirit-flame under the silver kettle and wondering what would happen next. The sound of Jasper's heavy trampling on the stairs pulled her wits together. He was much taller than Hugo. Jasper Mortimer had been tall. His face was like that of the portrait which peered over his shoulder: the portrait of Hugo Pomfret the Gunpowder Conspirator, which, on the day after the fire, had been found face-downward in the mud of the moat. "But stronger," she thought. "That is what *I* have given him." She said:

"You prefer Indian, darling, don't you?"

"I don't want any tea, Mother."

"You ought to have some after a long journey like that. Don't be contrary, darling."

"I want to get this matter straight, first of all."

"Well?"

"I mean about Wilburn and all that. He stole our insurance money."

"He lost sixty thousand pounds of it. We'd spent most of the rest."

"But it's all gone, anyway?"

"Yes, there's none of it actually left."

"Yet you're going on with the building?"

"Of course."

"But how *can* you do that, Mother?"

"We've modified our plans. The new ones won't cost so much."

"Major Powys said . . ."

"I don't want to hear what he said, Jasper. Major Powys can't say it was my fault that poor Ernest Wilburn committed suicide. Major Powys can't object to my using my own money—or what is left of it—on White Ladies."

"But *I* can object, Mother!"

"You, Jasper. Why, what has it to do with you?"

"I can try to stop your making a fool of yourself, anyway."

"Whom d'you think I'm doing it for, Jasper?"

"God only knows!"

"I'm rebuilding White Ladies for you . . . for you and your children . . ."

"That's all very well!"

"Please listen to me. When you're older you'll realize . . ."

"I'm old enough now to realize what a mess you're making. Oh, Mother . . . !"

"Listen! Your father made me his trustee. I know, just as surely as if he were alive, what he would have wished me to do, and I'm doing it. His money—*your* money—the money to which you had a right after me —is gone, every penny of it except what I put into White Ladies, as my duty, before the crash. Now I'm using my own instead. For your sake, Jasper. If I can possibly manage it, you're going to live in White Ladies."

"But I don't want White Ladies," he cried, angry tears in his eyes. "I don't want the damned house, I loathe the very sight of it! I tell you, there's something horrible about it. It's always been unlucky. Nobody ever succeeds directly. You know that quite well. I wish . . . I wish I may never set eyes on it again. You're mad about it, Mother—Major Powys

was right when he said you were mad. You've let
it ruin your life. Now you're making it ruin mine.
Do you think it's much fun for me to look forward
to having the weight of a beastly great place like that
hung round my neck till I die? I don't want it, I tell
you! I want to live my own life. I know just what I
want. And you're taking it away from me, just to
satisfy . . . oh, lord knows what you want to satisfy,
I'm hanged if I do."

He flung his arms wide in a gesture of despair,
and left her.

Bella heard a clatter of falling walking-sticks in the
hall—his anger made him clumsy—and then the
violent shutting of a door. She sat on, over her cooling tea, until Mr. Beaver, dancing into the room on
tiptoe, discreetly and apologetically removed it un-
tasted. No doubt Mr. Beaver had been much entertained by their quarrel. That was the worst of these
small houses in which there was no such thing as
privacy. In any case he must certainly have heard
Jasper's noisy departure.

Poor Jasper. . . . At first she had been angry.
Later, touched by the childishness of his petulance, she
had felt even more sorry for him. When he flung out
of the room she had wanted to run after him and take
him in her arms and comfort him. Now she felt neither
angry nor pitiful—but profoundly shocked, disappointed, hurt. Of all his tirade she remembered only
one monstrous sentence: she heard it again and again.

"I don't *want* White Ladies! I loathe the very sight
of it!" Incredible! Why, if he had said that he
loathed the sight of herself she could have understood
it more easily. Was this the sole result of all her
tuition, of the unceasing care with which, from his very
babyhood, she had tried to saturate his mind with the
idea of White Ladies, to make it the central and predominant interest in his life? Would it have been
better, she wondered, if she hadn't forced it on him,
if she had allowed him to discover it for himself? Was
this rebellion the kind of automatic reaction which
makes the children of free-thinkers devout and drives
the children of the devout into atheism? Or wasn't
it, perhaps, nothing more than the blind selfishness of
youth which knows only its own ends and at the least
frustration hits out blindly, recklessly, without caring
whom it may hurt?

This last was the explanation she found most comforting. If she could regard Jasper's sudden fury as
a childish tantrum out of which, when the storm had
subsided, he would return to her abashed and
repentant, there was some hope that, given the un-
assailable logic of her position, she might make him
see reason.

For of the fact that she was right, incontrovertibly
right, there was no question in her mind. Even from
the material point of view on which, coached by the
Powyses, he based his opposition, she knew she was
right. A ruin was worth nothing to the estate, it even

reduced its value; while a house, once made habitable, would add far more to that value than the sums she spent on Courtenay's modified plans. After all, she told herself, the run of bad luck from which she had suffered couldn't last for ever. Even the luck which had beaten Ernest Wilburn might change, and the investments which Mr. Chafey regarded with such smug pessimism still turn up trumps. Wilburn, at least, had been a man of courage and imagination. Supposing that these qualities, with which her own nature had a certain spiritual kinship, should finally be justified? Then Jasper would need no persuasion to change his tune. That, of course, was a gamble; but wasn't all life a gamble? And was a life like poor Mr. Chafey's, which declined to take any chances, really worth living? If she handled Jasper gently, patiently, tactfully, she felt certain that he would "come round."

For the present, at least, he showed not the least sign of doing so. That first evening of his holidays was by far the most uncomfortable they had ever spent together. They dined in a mortal silence which none of her attempts at easing the strained situation could break. It was unlike Jasper, she told herself, to sulk, though she remembered that Hugo had been subject to moods of this kind. Sitting opposite him at the dinner-table, she watched his face. There was no softness in it—only the sullen obstinacy of a thwarted child, or rather the obstinacy of a child in the features

of a man. Again and again she was struck by his flashes
of resemblance to Hugo the Gunpowder Conspirator
and to Hugo her husband. Like the later Hugo in
similar circumstances he drank more wine than usual,
impatiently signalling to Beaver to fill his glass; and
this disquieted her, though she dared not humiliate
him by remarking on it, for she remembered the story
of his father's drinking in Capri. His face looked hot
and suffused above his white shirt-front. As he
gobbled his dinner she saw the blue vein in the middle
of his forehead swelling, as though the anger which
his sulkiness concealed were swelling too. When they
had finished and she went to the drawing-room, he
rose but did not follow her. She waited patiently till
she heard him tramping upstairs to bed. It was the
first time in his life that he had not kissed her good
night.

All the rest of Jasper's holidays was shadowed for
her by a prolongation of the same unhappy relation,
by the silent conflict of two natures equally strong
and equally convinced of the justness of their attitude.
What troubled her most, in secret, was his inaccessi-
bility, his shying, like a wild animal, at the
least approach to emotional contact. Whenever
the subject of White Ladies arose, by chance or
by her deliberate intent, he veered off and shirked
it. It was quite clear that he shrank from discussing
it any further. He had opened his aggrieved heart
and said his say once and for all. He recognized the

temper of her spirit and knew that he could not break it. There was no more to be said; but the forbidden topic lay like cold steel between them and separated them.

They went their own ways. During all those three weeks Jasper carefully avoided setting eyes on White Ladies. He spent most of them fishing in the company of his Wychbury cousin. Bella would have preferred his frequenting any other, for she suspected that the parson belonged to the Powys faction and continued to foment his resentment. Even so, she realized that Jasper was happier away from White Ladies, and his happiness was more precious to her (for she loved him) than all other things, save one.

She consoled, or perhaps imagined that she consoled herself, with a devotion more constant than ever to the progress of the work. Courtenay came down every week, and whenever Jasper knew he was coming, he absented himself for the night. On the whole this was just as well, Bella thought. Jasper persisted in regarding Courtenay as her evil genius, and if the two had met there might possibly have been trouble. Possibly, and yet hardly probably: for Jasper's deliberate absence was only an example of the Pomfret nature's instinctive dislike of facing facts.

It was almost a relief, she reluctantly confessed, when he returned to Eton; for the imminence of his silent resentment had weighed on her night and day. When he was gone she felt able to throw herself into

the supervision of the building with a clearer conscience. Even the work itself appeared to move more
freely after his grudging presence had been removed.
That was sheer fancy, of course: but in fact, it had
now reached a point at which the results of the contractors' labours and her modified expenditure began
to be seen. Externally, at least, White Ladies had
recovered its former aspect of untroubled beauty. The
rainfall and sunshine of three years had washed and
bleached the sooty defilement of the fire away. Three
lavish springs and a third rich summer had restored
the surrounding greenness. When she gazed at the
house from a distance Bella could hardly believe that
it had altered a hair's breadth since first she saw it.
Whatever she might have lost—and in her ardent
heart she still trusted that her losses, even the loss of
Jasper's confidence, were not irremediable—that, of
itself, was a sufficient reward.

She was already beginning to think about furnishing
part of the house, her designs sustained, in this, by
the news that a number of the rubber plantations in
which Wilburn had sunk her money were gradually
coming into a state of production and paying dividends. She was thankful now that she had resisted
Mr. Chafey's lugubrious advice. The motor-car trade
was beginning to boom as well—Pearce-Tregarons
paid fifteen per cent—and even Hayseech, thanks to
Admiralty orders, showed a healthy balance that year.
If things went on like this, Jasper might still have

his beat on the Dee!

During the summer, his last at Eton, he had written to her regularly. His letters, dutiful and awkward as ever, encouraged her to think that he might possibly have repented of his outburst. When next he came home, she determined, she would no longer allow him to avoid the tender subject. All the persuasion of her love should be enlisted to reinforce the arguments of her reason. She would greet him tenderly as if there had never been any difference between them, and entreat him, not as a right but as a favour of love, to come with her and see what she had done for his sake. They would walk down together, she told herself, through the summer evening, and she would show him the miracle her piety had performed.

"Now see what I've done, my darling," she would say. "Look, White Ladies has come to life again! There it stands, renewed, as lovely as you remember it before any of these dreadful doubts and suspicions came to separate us. I held on to it for your sake in spite of everything and everyone. Now kiss me and tell me you love me and that I was right."

The prospect of this tender scene, so often rehearsed, entranced and encouraged her more and more as time hurried onward. She had imagined it so vividly and so frequently that, when the day of his home-coming arrived, she could hardly believe that it had not already taken place. She looked forward to seeing him with a tremulous, pathetic eagerness. In a few more hours, she told herself, all would be over, and all would be well.

Gibbs drove her in the car, as usual, to fetch him from Worcester. On the platform she hardly recognized him. He was taller—would he never stop growing?—and had actually encouraged a moustache. He was a finer-looking man, she told herself, than Hugo had ever been. She hurried to meet him. He bent down and kissed her clumsily. She looked in his eyes and saw, with dismay, that the shadow was still there. "Perhaps he feels leaving Eton," she told herself. She thanked heaven that, this time, there was no builder's lorry on the road!

All through the drive she tried to engage him in happy and trivial conversation. He answered her, sometimes smiling, but his smile was wry. After tea the tension became intolerable. She felt that the moment for which she had waited was at hand. Whatever the issue might be she must take her plunge. She felt shyer, more physically intimidated, less mistress of herself than ever before in her life. Trembling almost, she went over to him and put her arm round him.

"I have a surprise for you, darling," she said, laughing nervously as she spoke.

"A surprise? What sort of surprise?"

"Come with me and see."

"All right. What's the mystery?"

She waited in the north porch while he found his

stick. The night-scented stock was beginning to diffuse its perfume. (She had scattered seeds saved from the plants that grew between the fire-blackened flags at White Ladies.) Now, the scent reminded her of the dusks of that one perfect summer when they had walked to and fro so happily, so utterly united, and leant on the balustrade above the glimmering moat. Jasper came to her side and broke in on that dream. "Ready!" he said almost cheerfully.

They walked away from the farm together. Bella hardly dared speak, the coming moment seemed so precarious. They passed through the woodland belt.

"Where on earth are you taking me?" he said.

The moment had come. She held his arm gently.

"I'm taking you to see your house, darling," she said. "It's finished at last."

He broke violently away from her. It was as though the bitter repressed emotions of a whole year had suddenly found vent.

"How dare you play a trick like that on me, Mother?" he cried. "What do I care whether it's finished or not finished? I don't want to see it. Haven't I told you I loathe the place from the bottom of my soul? Don't you know that I hate every stone of it? Isn't it enough for you to have ruined my life without rubbing it in?"

"Jasper, darling, your life's not ruined," she pleaded, half laughing. "Why, your life's not begun."

"You've ruined it before it's begun. The whole

world knows you've ruined it. Everyone laughs at me, just as you're laughing now. . . ."

"My sweet child. . . ."

"Well, aren't you laughing? Do you want to know what I'ld do with White Ladies if I had my way? I'ld take half a dozen tins of petrol and set it on fire again. I'ld see that it burnt to the ground! And this time, thank God, you wouldn't have any more of my money to waste on it!" He glared at her: the great vein swollen, his mouth shaking, tears in his eyes.

"Jasper, Jasper. . . . How can you?"

"Oh, for heaven's sake leave me alone. I'm sick to death of you and your damned White Ladies." He gasped and recovered himself. "By the way, may I have the car after dinner to take me to North Bromwich? I have to catch the midnight train for Glasgow."

"For Glasgow?"

"Yes, I'm going to fish with the Powyses up in Argyllshire. Gervase asked me a week ago. Didn't I tell you?"

"So they've been at you again."

"You've no right to say that, Mother. Mrs. Powys is my half-sister, isn't she? I think she's a jolly nice woman, too."

"You're easily led, Jasper."

"Am I, Mother? Just try me and see! As a matter of fact I think I know my own mind as well as you. On some subjects, anyway. Now I should like to call in at Wychbury on the way and talk to the vicar about flies."

He was gone without another word, before she could stop him. Bella walked back slowly to the farm. By escaping from her in this way he had left her strangely impotent. This encounter had all the appearances of a signal defeat. She refused to accept it as such, as anything more, indeed, than a proof of mistaken strategy on her part. It had been useless, she realized now, to appeal to a sentiment which, merely because it had dominated her own life, she had foolishly imagined to be equally important in his. She was compelled at last to accept the fact that White Ladies meant nothing to him, or rather that he considered it as the hateful source of all those imaginary wrongs with which the Powys influence had infected his mind. He was by nature as obstinate as herself or as poor Hugo. When once an idea became fixed in his mind (as in hers) it was hard to eradicate. The root of the trouble, no doubt, had been his long separation from her at Eton, during which Sibell Powys and her husband had "got hold of him," and his friendship with the Powyses' ally, Mr. Pomfret of Wychbury, which she would certainly have discouraged more strongly if she had been half awake. It was her own fault, she told herself, that she had let White Ladies absorb the attention which she should have devoted to Jasper. She had been stupid not to grasp the fact that he was drifting away from her—so far away that, at this moment, he seemed almost lost to her. Not quite lost, she thanked heaven. There still remained in her armoury one weapon, the most powerful of all, which in her foolish single-mindedness she had neglected to employ: the natural love which united them as mother and son. Reason and sentiment, the arms on which she had vainly relied, had bent in her hand. From this moment she decided to discard them in favour of the more obvious personal appeal. If she had him to herself for long enough, she felt certain that her love must prove stronger than all the Powyses' machinations. If only she could stop his joining them in Argyllshire! To attempt this, she told herself, would be another bad move in strategy: he was so sore and irritable and suspicious of her at the moment that he would certainly resent it. But when he came home. . . . Then, at least she would know what to do. "I shall not mention White Ladies," she thought, "and I may even have to bribe him. What does it matter humiliating myself, so long as I make him my own again?"

On her way home through the woods she was less conscious of the wound Jasper's outburst had inflicted on her than of a rising hatred against the various enemies who had instigated and seduced him. She loved Jasper too deeply to be angry with him. The conflict began to disclose itself as a pitched battle over his captive spirit between herself and the Powyses, a battle in which she was prepared to employ every means, fair or foul, which might secure her ultimate victory. For the first time in twenty years White Ladies ceased to be the most important thing in her existence.

As she approached the Home Farm she began to feel nervous. So much might depend, she believed, on the first steps she made in this new campaign. She decided that it would be wiser not to thrust herself on him. When they met, as they would at the dinner-table, she would make no allusion to the shocking events of that afternoon; she would be gentle and loving and sympathetic, recapturing, if it were possible, the serenity of those unclouded days before the fire and its sequels, in which they had shared every interest and every thought. She would encourage him to enjoy himself with her enemies in Argyllshire; she would be lavish with money and convince him that her love grudged him nothing. It was important, she told herself, that her outward appearance should match this forgiving mood. When she went up to her room to dress she chose, with conscious subtlety, a frock which, in happier days, he had said he admired.

By the time that she came down to dinner she was convinced that she had herself and the new situation completely in hand. She sat in the drawing-room, waiting for him to appear. Mr. Beaver superbly announced that dinner was served.

"Mr. Jasper has not come down yet," she told him. "We'd better wait."

"Mr. Jasper, madam? Mr. Jasper's gone off in the car with Gibbs."

The first blow of the new campaign had been struck. It staggered her.

"Of course. I forgot. How stupid of me," she said. "In that case I'll begin."

For the next week she eagerly awaited a letter from Jasper; but no letter came from Scotland, not even a post-card. She supposed he was enjoying himself with the sea-trout, and was glad to think so. She went quietly on with her work at White Ladies. It was a blessed resource in the absorption of which she could almost—but not quite—forget about him. The new furniture for the Great Hall arrived. Courtenay had been clever in finding her pieces that resembled the old ones. When it was all in position she brought in flowers from the garden and arranged them. "If he could only see it now!" she told herself wistfully. But the pleasure she felt was secret and solitary. She was prepared, when he returned, to abandon these intimate luxuries and even to forget about them. White Ladies was as dear to her as ever, but Jasper came first. It was impossible, it seemed, to enjoy one without the other.

In the middle of the second week a convulsion shook the world. England declared war on Germany. For a long time she had not read any newspapers. In her abstraction and solitude the possibility of war breaking out had not occurred to her, though the miraculous revival of Hayseech and the hint that Henry Fladburn had given her might have warned her that desperate events were at hand. When Beaver, with a solemn face, brought the news, it did not seem to have any grave personal significance. Only one thought came into her mind: that Major Powys, who had only lately retired, would probably be called up at once; that the lodge he had taken in Scotland would be abandoned, and that Jasper would come home. Jasper himself, thank heaven, was not yet eighteen and therefore not likely to be involved.

Three days later she heard from him. Major Powys, he said, had gone southward hurriedly after receiving a wire from the War Office. Gervase and he had decided to stay on at Loch Avich until after the "twelfth." It seemed a pity, since they had paid the rent of their moor, not to shoot the grouse. He expected to stay in Scotland for another fortnight.

Naturally, as soon as we heard the news [he wrote] *I asked Oliver* [that was Major Powys's name] *if there was any chance of my getting a commission in his regiment, but he says that is quite impossible until I'm eighteen. Four more months to go!*

Four months! By that time, as everyone agreed, the war would be over. Though she wished him no harm, it was a relief to feel that the sinister influence of Major Powys had been removed.

One evening, when she came home from White Ladies, Bella was astonished to see a pile of luggage,

a gun-case and a bundle of fishing-rods in the hall.
She ran straight up to Jasper's room, but found it
empty. She rang for Beaver, who appeared in the
process of finishing his tea. Mr. Jasper had come
home? Where was he?

Mr. Jasper, he said, had arrived hurriedly in a hired
car from Bromsberrow. He had dumped all his
luggage in the hall and set off immediately.

"Did he leave any message for me, Beaver?"

"No, Madam. Not a word. He may possibly have
left a note on your writing-table."

But Jasper had left no note.

Her next news of him came in a scribbled letter
from London. He was dead sick, he said, of hanging
about like this, so he had gone to the first recruiting-
office he saw and enlisted as a private. They didn't
make enquiries into your age, he said, provided you
were fit, and the doctors had passed him without any
hesitation. The training was a bit tough and the
company odd, but on the second day he had palled up
with another Old Etonian. It was a tremendous relief,
he said, to feel one was actually in it at last, and he
knew she must approve of what he had done. His
father had joined the Imperial Yeomanry when he
was over fifty, hadn't he? It didn't matter a bit being
under age; as soon as he was eighteen he would get
Oliver Powys to back his application for a commission.

Bella drove off at once to Worcester and consulted
Mr. Chafey. He agreed that Jasper's enlistment had

been illegal; but everybody in these days, he said, gave false ages, and if it was only a matter of months the authorities made no difficulty. He thought that Bella had every right to be proud of her son. He was bound to say that if he had been in Jasper's shoes he would have done the same. It was easy to say that, Bella thought, when you were sixty-eight.

Jasper wrote to her once again from a training-camp in the north of England. When she wired back, proposing to visit him, he replied that it wouldn't be any good. The camp was in the middle of the moors (lots of grouse about, but the birds were as wild as hawks and packing already) and so isolated that there was really nowhere to stay. Besides which, the battalion was due to move any day, and leave was scarce. If he got a spot of it he would certainly try to dash home, and if she sent him ten pounds it would be useful. He was loving this life.

That wet winter of nineteen-fourteen was a dreary time at White Ladies. In spite of the catchword "Business as Usual," it was difficult to get workmen. All the painters and carpenters who had not enlisted were being rushed into aeroplane-works and munition factories. On Courtenay's advice Bella decided to suspend the work. On the whole, she told herself, she was not sorry to do so. All the savour had gone out of it; she could think of nothing but Jasper, and even the spirit of the beloved place no longer consoled her.

There were times, indeed, when its ghostly desolation oppressed her, when its very loveliness seemed tinged with mockery like a wry smile. Even so, she was happier there than anywhere else, submerging her thoughts—and, above all, the reproachful memory that at the moment of their parting she and Jasper had been divided—in a sort of meticulous piety over trivial things: putting berries and dead beech-leaves into vases in the Great Hall, setting pictures straight, shaking out curtains, hunting for moths. It was rarely that she moved afield. Gibbs's small store of petrol had dwindled, and no more was obtainable. She haunted White Ladies with a devotion that seemed to her ghostlike, wandering over the great silent house with the purposive ineffectuality of a lost spirit.

It was so terribly silent that, often, the least sound made her jump. One day, when she was making her usual tour of the first-floor bedrooms, she was startled by a sound that brought her heart into her mouth: a dry rhythmical sound, like the tapping of a stick on a flagged floor. It was only, in fact, the tapping of a blind-cord's acorn, agitated by the wind, against the window-frame; but it instantly brought into her mind the memory of little Miss Penney. And though she laughed at her own sudden fear she couldn't help reflecting how she herself, at that moment, resembled that little sinister figure which she had last seen shrivelling up like a spider on the flats of molten lead. She herself, she reflected, was almost as ghostly and lonely, condemned to haunt, in her restless peregrinations, the same empty rooms and corridors for the rest of her life. When she returned to her warm room that evening her skin still prickled with gooseflesh. She sat shivering in front of the fire. And what wonder? she thought, since the heart which should have warmed her body was empty and dead as White Ladies itself.

At the Battle of Neuve Chapelle, in March nineteen-fifteen, Private Pomfret, J., No. 16839, was blown to pieces by a shell of high-explosive.

The news came to White Ladies after a month of silence. Bella knew what was in the telegram before she opened it. The whole household knew. It came on an April evening when thrushes and blackbirds were in full song and young rooks already babbling in the tops of the elms. Bella read the telegram and handed it back to Beaver without a word. She stood gazing out of the window and seeing nothing, stricken and tearless. Inside the house there was no sound at all, until suddenly one of the maids in the kitchen broke out into hysterical sobs.

This irruption of trivial sound freed Bella's mind from the stony trance in which it was frozen. She turned from the window and moved unsteadily to her writing-table. She sat there, the pen suspended in her hand, with a blank sheet of paper before her. Then, without conscious volition, her dead fingers began to write.

Dear Mrs. Powys, (she wrote)
  I have just heard that my son has been killed . . .

The pen ceased to move. After a long time, like the jerking pencil of an automatic writer in a trance, it began again:

White Ladies, as you know, will ultimately pass to your boy, Gervase. I have the right to stay here as long as I live, but I have no more wish to do so. I am going away at once, and you can take possession of the house and the estate whenever you wish. All you need do is to communicate with Mr. Chafey, the lawyer in Worcester, whose firm has always handled the family business. Everything will be in his hands. I am sure you will be kind to old tenants and servants of your father's, such as Shelton the keeper, who is a good faithful man . . .

The pen stopped, as though the impulse which drove it had died out. After a long interval it moved on again, precipitately:

I hope you and Gervase will be very happy at White Ladies.

> *Yours sincerely,*
> *Arabella Pomfret.*

She folded the letter, addressed the envelope and

x*

stamped it. The sound of sobbing in the servants' quarters had ceased. While Bella had been sitting at her desk the sky had darkened. The babble of the young rooks had subsided. She heard nothing now but the note of one sleepy thrush and the distant bleating of lambs. When she had scribbled a note of instructions to Mr. Chafey, she rang for Beaver and asked him to send for Gibbs. By this time the thrush had stopped singing, the lambs, too, had settled to sleep. Gibbs appeared, his face harrowed and ghastly in the gloom. He was wearing an armlet which showed that he had offered himself for service under the Derby Scheme. He struggled with words to express the pain they shared, for he was devoted to Jasper. Bella answered him shortly, almost cruelly. She could not trust herself to hear what he wanted to say.

"I am going away, Gibbs," she said. "You have some petrol?"

"Very little, I'm afraid, madam. Only what's left in the tank."

"I want to go to Hayseech . . . to Halesby, I mean . . . to Miss Mortimer's. Do you think we can get there?"

"Just about, I should think, if we go by the shortest way, through Sheriff's Bayton."

"I shall be ready in a few minutes' time, then. You can bring round the car at once."

"Very good, madam."

Bella went upstairs to her room and packed a small suitcase of night-wear. Even if she had been able to think, there seemed to be nothing else that she wanted to take away with her: the possession of material things had no longer any importance. By the time she had finished this perfunctory packing the car was standing at the door. Night had fallen.

Gibbs wrapped the rug round her with something of the mute tenderness he had shown her on the night of the fire. He switched on the headlights and they drove off through the woods. In the level beams of light moths fluttered feebly: even night was full of the resurgent life of spring. The car turned to the left. Black yew-hedges rose on either side of it. When Gibbs spoke of the shortest way she had not realized what the shortest way was. Now the lights of the car, stealing silently forward, illumined the pallid, phantasmal shape of the Palladian gate-house; they flashed back from its broken windows, still unrepaired, and she remembered how, twice before, she had told herself that she ought to put them in order. Now that was all over: she would never see them again. The car crawled into the shadow of the arch and jolted under it—even as the bodies of all the dead Pomfrets (save one) had passed through. It was under this broken gateway, Bella remembered, that she had pushed her bicycle on the day of her first approach to White Ladies. Under that gateway, still broken, she left it. Such had been the beginning, she thought, and such was the end.

Now a heavier darkness closed on them. Gibbs drove slowly, husbanding his petrol. They climbed out of the darkling plain towards the lip of the basin in which the Black Country smouldered. As they surmounted the crest of the hills Bella saw that the whole of the sky in front of them was flushed with a blood-red glow. In the middle distance one small patch where the smoulder was concentrated burst suddenly into flowers and exfoliations of flame. That fierce blast arose, as she guessed, from the furnace-throats of Hayseech.

EPILOGUE: OLD STYLE

THOSE faint stirrings which the stimulus of Wilkinson's new patent steel had aroused in the body of Hayseech during the last years before the war had developed, after its outbreak, into an activity such as the valley had not seen since the days of Jasper Mortimer's triumph in eighteen-seventy. In this last and most bloody manifestation of the iron age, its accumulated mechanical equipment, much of which had lain idle for years, found the final justification for its existence.

In the first year of the war there was no kind of mechanism designed for the production and shaping of metal—no crucible, no mill, no hammer, no stamp, no press—which could not be adapted to the fashioning of deadly merchandise. Even the dumps of scrap-iron and other metallic debris which cumbered Hayseech were reclaimed and swept into its greedy furnaces. Other companies, caught unawares and scrambling for the gold which the nations poured forth so recklessly in exchange for munitions, were hurriedly expanding, running up makeshift shops and factories to house their machines. Jos. Tinsley & Co. had the start of most of them. Their vacant sheds stood only waiting to be used.

Nor were they long empty. Men were anxious (and little wonder!) to find reputable shelter in a protected industry. A human river poured in through the gates of Hayseech, to be absorbed immediately, like a stream that flows into sand. By the end of the war's second year the pay-roll had swelled to more than three thousand men, working double shifts. All the furnaces—even such as had been abandoned as obsolete —were in blast. Every workshop was filled. By day and by night, unceasingly, the fusing and forging and rolling and stamping of metal went on, producing those multiple elements, grotesque and complicated, which made up the monstrous equipment of the military machine: components of motor-chassis and tanks and railway-wagons; light alloys for aeroplane engines; drop-forgings for crank-shafts and limbers; tempered steel for swords and bayonets and helmets; light castings for bombs. And shells, shells—eternally shells! By the railway-sidings the sharp-nosed missiles stood waiting (though never for long) like truncated organ-pipes, until, loaded and stacked, shunting engines hauled them away to the branch line at Mawne Road, where more powerful monsters took them in tow and whirled the laden trains southward, roaring through the night. Over this hot and complex mechanism the cool brain of one man presided: the brain (and the tireless spirit too) of James Wilkinson: clear, care-worn, indomitable. His steady hand held the weapon Jasper Mortimer had forged.

Apart from its distant reverberations, whose echoes haunted her senses even when she slept, and the red glare in the sky at night which now never faded, Arabella Pomfret knew little of this incessant activity and cared for it even less. When, with Gibbs's last pint of petrol, she had driven up to Miss Mortimer's house, she had little idea where she was or why she had come there. After the fire at White Ladies, though her body was exhausted, her mind had been clear; after this greater catastrophe it was only her mind that suffered. Its last conscious effort had carried her to this friendly door. She stepped out of the car with a brain bemused and shattered, incapable of thought or of speech, incapable even of feeling. It was Gibbs, not she, who broke the news to Miss Mortimer. By the time she had realized it, Bella had vanished, like a ghost, upstairs. They found her there, standing and staring at the red sky through the spare-room window. Aunt Harriet and old Helen between them undressed her and put her to bed.

For a fortnight she lay there speechless and almost lifeless; she had nothing she wanted to say, and did not wish to live. But slowly, life, with its obstinate cellular will to survive, got the upper hand of her. It was a victory of matter over mind which the mind resented. People who saw and heard her were under the illusion that the woman who moved and spoke was Bella Pomfret. Only that woman knew that Bella Pomfret was dead. They were so good and so kind to her that—apart from the effort—it seemed hardly fair to disillusion them. Things like that didn't really matter. Nothing mattered much. It meant nothing to her, for instance, that, during the last nine months, the value of her holding in Hayseech had been multiplied fivefold; that all Ernest Wilburn's wild-cat flutters in rubber, and above all in copper, had "come off"; that, in fact, she was richer now than ever she had been. It meant nothing to her—and this was far more strange—that Sibell Powys and her son had taken possession of White Ladies.

At Witley Lodge nobody ever spoke of White Ladies. Aunt Harriet had decided that it was much better that Bella should not be "reminded of things." She herself had no wish to mention it, confessing, in confidence, that she had "never liked that place"; there was "far too much water about it" (one night there had been far too little!), and people who were compelled to live there, or rash enough, as she had been, to make a long stay, would certainly pay for their folly in rheumatism. Quite apart from these deep-rooted feelings, the whole incident of White Ladies was a little too recent in date to occupy an important position in Miss Mortimer's uncertain memory. No major event of the last twenty years had the definition or even the interest of trivialities which had taken place during the previous fifty. Among these her memory moved with the instinctive assurance of one who descends a familiar stairway in the dark, without having to count the steps or grope for a hand-rail; but later adventures, such as her crossing of the Alps, had sunk back into the same historical limbo as Hannibal's, and though sometimes—her swollen and knotted fingers shakily pouring out tea—she might be heard to declare that the population of the world was divided into those people who had visited Rome and those who hadn't, the Eternal City was actually labelled in her memory as the place where one had to send abroad for Garibaldi biscuits. The passage of time had not improved her opinion of the continent of Europe (whose uncivilized inhabitants had dragged her own country into war and made rationing-cards necessary) or, indeed, of any other place at any great distance from the Hayseech works. She still regretted the sale to Jos. Tinsley & Co. of the house on the "bank," from which one could see and smell and hear them, only consoling herself for the loss of it with the thought that it was now inhabited by Mr. Wilkinson who, though never to be compared with her father, had certainly tried to maintain the Mortimer tradition. The world, she frequently declared, would be a much happier place if people would only stay where the Almighty had put them and not yield to the modern habit of "gadding about."

This was why she so strongly approved of Bella's return to Halesby. Though Bella hadn't been born—as, but for her mother's elopement, she might have been—with the smoke of Hayseech in her nostrils, she certainly belonged there. Aunt Harriet regarded her, in fact, as a prodigal somewhat tardily returned, one who had tasted the discomforts of the outer world and should now, thank heaven, know better: even more as—after herself—the sole living representative of the Tinsley-Mortimer stock. It was a pity, Aunt Harriet felt, that marriage had changed her name—and so much for the worse!

Bella listened to these strictures with some amusement. It was a good sign—though she did not realize this—that she could be amused. And indeed, when the violence of Aunt Harriet's native dogmatism had been discounted, there appeared to be a basis of reason in what she maintained. Bella was not actually happy at Halesby—it was too much to expect that she should be happy anywhere—but she was probably less unhappy there than she would have been anywhere else. She felt mortally tired. Sheer nervous exhaustion, the doctors said, was at the root of her disability. Not unreasonably, after all, when she came to think of it; since her life, from the moment when she succeeded to the Mortimer fortune, had consisted of nothing but a series of predestinate struggles in which she had sought to impose her imperious will on refractory time and circumstance. In the end time and fate had beaten her and worn her out. That spirited contest was over, and she shuddered at the thought of renewing it. She was now—for the war rolled unendingly over her head almost without her knowing it—in her forty-eighth year: two-thirds of life gone! On the downward slope, people said, the progress of time gathered speed. In a little while, she knew, she would be an old woman. Well, she had lived her life, a life more vivid than most, and it would be equally useless and churlish

to resent the coming of old age. It was her duty no
less than her fate to submit, to relax, to subside.

And where else in the world, Bella asked herself,
could she have found surroundings more suitable for
this unusual passivity than in the placid company of
those two ageing women at Witley Lodge, in this
atmosphere instinct with untroubled thoughts and slow
resignation? Here no day was unlike the last or the
one that followed it. Even the seasons passed by
almost unawares in that little garden, where green
entered protesting, as it were, against spring's
sulphurous mists, where the bark of the trees was
blackened and their young leaves blighted by hot
winds and caustic exhalations blown over them from
forests of smoke-stacks. There was no grace in this
life, and little enough of beauty. (Bella did not regret
this; for beauty, she knew, still had power to wound
her.) But peace there was, of a quality that passed her
understanding, and solitude, which was what, above
all, her bruised spirit craved.

Visitors broke that solitude rarely. Miss Mortimer
had never "mixed" with the Halesby people, and in
those days the neighbours of her own caste, Hingstons,
Hacketts and Willises, were too busy making new fortunes out of the war to remember her existence, quite
apart from the fact that since the company's reconstruction and the transfer of power from the old
family's hands into Wilkinson's she had forfeited her
claims to membership of their society.

Their only regular visitor at Witley Lodge was James Wilkinson himself. Bella found that Aunt Harriet and old Helen regarded him as a friend of the house. He was still living alone, with a housekeeper and an invalid soldier who acted as chauffeur, in Jasper Mortimer's house on Hayseech Bank. He had got into the habit of visiting Aunt Harriet partly, no doubt, out of natural kindliness, partly, also, because he still reverenced the tradition which she represented as old Mortimer's daughter, and partly, again, because he felt in the backwater of Witley Lodge that slow peace, that detachment from the currents of everyday life which Bella herself had found so grateful. It was the only refuge of the kind available within a few minutes' walk of Hayseech, in which the fume and noise of the works could be lost and forgotten.

He had need of some such sanctuary in those harassing days. Many men would have staggered and cracked beneath such a monstrous burden as the solitary direction and control of Hayseech in wartime. When he walked over the smoke-scarred fields to Miss Mortimer's house he was able to leave these strains and anxieties behind him, to immerse himself in the minute preoccupations of that still and virginal existence (as a man exhausted by heat slips into a placid pool) and to return to his cares refreshed.

In the first months after Bella's coming to Halesby he had felt her presence at Witley Lodge an embarrassment. Even when she was silent, the immanence of her dumb desolation affected him. He was naturally awkward of speech, and however deeply he felt for her, the mere shadow of her tragedy reduced him to silence. As life slowly returned to her, Bella guessed the reason of his shyness and began to reproach herself for being the cause of it. She was disposed to like James Wilkinson—she had always respected him —and the proclaimed admiration of Aunt Harriet, in whose eyes, as the restorer of Hayseech, he had become the most important male inhabitant of this planet, encouraged her liking. He was very different, she found, from the intense young man (he had only been thirty-two in those days) who had so grimly discouraged her first investigations of Hayseech. The passage of twenty-two years had narrowed the gap between them, and he was actually younger now than Hugo would have been if he had lived. Prosperity and confidence in his own powers had softened his original angularity and made his attitude, oddly enough, not only gentler but more humble. In the end, when that first period of awkwardness had passed, Bella looked forward to his visits. It seemed strange to her that a man whose mind and personality were, in their own strange way, so attractive, had never married. Compared with Aunt Harriet, he and she were so much of an age that they began to share a separate intimacy. At times, indeed, Bella was almost afraid that the old lady might be jealous. Wilkinson was now the only man who entered either of their lives.

This, of itself, was enough to make her think of him more than she would otherwise have done. As their friendship increased—it could only be friendship, she told herself—he began, more and more, to make her the willing confidante of his triumphs and his anxieties. Now that her brain had recovered a part of its energy, Bella was pleased to find it capable of keeping pace with his vital intelligence, proud to feel that she had his confidence, and flattered to know that, at times, he deferred to her judgement. For herself she had no more ambitions nor even hopes. All her natural vitality, whose secret springs slow time had replenished, found a vent in seconding his. His career —and, through him, the present and future of Hayseech—gradually became its sole object and vehicle. She planned with him, hoped with him, suffered with him, and knew with pride that he was happier and stronger for her sharing. She was not altogether surprised when, at the end of the war, he asked her to marry him. Not surprised, but, somehow, to tell the truth, a little shocked. . . . Since coming to life again she had got into the habit of thinking of herself—not exactly as an old woman, but as a person detached, and no longer interested in ordinary human relations. Of all possible emotions love had seemed the least likely to disturb this dispassionate state. Many years ago—the war-years surely counted for treble—when her encounter with Henry Fladburn at Wilburn's creditors' meeting had tempted her to play with the chance of accepting his tardy amends, she had rejected it instantly. She had told herself that if she married again it must be for love. But no man could be expected to fall in love with a woman of nearly fifty, and the idea of her falling in love with James Wilkinson had not even occurred to her.

Even so, when he asked her to marry him, she could not treat him roughly.

"What could have made you dream of our marrying, James?" she asked him calmly.

He smiled. By this time they knew each other so well that there could be no question of any lack of candour between them.

"The most natural reason of all: that I love you, Bella."

"What is there in me that anyone could love?"

"Now you're asking too much. If you'll give me a year to talk I might possibly tell you."

"But people don't fall in love at our age, my dear."

"They can remain in love till they're our age. I'm here to prove it."

"What do you mean?"

"That I've been in love with you for—let me see—twenty-six years. More than half your life. I fell in love with you instantly on the morning when you first ordered me about in the old office at Hayseech. And I'm afraid I've been in love with you ever since."

She pondered. "Is that really true, James? No. . . .

I know I shouldn't have said that; but . . . Well, nothing happened at the time . . ."

"How could it? You left Hayseech almost immediately and fell in love with somebody else."

"No. It wasn't that. I never fell in love with anybody."

"Shall we say 'with something'?"

"Yes. That would be nearer the truth."

"The result was the same in any case, Bella. I had to lose you. I, too, *faute de mieux*, fell in love with something: to be precise, with Hayseech. And I've been faithful to both my passions. Fidelity is one of my strong points as well as yours."

"With regard to Hayseech, I let you down badly, didn't I?"

"Very nearly. Not quite. You had helped me in the beginning. When your love for White Ladies clashed with my love for Hayseech, you did what your nature compelled you to do. Being tolerably single-minded myself, I understood you—almost sympathized, in fact."

"Yes. . . . You're wonderfully understanding."

"Isn't that a good reason for marrying me?"

"It's one good reason. There are others, of course."

"I'm prepared to expect the others, if you don't keep me waiting too long. What are the reasons against it?"

"Well . . . I don't think I love *you*, James."

"You've not thought about loving me, Bella. Are

there any more?"

"Less important ones, yes. I don't think I should leave Aunt Harriet. She's terribly shaky nowadays."

"But why need you leave her? Why couldn't she live with us?"

"She could. But I don't think she ought to. People of her age and her state of health don't stand transplanting. I think she ought to stay here as long as she lives. In my old age, you see, I've developed a new sense of duty. I've been a selfish woman: perhaps it was just about time."

He sighed. "Well, at least you'll remember what I've told you."

"Of course. And I'm very fond of you, James."

"Well, that's better than nothing."

"But I don't like Hayseech. I never have liked it, you know."

He laughed. "After all, it's not used you so badly, Bella."

That was all.

Later, thinking it over, Bella felt she had used him ill—less well than his devotion deserved. She found it puzzling to think that this man, whom she had known in a casual way for so many years, had loved her for a quarter of a century. Yet, knowing him as well as she did, she could not disbelieve him. There was no man in the world on whose word she relied so completely, no man who had given her more reason for trust and for admiration. Did she love him? That was a question she had already answered candidly. If love were the emotion she had felt for Henry Fladburn, she certainly did not. Could she ever love him? Never in that fashion, she told herself. The first love of youth was like the perfume of youth itself, as intoxicating, as evanescent. Even so, she remembered, without that kind of love, her married life with Hugo had been generally—and at times supremely—happy. James Wilkinson was a better and a bigger man than poor Hugo in every respect. In his strength, in his stability, she knew he was much nearer to herself. His companionship, in these latter years, had added enormously to the richness of her life. She knew that she had reached a stage in which her own strength was not self-sufficient, when it had become a comfort to feel that the strength of another human being was at hand to support her loneliness. Perhaps he felt that, too. And old age was bleak . . . terribly bleak. Even in Aunt Harriet, who asked so little of life, she was aware of its bleakness. . . .

"Perhaps, some day, I might marry him, if he still wants me," she thought.

But though their companionship continued and became, now that she had accepted the idea as a possibility, even more essential to her, James Wilkinson did not mention the subject again.

In the middle of the following winter, Harriet Mortimer died: suddenly and mercifully, of a stroke like that which had killed her father. Bella bore the blow firmly: indeed it was less of a blow than a solution, for during the last few months of her life the old woman had grown pitifully childish. Bella was well acquainted with death, and in this case death of itself had no terrors. They buried her quietly in Halesby churchyard by the side of her parents. During the grim preliminaries Bella was more grateful than ever for James Wilkinson's help. She and he and old Helen, who was more dazed than hurt by the event, were the only mourners.

After the funeral Bella lived on alone for a while at Witley Lodge. She had told herself that as soon as Aunt Harriet had died she would leave it and settle down quietly somewhere in the country: not in Worcestershire—that landscape was too full of ghosts —but in the south of England. But when the time came she found herself faced by an odd disinclination to move, to which the prospect of leaving her only friend contributed. Hayseech, as she knew, was passing through difficult times; for the sudden post-war boom had begun to dwindle. In the stresses of readjustment she felt that it would not be fair to leave him alone. He relied on her company so much, and in her power to help him she found her greatest joy. Even his splendid strength began to show signs of flagging. Though he firmly denied it, she knew he was tired to death.

One evening in early autumn when he came up to the Lodge she was aware of a sudden change in him.

He seemed to have recovered most of the vigour he had lost. He was gay and boyish.

"Come into the garden," he said, "I want to talk to you."

They went out and walked, arm in arm, across the small ragged lawn.

"I've come to ask you the same question again," he said. "I want you to marry me, and this time I believe you will."

She smiled. "That was clever of you, James," she said. "If you still want me, I'll marry you."

"If I want you! You know that I've never wanted anyone else. But before I said that, I proposed to lay down conditions."

"Conditions? That sounds rather frightening, my dear. What on earth do you mean?"

"A man cannot serve two mistresses. I've resigned from Hayseech."

"For my sake? You shouldn't have done that, James. If you want me to stay here, I'll stay with you. You might have known that."

"Yes, I think I knew it quite well, but I made up my mind some time ago. I believe I've done all I can for it."

"Of course. You've done wonders."

He laughed. "My dear child, will you never stop flattering me? And you see, if we leave Hayseech—and I've no more reason for staying here—we shall have to live somewhere. I've been engaged in some secret researches into your family history. You know, of course, that your grandfather came here from Shropshire? It's a pleasant county, and not altogether too far from the remains of my interests. I've found an old Mortimer house, not far from Cleobury, nestling close to the foot of the Clees. I was attracted to it for sentimental reasons. It's not too big, and the place has been modernized. There's not too much land. I think you would like it."

"We might drive over and look at it."

"We will. But here comes my confession. I've bought it. Do you mind? Do you think that was dreadfully rash of me?"

"Of course it was dreadfully rash—but dreadfully like you. I believe you'll hate leaving Hayseech, James."

"With you, my sweet darling? Never!"

"After all, haven't you given Hayseech the best years of your life?"

"The best years? Oh, Bella, how dare you say such a thing? The best years are beginning!"

Bella Pomfret smiled. "Yes . . . I feel that too, now," she said.

CRAYCOMBE HOUSE. *November 1st, 1934.*
CASA FRAITA. *April 8th, 1935.*